The New

Prosperity

Museum

A Novel

by

Edward Averett

The text of this book is set in 11-point Georgia Font.

Excerpts from the following, all in the Public Domain, are part of this book: *The Velveteen Rabbit,* Marjory Williams, 1922, Chump Change; *The Adventures of Sherlock Holmes,* Sir Arthur Conan Doyle, 1892; *Animal Farm,* George Orwell, 1945, Britannica; *The Black Stallion,* Walter Farley, 1941, Random House;.

The Library of Congress has cataloged this book as follows:
Averett, Edward 1951 –
The New Prosperity Museum/Edward Averett
First edition, February 2023
Summary: Henry James George is plunged early into the mysterious ways of the Skookumchuck Triangle in this coming-of-age saga of a small-town boy with a magical gift who seeks to find meaning in life via his long-term relationship with the New Prosperity Museum.

ISBN 978-0-9989359-8-0
1. Magical realism–Washington (State)–Fiction. 2. Indigenous mythology–
3. Small town/rural– Baby Boomer customs–Fiction.

Wellborn Books, USA
Wellbornbooks.com

For Patricia Eileen Averett,
who had first-hand experience with Skookumchuck

*There are more things in Heaven and Earth, Horatio, than
are dreamt of in your philosophy.*

-William Shakespeare, *Hamlet*

PART I

THE POWER

PREQUEL

John George was watching Arthur Godfrey's Talent Scouts at Anderson's Department Store when Henry was born on a rainy first night of spring in 1950. He had stumbled there from the Rochester Tavern three doors down where he and Uncle Ray spent the afternoon arguing over the war. As usual, John had grown drunk and pissy and fell out the door, leaving Uncle Ray to blather on with the other patrons about Anzio until Aunt Peg got the call from the nurse about the crowning baby and Ray left to do his duty.

John sat in front of the brand-new boxy Sylvania, hammering on his pants. He was an unsatisfied man, having relinquished his marital bed on the advice of his beloved Alice's OB-GYN, who insisted any sexual activity after five months would mark the baby for life. As a result, Alice happily spent her pregnancies at home reading book after book she ordered from the library and had delivered by the friendly rural bookmobile. Anne was her Marjorie Kinnan Rawlings baby, Henry her John Hersey and William Faulkner, and Suzanne absorbed the prose of Ernest Hemingway. In between Suzanne and Henry, Alice suffered a mid-term miscarriage that John always blamed on Norman Mailer.

At the department store, John said, "I don't know what the heck to do." When Anne came into the world, he had avoided all this emotion by hightailing it to Serpent Heaven with Uncle Ray and carting home the boa constrictor Uncle Ray bought for a song when the owners went into bankruptcy protection.

Now, his body was slick and dripping from the torrent splattering outside. With his hair plastered to his face, and his chin sunk deep into the lapels of his coat, he resembled a tired sewer rat. In his fingers, he held a pair of spoons he was tap-tapping on his knee to the rhythm of the boy he was watching on Arthur Godfrey's show.

Oleta Anderson stood and walked over to the door, snapped the lock shut and flipped the cardboard OPEN sign to CLOSED. On the way back, she said, "She comes from good stock. She's going to plop that baby out easy as pie." Oleta even made a plopping sound with her hands. She stopped to test the customer coffee pot, which gurgled in its percolative death throes.

"You do it for those of us who can't," Ike finished. He took the cup his wife offered.

Oleta tried to hand one to John, but he waved it off. He had stopped looking at the TV and now stared out into the abundant rain. "I wonder how it's going?" Oleta asked, scalding her bottom lip.

The sounds coming out of the maternity ward at St. Joseph's Hospital in Olympia were otherworldly. That's because panic was setting in for Alice George. The head nurse had bisected her body with a blue curtain, and she could no longer see what was happening lower down.

"She died," Alice suddenly cried out.

"Who died?" said the nurse.

"My baby. You know. That girl." She stopped, squinted. "Wait, no, that's not right. Okay, the one in Steinbeck's book. The girl whose baby died in childbirth." The nurse peeked around the curtain and confronted her charge. "You mean Rose of Sharon?"

Alice nodded. "Roseasharn. My baby. I mean, her baby."

"Oh Lord," the nurse said. "Mamie, put a little more in the syringe, won't you, hon?"

Henry was born a squalling eight pounds five ounces and, like most boys delivered in his time, had only a few minutes to enjoy his foreskin. Snip-snip and he was equipped like every other dog in the pack.

They brought him back to Alice swathed in cotton. The nurse handed him to her, but Alice hid one arm under the blanket as the fingers on the other fumbled with her lip.

"Mrs. George," the nurse said. "Here's your new baby boy."

Alice peeked from under her lidded anxiety. "Do you think I could have just a few more days without him?"

The boy was christened Henry James George. The kid with three first names. Alice forever said he was the namesake of the great novelist. Her husband, on the other hand, was not a reader.

But Henry was. He walked at ten months, said his first sentences at fourteen months. Read his first novella at age three. Okay, maybe three and a half.

"He's special," Alice said. "He may be a miracle. Someday we'll all read about this boy."

But his older sister, Anne, a red haired and unruly fireplug, did not agree. She thumped him a good one whenever she got him alone.

"You're ruining it for me," she said as she kept a knee on his temple, daring him to scream. "They like me, stupid. Me, me, me." Not good with others, Anne taught Henry to be discreet with his reading gift.

"Stop torturing your brother," Alice would say as she sped-read through another John O'Hara. "He can't defend himself."

"Hear that?" Anne said. "You can't defend yourself. Follow me, that's all you need to know." Then she grabbed his book and flung it into the fireplace.

Henry hurried over to get it, brushed the dark ashes off its cover. This wasn't going to be easy, his young brain deciphered.

ONE

The Georges didn't know what they had in their little boy until a brilliant sunny day in the late spring of 1953, shortly after the birth of their third —"Where have you hidden those French letters, John?"— Suzanne, was born. John and Alice, on the verge of a psychotic cabin fever after months of mind-altering drizzle, packed the car. They were headed to Quinault on the Washington coast, where John could dig clams and Alice could start *A Tale of Two Cities.* "It was the best of times, it was the worst of times," she read from the passenger side as they bumped along the coastal road, catching glimpses of the gray-green Pacific Ocean between the wind-bent evergreens.

"You said it," John said smartly while Suzanne spit up on the seat between them.

Alice had her window rolled down, dreaming of other venues. More and more she could do that, be there and not be there, just lift off and float away. She hung her arm out and her hand moved like a dolphin diving and then breaking the surface as she stared at the words on the page. The breeze ushered in the intoxicating scents of wild rhododendron and foxglove.

But soon, Suzanne started crying and John began to whistle *Vaya Con Dios,* first *sotto voce,* then loud and off-key. So off-key that Alice, having dropped from the lofty heights, slammed the book closed and glared at him.

Because of this, they didn't notice the fresh drama developing in the back seat. Henry, now three and a towhead, clutched desperately at his neck as if someone had coiled a rope around it and was tugging upwards. He kicked his feet and yelped.

"Cut it out," Anne shouted. No angel, this one.

"What is it?" Alice asked. When she turned around, she witnessed her only son rise from his seat and become wedged into the DeSoto's deep and wide back window well. Anne screamed and hugged her door.

"What's happening?" Alice cried. "John!"

The car came to a careening stop. John jumped out and yanked on the back door, nearly spilling Anne onto the ground. He reached around her and grabbed an arm. He played tug-of-war with whatever had hold of his son until Henry finally leapt at his father and they both tumbled backwards.

Anne screamed once more. "Are we at the circus?"

"It's okay, it's okay," John assured everyone. He stood and brushed the dust from the front of his pants. He took hold of Henry and pulled him to his feet. "You all right?"

"What had me?" Henry said. "And why did they say those things?"

"What things?" his mother asked.

But when he tried to re-capture them, they drifted away. "Where are we?" he said instead.

John took his bearings. "Just passed that little Dari-Freeze outside of Aberdeen."

Henry coughed; the pressure was now completely gone. He could breathe again.

After John settled Henry back in the car, he and Alice stared at each other, as if there was a secret about life on the Inland Coast they should consider telling their kids.

Alice broke the silence and said, "That was odd. You don't think..."

John shook his head. But as he started the car Alice put out her hand. Had the event given her point of view a 180-degree twist? "Let me," she said, and both Anne and Henry gawped. They may have had good reason.

John was always the driver, by default of course; this was the 50's after all. But Alice lately had been hatching different plans for her future. John had wanted children. Okay, but in return, how about some mobility for Alice? She wanted the power of the wheel sliding in her hands. She wanted to rule the world, or at least the county highways.

She was a wretched driver but knew how to be charming. She failed the test twice and informed her husband that surely there must be something wrong with the car. John dutifully spent the rest of the afternoon under the DeSoto's hood, fixing every conceivable connection that could go haywire. When Alice took her third test the examiner, left in shambles and eager to be shed of her death-defying charm, gifted her with legal status. Not surprisingly, she took her passing grade as *carte blanche* to drive as she damn well pleased.

Living on unpaved rural roads, Alice found every chuckhole, every mud puddle, every immoveable protrusion of granite, and rattled her children's teeth in such a way as to make any dentist worth his salt a wealthy man. In the back, the children clutched at the pull straps, trying to keep the road and each other in focus as their mother chatted on about Adlai Stevenson and Jaye P. Morgan.

She was fond of current events and, since John wasn't much for that kind of gab, she now had no one else to talk to about them. Her Rochester Daily Living Club booted her out after she grew too hot under the collar with Margaret Livingston who, in giving a book report to the study group on Pearl S. Buck's *The Good Earth*, called it a communist plot and full of sexual innuendo.

Alice rose to her feet, face red and getting darker, and roared, "Innuendo, hell! They fuck in that book! As has every individual in this very room."

"Yes, my dear," said Margaret Livingston, her panties bunching a bit. "But never with the Chinese."

And all this, tsk-tsk, right on the heels of Alice's attempt to get the ladies to write a collective letter of praise to Ray Bradbury for his daring tome: *Fahrenheit 451*.

Alice, now blackballed, ("Hon, we simply haven't the strength to listen to another one of your critiques") became a loner in the inland farm country of the coast of Washington State. But it seemed to bother her not a whit and she often could be found tucked away in some corner of the barn, a book opened in her lap, the straw arranged around her head like a golden pillow.

Now, a rigid caution invaded the DeSoto, as if a large serpent were slinking its way from the front to the back seat and sliding along the windows, on the hunt for those not paying close enough attention.

"Turn right," John said to a wife who casually ignored him. He swiveled in his seat and looked through the back window. "Right. I said right."

"Indeed, you did," Alice said as she pushed harder on the accelerator.

After about ten minutes, she slowed and looked around. Nothing seemed familiar to her yet, but she would not disclose this to her husband.

"Where are we?" said Anne.

"Well, we're almost at the right place," John said. "We'll be dropping your mother off for good ahead there."

Alice slowed and stopped; all heads pivoted to the right. In the early 50's, the sanatorium called The Cedars still existed in Cosmopolis, Washington. It towered above a grove of its namesake, a three-story imposing white frame affair that looked exactly like a hospital for the sick and insane should look, like a head nurse, all bosom and substance and authority. It was the place to send someone with tubercular lungs or bones or eyeballs, a place where others decided their fate, allowing families to rest easy. The sanatorium was also a home where the elderly could slip into the warm bath of senility and no one on the outside was ever the wiser, physical ailments being preferable to mental and all. But the George family was not there yet, not to the point where Alice's father crumbled at the death of his wife.

"This isn't the beach," Anne said. "What is it?"

"This is where the good people take care of the sick. Alice said. "Your grandmother is a volunteer here."

"Well, it's a sad place, that's for sure," John said, but Alice shushed him with a finger to her lips. Meanwhile, Suzanne amplified her wails and the two in the back rolled their eyes.

By the time Alice found the elusive road to Moclips, they were all certain Suzanne had set a new American record for crying. She was to be forever a colicky baby, one needing special attention according to Dr. Spock. What is colic, John once asked, but no one ever had a good enough answer for him.

In the DeSoto that day, John tried whistling again, but Alice quickly cut him off. "Don't blame me for this," she said.

"What does Spock say?" he countered.

"Spock says maybe you should keep out of it." She looked back to the road again, but Suzanne shrieked even louder. "Could you at least hold her?" She watched John as he anxiously placed Suzanne against his chest. "And the nerve of you, thinking I hadn't checked with Spock on this problem."

John shrugged, got out a couple of whistled notes before catching himself. "I take it nothing worked," he said.

She didn't answer. During the first few months of Suzanne's life dark purple half-moons bloomed beneath all their eyes.

Once in Moclips, Alice careered north. Their favorite beach was about five miles further. The rip tide was tricky at times, and it was too far into the Quinault reservation for most, but relaxingly far enough away from the crowds for this family. They parked and all four doors swung open at once. After John laid Suzanne on the seat, he grabbed the pail and shovel from the trunk. Alice hauled the picnic blanket while Anne and Henry sped down the trail to the sand. They still weren't used to Suzanne, and it fell to Alice to trudge back and retrieve her new daughter from the front seat.

John fancied himself an expert huntsman, and after he changed into Bermuda shorts, he stalked the beach, small square clam shovel in hand, head bent, looking for tiny blowholes in the sand. He had a fine eye, but his timing could be unnervingly off. Anne and Henry followed him while behind them Alice changed into her black one-piece.

It wasn't long before John held the children back as he crept to a likely spot. Stepping carefully beside it, he spotted the bubble of an escaping razor clam. Like a dog to a mole hole, he pounced, and soon gobbets of sand flew left and right. Despite his earnest attempt, he lost this clam to its wily superiority. Sometimes he was more successful, only to be faced with a shell severed into a thousand greenish-yellow pieces, which the screaming gulls snatched within seconds. Anne and Henry soon tired of John's escapades and turned to their favorite spots along the shore. Henry collected shells and the tiny purple carapaces of crabs, while Anne revisited her task of digging to China. She was all curly red hair, brawn and rebellion, and every time they came to the beach, she moved around enough sand to build another Grand Coulee Dam.

Henry had secured a good pile of shells. John was far down the beach, two or three keepers rattling in his pail. Alice lay on her back, shading her eyes, her face in her book. Suzanne screamed in the shade a short distance away.

Anne had just reached Singapore on her lonely spelunk to China, but Singapore was quite far enough. She stopped for a moment and leaned on her shovel. She stared at the baby and looked increasingly irritated. She dug out another few shovels full of sand till the baby's cries distracted her again. She threw her tool aside and stomped over to where Suzanne was lying. She grabbed her the way Anne grabbed anything living, with no thought to a heart beating in the body. She dragged Suzanne fishtailing across the sand to the hole she'd just dug. With little ceremony, she dumped Suzanne in.

"There you go," she muttered. She grasped her shovel and started flinging moist sand over the top of Suzanne.

After a moment, Alice abruptly tilted her head. It was undoubtedly the eerie quiet she heard. Her eyes narrowed on Henry, and he quickly pointed his chubby three-year-old finger at Anne. He had no choice and would forever regret it. Even though the sand had covered Suzanne's mouth and given them peace for the first time in weeks, he had to.

But it didn't faze Anne. Like some high priestess in mid-chant, she was focused only on her grisly job, and it took a good deal of Alice's strength to wrestle the shovel away and toss it into the trees. Alice dropped to her knees, bulldozed her hands in the hole and gently pulled Suzanne from her sandy grave. She frantically brushed grit from all her parts and hoped for the best. But Suzanne was mute.

"John," she called. "John!"

John looked up from yet another empty blowhole and saw everyone jumping around. He ran to them.

"She's not breathing," Alice said. "She's dead."

He put his ear directly over Suzanne's mouth. "She's not dead. Nobody's dead."

The baby was a little blue, but alive. There followed a lot of shaking and spanking and defiant stares from Anne, and for a while it looked as if hysteria might reign there on the Quinault beach.

"I'll get you," Anne said, but nobody cared because the reality was the plain fact: Suzanne was not crying. Not a peep. In fact, the family was so focused on Suzanne, they did not notice Anne as she slipped behind a dune and disappeared.

John snatched Suzanne from his wife and stared into her face. He patted each of her arms, breathed into her mouth. Nothing came forth but the tiniest batting of her eyes.

"We'll do this like normal people," he said. "Alice, you fold the blankets and towels and get the basket. Henry, take my pail and shovel. And Anne, you gather the toys. We'll just go back home and figure out what we can do."

Alice was tucking Dickens in between the folds of her towel when she stopped and searched around. "Is Anne already at the car?" she said.

"I don't know where the hell she is," John said. "She can be in Timbuktu for all I care. She almost killed her sister."

Alice looked down at Suzanne and let out a scream. "My God! That's it. She's got brain damage! Where's Spock?" She tore through the basket, tossing aside pickles and carrots and cold wieners, finally latching onto the book.

"Brain damage, brain damage," she muttered frantically as she flipped the index pages. "Oh, my God, it isn't here."

"Look for lungs... breath... anything," John said.

"It's not here," Alice said. "Henry, Anne, come on, we need to go to the doctor. Quick."

Henry ran ahead and waited for his parents. They argued all the way while running to the car. John jumped in and started the DeSoto.

"I think we dodged a bullet with this one," Alice said.

It was Henry who noticed: "Where's Anne?"

"I swear," John said, shutting off the engine. "When I get my hands on her." He headed for the beach at the same moment Suzanne began to wail.

Alice put her hand on her forehead, an elbow on the window frame. "I don't know, I don't know, I don't know," she said. One hand fell to the seat and grabbed Dickens. She handed it over the seatback.

"Hankie, could you?"

He took it from her. "Should I read it?"

"Would you?"

And he did. "It was the best of times, it was the worst of times." His little boy voice figured out even the hardest of words. They made him tingle; a slight buzz crossed his brain. He recalled the day these fuzzy words came into focus for him, like an SLR camera. It was as if he had opened the giant hole in the world that contained all the secrets.

Now, Alice closed her eyes and listened. A smile grew on her lips. And, most interestingly, Suzanne's voice lowered to a tiny peep and then she stopped crying altogether.

"See there, Hankie," Alice said. "She loves the classics too."

While his father's family gave Henry books about little ponies and engines that could, not one of them sparked anything in him. Alice always tossed them in the trash and gave him the great novelists. Whenever she passed one of them to him, as now, he would feel a strange sensation. It started in his hands and traveled everywhere. He grew excited as it charged through him. And that feeling of power came to fruit there in the DeSoto on yet another miserable day at the beach.

"Ignore the naysayers, Hankie," Alice always said. "They don't appreciate what's good in life."

He cleared his throat and filled the car with the monotony of his soothing little voice. Suzanne's eyes fluttered and closed. Before long, time created shadows which fell across the page as Henry read and read.

When one shadow wouldn't leave, Henry finally looked up. A man stood backlit by the blazing sun.

"Who are you?" Alice asked.

When both Henry and Alice emerged from the car, the man stepped back a few feet. He was tall and thin, wore jeans and a T-shirt.

"Have you seen my husband?" Alice said, rearranging Suzanne at her shoulder.

"Come with me." He indicated with one hand that they should follow and turned toward the beach. He took long, purposeful strides.

Alice hurried to catch him. "Did he find my daughter?"

Henry studied the man. A single braid trailed down his back, tied with a bit of cloth decorated with tiny whales.

"I seem to be missing both my daughter and my husband," Alice said. "Can you tell me anything about them?"

"Yes," the man said. "Follow me."

They passed the hole Anne had been digging and took the path to the left of the old bent tree. The path opened about thirty feet later onto the spreading sands. Henry immediately spied a cluster of people about a hundred yards down and a glimmer of understanding took shape.

"My," said Alice. "It's a busy day."

Henry broke into a trot and then a gallop. The closer he got, the more certain he was; no amount of reading was going to quiet his family for a long time.

John was on his knees in the wet sand. Anne, on her stomach, was not moving, except for a shift of her shoulders as her father worked to resuscitate her by pressing strongly on her back and pulling on her arms.

"Come on, come on now," John pleaded as he pushed and pulled. "Annie, do as your father says." Push and pull.

Henry slowed and crept to the side. Before his mother screamed, he could see his sister's pasty face, her blue lips. He turned away.

"Oh no," Alice said. She screamed again and fell to her knees, setting Suzanne aside. She moved in close to her husband as he worked. "Keep going," she said. "Please."

Henry turned and stood transfixed. Curious thoughts flew across his brain. He wondered if he should blame the book for this tragedy.

Later, Henry couldn't get rid of the images of Anne lying face down in the wet sand, or of those lovely Quinault tribal members lifting her gingerly, holding onto Alice so she didn't fall screaming to the beach, or of one man trying to explain to Henry about rip tides and how to recognize them and stay on the shore. Such a sorrowful event you would think would be the defining moment of Henry's life. But it wasn't.

TWO

A day four years later was Henry's defining moment. It had the potential to release him from his grief. Or add to it. Henry's entire life has spun on the axis of this incident.

Henry and Wayman Simpson left one summer morning to go on safari. They were close friends although Wayman was two years older and a bit of an anomaly on the Inland Washington Coast. He was a large boy and growing larger by the year. Most kids were afraid of Wayman because of his mumbling, almost incoherent ways, but Henry wasn't.

It was cool outside but threatened to become hot by the time they got to Tanganyika, so they wore sweatshirts early that they could later tie around their waists when the sweating began. They thought of themselves as free men, free to roam the hills and valleys until they were called home by their mothers.

They took the Tulane Road through Kenya and then veered off on the dirt logging track and started the uphill climb to Zanzibar. When they came to Ike and Oleta Anderson's timothy field, Henry, like the sprinter he was, ran ahead a hundred feet and turned to take in the expanse of the Serengeti spread out below. Sure, it was only a slice of the Inland Coast, and the rolling hills below would never see a lion or a cheetah run free, but what magic was there in acknowledging the Tilford's chicken coop and the rusted '27 Ford grazing in the Waxman's meadow? In keeping with the requirements of his waning innocence, Henry heard the lowing of the gnus and the growling of the lions as they made their way across the valley. Wayman was naturally slower and took long, tired strides, his chest heaving, as he slogged the pasture slope. Henry ran farther. He prepared to turn and criticize his friend for his sloth when he heard Wayman sputter.

"Hankie, Sec a rest to need we think."

Henry stopped, puzzled. "What?"

Bent over, his face washed in red, and hands on his knees, Wayman was a human oil rig about to pump some crude.

"What did you say?" Henry said.

Wayman straightened; sweat dripped from his chin. "Weird feel I," he mumbled. "Going get just."

Henry shook it off, breathed in the competition and bounded through the hay, shouting to the sky. He knew he had the race won; the victory wriggled like a garter snake in his palms. He held high his arms as if breaking the tape at the finish line. The hairs on his neck rose and he felt something like a lightning strike close by. He stopped and once again turned to face his vanquished foe.

But Wayman was not there. No big bobbing head, no torn jeans and T-shirt. Henry flashed eyes around the field but didn't see him anywhere. A bitter dose of consequence dribbled down his throat.

Above, the sky was still a brilliant blue, the birds still sang and swooped through the trees. No angry dark tornadoes of clouds formed; no ravens perched menacingly on maple branches. But no Wayman. Henry scrambled back to where he last saw his friend. Two meandering swaths cut through the timothy, but while Henry's continued to climb the hill, narrow and consistent, Wayman's did not. Henry dropped to his hands and knees and examined the place where his friend's trail stopped.

"Come on now, Way!" he called. "Come out!" His pulse thumped as again he felt something prickly grow along the hairs at the nape of his neck. He sniffed and smelled a peculiar fragrance, smoke and cologne and food on the verge of being left in the refrigerator too long. "Okay, you win!"

Even though it was warm out, Henry shivered. On impulse, he galloped through the grass to search the edges of the field, checking in the scrub maple and alder. He thought Wayman might have turned tail and run back—he was jumpy around the idea of African predators—but there were no other trails in the hay. Just the two, and Wayman's wasn't going anywhere, forever.

Henry looped around the meadow in ever-decreasing circles until he finally plopped down, corralled his legs and waited. As the day wore on, hunger chewed at his gut, and he nibbled on the sweet ends of the timothy. Toward dark, the DeSoto made a wide turn at the logging road, and he stood to wave. Alice emerged, white blouse, dark pants, wire glasses perched on her nose. She hiked to him.

"What is it, Hankie?" she said, gripping his arm. "What are you doing here so late?"

"Waiting for Wayman," he said.

"And where is he?"

"I think a lion ate him."

"A lion? Be serious now."

He explained what had happened, and for a woman who had devoured fiction all her life, she didn't seem to take it in well.

"A child can't just disappear, Hankie. It's simply not possible." But she checked herself, what with the memory of Anne and all.

Dusk crawled over the hillside. Bats swooped from the trees while crickets chorused a few feet away. Alice sank to the ground and faced her son.

"This is not funny," she said. "This is life changing. Think hard. I want you to tell me where Wayman is."

Henry related the story so many times that tears of frustration bubbled in his eyes.

But this didn't stop her. Over and over, she asked, "Where is Wayman?" unwittingly laying down the hard wire for the trouble Henry would experience throughout his life. By the time she pulled him away from the field, it was dark.

Alice drove to the Simpsons' where she called the police and Wayman's parents interrogated an already battered Henry. Mrs. Simpson was indeed impatient and folded her arms so her muscly biceps inflated like rising bread dough.

"Listen, you little prevaricator," she said. "You little friend of Satan." She pulled at his lower lip, making him cry again. "What did you do with my boy? Huh? Tell me."

"Nothing," he whimpered.

"You know what I think? I think you've always had a bad taste for my son. I think you've been planning this."

"Preposterous," Alice snapped. "They're children. And good friends."

But Mrs. Simpson inhabited a pre-grief daze. "Preposterous, huh? Lizzie Borden was a child. The Bad Seed girl, she was a child. It happens."

"Lizzie Borden was an adult," Alice said.

Mrs. Simpson ignored her and peered down at Henry again. "And there's no one your own age to play with?"

"He lives close," said Henry.

"It's on account he's adopted, isn't it?"

"Wayman's adopted?"

Before Alice could react, Mrs. Simpson clipped Henry on the ear. "Spill the beans," she commanded. "Confess and face the wrath of God." She crowned her cry with: "Are you an Injun?"

"Stop yelling at me," Henry said, but it didn't stop her. Finally, Alice planted him behind her so Wayman's mom couldn't touch him again.

"Enough. Let's not get into it."

Sheriff Godfrey eventually showed. His belt was so heavy with pistol and bullets, he had to yank on it to keep the uneven load from pulling him backwards. He was friendlier than Wayman's mom.

"Now, okay Henry," he said, after he'd seated the boy on the couch. A sprung coil poked Henry in the rear. "Kids just don't disappear like this. Like, you know, like..." He turned to Wayman's father. "What the hell am I trying to say? In the blink..."

"...of an eye," said Wayman's father.

"Yeah, yeah. That's it." He patted Henry on the leg. "Kids just don't disappear in the blink of an eye. It only happens at the movies. With aliens or giant bugs or the like. And it doesn't happen here in Rochester."

"Oh yes it does," said Mrs. Simpson, but the sheriff put a finger to his lips.

"Or it takes a lot longer," added Wayman's father.

"Have you been to Hurricane Ridge lately?" Mrs. Simpson said.

"Hurricane Ridge?" said Henry.

"He's not old enough," Alice said.

"Does the name Sander Wirkkala mean anything to you?" Mrs. Simpson said. "Ain't you got some body part of his in your freezer, Sheriff?"

Mrs. Simpson's question stopped the cryptic argument instantly.

"There was something," Henry eked out, and the rest of them moved in closer. "It was like...it was like he started talking backward."

"Ah-ha!" Mrs. Simpson shouted. "Injun talk."

"Backward?" said Mr. Simpson.

Henry tried to free himself from the spring. Seeing this, Sheriff Godfrey, perhaps frightened by this latest revelation, stepped back and fumbled with his holster.

"Whoa now," said Alice. "There's an explanation for this; we're all just too upset to see it clearly." She gathered in her son. Her arms trembled around him.

Mr. Simpson executed a three-point turn in his chair and took off for the kitchen. He sniffed as he left.

Outside, Alice put Henry in the front seat of the DeSoto. She leaned in. "This may not be the best thing to be talking about."

"Okay," said Henry. "But what happened?

"Someday you'll know. But now is not the time. Just understand, sometimes unusual things happen here."

Henry stared silently out the windshield as his mother drove home. He couldn't help but remember the voices he heard in the back of the DeSoto on the day they lost Anne.

About a hundred yards from their driveway, Alice pulled over. "Some parts of life are just impossible for most folks to figure out," she said. "You know, like you reading the classics."

"The classics," said Henry.

"And remember what happened to your poor sister?"

How could Henry forget?

Alice put the car in gear again and slowly eased onto the road. "Someday," she said. "But not today."

Eventually, Mr. Simpson came to his senses and stopped blaming Henry, but his wife took every opportunity to finger him as a murderer.

In the candy section at the Super-Valu: "Keep it up, eat hardy and get fat, little Adolf," she said. Or at the Trailways Station/Postal Outlet from across the street: "My boy rots away six feet under out in Nowhere land and you, yes you can walk around free as a god-blessed bird!"

Henry was paralyzed, humiliated by the attention. Even when he was with his mother, he saw her sidelong glances, sensed her ambiguous feelings. Was there no one who would believe him? No place he could go?

"To hell," is what Mrs. Simpson suggested.

The uproar eventually died down. A month later, Henry gathered his courage and rode his bike to the scene of the so-called crime to take a new look on his own.

It was early and quiet and a little cool, summer on its last legs. Dew covered the timothy, now sporting a crewcut from its final harvest. Henry laid his bike at the side of the field and walked out into it. As he did, he felt a sensation of movement, like each corner of the pasture was curling in toward him. He cupped his hands at his mouth.

"Wayman!"

There was no answer, of course, and he never expected one, but he watched the word as his voice took flight on its own, not really an echo, more like a relay of different voices as if each hill had another "Wayman" perched on it to carry the message farther and farther away into a future he knew nothing about but one the gods were busily assembling for him.

And perhaps as a part of their curious work, a few minutes later an old black Plymouth rattled along the dirt road. It parked near his resting bike and a woman struggled out of it, standing for a moment by the rounded bustle at the rear. Her hair was black and gray and brown and hung un-brushed to her broad shoulders.

She wore a black dress with an ironclad bodice and shoes also black and heavy in the heel. She was sixty years old, and her body bore the signs of having lived through all the changes of those years: Her back bowed slightly from the Depression, her face pockmarked by acne possibly a reaction from the shellings of the wars, her voice thick and gravelly from shouting in support of some temperance cause.

She was Encarnacion Obregon, a healer, a Washington *curandera,* whose only potions were soup, and a pair of knobby hands. For years she had bounced into driveway after driveway on the Inland Washington Coast on her errands. She charged a fee for her work, and the price rose every year as fewer people relied on her intuitive expertise and turned toward more conventional forms of treatment. Supply and demand, you see.

She spotted Henry and began climbing the hill. At a point very near where Henry last saw Wayman, she stopped and whirled around.

She raised her crepey arms and delivered a common one-word expletive: "Skookumchuck."

Henry was at once startled and intrigued. He'd heard of this woman but didn't know her. The beginning of an ache gathered in his chest. She continued walking toward him and the closer she got, the harder his heart hammered. Finally, they were face to face. Her eyes of pure obsidian peered into his. His feet wanted to turn and canter away, but those eyes, like magnets they were.

"Are you ready then?" she said.

"Don't hurt me," he said.

"No one is going to hurt you."

But his face puckered and froze into a rictus of despair. He flinched when she laid a leathered palm on the top of his head. "I think you know what I mean." She explored his scalp for a moment and then snatched her fingers back. "It is you."

"What is me?"

"You're next," she said. "After me."

"I don't know what you mean."

Now, her face fell a bit and she clenched her brow. "Of course, you know what I'm saying. You were out here. You witnessed it when the boy set sail."

"Huh? You mean Wayman?"

"No. I mean you. Skookumchuck has chosen you. You are to set the world straight again for us natives."

He met her stare once more; the shiver was now a full-fledged tremble. "Do you know where Wayman is?" he asked.

She moved her face in such a way now he could not avoid her piercing eyes. In them, he saw his own face, relentlessly scared. "Do you see?" she said. "You've been chosen. Haven't you been waiting?"

And he did see. The whole cataclysmic event of a lifetime was played out in her left eye. There he was, running carefree up the slope with his friend. Wayman was still those few feet behind him, but wait, there was a change. It was Henry who stopped and began to speak. And it was Henry's body that floated briefly and was spirited away, pitching and yawing. One moment a normal panicked human form, the next, well, particles of dust. Henry sucked in a difficult breath and jumped back.

Mrs. Obregon smiled. "What?"

"Am I here? It was me who got lifted to the sky."

"You?" she said. "No, it was the white boy."

"I'm the white boy."

Her forehead did its squeeze of concern again. "Oh my," she said. "So, you're not native?"

"No."

She tapped a finger against her cheek. "Some mistake's been made." She turned and crossed her arms and muttered to herself. "What to do, what to do?"

Meanwhile, Henry felt the need to pee. He crossed his legs. Was it possible he was secretly a Chehalis Indian?

Mrs. Obregon whirled back around. "But there is proof. Do you see?" And the scene changed in her eyes. There Henry was, in the back seat of the DeSoto, his body climbing to the window well on that fated trip to Moclips.

"I see," he stuttered. "I remember."

"This is a problem maybe," she said. "It should have been you who was taken. But it wasn't. I want to know why your friend is gone and not you."

"I don't understand," Henry said.

"Good." She turned to go. "But you will one day."

As she was leaving, he called after her. "But what's going to happen?"

She came back, pulling his chin to face her. "Skookumchuck is a powerful force. The one who is chosen can do amazing things. He can heal people. He can send people to other realms. He can bring them back. He can give strength to the tribe. He can compensate for the fact we Chehalis never signed a treaty and still they took everything away from us."

"All that?" Henry said.

She nodded and walked off again, but at the edge of the field, she spun round once more and said, "Be ready then. I guess." She shrugged her shoulders and slipped in the car.

"Wow," Henry said. He wobbled but managed to stay standing until long after she chugged off in her Plymouth.

THREE

Some months after Henry's grandmother met her maker on the dogleg to the left of the 13th fairway of the Lewis County Golf Course, Grandpa took to drinking and midnight conversation with the remaining Ayrshires in his dairy herd. Given this, the family decided to send the old man to The Cedars. They all prepared for the problems that had to follow such a change. But with barely a flinch, Grandpa took to the sanatorium like a conquistador to gold and his antics made him the darling of the nursing staff and the absolute embarrassment of the George family's life. Alice George felt duty-bound to visit him at least once a week and so, piled her kids into the back seat of the DeSoto and drove the forty-five miles to The Cedars.

When they arrived, Alice quacked to the children, and they made like a duet of obedient ducklings as they waddled into the building behind her. Alice wandered off after instructing them to sit calmly in the waiting room and entertain themselves.

Suzanne, at three and barely able to make a dent in the world, sat with her legs tucked next to the sofa in a finishing school manner until her brace—never send a three-year-old to tame a stallion—grew heavy and her leg quivered and bowed.

Henry grew tired of watching his sister and climbed the back of the sofa. He looked through the window at the nurse who sat erect in the office, hair curled under and tied with a bow. She typed methodically on pieces of thin cardboard stock, her eyes not moving from the typewriter, until a muffled voice came over the intercom and she frowned and stood.

She was normally the one assigned to search out Grandpa because she was so patient and kind about it whenever she located him. This time, Henry secretly followed her down the hallways, happily listening to the way her nylons harmonized at her thighs and calves. Children were normally allowed access to only one of the wings; the left bosom of that structural head nurse, but at this age, Henry was a fine tease and took great pride in hiding from the adults in charge. The banned wings were filled with zombie-like creatures shuffling back and forth and up and down, and he slalomed through them with an endearing grace as he raced past the doors.

"Stop him," an orderly called. "He's getting away!" It was if Henry were one of those special people doddering in the hall. Before he got far, a volunteer from the Humptulips High School worker pool captured him and carried him upside down to the waiting room.

As usual, Grandpa was in found in the closet of someone else on the road to dementia. Returning with the typist, he was like a mountain man at a dance, the way he watched his own feet shuffle and jump, as if they belonged to someone else, someone even more fearless and agile.

Grandpa played peek-a-boo with his gown all the way down the hall and then crawled back into bed, waving off any tired maxims from the nurse who attempted to coddle him. When the typist had padded away, Grandpa and Alice spoke to each other in the timeless reversal of roles they had now adopted. Alice's frustration grew as she dabbed at her eyes with a lilac hankie. "Oh, Papa," she said. "I miss my true Papa." She bent to kiss his cheek and then, clutching her purse, said, "Well, I think I'll go get the kids; you know they miss you, too."

Being the younger, Suzanne was first, and once inside her grandfather's room, she walked carefully over to his bed, stayed mum as she stared at him. In seconds, Grandpa rolled over to face the wall. Suzanne shrugged and left, calling for Henry out in the hallway.

Scrape-scrape barked his shoes as Henry soldiered across the wood plank floor. "Hello, Gramps," he said, saluting. "Guess who?"

Grandpa rolled back over and eyed him, and Henry laughed because he could see all the way into Grandpa's nose through a forest of wiry hairs. The old man squinted, then raised his brows.

"Ye resemble ye wee mother," he said.

"I do not," said Henry. "That lady's a girl."

"Sometimes boys look like girls, girls like boys. I seen it in them movies they showed us in the conflict." He crooked his finger and beckoned Henry over even closer.

Henry climbed on the bed and put his ear next to the old man's mouth. "It's happening to ye, ain't it?" Grandpa said.

Henry jerked back. "I don't get it."

"Oh, I knows better. Ye gets it. Everone stay put in your wee family? Everone counted for?"

"Sure, Gramps."

"Make sure ye keeps the eye on them. Soon, ye know what I be speaking of."

"Will do," Henry said.

"Ye ma still reading them goddamn books?"

"All the damn time," Henry said. "Goddamnit."

Grandpa wrinkled his nose. "Ye grandma's fault. What did her name be now?" He fought with his sievy brain, then flapped his lips. "Say, who be that girl was just in here?"

"Suzie," Henry informed him. "You know her, she's my sis."

"Used to be another."

"Yeah," said Henry.

"Big gal. Big feet."

"Anne."

"Where she be? Give her away maybe? One of them trades?"

"Tide got her," Henry said.

Grandpa nodded. "Had me a boy, me thinks," he said. But again, he closed his eyes and tried to recall what he wanted to say. He snapped them open. "That man who hang around ye ma."

"My dad."

"Hmm. He still pissing in the shed?"

"Yup. Into that old funnel. Goes out through a hose. But Gramps, tell me about that river."

"What river?" he said. "That damn Chehalee? That Hamma Hamma?"

"No, not those damn ones. That damn River o' Life."

Henry snuggled in even closer, listening to the thub-dup rhythm of his grandfather's old heart. Thub-dup. Thub-dup. The pair was happy.

"Here it is, young whickersnacker," said Grandpa. "The River o' Life. In the winter, she flood. In the summer, she ebb. In between, ye got ye quilibrium. Everone, even ye fish, like ye quilibrium. Ye look for her. But don't count on her. Somebody, and you know who, always pull a wee flood in summer or visey-versy, if ye know what I mean."

"The other thing, Gramps. Don't forget." Henry loved this part, although was not sure why.

"Careful of ye Chehalee."

"That river?"

"No, ye damn injuns."

"Why so?"

"They get ye if ye not careful."

Henry giggled and patted his grandfather.

The Cedars closed soon after Grandpa died. For a while, the forest around it was for sale, threatening the old structural nurse with execution. Then an earnest faction of ladies with money and time— The Bi-County Sorority of the Home and City Improvement League— came to the rescue. These women who had all been volunteers at The Cedars, loved their place, loved their time in history, were frightened of seeing it pass into nothing. At a special meeting, they unanimously agreed to buy the land and the building and save the old gal's life. What else could they do with all that timber money anyway? They might have had a touch of crazy as well.

Their vision was realized with the opening of The New Prosperity Museum, which they filled with the artifacts of postwar America, hope and ambition and plum luck mostly, but *objets du jour* as well. At the time, the Pacific Coast was stocked with Enchanted Forests and Dinosaur Haunts and Old West Towns, and they were advertised for miles with cement replicas of Triceratops or Boa Constrictors or Covered Wagons. To get to The New Prosperity Museum, you took the highway to Cosmopolis and then turned east on the back road as Alice had the day she commandeered the wheel of the DeSoto. In a short while, there came a billboard planted in the soil opposite the entrance. On it was displayed a picture of a mom in a fitted black suit, blonde hair peeking out from under a pillbox hat, and a dapper dad in his gabardine and fedora. And their three children, two boys and a girl. They were all standing around a new 1951 Buick Roadmaster with four portholes and the Dollar Grin smiling like the Cheshire cat. *Come See Your Future In The Past*, it said. *At The New Prosperity Museum.*

FOUR

Both Ralph Underwood and Henry had Mrs. Winkle as their fifth-grade teacher. She was their generation's biggest supporter. Though her subject was entitled American History, Mrs. Winkle far preferred talking about contemporary issues. She walked around the class in her sensible low heels, suit, and hair coiffed like a helmet for the times.

"Pay close attention," she said as she pulled down the map of Washington State and secured it to the nail driven in just below the chalk tray. "This may be the most important thing I ever tell you." With her rubber-tipped pointer she rapped on Puget Sound. "You are the blessed children of the future. You will be the beneficiaries of the most wealth, the most natural resources, the strongest armies, the soundest form of government, the most highly developed health system in the world." The students had heard it all before. True to form, it was Ralph Underwood who spoke.

"Rubbish, Mrs. Winkle," he said. "I mean, with all due respect, it will be technology that takes us places we've never dreamed of."

"Yes, as you keep saying, Ralph," said Mrs. Winkle, her patience about to spring a leak.

"Technology will help us leap forward into the future. It will make our lives easier. It will solve the big mysteries. And..." The class waited, their collective breath baited, especially that of Anita Bush. Ralph winked at her, and Henry felt hope drop from his soul. He secretly crossed his fingers on both hands, each for the possibility of winning Anita's love.

Ralph kept talking, as he was wont to do, but Henry drifted off. He was mesmerized both by the tip of Mrs. Winkle's pointer, tap-tapping on the laminated map and by sweet Anita, the little blond future love of his life. Ralph's voice slowed from 45 rpm to 33 and 1/3. The room grew fuzzy. Except for the map. There was Puget Sound, all right. And above it, Vancouver Island. An insight plowed into Henry's brain like a burrowing screw fly maggot: Vancouver Island was the fat bumpy penis, Puget Sound, the compliant receptive vagina. Henry didn't understand why no one else could see it. There it was in plain sight. Without anyone realizing it, Canada was screwing the U.S.

"And that truth will play out for us all," Ralph said.

"Canada is screwing America," said Henry. Anita's face turned tomato red.

Mrs. Winkle had had a long day. "Thank you, Ralph, for that entirely unoriginal, insight. And as for you, Henry George. Here's a ticket to Principal Peterson's office."

Which all led to the moment on a February day in the lunchroom when Ralph stopped by Henry's table and invited him over to his house on Saturday night. Henry spit pigs-in-a-blanket into his napkin.

Later, when he told his mother, she put down her book and got to work. "You know, Hankie," she said, pulling clothes off the top of the rickety wooden dryer rack. "Ralph Underwood is a discovery waiting to happen. I think you may have scored some points here."

"Maybe," he demurred. But on the inside, he was excited at the possibility she might be right.

Alice helped him pack a knapsack with some pajamas, tooth sundries, and clean clothes for church, should the Underwoods decide to take him.

"What have I always told you?" Alice said.

"Brush as often as possible?"

"No. See as much of the world as you can."

"Okay."

"And I'm here to tell you the Underwoods are a whole different world. The truth is, no George has ever spent the night at their place. You're sailing into uncharted waters. Make sure you take along a pail in case you need to do some bailing."

Henry wondered what it would be like to be at someone else's house again, to talk with a contemporary outside of school, to start really living instead of being the boy at the back of the class who was hardly ever called on, who sketched pictures from memory of his dead sister, not to mention the murder rumors. It had been a difficult four years, if not just for the energy expended to keep away from Mrs. Simpson.

Alice motioned him over. "Sit down," she said. "Now, when Mrs. Underwood brings in the salad, do you know which fork to use?"

"There's more than one?"

Alice rolled her eyes. "I was hoping you might have learned table manners by now. Hold on." She hurried back carrying *Pride and Prejudice* and dictated to him how one acts in sophisticated company.

"I'm eleven, Mom," he reminded her.

"Mmm-hmm," she muttered, adjusting his collar. "And if you read more, you would know several French kings began their reigns at that age. And believe me, they knew how to ask politely for the baked *pomme d'terre.*"

"Maybe you're right," he said.

"Listen, Hankie. You have a chance to succeed. You can go places, do things. I can see you traveling to different countries, making friends wherever you go. We should start saving now so you can go on a sojourn when you graduate."

Her excitement captured Henry as well and by the time he left on Saturday night, he was certain he knew enough to fling his family high into the stratosphere of the special Rochester society called Underwood.

They lived about a half mile out of town on the road to Porter. Their home was a white rancher which gobbled all the ground around it. There was a rumor that either Mrs. or Mr. Underwood came from money back East, but no one had yet verified it.

Mrs. Underwood greeted him in the hallway amongst a forest of potted palms. Soft green carpet covered every floor but the kitchen.

There were five of them; Mom and Dad Underwood, both teachers in Rochester; an older brother, Robert, in high school who was the escort for the Homecoming Queen and a citizenship award winner; an older sister, Natalie, who spoke French fluently and wore a beret to school; and Ralph, who was, of course, the wizard in Henry's class. Each one of the kids had a bedroom and there was a family room to boot. Ralph showed Henry all around the house while his mother retreated to the kitchen. How perfectly synchronized was this family.

The walls were filled with pictures of all the Underwoods, the parents' diplomas—both graduated from the University of Washington—and even the cocker spaniel's pedigree and picture were there. Mrs. Underwood came into the family room with a tall glass of lemonade and handed it to Henry.

"We're so excited you've come to visit us," she said. Henry couldn't keep from looking at her short dark hair, lips full of rosy color, dazzling smile. He knew her from school, naturally, but he'd never been in her class.

"How is your sister?" she asked.

"Fine," Henry said. "She's keeping a positive attitude."

Mrs. Underwood cocked her head. "She's such a sweet girl. Such a little soldier. Is there anything else I can get you, Henry? Our house is your house."

"No, thank you, ma'am. I am at ease." Perhaps a little too much Austen, but impressive, nonetheless.

Mrs. Underwood left in a swirl of dress.

"So, Henry," Ralph said, rubbing his hands together. "Let me show you some very interesting examples of my pursuits."

In Ralph's room, they ducked under the model airplanes hanging from his ceiling. The space was about twice the size of Henry's and full of clutter. But it was the good kind of clutter, the educational kind. Besides the model planes, he had an aquarium and a terrarium with live salamanders wobbling around inside. On the windowsill Henry was excited to see a ham radio set.

"I've always wanted one of these," Henry said. "You can talk to people all over the world." Ralph promised they could try to tune into Japan, or at least the International District in Seattle. Henry practically clapped.

Alongside his bed was a calendar showing Ralph's daily schedule: brushing his teeth, reading his library book. He even set aside several seconds for urination.

"This is from our trip to Disneyland," he said. Ralph crowned his head with a pair of mouse ears. He screwed up his mouth and made his front teeth protrude. "Got some cheese?"

They toured around the room, opening drawers, digging into file folders, reading the labels off 45 rpm records. Ralph showed him how his stock was doing on a makeshift tickertape. By dinnertime, Henry was exhausted.

The table glittered as Mrs. Underwood sat Henry at the opposite end from Mr. Underwood. "A place of distinction," she called it. Henry followed suit as each member of the family pulled the linen napkin from beneath the utensils and flapped it once before placing it across their laps. It was a big spread. Plenty of foods Henry had never seen were passed around the table: lima beans, steamed carrots, potatoes au gratin, and the entrée, which was a different play on beef than Henry was used to. Mrs. Underwood sliced off a fat chunk of roast and placed it gingerly on his plate.

It took a while and a few surreptitious sniffs to orient himself, but it was not the food that left Henry flummoxed all evening. It was the way this family conducted itself.

"Darling," Mrs. Underwood said to her only daughter. "Did you finish your book report?"

"*Oui,*" said Natalie, between spoonfuls of spuds.

"Natalie is so impatient," Mrs. Underwood told Henry. "She couldn't wait for the library to order her book of choice, so she wrote one herself."

Henry glanced over to Natalie. She was the best looking of the lot and seemed a bit serious, like his sister, Suzanne. And what about the beret? Natalie sighed deeply, already tired of the whole conversation. "Boring," she said under her breath.

"Well, be sure and let me see it," Mrs. Underwood said. "I'd like to check it off before you turn it in."

"Unless it's in French," Ralph said. "You can't speak a word of it, Mom."

"Why yes I can," said Mrs. Underwood. She turned once again to her daughter. "What is the word of the day, sweetheart?"

Natalie chewed slowly, while the rest of them held their forks in mid-air. When she sat back and took a deep breath, it was as if the whole table leaned forward to listen.

"*Chapeau,*" she said, her nose poking slightly higher.

Henry could sense lips moving around the table, so he did the same. *Chapeau, chapeau, chapeau.*

He munched and learned throughout the evening at the Underwoods. Learned more than he wanted to. Around dessert was when Mrs. Underwood nudged Ralph's shoulder. "Well, have you asked our honored guest yet, honey?"

"I was waiting for later," Ralph said.

"Strike while the iron is hot is my motto," Mr. Underwood said. He placed the pad of a finger on the table and made a hissing sound.

"Okay," said Ralph. "You know I'm in Mr. Peterson's special library class, don't you, Henry?"

Henry nodded.

"Only those who can read over 400 words per minute can join," Mrs. Underwood said proudly.

"We have to do a special project."

"For the entire semester," Mrs. Underwood interrupted.

"Mom," Ralph complained.

"Sorry, love."

"Anyway, it has to be a project about people."

"A sociological study," said Mr. Underwood.

"Oh, *chapeau*," said Robert.

"You guys," Ralph said. "Can I talk, please? You see, Henry, a sociological study, well, it's probably more anthropological, requires me to watch a group of people or a person for a while so I can say scientific things about them. It's how we understand the natives of the South Seas and in Africa too."

A piece of roast slid off Henry's fork onto the table. "Most interesting."

Ralph set him with one of those great Underwood smiles. One day the world would see that smile and associate it with billions. "So, are you interested?"

Henry looked around the table. They all stared at him. "Well, sure, I guess so," he said. "But I'm not great at the writing part."

"What? Oh, you don't have to do one bit of work, Henry. Just be you. You are all I need. Once in a while, I'd like to come over to your house. Maybe we could go to the show together. You know, just do the stuff you usually do."

"That would be neat," Henry said. "It would sure make my mother happy."

All the forks hit plates once more.

"I'm glad it's you," said Mrs. Underwood. "I've always thought your family was, well, special."

"We've always liked you too, Mrs. Underwood."

"*Merde*," said Natalie. She frowned when Henry looked at her.

"I must say, we were all intrigued by the story about the Simpson boy," Mrs. Underwood said.

"So, tell us, Henry," said Mr. Underwood. "He just disappeared?"

"Well…" Henry's throat went dry, and he raised his glass of milk.

"Oh, honey," Mrs. Underwood said. "You're embarrassing him."

"Embarrassing? Pshaw," said Mr. Underwood. "Don't worry, son, there's not one of us who believes it was murder."

"*Merde*," Natalie said once more.

"Lunacy," said Mrs. Underwood. And she fixed a cautionary look on her husband's face. Apparently, one didn't discuss disappeared friends at dinner. "My word, to think some Indian legend would motivate good people to doubt your truth."

"Huh?" Henry cleared his throat. "Anyway, we were walking in the Andersons' field by Porter. One minute I'm talking to him, and the next, he's gone."

"Did you smell any trace of ozone?" Ralph said.

"Of what?"

"Like what's in the air during a lightning storm."

"What are you thinking, Ralph?" Mr. Underwood said, resting his chin on his hand.

"Spontaneous combustion," he said.

"And what do you have to support your theory?"

"Not much. We have to rely on self-report on the part of the subject."

"And that is?"

"Notoriously unreliable." Ralph scored an imaginary point in the air.

"That's my boy," Mr. Underwood said. The family all looked at Henry, their eyes penetrating. He smiled nervously. "Glad to have you on board, son," Mr. Underwood added. He patted Ralph on the arm. "What have you learned from this?"

Ralph thrust out his chin. "I think I've learned if you have an idea, there is always a way to make it bear fruit."

"Looks like you got yourself a real *citron*," Natalie said.

Robert laughed and a glimmer glowed on Mrs. Underwood's lips before she shook her head in reprimand.

Henry debated whether he should bring to light the issue of what happened on the Tilford's meadow the day he returned to the scene of the crime, and had decided against it, but these people, this group giving him his head, won out.

"You want to hear something funny?" he said to the table. Then he told them the story of Mrs. Obregon mistaking him for a native and what it meant in terms of Skookumchuck. He kept talking, blissfully unaware the entire table had grown quiet and now stared at him.

When he finally noticed, he said, "What?"

"Skookumchuck," said Mr. Underwood. He squinted down the table. "Are you an Indian, son?"

"No. I'm pretty sure I'm not."

"I believe Mrs. Obregon is native," said Mrs. Underwood.

"What exactly did she say?" Ralph said.

And Henry told them, word for word, what he could remember. He had them, he knew. They awaited each sentence with great anticipation, it seemed. He liked it, liked having control over this family. But it was short-lived. Soon, Mrs. Underwood frowned and said:

"Could we maybe talk about something else?"

"Yeah, we don't want Henry to send us to La-La-Land," said Natalie. "You know, like Wayward Simpson."

"Wayman," Henry corrected.

After dinner, Ralph and Henry went back to his room. Ralph sat Henry down on the bed, adjusted his glasses, and reached for a lined tablet. "Let's get started," he said. "I would like the exact time of your birth."

"Boy, when this family makes friends, they end up knowing you through and through." Ralph only stared, so Henry quickly said, "March 21, 1950. Eight forty-eight p.m. There was rain and my mother wasn't happy."

Ralph scribbled like a stenographer. "Length? Weight?"

"I don't know."

"Did they have to suck mucous from your throat or did they slap you on the behind?" Henry's mouth hung open. "I'll maybe have to get some of these from your mother," Ralph said.

"Okay."

Ralph grilled him for much longer than an hour. He found out things nobody else knew. But when Henry dove deeper into the secret of his power, Ralph stopped scribbling and snatched the dark-rimmed glasses off his nose.

"What did you just say?" Ralph had been such an effective interviewer he had pulled out of Henry information he was both most proud of and most afraid to tell.

"Nothing," Henry said. "I don't really want to talk about it."

Ralph opened his mouth in a faux yawn. "Maybe I didn't mention this before, but everything you say is between you and me. It's like a lawyer and client relationship. If I were your lawyer, would you trust me?"

"Probably," Henry said.

Ralph raised his glasses again and sat poised with his pen. "All right then."

The words oozed out like molasses. "I can heal people."

"You said something like that at dinner, you know." Ralph paused. "You can really heal people." Not a question, a slicing statement.

"Yes."

"Do you have proof?"

"Yes."

"Well, come on then, out with it."

"My sister," Henry said. "Suzanne doesn't wear her brace anymore."

Ralph tapped his pen on the pad. "You say the reason your little sister doesn't wear her leg brace anymore is because you cured her?" When he came closer, his breath smelled of bay leaf. "Didn't she get thrown off a horse?"

The question itself bucked Henry back to one summer day when Suzanne was three years old. She and John drove off in the truck and came back with a monster of an animal, so fierce and proud it took Henry's breath away. He stayed on the porch as John led the horse to the middle of the lawn and let it go. It pranced away in a wide, regal arc and stopped, its great white eyes challenging everyone.

John, like a circus ringmaster, escorted Suzanne out to the lawn and left her there. She was skinny and knobby, but she stood, one leg out in front of the other, not betraying an ounce of anxiety. What happened next Henry would always keep as a memento of the power of girls. This little creature moved her dress aside, licked her palm, and smacked it hard against her skinny thigh. "Come, Whipper!" she called. "Come, boy!"

And the horse, this bold Arabian stallion, put his ears forward and walked slowly toward her, head lowered and whinnying like a beaten dog until he got close enough for her to scratch him behind an ear.

Relief sped around the George farm, and it was with the family's blessing Suzanne was allowed to halter the horse and lead him back to the shed John had built. "He was whip trained," John said. "Anybody can keep him in line."

It wasn't until later, when John was irritable and tired of helping Suzanne onto the horse's broad back that the accident happened. Henry was upstairs in his room when he heard it. His father's shout, the horse's reply, and the great, dusty whump!

The horse was up quickly, but Suzanne stayed down, holding her leg, screaming. Hardly a minute passed before John ran into the house, grabbed his 30.06 and put an end to the horse's life. He scooped up his wailing daughter, carried her across the lawn, like a pilgrim to a blessed shrine, singing with tears crowded in his eyes:

"Hush, little baby, sleepy time's a comin'.
Hush, little one, sleepy time is here."

Suzanne was quieter after the accident. Meanwhile, John spent two nights out in the barn, thinking of his lost Anne, and fashioning a leather and metal brace to fit his injured daughter.

Back in the bedroom, Ralph Underwood grabbed Henry's arm. "How did you cure her?"

Henry winced as he said it. "I read a book."

Ralph's eyebrows hoisted high, but he remained calm. "What did you read?"

"The Black Stallion."

"So, you think Walter Farley has a secret power to heal the sick?"

"I don't know. I just know it worked."

"But it had to be Walter Farley because of the horse connection."

"I don't think so. I could have read her anything."

"The newspaper?"

"Something she likes."

"Oh boy," said Ralph. "I have just one more question. Do you know how rich it would make you if you could cure sick people?"

"Oh, I don't think I'd want to get rich for doing good."

Ralph smiled mischievously. "You are going to make such a good subject for my report."

Henry was thrilled. He felt the loving arms of this family hugging him tight. Then Ralph's sister walked by the room and peered in.

"Hi, Natalie," Henry said.

She fake-spat on the floor. "Suck my dick, you fucking assassin."

"But..."

Natalie hurried down the hall.

Ralph shrugged. "She's not what she looks like."

Henry stared at the doorway and nodded his head.

Mrs. Underwood came into the room a few minutes later and asked if Henry wanted her to call his mother.

"It's okay," he said. "I already brought all my necessities."

"I mean for your ride," Mrs. Underwood said. "Or I suppose Mr. Underwood or I could give you a lift."

"I'm not spending the night?" Henry was one-third looking at her, one-third at Ralph and maybe a third on the lookout for Natalie.

Mrs. Underwood stood perplexed. "Did someone tell you were invited? Ralph, did you tell Henry he was spending the night? You know the rule."

"I didn't," he assured her. "We never have sleepovers on Saturday night, Henry. It's family night."

"Oh, that's perfectly okay."

"Let me take you, sweetheart," Mrs. Underwood said, and she would hear none of Henry's protests.

She drove him in the station wagon, a white scarf protecting her Saturday hair. She chatted politely. Henry rode along in silence. How would he explain this failure to his mother?

Mrs. Underwood dropped him off at the end of his gravel driveway. "It's been most pleasant," he said to her. "I am half agony, half hope."

Mrs. Underwood wrinkled her brow for a moment and then brightened. "Why, of course, it's Jane Austen, isn't it? Good work, Henry." She tightened her scarf and added, "Listen, about Skookumchuck. You see, it's a legend. Sure, some people have disappeared to God knows where, but I don't think you need to take it seriously. You're not a native boy, therefore it doesn't apply to you."

"Okay," Henry said, and watched her drive away.

He dawdled there at the end of the driveway, divining excuses and telling them to the bright stars. Mrs. Underwood didn't want to give him her cold. They were too embarrassed after their dog bit him. They didn't like realizing he turned out to be smarter than Ralph.

Eventually, none of these lies made him feel any better. And he had disclosed his power to Ralph. What would happen now?

He made it to the porch where he sat, listening to the goings on inside, voices coming from the TV, an occasional grunt from his father. None of it sounded too supernatural.

After a while, he rose and peeked through the curtain. There was his dad, eyes slipping closed, palm pushing his cheek into a grotesque shape. His mother sat on the other end of the couch, legs crossed at the ankles, a book open. She read quietly, as if there were no TV droning on just a few feet away.

Finally, Henry pushed inside and dropped his knapsack near the sofa. John opened one eye and took the measure of his son before nodding off again. Alice closed her book.

"What are you doing home?"

He sat between the two of them and flirted with how he would explain.

"Henry?"

"Screw Austen," he said.

Shocked, Alice set her book down.

Unable to bear her blazing eyes, Henry finally said, "I just don't think I'm Underwood material."

FIVE

The truth of the statement came a few months later. Was Henry's initial presumption about Ralph Underwood to become fact?

Ralph was asked to present his sociological study at a school assembly. Of course, he didn't use real names, and of course the facts were disguised. But really, how many kids in town had been accused of murder by age seven?

He only made it halfway through the presentation. But even during this time, Henry watched the kids around him point, heard them giggle. He noted whispers of "freak-boy" and "weirdo." Voices eventually rose to such a pitch that Principal Peterson had to stop Ralph on several occasions. But trooper that he was, Ralph soldiered on and surprised Mr. Peterson by reaching his conclusion far before the end of the speech.

"At a gathering of jurors," read Ralph. "Meaning my family, heh-heh. We agreed, especially my sister, Natalie, that the evidence pointed to one faultless conclusion. Citizen B was the guilty party in the case of the missing boy."

"Enough," said the principal, and Ralph looked up from the page.

A pause followed, and then, like a Skookumchuck squall, a few drips and drops of applause built to a deafening deluge. Either Ralph and the rest of the Underwoods had been spot on in this conclusion or these students would clap for anything. The former seemed to have been true.

The principal scooted Ralph aside and raised both arms to quiet the crowd. "Even though he did excellent work on the research, the conclusions are theoretical. And remember, we don't actually know who Ralph is talking about."

But they did not remember the theoretical part. For years after, kids stopped Henry in the hall and asked if they could hire him to do a hit or heal their pet collie. So much for Mr. Underwood's statement about the family's belief in Henry's innocence. This would surely put a crimp in his plans to be a blessed child of the future.

Henry kept his mouth shut, though. He was grateful Ralph hadn't yet learned about what Henry did for his own mother.

Not long after Henry's visit to the Underwoods, Alice's behavior turned peculiar. It took a while for anyone to notice, since she had always been distracted. She usually cooked dinner with a book in her hand, she slept with one open on her chest. The bathroom was full of novels whose colorful spines leapt out of the wooden magazine rack. The DeSoto's glove box held at least one classic shoved in crosswise. She normally spoke in unwieldy literary terms, quoting favorite characters as if they were her best friends.

It was on a day in summer when Alice disappeared, and Henry had to search her out. He found her sitting on top of the big rock next to the creek that ran year-round on their property. "Mom?"

"Oh my," she said. She smiled weakly and climbed off the rock. She took him in her arms. "I think you already understand how I've been feeling. I'm not well, I believe."

"I know," Henry said.

"Maybe you understand and maybe you don't. I could teach you about depression and you could understand better. But I'm afraid I don't have the energy. Oh, shoot. You know what I really should be teaching you? How to make a hamburger. That's what life is about. They're not complicated, and they allow extra time for books."

Henry's stomach growled as she led them away from the clearing.

As it turned out, Alice did teach him about her signature dish: the burger. He learned to flatten, pound, edge, round and fry one better than anyone in the family. John always asked for seconds. It was a fascinating hobby and Henry liked feeding the family until necessity took the fun away and it became a chore.

After their conversation in the glade, Alice was buoyed for a week or so, but when the next wave hit her, it was far more powerful, and swept her miles out to sea.

She did not read another book that summer. Instead, shackled to her bed and propped against the pillows, she mumbled some soliloquy from Shakespeare and watched the tops of the fir trees as they bowed in the wind.

Since it was summer, she was not missed much, only by John who grumbled in the mornings as he fought with the percolator.

"Fucking Russians," he was heard to say, although he had no idea who was responsible for the manufacture of the pot.

The kids slept in and later were off creating some variety of mischief. Since Henry was now making the burgers, life mostly chugged along as before.

It was like this for days. Alice only rose to shuffle to the bathroom. Each day her footfalls sounded like less and less. When John arrived from work, he bounded the stairs and pleaded with her as he paced from one end of their room to the other.

"Just one little burger," he begged. "One. It's all I ask." But there was rarely anything back. "Her goddamn blues got me whipped." He staggered down the stairs and searched the cupboards for any leftover whiskey.

Suzanne wandered the house, wearing the same clothes day after day, occasionally calling out for her mother to no reply.

They all did their best until the day the bookmobile putted into the driveway. This stop had always been the driver's favorite because Alice spent time talking about books and his career goal to be a veterinarian. Now, the driver hopped out of the truck, sliding open the door. He leaned against it, digging out a pair of newer novels. His smile faded slowly as he realized Alice wasn't rushing down the stairs.

Seeing his disappointment, Henry knocked on Alice's door requesting she at least see what he had to offer. It spoke to her sense of fair play that she crawled out of bed and waved to the driver.

He held the books aloft. "Mrs. George, I finally got the Harold Robbins we were talking about."

"Hello, fair traveler," she said. "Have they stabled your steed?"

"Uh, Mrs. George. The books?"

"The first thing we do, let's kill all the lawyers."

"It's the one you've been waiting for," Henry said. But he was mortified and gently crossed his fingers behind his back.

"Shall I leave them for you?" the young man asked.

She took a deep breath and spoke in two simple words the story of her summer: "Not today."

It got worse. But when his father started talking about Steilacoom, Henry knew it was even worse than he'd thought. Steilacoom was home to the state mental hospital and the name scared the wits out of every kid on the Inland Coast.

"No," Henry said, hoping his father might hear. "Not there."

But to there she went. Another few days of not eating, and Alice was unable to make it down the hall to the bathroom. They took her away in the evening. Henry and Suzanne crowded in front of their parents' bedroom window. They watched as John carried Alice, wrapped in an army blanket, to the DeSoto where he gently laid her in the back seat. The two siblings joined hands as the DeSoto backed out of the driveway. "She's never coming back," Henry said.

One morning two weeks later, John woke Henry from a sound sleep. He held the percolator and a can of Maxwell House, and desperation hung on his face. Henry grabbed the can and prepared the coffee and while it bubbled in the glass top, father and son waited at the table and listened to the percolator's music.

John was dressed in his dark blue suit, a white shirt, dingy at the collar, and a bright red tie. Soon, Henry poured his coffee, and John held it at his lips like a wary street beggar.

"Old lady Pinckney wants me to give her Buick its annual check-up out at the museum," he said, wiping his mouth. "You want to come?"

"'Course."

"There's one other thing. I want to stop by Steilacoom first and say hello to your mother." He dropped his head, braced it with his hand. "Still want to come?"

Henry thought of the long drive to Tacoma and across the peninsula to The New Prosperity Museum. He had wanted to check it out for years. "But maybe you want to be alone," he said.

"I could use the company. My whistle will dry out before I'm halfway there."

"What about Uncle Ray?"

"I don't want Ray." He touched Henry's forearm tenderly.

"Okay." Henry felt bouncy inside with the touch.

They left as soon as Suzanne awakened so they could drop her off at Uncle Ray's. Henry had changed into his slacks and blazer, even though they were too small. He took a few seconds to squat and stand so he could walk comfortably.

John didn't abide the freeway, so they took the county road that wound through Little Rock and the tall silos of the dairy farms. Henry clutched his hope for curing his mother's depression, a novel by William Faulkner.

The DeSoto was beginning to look like an anachronism, what with all the Impalas and Fairlanes and Falcons crowding the asphalt. It still purred, though, thanks to John's artistic hands. It motored them through Olympia without a hitch.

Even Henry trembled by the time they got to the hospital at Steilacoom. John parked in the lot, but instead of getting out, he braced his elbows on the wheel and looked through the windshield. The building was brick and as clean as bureaucracy could get.

Henry carried the book close to his chest as they walked across the lot. From one of the windows above, a radio played Frank Sinatra. At the door, John adjusted the collar of Henry's shirt and got down on his haunches to shine the scuffed crescents off his shoes.

A ruddy-cheeked nursing assistant directed them to a large sunroom at the end of a long wide hallway. It was crowded with sofas and overstuffed chairs. Light flowed in from the floor-to-ceiling windows, strategically run through with reinforced chicken wire.

John and Henry were the only visitors. They sat on the edge of a sofa, John twisting his hat in his hand while Henry fidgeted next to him. After an interminable fifteen minutes, Alice tottered in on the arm of the same jolly assistant who'd led them to the room.

Her cheeks were sallow, but otherwise she looked the same. She sat in one of the chairs on the opposite side of the coffee table. She shook her head in a kind of coy embarrassment, and Henry and his father squirmed like uncomfortable strangers. Finally, John went to her, kissing her full on the mouth while she held onto the inside of his shaking leg.

"Mr. Darcy," she said.

"Huh?" This from John who quickly looked over to Henry.

"It's Jane Austen," Henry said. He kissed his mother on the cheek, handed her William Faulkner.

She looked down on it as if viewing the fragile photograph of a long-lost friend. She petted the cover once. Henry held his breath, hoping for pure desire to overpower her. But it would have to come later. "I simply cannot," she said. Tears glimmered in her eyes.

"Mom, I didn't mean anything bad."

"No, no, it's not you." She cleared her throat and glanced around. "The doctor says books may not be good for me." She bit her lip closed. Her hand trembled as she returned Faulkner to him. "He says I can't tell the difference between fiction and reality. Do you understand?"

"Now, Alice," John warned.

"And he says I do something they call perseverate; I repeat things over and over again, and I know he's right. Sometimes, I can't get the Simpson boy out of my head."

John glanced sharply at Henry. "Alice?"

"Or Sylvia Treston. I saw that baby she gave birth to, John." She grabbed his leg even tighter. "I saw it. And, of course, my Annie."

Henry felt a familiar stab at his heart. How many more times did he have to hear his sister's name? It was like a knife now, sharper with each thrust. He hoped for some kind of miracle that would take the pain away. But time after time, no miracle came.

"Come on," John said. "The business with Anne's been years now."

"It's not business, John. It's more than that. She was more than that."

"It's okay, Dad," Henry said. But her tangential revelations disturbed him too.

"Oh dear," she said. "One sentence too many. Now I've spoiled your visit."

John touched the soft curls at her shoulders and denounced the doctor as an overpaid charlatan.

Henry wished his mother would say she was sick and tired of the place and wanted to come back home, but this was not to be. With the mention of Anne, Henry realized his mother's actual pain about it was a stranger to him. Alice ended by saying, "It won't be much longer, but I'm afraid not now. Ta."

After the friendly nurse whisked Alice away, John and Henry sat in the DeSoto for a long time, facing the side of the building, bearing silent witness. John finally cranked the gearshift to Low, but they were still quiet. Henry gripped the failed Faulkner as they drove through Tacoma, across The Narrows Bridge, and cut over the peninsula through Shelton, McCleary, Elma, and Montesano.

After a while, John turned on the radio and soon whistled out of tune to Connie Francis. Bright sunlight shone through Henry's window, warming his face. The wind smelled pure and fresh; the ocean air was thick with salty tears.

Before McCleary, John gunned it under a great canopy of cedars that hung low over the straight highway. They sailed through the shadows. Mere yards away from the shoulder porcupines and opossum waited for the sound of the engine to fade so they could waddle unimpeded across the road. Red squirrels skipped along the branches fifty feet high, and tiny and delicate wildflowers prospered in the rotting humus of the trees. Somewhere close, great flocks of goldfinch flew back and forth in bright yellow sheets, their wings reflecting the sun in flashes. The air there, the air everywhere on the Inland Coast, could support almost anything, could lift and float it across all horizons.

Riding through the small towns quieted Henry. They were not unlike Rochester, although most of them were pure logging towns. They all owned at least one tall, rusted cone at the shake mill, giant metal shuttlecocks with an endless trail of smoke drifting from the top. Young men drove second-hand pickups, cruising back and forth, waiting for an opening at the mill.

When they finally arrived at the museum, they passed the sign across the road.

COME SEE YOUR FUTURE IN THE PAST

Interesting, thought Henry.

The lot was filled with cars. John parked in the reserved space next to the Buick. He got out and changed into his coveralls. Henry loitered nearby, Faulkner still in hand, until John opened the jaws of the Buick and peeked inside.

"Don't get your balls in an uproar," he warned as he climbed in.

Henry heard the wide doors of the building creak open behind him. A woman walked out, all officiousness and lacquered hair. She was of his grandmother's generation, having that certain girdle-contained protuberance about her waist, the girth of dignity. She greeted John as an old friend. With John still under the hood, they chatted about the Buick.

It was a beauty of an automobile, a deep forest green. Henry studied it as the woman explained its deficiencies. He ran his slender hands into the teeth of the grill, pulling at the dry shells of grasshoppers and dragonflies and bumblebees. Despite a few scratches, it glowed with a patina of care.

Soon, John was leaning way in so one foot now swung in the air. The woman spied Henry chewing on his tongue and waved him over. "Have you seen the inside?" she asked.

Henry nodded. "But not since Grandpa died."

"I mean since we made it new." She brushed her hands together and held them out. "Come. Your daddy will be busy for a while. Let me show you what we've got."

Inside, the walls were stark and white, the floors smelled of new carpet. The cubicle where The Cedars clerk had typed and waited for messages on the intercom was gone, replaced by a dark cherry wood desk filled with the accoutrement of a busy person. On it, rested a large wooden box with the word DONATIONS stenciled in red along the side. The woman went to the desk and picked up a pack of Parliaments lying on the writing pad. She lit one, taking a long drag, one hand poised at her hip. She let the smoke curl from her mouth and ascend above her like a papal reveal.

"I knew your grandmother," she said, after surveying him for some time. "We were very close friends in the sorority."

"She died playing golf," Henry said. "It was her favorite thing to do."

Yes," came the studied reply. She placed the cigarette in an ashtray and held her hand out. "I'm Mrs. Pinckney. Rosal Pinckney." She cocked her head. "And you must be..."

"Henry James George," he said, grasping her meaty hand. "I have three first names."

"Well, Henry James George," she said, walking away from the desk and sweeping her arm out to the room. "Doesn't this all look grand?"

Directly ahead was the wide wooden staircase where Alice had always disappeared on the way to find Grandpa. Now, on each step rested a pot of red geraniums, soaking up the sun blasting through the tall windows at the landing. From there the stairs went off right and left, but chains were draped across both sides with a sign bearing the sober warning: NO ADMITTANCE.

"We're adding to it all the time," Mrs. Pinckney said. "When we get too large for the bottom floor, we'll go higher." She led him along a wide hallway. Halfway down, they ducked into the first door.

They now stood in a long gallery, well-lit by both the natural light from the windows and by sets of artificial ones placed at intervals on the floor. Henry's jaw dropped, and he let go of Mrs. Pinckney's hand.

"This is our Appliance Wing. Postwar till now," she said, a serious pride in her voice. "We combined a few old rooms."

Henry stepped to the first exhibit. On top of a pedestal about as tall as he was, sat a contraption that looked to be a giant plumbing pipe. A typed card explained it: Westinghouse Waste-Away.

Mrs. Pinckney laughed. "I don't suppose you have one of these at your house. You connect this under your sink and no longer have to contend with messy wet garbage. Turn the switch, and this little wonder chews it and carries it away." She nodded. "I just love Westinghouse."

"You can be sure," he said.

"If it's Westinghouse."

"I see it on TV."

"Oh, what brand do you have?"

He closed one eye, picturing the letters on the front of the cabinet. "Motorola. It belonged to Uncle Ray."

"Oh, well, not the best, you know."

"What?"

"Not to mind," she said.

Words crowded Henry's thinking and did not wait their turn. "This...is...like..."

She waited for the next word, a smile pasted in place.

"Home," he said.

"Oh, so you do have these things."

"No, not that kind of home. Different. Like a different planet, but still the same."

"It's curious," she said, "the same planet but also a different one you say?"

"But it feels right."

"Doesn't it?" She waited for more, but Henry's mouth was pinned closed. "Shall we proceed?"

Mrs. Pinckney led him from display to display, and he learned the names of the appliances she thought worth commemorating in a museum. He met a sleek, top-of-the-line roaster oven, a hot plate, a toaster that could launch the toast into the air, a cozy glow, tank cleaner, a mixer with three speeds, coffee maker, fan, iron, and waffle baker with the temperature gauge restyled to make it easier to see. Mrs. Pinckney caressed each one with pride.

Against the wall at the end of the room stood an Admiral refrigerator. Here she stopped. "I included this," she said, "because there was some feeling in the group that Westinghouse was over-represented. Oh, the younger ones in the sorority have a harder time understanding the grandeur of these inventions." She opened the door to rubberized displays of food. She pulled out the crispers desultorily. "You see," she said, "it's not to gush on about." Closing the door, she added, "And it's white, not even Apricreme, the exciting new go-with color of the 40's."

Henry heard his father's voice and noticed one of the gallery windows was open to the parking lot. John must have been under the Buick now, muttering to himself in the manner Henry had grown to recognize as his work monologue.

"This whore ain't got a prayer with old John B. George wrenching her nuts," he said. Pound-pound, tink-tink. "God bless, you old tit sagger. Take that. What the hell? Give me back a little of my own medicine, eh? Zip your lip, you old sow." And on he went.

Henry wished his dad hadn't used his raunchy *patois*, but Mrs. Pinckney seemed accustomed to it, for she ignored him and spread her arms to the room once more. "Don't you think it's fantastic to have these specimens all in one building?"

"It's special," he said. "Like home."

"Ah-ha!" exclaimed John through the window. "So, it's a dick you got, you old mare." Tap-tap.

"Well, it is my home," Mrs. Pinckney said. She leaned in conspiratorially. "It's where I hide my husband."

Henry snapped out of his daze. "Maybe I should go help my dad."

"But you haven't seen the other wings yet."

"Oh, I'll be back," he quickly said, not knowing how truly prophetic his attempt was to escape. "And thank you very much for the tour."

She put her arm around his shoulder and led him from the room. "Your grandmother spoke fondly of you, Herman."

"Henry," he corrected.

"She loved her grandchildren so. She was a woman with a lot of ambition. To go from the farm to the golf course is an accomplishment. To climb the ladder from the barn to president of the Bi-County Sorority of the Home and City Improvement League is the dream of a lifetime."

"We're so happy she died where she did," Henry said.

Plenty of visitors walked in and out of the rooms. Mostly blue and white-haired folks with feeble voices approached Mrs. Pinckney

"We'll chat later," she said to Henry. "I'm sure there's a big crowd in the Eisenhower Room." She drug the visitors along as they passed the Appliance Wing and made for a spot at the end of the hall. She let go at the door, smoothed down the front of her suit, and strode in. "Here we are, smack dab back in the fifties."

Henry peeked around the doorway. The walls, awash with red, white, and blue bunting, were crowded with enlarged photographs of Ike and Nixon, Ike and Mamie, Ike and Dulles, Ike and his cardiologist.

"Anyone here named Eisenhower?" she asked, before Henry turned and left.

She was clearly in her element as the queen of post-war America, with throngs of interested onlookers living on her every sacred word. And as Henry arrived at the lobby, he heard a different woman ask in a booming voice, "But why a museum full of things everybody has today?"

"Because someday," Mrs. Pinckney said soberly, "you will miss all the miracles you have now."

It was a banner day for the museum. Through the front door, Henry spied cars with plates from Oregon and Montana, and even the bronco buster from Wyoming pulled into the lot. He headed for the staircase as people piled out of them and stood with his back to the window at the landing. To both sides of him, the NO ADMITTANCE glared its red and white challenge. The doors below opened, the bell tinkled, and a new crowd moved to the table to sign the register.

Voices carried toward him with an echo making them seem miles away. "Did you hear that man out there?" a woman in turquoise pedal pushers asked her husband. She leaned in, giggling like a teenage truant as she repeated some blue liturgy John had delivered into the gaping maw of the Buick.

They milled for a moment; a few faces looked at Henry, as if he held the secret to their movements in this place. But, since it had already been a day without answers, he jumped the chain to his left and hurried up the next flight.

At the top, the tread of a thousand wheelchairs marked the floor. He crept ahead, Faulkner still in hand. He could detect the earthy smell of The Cedars, the faint residue of urine and medicine and sweat in one olfactory cocktail.

The artifacts emerged slowly; a portrait of John Kennedy against the wall, a similar one of Jackie on the other side of the hall. LBJ waved from a Cadillac before leaving his Texas ranch, and then Henry's busy eyes landed on a cluster of photos next to an open door; Pierre Salinger; Robert McNamara; Bobby, Rose, and Joe on the Florida yacht; and Pearl Bailey. He peeked into the room and saw shapes hard to recognize in the darkness. He pushed aside boxes and bed frames, making his way to the back where a drawn velvet shade covered a small window. He pulled the string and the shade flapped open, throwing the room into a stage of dancing motes. It was bursting with treasures, mostly new; the spiders had had barely enough time to string webs from the frames to the arm of a rocker.

These treasures seemed to be piling up, preparing for the passage of years it took to become a relic in The New Prosperity Museum. Henry could see these famous people that very night if he turned on the television and waited a while, maybe an hour, maybe a day. It intrigued him to imagine these artifacts lying in wait to make a new wing of the museum.

He pulled over the Kennedy rocker and sat in front of the window. He looked out at blue and green, the true colors of Washington State. In summer, if you lay on your back practically anywhere on the Inland Coast, you saw those colors. The cedars stood tall and proud and romantic, their heavy branches drifting like delicate fingers through the backdrop of a sky the color of a robin's egg. A fir and a pine were stern and prickly, the cedars waved at Henry. He settled into the chair.

He opened Faulkner and spoke the dense words in his brain, tried on the rich melodic dialect of the Deep South. He stumbled over names and phrases, but pushed on, finally rising to the rhythm. And in so doing, the conflicting emotions of the day coalesced into a single more manageable feeling.

He looked out the window. He was facing east, toward Steilacoom. Hmm. There was Suzanne to think about. Reading had worked for her. He ran scales to limber up his voice—mi-mi-mi-mi-mi-mi-mi and began to read aloud.

As he did, he imagined those words peeling off the page and floating up, out, and over the tops of the cedars, into a gracious blue sky where they caught the prevailing winds and floated across the Olympic Peninsula.

In his mind, he could see them go, those words his mother cherished; the ones his father had little use for. The words took flight, each one catching another and joining an endless chain of healing sentences wending east to Steilacoom where they would find his poor story-less mother and settle over her, creating the best kind of therapeutic heaven. He believed as he read, his mother's depression would lift like the words that streamed out the window.

He read for an hour, until his throat chafed and balked. He closed the book and got up from the rocker. Wading through the future relics, he came out in the hall again. Somewhere below, he heard voices, including John's, as he called softly for his son.

"You ready to go?"

Henry rubbed at his throat. "I think I am," he said.

It may have worked.

Within ten days, Alice was back home. When the bookmobile pulled into the driveway, Henry walked out preparing a speech about how the guy probably should not come back. But there stood his mother by the open door of the vehicle.

"Hi, Hankie," she said, smiling in her old way. Then she turned to the driver and said, "Give me a Carson McCullers, a John Hersey, an Irwin Shaw, and who's that one you suggested before...?" She tapped her forehead. "Oh, yes, Harold Robbins." The guy stacked one book after the other into Alice's outstretched arms until she could hold no more, and Henry had to take her place to handle the excess.

"What are you doing here?" Henry asked.

"It was a dereliction of duty," she said.

"But, how?"

"It's a long story. Hold on a minute." Back at the bookmobile, she pulled out her small suitcase.

"Anything else?" the driver asked, offering her a bit of carbon to sign for the books.

"I don't think so."

"Welcome back." The guy hopped in and drove off and Alice and Henry sat on the front steps, watching the trails of dust settle back on the road.

"Where is everybody?" she asked.

"Dad's in the toolshed and Suzanne went to town with Uncle Ray."

She patted him on the head. "You're all alone then?"

"But Mom, what did you mean by dereliction of duty?"

She leaned back against a riser. "I just got to thinking, how could I possibly leave them to fend for themselves? The doctor kept telling me what I wasn't supposed to do, and I got so tired of listening to him. I can hear the same right here at home, thank you very much." She closed one eye and looked to the sun. "Of course, the medicine might have had something to do with it."

Henry was not so sure. Every night since his day at the museum, he'd sat in his room and read Faulkner to the twinkling audience of the stars. Like radio, he figured the words would travel cleaner at night.

"I'm glad you're back, Mom. But why didn't you call us to come get you? I mean the guy in the bookmobile is nice and all, but we're family."

"I'm sorry, son. It's just that I had dreams of being covered in books and then the bookmobile came into my dreams and the rest is history. I took a bus. Are you mad?"

"Confused," Henry said. "But you shouldn't have worried. We were fending for ourselves just fine."

Her eyes clouded over in confusion until she understood. "Oh, you think…That's so sweet." She patted Henry on his leg. "I know you guys can fend for yourselves, but the poor books. What were they going to do?"

Ah, there she was. His mother had returned.

"I'm sorry about Wayman," he said. "I'm sorry it worries you. And Anne."

She caressed his cheek. "It's not your fault. It's nobody's fault. It's just there, you know, like a big rock in the road. But look at me now. All better."

Everybody guessed and secretly hoped, maybe she was. She took pills for a few weeks, but cast those out one day in the fall, and still she remained well. When he was sure of it, Henry climbed upstairs and reached for Faulkner, rubbing the cloth cover, petting it, getting the feel of it, like his mother was once again doing to any book she could get her hands on.

"I definitely have a power," he whispered.

He felt a certain ravenous need growing under his fingers. A pulsation. If not that, then pulsation's desperate aunt, throbbing. Like a parallel life trying to claw its way out. He understood then the effervescent power living on the printed page. And he knew intuitively he had to talk to Mrs. Obregon.

SIX

On the Inland Coast, rain wasn't a deterrent. It invigorated. It found the tears and cigarette holes in the most impermeable of gear and insinuated like the ganglionic fingers of a cancer. Henry turned his face to it and let it drop on his eyelashes and splash over his lips where he spit it out to the world. It was a warm and silken pleasure and he felt omnipotent as he rode his bike through the deluge. He was surfacing, as his grandfather used to say. "Folks always be surfacing, trying to get thee heads above thee goddamn water."

The road to Mrs. Obregon's was a long seemingly endless incline. The rain did not relent the entire way. The back wheel of his bike sprayed a narrow line of mud; he resembled a soggy skunk when he finally arrived in Porter.

If Rochester was small, you needed a microscope to uncover Porter. All the history there was lost or leaning toward the ground; sagging structures with bent and porous bones, made of cedar shakes long gone slimy with the humidity. On the road sat a small grocery with a couple of Flying A pumps, and inside, Henry learned where Mrs. Obregon lived.

Her cabin sat on a bluff above the road, surrounded by an apple orchard now in snowy bloom. He rested his bike against the bank and climbed the muddy trail battling the tangles of blackberry vines trying to keep him away. Smoke curled from a chimney that needed a good pointing. The frames of the wooden windows were flaked with the last of their red paint.

He knocked twice before Mrs. Obregon opened the door, her hair down around her shoulders, more grays now and fewer blacks and browns. At her feet, a fat calico executed figure eights and howled.

She surveyed Henry from head to toe before she said in a hoarse voice, "What is it?"

"It's me," he replied. "I'm here to talk."

"Ah," she said. A finger, bony and lined, pointed toward his chest. No sparks: she simply crooked it, and motioned him in.

The cabin contained two rooms; a living area with a kitchen, and a place to sleep. Through a beaded curtain, he noticed her bedroom, one entire wall a bookcase.

Mrs. Obregon stood on the rug; hands folded. She was dressed in a housecoat of many brilliant colors. "Tell me," she said.

"It's about my power."

She raised an eyebrow. "Your power."

"You know. What you told me about that day in the field after Wayman disappeared."

She seemed less than enthusiastic. "I see."

He explained as best he could, hoping she would understand what happened with both his sister and his mother. When he finished, Mrs. Obregon slipped to the kitchen table and returned with a box of oyster crackers.

"You'd better eat," she said. She shook them until he dove in and collected a handful of the tiny octagonal crackers. Before he could stuff one in his mouth, though, Mrs. Obregon was at his face.

Her eyes were darker than ever. "Remember Skookumchuck?"

"Yes, but now I don't think you mean the river."

"No. But it is time for you to know what I mean."

She joined both her hands at the thumb-tips and the points of her index fingers, so they made a crude triangle. "Come over," she said. "Touch there." She licked the web of one of her hands. Henry poked the spot and she said, "That's Aberdeen. Now there." She licked another spot where her long fingers came to a point. "That's Olympia." Now she kissed the web of the other hand. "And there," she said, "is Chehalis. All together, they form the perimeter of the Skookumchuck Triangle." She lowered her hands. "All the spaces inside, much can happen." She took hold of his wrist. "You remember what came to pass with your big friend?"

"I didn't kill him."

"He is not the only one."

"I get the feeling."

She told the stories of what she knew: the disappearing Wirkkala brothers and their toes aligned in the sand; Isabel White, who walked across her field on a clear day and vanished in a blinding flash of light;

Russell Viorst, born with a cow's hoof and a monkey's tail. Sylvia Treston gave birth at age sixty to a baby with no face. And on and on.

Henry sat rapt; memories of Wayman Simpson flooded him. His friend and his downfall. Mrs. Obregon ended with the story of Danny Fontana, the frog boy, who croaked and grew webs and slippery skin until his parents could bear it no longer and let him off at the side of the road in Olympic National Park with a case of Spam and a flashlight. He was never heard from again, except on dark nights when his ghostly croaks could be made out in the high winds on Hurricane Ridge.

"Wayman's mother told me some of this," Henry said.

He declined another offer of oyster crackers; the ones he already ate filled the spaces between his teeth. As he had believed before, he thought Mrs. Obregon might be disclosing a precious secret very few knew.

Seeing concern on his face, Mrs. Obregon said, "Ask."

"I don't understand. Why me?"

"This is the answer. With every generation, one is chosen. I am the chosen one of my generation. It is possible you are the chosen one of yours. You will just accept it for now. We don't control our world any longer, but we still have a mandate."

"Who's we? Do I belong to a club now?"

"We who are native can still affect the world."

"But I already told you, I'm not an Indian," Henry said.

Mrs. Obregon's face turned grave as she looked at him head to toe. "How is this possible? Of course, you are from the originals who populated this land."

"But I'm not."

Her hand shot to her chin, and she massaged it. "Now I'm the one who doesn't understand. The one who is chosen is always native."

"Don't get me wrong, I liked helping my sister and my mom. I like this job. I would like to be the chosen one."

Mrs. Obregon shook her head. "But I don't know what will happen. This isn't right." She looked him in the eye. "It could be sabotaged now."

"I don't like the sound of that," he said. "Sabotaged how?"

"I don't know. I have never seen this before. But if it's true, and you are not an Indian, then you'd best be careful."

"Is there something I need to do? Is there something I need to learn? Shall I take lessons from you?"

"Perhaps you need to be more careful than normal. Think of your power, if it is a power, as a revelation. Use it to define your broad strokes and your limits. And yes, don't walk with the medals of your accomplishments advertised on your breast. This is not a gift; it is a bestowment. Dust shakes out from elsewhere and sprinkles down on you. Do not take it lightly. Do not bend the waves of grace. You only fail if you do. And if you fail, you must answer to Qone."

"But what do I do...?" He paused. "Wait, Qone?"

"Yes. When you fail. In the meantime, I will be your touchstone as you learn. You come when I call. We will proceed as if you are native. As if you are needed." She stared deep into him again. "I didn't think it was possible, but it looks as if it is."

"What is?"

"As I said, you are not native. But never mind, it may have been decided."

"But..."

"Farewell for now," she said, leading him to the door. "As much as is possible, stay clear of the Triangle until it is time."

"But I live in the Triangle," he said, as the door closed solidly behind him.

SEVEN

Henry worried about the time when Mrs. Obregon would call for him. With the complication of not being native, he felt anxious about what could happen. But this did not keep him from wanting to go forward. He was tickled at the prospect. The first call came during a visit with his friend.

One day, John and Henry stopped by Uncle Ray's house on the way back from the museum so Henry could see Ray, Jr. Uncle Ray was not really his uncle, Aunt Peg not really his aunt. John and Uncle Ray had met in the service and continued their friendship long after the end of the war. Henry often wondered why Uncle Ray was his father's only friend.

Ray, Jr. was two years his senior, but by the time Henry was five, he'd seen more sunlight than Ray, Jr. would for years to come. He had a chronic respiratory disease, or at least that's what Mrs. Obregon said when she first examined him.

Her Plymouth sat in the driveway when they pulled up to the peeling white one-story clapboard house with its treeless yard. They caught Aunt Peg in the living room. She was a frail woman, taken to falling back into a chair if she had to stand too long. She had her head down. Near the stove, Uncle Ray stood over her, jabbing at the air with his finger.

When John tapped on the screen door, Aunt Peg quickly stood, arranging her apron.

"Junior's back in the bedroom," Uncle Ray said when Henry and his father came inside. "You might peek in and tell him to get off his duff. There's work to be done and it ain't going to get done if he spends all day pulling his pud."

Henry hurried to the bedroom, which was located next to the utility porch, where Uncle Ray kept his caged boa constrictor. Henry desperately wanted to peek at it, but at the same time he was fearful of the thing. It was bad enough to hear it through Ray, Jr.'s wall as it thumped onto the floor of its cage to stalk the mice Aunt Peg bought each week at Woolworth's in Olympia.

Henry knocked on the bedroom door. After a moment, Mrs. Obregon's deep voice invited him in.

"It's you," she said. "You heard from me, no?"

"No," Henry said.

"Well, you hear from me now."

Mrs. Obregon pulled the blankets off a wincing Ray, Jr. and he lay there, a thin shadow.

"Hiya, Ray," Henry said. "How you doing?"

Ray, Jr. wheezed when he spoke, always had, and sometimes his words were caught up in his rattling ribs. "I'm... better... today," he said.

Mrs. Obregon began to massage one leg, her hands practically encircling it whole. "He is a good boy," she said. "One day the sickness will vacate his body."

"My dad says it'll go away pretty soon," Ray, Jr. said. "You know my dad."

Henry did, of course, but wished he didn't. Right now, he watched Mrs. Obregon's hands. They gripped and released, gripped and released, as she talked on in her throaty way.

The pain slowly left Ray, Jr.'s face. He submitted to Mrs. Obregon the way he submitted to everything, as if he had no will of his own.

When she finished, Mrs. Obregon snatched a towel and wiped her hands. "A difficult case," she said. "But we shall see. Now, Raymond, I want you to stand."

Ray, Jr. looked at Henry and then back to Mrs. Obregon. "But..."

"Now, now, he is not in the room. Show your friend what you can do."

Very carefully, Ray, Jr. twisted out of bed and planted his big feet on the floor. He stood as if at attention.

"You're cured," Henry said. He saw all miraculous things as a cure now. "You can get out of bed. You can breathe. Whatever you had is gone. Yay."

"I'm not cured all the time," Ray, Jr. said. He crawled back into bed and pulled the covers over his shivering body.

"You rest," Mrs. Obregon said. She kissed her fingers and stamped them on his forehead.

"I have an idea," Henry said, and he pulled Mrs. Obregon aside. "What if I just read to him? You know, so he can get cured."

"Hmm," said Mrs. Obregon. "It would not work. He is my patient, and you are too young yet."

"So, I have to get better at it?"

Mrs. Obregon nodded. "I have called you and now you will come with me."

"I'm with my dad."

"You will come alone. I have something for you to do. This will be your first and we shall see how it works." She gathered her jacket and bag and left the room quietly, trailing a scent of soot and spices.

"You okay?" Henry said when the door closed.

"No." Ray, Jr. coughed as if to remind him. "Listen, you can't tell my dad about this."

"Okay. But why?"

"I don't want him to know."

"I won't then." Henry sat at the foot of Ray, Jr.'s bed and began to talk about the week's events. Ray, Jr. was especially interested in Suzanne, and these visits were really the only time Henry could talk freely about her.

"Poor Suzie," Ray, Jr. said. He had a special place in his heart for those kissed by fate. "Buried alive before she could walk. Rolled over by a horse."

"But better than she was before," Henry reminded him. "I cured her."

They heard a thump on the other side of the wall. Henry hurried over and plastered his ear against it. Ray, Jr. rose over the headboard and did the same. They listened to the snake as it oozed around its cage and Henry felt the kind of shiver he always did when he imagined being trapped in there with the scaly thing.

"Why does he still keep it?" Henry asked.

"To teach me a lesson."

Just then Uncle Ray burst into the room. Ray, Jr. slithered down into his bedclothes.

"Caught you," Uncle Ray said. "Hands off your little pricks." He yanked the shade, letting it flap endlessly on the roll. He put his big hand on Ray, Jr.'s forehead. "Not a lick of fever. Come on, move it." He drug Ray, Jr. out of bed and stood him on his scarecrow legs.

"There, see? Better every day." He grabbed the waistband of Ray, Jr.'s underwear and gave it a big snap. "Peggy! Get your butt in here and see this."

In a few seconds, Aunt Peg crept in through the doorway. She clutched at the jamb for support.

"Look at the boy," Uncle Ray barked. "He's out of the frigging bed. Tell me she ain't doing nothing for him."

Ray, Jr. wobbled, eyes closed, trying to smile.

"Now you get your damn purse and take out two bills and hand `em over to the little lady waiting out on the porch. Pronto!"

Aunt Peg flared her nostrils but left the room right before Ray, Jr. collapsed in a heap against his bed. Uncle Ray stood over him, frowning, before he roughly shoved him under the covers, and glanced at Henry. "Don't he look better to you?"

Uncle Ray left the room before Henry could answer.

"See you," Henry said to Ray, Jr.

"I've got to get out of here," Ray, Jr. replied.

John stood by the stove when Henry came out, his eyebrow raised in a perfect crescent. In his hand, he held a facsimile of the Lone Ranger's horse, Silver, rearing on its heels.

"You be sure Suzie gets it now," Uncle Ray said. He stood by the window, his meaty finger slitting the Venetian, watching Aunt Peg and Mrs. Obregon make their transaction on the front steps.

"I will," John said. "Only she doesn't need any more damn horses."

When Mrs. Obregon disappeared down the road, they left via the back door. Uncle Ray and Aunt Peg were having words on the porch when John gunned it out of the driveway.

EIGHT

As soon as he arrived home, Henry hopped on his bike again and made the trip to Porter. Only this time the sun was out, and he could smell new growth bursting out of tight buds. His fear had flown, and he felt an approaching state of self-containment.

Mrs. Obregon's door was open. A woman and a young boy stood just inside. The woman bit her lip; the boy's face was washed out, nearly lifeless. "At last," said Mrs. Obregon from behind them. She motioned Henry in.

"This is Simon," said Mrs. Obregon. And as if Henry had pricked him with a pin, the boy shrunk back.

"We came all the way from Portland," the mother said. "All the way. Traffic was fine."

"But..." Henry said while Mrs. Obregon waved her hand like a wand.

"They have come to see you because nothing else works," she said.

The mother's eyes filled with tears. "I don't want him to be lost."

"I see," said Henry. He checked himself. Still no nerves. A good sign. "What then?" he said.

"Simon has leukemia," the mother said. "He's had it practically all his life. He was a healthy little baby and now he's down to this." She pushed the boy out further in the room. Simon was short and skinny. His face looked as if it hadn't entertained a smile in years. He bowed his head so his chin was pinned against his T-shirt. He wore athletic shorts and flip-flops.

"I try to expose his body to as much sun as possible," his mother continued. "I'm a big believer in the healing power of the sun."

Simon's lip trembled. His pupils shot to pinpoints.

"It's okay," Henry said in his best soothing voice.

"He's not wearing a white coat," Simon wailed, and he turned and buried his face in his mother's stomach.

Henry took Simon's hand and gently pulled him from his mother. He led the boy to the bedroom where he laid him on Mrs. Obregon's lumpy bed.

Simon's mother said, "How long will this take?"

Mrs. Obregon put a finger to her lips. "It will take as long as necessary." She steered the woman out of the cabin.

Simon's arms were rigid at his side. "Is this going to hurt?"

"No, of course not," Henry said, though he had no idea what would happen. "Are you warm enough?"

"I don't feel anything."

"What do you need?"

Simon didn't hesitate. "I need to go home."

"You will. But give me a chance first. Do you have a favorite book?"

"No."

"Do you read?"

"Not really."

"Don't your parents read to you?"

"Yes, but it puts me to sleep, and I don't remember it."

Henry glanced to the wall of books. He ran a finger along the spines that sat ready for him. They seemed almost to sing, "*Pick me, pick me, pick me.*"

"What are you doing?" Simon asked.

"Consulting the books. Do you like cars, Simon?"

"No, they scare me." It took a long time to answer, but he eventually said, "I like animals."

And there it sat, sparkling almost, like Tinker Bell's dust. So wrong, of course, for a boy of nine who was not Henry James George, but what was Henry to do? He pulled it off the shelf. "We'll try Mr. Orwell."

He sat in a chair of the proper height, so the words had a clear shot at his patient. Henry recalled the ritual his mother went through when selecting a book and he mimicked her now. He petted the cover, holding it to his head before giving it a big, healthy sniff. "Oh yes. This is the one for you."

He began to read from *Animal Farm*. It was enjoyable to be reading to someone in need again, to feel worthwhile and wanted, and Henry imagined it was much like riding a bicycle; the words, the inflections, the cadence were so familiar, he knew he would never forget how it was done. He lost himself in a world that had always protected him. For his part, Simon lay very still, staring at the ceiling.

Henry stopped somewhere in the middle of the book. He thought Simon had fallen asleep. But the little boy said, "Keep going." It was in this moment the peculiar feeling came over Henry.

It was so subtle he might have missed it, this crawling of his skin. It started in his feet and flushed his calves. Like someone had shot him with a needle, and the medicine was streaming through his veins. It was not an overt pain, rather more diffuse. Henry let it wash over him as he read. When it finally disappeared, he was left feeling dizzy.

It's nice," Simon said.

A half hour later, Henry read the last sentence.

Simon sat straight. His eyes still sunken, his skin pallid, he said, "Those words can sure strangle you."

Henry thought it an unusual turn of phrase, but then again, he'd never had cancer and didn't know what it did to little boys. "Words have a mind of their own sometimes," he said. "They can be little devils."

"I don't like devils," Simon said, sliding off the bed. He stood for a moment and looked around the room. "It's like the biggest cave."

Outside, Simon's mother rushed to greet her boy. She examined him closely, pulling an eyelid here, checking a finger there. Disappointment spread on her face. Her shoulders hunched as she turned to Henry.

"Thanks for trying anyway."

After they left, Mrs. Obregon was the first to speak. "You are tired, no?"

"Very." But it was more than that. "Something happened."

"Tell me."

"I don't exactly know, but I need to lie down."

Under the watchful eye of Mrs. Obregon, Henry spent the rest of the afternoon on the very spot Simon had just occupied. He told her he felt uneven and sick. Occasionally a pain in his gut hurt like a herd of pinpricks. The nearest he could come to explaining it was that while he was reading, it felt like he'd brokered a deal; something from Simon for something from himself. But there rose those odd murmuring voices in the background just like in the Buick at the

Aberdeen line all those years ago, and it was as if they had not given their permission for the transaction. Angry, backward voices.

"Like Wayman before he left?" she asked.

"Maybe. They scared me."

Henry didn't like the look that developed on Mrs. Obregon's face. She seemed disturbed, unsure. "We'll have to see," she said.

"Is it Qone?"

She didn't answer when he needed her to. Something as fishy as a Satsop salmon was going on with his life. Who was Henry James George after all?

Eleven years old and already asking the big question.

That night he awoke. The moon was full and white, sending a block of light into his room through the wide space in the curtains. He looked out the window, his elbows planted on the sill. Moonlight painted the fields around the house, coaxing a phosphorescent glow from the new grass. When the wind came up, the blades swelled, giving the illusion that he was on a mighty ship in the middle of a restless sea.

He hated the horse whose bones lay under the sod in the middle of their field. He cursed it from his window, even conjured its ghost in the pasture. There it stood, shiny and dark, bending its thick and muscular neck to tear at the grass. When its head rose, roots hung from its mouth as it chewed noisily, unrepentant, it mocked Henry.

"You should never have come here," he said.

He opened the window and felt the chill of the April night. He snapped his fingers and slapped his thigh. The horse vanished.

He leaned out and looked at the stars. Mrs. Obregon's first words came back to him, "It is you." They seemed innocent, but a warning lurked somewhere inside them that he couldn't parse.

The strange sickness he'd felt could be a temporary sign. Now he was renewed, stronger even. Whatever the feeling that crept over him, he knew he could survive it and move on. He knew that surgeons probably felt tired after a long surgery. Painters after a day in front of the easel. Singers felt tired after hitting the high note all concert long. Henry James George felt drained after attempting a cure. And after ministering to Simon, he wanted to help more than ever.

This must be how it worked: you think, you see visions, you make decisions, you read. Could it be any clearer? Suddenly, the River o' Life was not so murky after all.

Did he need more proof than Suzanne and his mother and this unknown boy? He didn't know it yet, but he felt Simon was cured. Sensed it in a part he had never met. Take that, Ralph Underwood. It was not all logic and computers and technology, at least not any kind of technology Ralph Underwood would understand.

But Henry had to be careful. Arrogant words perched on his tongue and wanted to jump out to the room, but he did a good job of keeping them in. He knew what they were. It was a warning. Those murmuring voices were a signal to be heeded, when you dabbled with magical fire.

"Okay," he said to calm himself. "All right. I'll be careful." But he was thrilled, and everyone knows a good thrill heeds no warning. This was surely it. Just like Mrs. Winkle had told them. He was now a blessed child of the future. He'd finally found the one thing that would change his life. Soon, no more the murderer. No more responsibility for his sister's death. No more the boy kids shied away from. He was now just like Mrs. Obregon. A *curandero*. It wouldn't be long before everyone would clamor for his power.

NINE

The news was all about the first American in space. Forget Russia, planes hijacked to Cuba, the new president. Alan Shepard was everywhere, so even in *The Oregonian*, Portland's big newspaper, it wasn't until page eight where you could read this:

LOCAL BOY CURED OF CANCER

It was so unbelievable few read it. Ho hum. Something spiritual. Something with snakes and tongues, perhaps? No one got cured of cancer. No one.

But someone else read it. Read it and read it. Then she found her delicate scissors and excised it carefully from the paper. Two and one-half column inches of mystery. But she knew what it was about. Knew it, and her brain wouldn't let it rest. Had not let it rest for four long years

Henry didn't read it; the Georges didn't subscribe to *The Oregonian* and papers closer to them didn't cover it. John preferred his news from the lips of trustworthy anchors on the television. Alice wouldn't dare spend her reading time on anything pulpy. So, the Georges were ignorant to the so-called facts laid out by the area's biggest newspaper. But of course, there was someone better than a newspaper and Henry pedaled to meet her. He asked about Simon and the outcome and Mrs. Obregon broke into the first real smile he had ever seen from her.

"He is well," she said. "He has been cured."

The news hit Henry like a soft caress, pleasurable and electrifying at the same time. His future opened to him as a wide and plentiful opportunity to help the entire world.

"I want this," Henry told Mrs. Obregon.

"Good," she said. "It will work if it works."

Henry sat on his bicycle on a sunny June morning. All around him the flowers, the shrubs, the trees were blooming red, white and pink. A bud was bursting inside him as well. Cataclysmically bursting; if he knew the word, that's how he might describe it. A feathery, tickly, tendril-y expansion in his chest. In a few more years he might even call it orgasmic.

He took off, pumping life into the bike and himself. Word from Mrs. Obregon about more work was like being shot with hope; prickly at first and then a spreading warm joy. He looked at the sky and wondered what it was like for that astronaut to be blasted so far and to plummet back to earth so fast. A metaphor for fame that he ignored because he was still pre-fame.

But he wanted more. The bodily sensation he'd experienced with Simon had not returned. It looked to be wide open for the *curandero* now. Someone at *The Oregonian* knew. Eventually, Henry would like everyone to know.

For now, he would especially like his classmates to know. Because then he would be free of the tag, that slander perpetrated by Ralph Underwood, that Henry had caused his best friend to disappear from the earth. If he didn't do something now, that blight was going to haunt him for the rest of his life.

Henry sped straight along the Tulane Road until he spied Mrs. Simpson at her mailbox, the arched lip of it pulled open, sorting through letters. She wore her coveralls with one strap hanging over her chest. Her hair sported tight French braids. Deftly, he steered to the other side of the road.

He'd seen documentaries about the big cats of Africa, and they moved much like Mrs. Simpson did now, a gathering of muscles at the joints, a determined push off from a solid heel. In seconds, she had leapt across the road and grabbed onto Henry. Henry bleated out like one of those impalas might when fate dealt it such a hideous outcome, and he lost his ability to steer the bike. Three seconds more and he was in the ditch, mangled in with his machine whose front wheel now spun in an ever-slowing revolution.

Mrs. Simpson was on top of him, wrenching his neck so that his lips were only inches from hers.

"You did it, didn't you?"

"I don't know what you're talking about."

The buckle on her strap bit into his neck. She jammed her hand in her top pocket and pulled out a tiny piece of newsprint. "This was you."

Henry tried to get his eyes to focus but could only make out the word, Cured. He couldn't nod, couldn't shake his head, so he merely said: "Help."

She held onto him a bit longer. "I know this was you and you know how I know? I got a message from my son. And you know how I know it was from my son? A mother knows."

Finally, Henry could get a good look at the article. "Oh," he said. It was the first time he'd seen it and took a moment to read it all. When he was finished, he couldn't keep a smile from his face.

"Yes, oh." She drug him off the bike. She shook him until his foot, tangled between two spokes, broke free.

Henry looked both ways along the Tulane but saw no help coming from either direction.

"So, here's what I'm thinking," said Mrs. Simpson. "I'm thinking if you can murder somebody, if you have those special abilities, then you can un-murder them too."

It might have been Henry's first experience with true crazy and it made him want to piss his pants. "I didn't murder anybody."

She grabbed him by the shoulders and shook him again until spit strung from his mouth. "Listen, you little ditch rat. Don't you get it? Haven't I been clear enough? I don't care what you think. I don't know how you did it, but I know you cured this here boy from the cancer. Probably with that old Injun woman would be my guess, but I don't care about her either. What I care about is getting my boy back. And you're going to do that for me, aren't you?" More shaking, more rattling eyeballs. Then she let him go for good.

Quickly, Henry drug his bicycle back onto the road. The handlebars were cockeyed, but he wrenched them back to true. Mrs. Simpson crossed the road and collected the mail scattered in front of her driveway. For a moment, they squared off from opposite sides of the battlefield.

"It's going to happen," Mrs. Simpson said.

TEN

It had to come out. Six cures could not lie dormant and unappreciated for long. The woman from Olympia whose rickets disappeared was overjoyed, and her neighbor who watched her friend crack bones for twenty years couldn't wait to tell her bridge club and her bridge club, individually and collectively spread the news until a doctor got a whiff of the scent and then another and then the biggest prize of all, a television reporter opened the gift of a human-interest story to beat all human-interest stories.

She was the one who located Henry.

They met on the hottest day of the year. A cloud of humidity had dropped over the George farm and wrung seas of liquid out of everyone. Except for Miss Bright, the promising cub reporter from the Seattle news station KKYI. She was as clean and crisp as a nun in an air-conditioned convent.

The Georges all sat in their homemade Adirondack chairs on the coolest side of the house. Alice's index finger held her place in a book she guarded in her lap. Suzanne was overdressed in something blue with an empire waist. One tiny high heel anchored her in the grass.

John gripped the slivery arms of his chair. Sweat poured from every follicle. His smile was forced but obliging.

"I cannot and will not create chaos for this family," Miss Bright said. "That is not my intent. I as much as anyone know the power a simple TV message can have. For that reason, I would like to treat this as an anecdote, a footnote at the bottom of life's page here on the plains of Inland Western Washington."

"Uh, we agree," said John.

Henry, who started out wearing his best Sunday trousers and vest, clodhopper shoes and a clip-on tie, had divested each, one by one, as if involved in some peculiar strip poker game. He was down to a T-shirt and pants and still he had dehydrated like a sun-blasted apricot. He'd been here before, albeit in the Rochester Elementary auditorium listening to Ralph Underwood destroy his life and, even though he was sure Miss Bright was trustworthy, there was history and rotten luck to consider.

"He's called a cure-an-dare-o," Suzanne said, unprovoked.

"See, that's the thing," said Miss Bright, who drug over her chair and plopped in front of Henry. "How is that possible? I mean, no offense, but you don't look the part of a, what is it, Mexican mountain shaman."

"What?" Henry said.

"How did you get to be what you've turned out to be?"

"Practice?" said Henry.

"I must say," said Alice. "That's a question even the best adult finds hard to answer."

Miss Bright shrugged. "I know I got here through hard work and determination."

"Good for you," Alice said. She bit at her lip until it trickled watery blood. "Perhaps we should get this over with before we all melt into nothing."

It went rather well. Each of the Georges got a word in about their reaction to their brother or son. And Henry was appropriately self-deprecating and humble regarding his gift. Miss Bright was satisfied. It may have been the last time the Georges stood together as a solid family unit when they waved at the news truck as it made its dusty way down their road

It was not pandemonium; it was pandemonium's close cousin, hubbub. In any event, Rochester would never be the same. At last, and not a moment too soon, they had a hometown boy to celebrate. Locally, Henry was a star. Regionally, he was a name not yet whispered in hope, but recognizable, nonetheless. Nationally, perhaps in due time.

Cars careened along the Tulane and slowed as they neared the George place. Heads popped out of windows; cameras focused in shaky hands. Henry contended with this, but the first time he mounted his bike for Mrs. Obregon's, he was met on the road by what could only be called a rural traffic jam. People wanted autographs. They wanted him to tend to their sick aunts. Henry retreated to the barn and hid in a horse stall.

Alice followed him in there one day and sat quietly on the hay. She studied her son, pulling her wispy hair back and tucking it securely behind an ear. "We can put an end to this," she said.

"How?"

"You can stop doing what it is you do."

"But I don't want to. Mrs. Obregon thinks I've been chosen."

Alice shook her head. "That woman can be a bit hysterical. Who does she say has chosen you?"

"I don't exactly know. Somebody named Qone?"

"Oh my," said Alice.

"Only I'm not Indian so there could be a problem." He pushed himself further against the wall. "You don't believe it's true, do you?"

"On the contrary, I know what you did for that boy who was dying. No, it isn't that I don't believe you have something. I just don't know what or how or whether it's good for you."

"I don't want to give it up. It's important to me."

"Fair enough. But could we be a little less public about it?"

Neither Henry nor his mother had any idea what was being meticulously planned not that far down their own Tulane Road. A mother scorned, and all that. Something lurked.

Aunt Peg was ordering fall bulbs from the hardware when she spied the note on the community bulletin board, right next to the worn one asking patrons to please not urinate in the corners. This was what it said:

A MIRACLE WILL HAPPEN ON SATURDAY AUGUST 26
WAYMAN SIMPSON WILL FINALLY COME BACK HOME
WATCH ROCHESTER'S FAMOUS HEALER
HENRY JAMES GEORGE BRING HIM BACK
THE EMPTY LOT ONE O'CLOCK

Aunt Peg thought Mrs. Simpson was at her crazy tricks again, but when she stopped by the Super-Valu, the same notice was tacked on that community board. And at the post office. And, as it turned out, on nearly every telephone pole in the greater Rochester area.

If Rochester were a bumblebee, it would have been buzzing loudly. They all, of course, knew about Henry and his power, but none had seen it in action. It was better than Squaxin Days, even with the fireworks. Plans were made by nearly everyone to hold the 26th open.

For her part, Mrs. Simpson did an extra cleaning of Wayman's old room. She picked gladiolas from the patch against the shed and set a pitcher of them next to his old bed. She oiled the squeaky wheels of her husband's chair and hummed a proper tune: Dvorak's "Going Home."

Aunt Peg called Alice to tell her of the curious invitations she'd seen. Alice drove in and inspected the evidence. There was little to misinterpret. She consulted John when he got home.

"The hell you say," was John's reaction. "This I've got to see."

At dinner, Henry found out what the others already knew. Alice took one of the notices and passed it to her son.

"Do you know anything about this?" she asked.

As he read, Henry felt a cold steely claw latch firmly to his cranium. He feared he would be lifted from the table much like he was in the DeSoto those years ago. But it loosened its grip as he considered what the notice said.

"Of course, you'll not be doing this," Alice said.

"Of course," echoed John.

Henry set the paper aside. "I want to be normal."

"There," said Alice. "That settles it. I'll call Mrs. Simpson and put an end to this."

"So that's why I should do it." It was a perfect plan. And the best part was that other people would watch the miracle happen. When Wayman Simpson fell back into Rochester, it would be as it was before. Not that he knew for sure that bringing someone back was part of his power, but he had a feeling.

"I want to be normal," he repeated, louder this time.

"I want you to be safe," said Alice. "John?"

He leaned back in his chair. "I say give the kid what he wants. Might be a long time before normal comes calling round here again."

Alice stared him down, but John was helping himself to seconds. For his part, Henry felt more optimistic than he had in years. Normal was just around the corner. Alice, on the other hand, fingered her book over to her plate and opened it. In a moment, she was lost someplace else.

In the name of all things hopeful, Henry appeared in Rochester on Saturday August 26th. He wore the emblem of his arrival: his dress pants, a bit high-water for the times; a pair of brogues that cramped his toes like those of a concubine in the Song Dynasty; a short sleeve white dress shirt whose third button was not the same as the rest but not so different that it was immediately noticeable; his belt lolled like a leathery tongue; and his ubiquitous black and gray slant stripe clip-on tie hung slightly askance. His hair was trimmed and pomaded with Wildroot cream oil, which curdled as he walked the humid main street.

Lawn chairs of all shapes, colors and sizes lined the street. Umbrellas shaded the older folks, some of them with coat hangers to keep them rigged to the chairs. Pedal pushers and cut-off Levi's dominated the fashion scene. So many people for such a small town. Henry knew about half of them.

He hesitated only when his father parked the DeSoto in the elementary school lot. Something pulled at him, a first warning perhaps, but it passed. He would do this. Not because of Mrs. Simpson and her fiery temper, but because it was just and honorable. His certainty of success buoyed his family who accompanied him as far as the Rochester Tavern where Henry informed them he needed to go the rest of the way alone. He felt like a Western sheriff, uncertain who or what destiny awaited him at the other side of this capricious corral. But it wasn't long before the cameraman dogged him while Miss Bright thrust a microphone in his face for a pre-miracle statement.

They let him be when he came to the vacant lot, a weed-heavy piece of ground littered with wrappers and non-returnable bottles. To one side, a rusted burn barrel leaned against a wall. Today, a big wooden chair, a throne really, sat in the very middle of it. A tiny end table hugged it close. On it sat a small glass, half full of water, a ticking clock with a phosphorescent dial, and a thin hardbound book of about sixty or so pages. It was seeing this book that stopped Henry at the edge of the lot. For the first time, he felt a nibble of doubt. He had no hand in selecting the book. Would that make a difference? He'd never brought anyone back. Would that work?

The mayor was there, and while you might have expected him to be dressed in finery more befitting the occasion, he wore a pair of loose-fitting cords and a checked short-sleeve shirt unbuttoned halfway down his torso. A microphone whose cable trailed to a boxy speaker on the edge of the lot, hung from one of his hands.

"Welcome," he said to Henry, and stuck out his free hand.

Henry took it. "Hello."

That's when Henry saw Mrs. Simpson. She stood on the opposite side of the street. Though the sun was blazing, she wore a bonnet type contraption on her head and was tip to toe covered in a dress that would be more comfortable on, say, Laura Ingalls Wilder. She held her hands together in supplication. Mr. Simpson sat at her side, his own umbrella protecting him from the glare.

The mayor handed Henry the microphone. "Now we all want to be sure to hear what you've got to say, young man," he said.

But Henry gave it back. "No, it has to be me. My voice."

"Sure, it does," said the mayor. He checked his watch. "Well, it looks to be time."

Henry walked over to the chair. He peered at the book. Not meaning to, he laughed out loud. *The Velveteen Rabbit.*

Of course. What else would Wayman enjoy? Not the school's best reader, still, he adored this book. Henry picked it up as he sat on a straight wooden chair. He held it out and smiled at the picture of the special stuffed rabbit and thought about its meaning in the world. The cover was well-worn, dyed with old sweat on its edges. Henry held it to his nose and took in a big lungful. It smelled like, well, Wayman Simpson. He flipped it open and fanned the pages. One of them had a half-moon tear in the upper right corner. The breeze tickled his face. He looked at the crowd lining the edge of the lot. He hoped this was the spectacle he would be remembered for. The clock on the table hit 1:00 and Henry started to read.

In a proud, ringing voice, he told of the Christmas present that appeared in a stocking one day. People in the street immediately nodded along with the story:

'There once was a Velveteen Rabbit, and in the beginning he was really splendid.'

It was the greatest moment yet of Henry's life. Better than watching the words float across the Olympic Peninsula. Better than reading about his triumph in the newspaper. He felt victorious, immortal, maybe even evangelical and his audience was real and sincere and exuberant. These were his people, and they were listening to him. They believed him. They saw him now for what and who he was and was about to become. Henry, the local *curandero* who had crawled out of his slimy bog of alleged criminality and was about to make things right. It was working. Soon, he would see his friend.

When he finished the story, the crowd erupted into cacophonous applause, so much so that Henry had to stand and acknowledge them with a tip of the book at his temple. The applause lasted for minutes, built to a crescendo and then calmed. People clapped more slowly as they swiveled their heads around, looking for Wayman Simpson.

When the ovation had finally stopped, the mayor stepped forward. "How does this work now?" he said.

"Maybe he drops right out of the sky," suggested Suzanne. The mayor automatically ducked and squinted at the sun.

"Is it not instantaneous?" asked Miss Bright.

"No, it takes time," said Mrs. Simpson. "Ain't that right, Henry? Henry?" She licked her lips with a rapid-fire tongue.

"Well. It took quite a few days for my mom." Now that he had stopped reading, his heart rate was returning to normal, and he could breathe more easily.

"Didn't take more than a day for that little feller from Portland," said someone still lingering out in the street.

"I guess it depends," Henry said.

"Maybe he's afraid," Mrs. Simpson said. "Yeah, that's it. There are too many of you around here. Ain't that possible, Henry? Too many." She turned to Miss Bright. "And he was always scared of cameras. Why don't you shoo and give him some breathing space?"

Miss Bright frowned. "If he does return, Henry, will you let me know?"

"Oh, he'll return all right," said Mrs. Simpson.

People started drifting. A row of concession stands beckoned further up the street. Soon, everyone was gone except for John and Alice and Suzanne, Uncle Ray and the Simpsons. Mrs. Simpson stared deep into Henry's eyes.

Henry fell back into the chair, his legs shaky. Maybe he had been more anxious than he thought. "Here's your book," he said to Mrs. Simpson.

She snatched it and spent a few seconds studying the cover. "I don't know why he liked this so much."

"It's about loyalty," Henry said. "That's Wayman."

"You think so, do you?" Mrs. Simpson turned to go but had second thoughts. "Loyalty, you say? Huh. To you maybe. Not to his father and me." Then she walked away.

ELEVEN

As he made his escape from the debacle of the empty lot, Henry heard the whispers. "Fraud. Phony. Conceited jerk". It was an easy enough way to think. After all, despite the extensive buildup and promotion, a half hour after the reading, no Wayman. Only a few hours later, Henry was lying in his bed in the deepest of funks. By his calculation, the reading had to have worked because he felt the strange bodily sensation while he was doing it. But what went wrong? He was back to thinking maybe it was the book after all. He hadn't chosen it. What was he going to do? With this failure, how would he redeem himself?

That night, when he finally dropped off, a curious story unfolded. He awoke to a thump against the side of the house. Not a big bang, but an almost gentle whoomph. He raised his head and tried to look through the window to see if a storm was closing in, but the darkness blinded him to it. He lay back down. Then, the faint sound of a rhythmic scraping that felt closer and closer until finally, a tap on the window.

Henry bolted upright, grasping for the switch on the lamp. "Who's there?"

The tap-tap at the window sounded again and this time he saw actual fingers doing it. "Hankie? Is this still your room?"

He knew the voice, of course, and every air sac and corpuscle in his body cried out. "Wayman!"

"Let me in."

Henry leapt out of bed in T-shirt and underpants and flipped the window lock, pulled it open, and Wayman Simpson tumbled into his bedroom. Wayman caught his breath and when he stood, it was as if he would never stop rising.

Even though he was always tall, Henry was amazed how much Wayman towered over him. "How?" Henry sputtered.

"Puberty, bud," said Wayman. He wore a logger's tin pants, a flannel shirt and a pair of heavy boots that would trip any other kid. "You got a washer?

"But where? How?"

"It was you who did it, Hankie." He sat and started unlacing his boots. "Little jerk."

At last, at last, Henry thought. "You disappeared into thin air. I've been waiting and waiting for you."

The other boot got Wayman's attention. "That's funny. I haven't been waiting for you."

"They think I killed you."

Wayman toed the other boot off and unraveled the socks. He stood again, unhooked the bibs on his pants and wiggled them to the floor. Underneath was a healthy pair of well-used long johns. "In a way, you did."

"What does that mean?"

The flannel came off before Wayman, slowly and deftly, unbuttoned the long johns. He shrugged out of the arms and then pulled off the rest. Now he stood large and naked in front of his old friend.

Henry looked away, but not before he noticed puberty had indeed visited Wayman Simpson and touched him in the important areas. When he glanced back, Wayman was holding out the clothes.

"They itch something fierce," he said. "And the pants, you're not supposed to wash them, but if you turn them inside out, you can do it."

Henry took them downstairs, creeping all the way. Although he wanted this news to spread, for now he wanted no one else privy to it. The washer was far enough away from his parents' bedroom that its noise would not wake them. He turned the stiff pants inside out and threw everything in the machine.

Back in his room, Wayman sat in the chair, legs spread out, hands folded over his abdomen. "You want a shower?" Henry asked. "Do they take showers where you come from?"

Wayman pooched out his lips and nodded. Henry led him down the hall, found a towel and warned about noise. In a few minutes, Wayman was back, rubbing his wet hair into a tall crewcut.

"You owe me an explanation," Henry said as Wayman lounged on the bed.

"Okay, shoot. I know everything now, so this should be easy."

"Number one: Where have you been?"

"Does the first one have to be the hardest? The answer is I'm not sure."

"You said you know everything."

"I do."

"So, where were you?"

"I told you I don't know. See, I do know everything. I even know what I don't know."

"How did you get back?"

"It was you. You and that book and that crowd in town."

"But you didn't show."

"Oh, yes, I did. Only, who am I to come prancing into the middle of everybody? No siree Bob, that's not for me. I hid until all the lights went out."

"It really did work," Henry said to himself. He felt relieved he hadn't lost his power.

"There I was, minding my own business, working in the woods and poof, gone. Pissed me off, Hankie boy. And right before lunch too. I thought I was done with the disappearing crap."

"Working in what woods? You're not old enough."

"I don't know what woods. But yes, the woods. And yes, work. My mom gave you that book to read, didn't she?"

"Yes."

"I knew it. Hey, hold on a second, so you're the guy they're all talking about."

"Who's talking about?"

"They. Everybody. The other people there."

Henry felt the frustration he always felt with Wayman, only different. It was like Wayman had found a good excuse for his lack of knowledge and understanding. But this boy-man, this near stranger sitting in front of him hardly seemed the same person who disappeared in 1957.

"And you best be careful."

"Of what?"

"There's some Indian guy who runs the place. I don't think he likes you much."

"But I never did anything bad to the Indians."

"I'm just telling you," Wayman said.

"What was it like?" Henry said. "You have to tell me. You were here and then you weren't."

Wayman cocked his head. "Like I was one second all together and the next, breaking apart. I'd say I was floating, but it was faster than that, like being in a super-fast elevator."

"And you get off in heaven?"

Wayman showed once crooked teeth that were now perfect. "No God there, I have to say. Or who's the other guy? St. Peter. None of the big ones from church. Maybe that Indian's a god."

"You must have met someone."

"I did. You ever hear of Russell Viorst?"

Henry recalled his first conversation with Mrs. Obregon. "Cow's hoof? Monkey tail?"

"Yep. Boy does that thing get in the way. Nice Indian fellow though."

"But where is it? Can't you at least tell me that?"

"It's just..." Here his eyes narrowed, and it looked to be an idea he had struggled with before. "It just is."

"Please tell me."

Wayman scratched at his stomach, and it sounded like sandpaper. "Okay, you're not going to like it, but here goes. At first, I didn't know where I was, and it was scary, but everyone else already knew me and I got used to it. Now, it's not a big deal where it is or what it is."

Henry couldn't get his brain to accept this. "You're going to leave me in the dark?"

"Listen to me," Wayman said. "I was here the whole time. Here in Rochester, but a different Rochester. That's all I know. That's all I can say." He uncrossed his legs and then crossed them the other way. "Well, maybe one more thing. You got anything to eat?"

The pants made noise when Henry moved them to the dryer, but the long johns muffled them enough to keep Henry's parents in bed. When it stopped, Henry brought the clothes back.

"Do you want to spend the night?" he asked. "Tomorrow we can go to your house. Boy, I want to see the look on your parents' face. Your mom, she's the one who arranged the whole reading. She misses you."

"Uh, no," said Wayman. "The whole reason I came here is I don't know how to get myself back."

"You don't want to stay?"

Wayman started putting on his clothes. "I like it better there."

"But you have to stay. You're my proof I'm not a killer. You have to tell everybody you're alive. Stay, and then go."

Wayman thrust his arm into one of the legs of the tin pants, grabbed the cuff, and pulled it back through. He repeated it with the other leg. "I think it would be worse for my parents if they saw me and I left again. And if anybody else finds out, they'll spill the beans to them. I can't let anyone know. And you can't, either."

Henry laid his hands flat on the bed. "Please, Wayman, I've been counting on you all these years. You have to help me. Please?"

Wayman threw on the pants. "There's something you've got to understand. I don't know if you remember, but life here wasn't exactly the best. You were my only friend, and you were practically a baby. Now, where I am? It's still the same but my favorite dream come true. Nobody cares what I am or how long it takes for me to tell a bad joke. Besides, there's girls there. And they think I'm a stud."

"So what."

As he buttoned the flannel shirt, Wayman studied his friend. "Yeah, I guess you wouldn't know about that yet. But, girls, Hankie. It's a whole different world."

"There are girls here."

Wayman sat and pulled on his socks, then started with the boots.

"I need you," Henry tried. "Please."

Wayman stopped the lacing about halfway on one boot. He tousled Henry's hair. The hand felt wide and heavy.

"We're different," Wayman said. "It will never be the same. It can't be." He put out his hands next to each other and quickly split them apart before he banked them to the right like a pair of fighter jets. "You and me used to be on the same road, and it's like we're still tracking each other, but it's like two trains racing side by side. We'll never come back together at the end."

"What are you talking about?"

"Don't worry so much." He patted Henry's head again. "We'll always be side by side, but we won't cross." He started the laces once more. "Anyway, that's the way they explain it."

"They?"

"Don't ask." Wayman said. "It'll only confuse you."

Henry crossed his arms hard at his chest. He wanted to be more mature about this, but it came rolling right out his mouth. "Then I won't help you."

Wayman pulled the cuffs of his pants and stood, shaking them out. He took Henry's chin in his hand.

"You will help me because we're friends and friends get their friends what they need. And I need to go back." He let the chin go. "So, where's the book?"

"At your house," Henry said.

"Damn."

"Your mom wanted it back. I think she uses it to remember you by."

"Well, you have to get it."

"Me? Now?"

"Of course, you. Of course, now. Haven't you been listening? I need to get back."

At midnight, Henry descended the ladder. Dew made his sneakers slippery. Wayman waited at the bottom. All was quiet under a star-filled sky.

They crept to the barn where Henry pulled out his bike. "How?" he said, but Wayman had already stolen it from him and mounted the seat. His feet were flat on the ground on either side, with plenty of room to spare at the seat. He patted the handlebars and when Henry balked, lifted him and settled him on top of them.

"Watch that bolt," he said.

Wayman wobbled them out to the Tulane Road, and they picked up enough speed to stay balanced. Henry felt Wayman's hot breath on his neck as he labored along. Eyes used to the darkness now, clumps of alder and scrub fir loomed like washed out soldiers guarding the side of the road. Henry still felt tilted, but wouldn't it be grand if this were him and Wayman on a normal late night, sneaking out like kids were wont to do?

In minutes, they arrived at the Simpsons' driveway. Wayman balanced the bike again with his big feet. "I can't go in there. I'll wait here. You get the book."

"But where is it? How do I get in?"

"Five will get you ten it's by my bed. Just go." Wayman pushed him off the bike.

Henry kicked at the gravel as he stumbled to the house. Mrs. Simpson was known as a night owl, but there were no lights shining through the windows. Henry skirted the cellar doors and the oil tank and climbed to the back door. The knob turned easily in his hand.

Poking his head in, he smelled the remains of dinner and cigarette smoke. He eased his way into the kitchen and closed the door as silently as he could. He stopped for a moment to get his bearings. He thought, parents left and Wayman right.

But as he crept through the kitchen, a light flashed on. He fell back against the table and knocked over a vase.

Mr. Simpson sat in his wheelchair. A pistol trembled in his hand. "I had a feeling," he said.

"What feeling?" Henry clamped his legs together to keep from wetting his pants. He stared at the gun.

"I had a feeling my boy would come walking through that door tonight. He was always a latecomer and I figured he just got lost on the way back."

"Reggie?" It was Mrs. Simpson, standing at the mouth of the hallway, tightening the sash of her robe. She noticed Henry. "Ah, a burglar."

"No," said Henry. "It's not what you think."

"Then what is it? Please tell. I can hardly wait."

Henry thought fast. He had a jewel case of options, none of which seemed reasonable. He snatched one that sparkled. "I wanted to read the book again, just in case."

"Wayman's book?"

"Yes. I'm sorry, but I woke up thinking about it."

Wayman's parents looked at each other. There was more than sleep in their eyes. For the moment, suspicion bested hope. "Why are you really here?" Mrs. Simpson asked. "Haven't you done enough as it is?"

"I really really want to help. I think if I can read it one more time, Wayman will come back."

In a complete turnaround from her usual treatment of Henry, Mrs. Simpson slid over in her mules and gathered him in. "You've come with your heart in your hands. Reggie, he's here to repent."

Mrs. Simpson's chest smelled like Vicks and it cleared his sinuses with one healthy noseful. He tried to talk into her bosom.

"Let the boy breathe," said Mr. Simpson. "Hell, you suffocate every fellow you meet!"

She held Henry out in front of her. "You still got your voice left after today?"

Henry shrugged. "It takes it out of a guy," he said. Mr. Simpson lit a cigarette and clutched the burning match, just staring at it, until it faded out.

"Come with me," Mrs. Simpson said, as she corralled Henry and led him down the hallway to Wayman's bedroom. It was much as he left it; a picture of the first monkey in space adorned one wall, a basketball and football lodged in a corner on a table. A light green cowboy bedspread, a teddy bear resting on it. Mr. Simpson rolled to the doorway and took a puff off his cigarette.

"Boy's older now. He comes back, he's not going to like this. Ought to hang a picture of that Monroe woman. Will make him want to come home faster."

"Hush," Mrs. Simpson said. She grasped the book that rested next to the vase of homecoming glads. "You know what I think? I think a boy like you must be so tired of reading to other people."

"Oh, I don't mind. But I need a moment."

"Oh, you need...oh my..."

"I need to be alone."

"Yes, you do," said Mrs. Simpson.

Henry waited for Mrs. Simpson to leave. He ran to the window and peeked through the curtain. He could barely make out his bicycle, but was relieved to see Wayman still astride it, picking his nose.

Inside of a minute, he was back standing by the bed when the knock came on the door. Mrs. Simpson pushed it open and stood, backlit, with her hands clasped at her cheek. From out of her chest, she pulled a handkerchief and dabbed at her eyes. "Thank you," she said. "You dear dear boy."

Behind her, Mr. Simpson sat in the doorway, a different cigarette in his hand. The light was so bright around him he resembled one of those interviews on TV where they hid the identity of the speaker.

"You may begin," Mrs. Simpson said. She sat on the end of the bed, signaling Henry to sit as well.

Henry cleared his throat and opened the book to the first page. He heard all sorts of voices of caution speaking to him before he had even gotten out one word. What was he doing? What might happen? What made him think he could send Wayman back to the land he came from? Before he started, he blurted out, "Wait!"

"Wait what?"

His face flushed pink, his hope grew rust.

Mrs. Simpson felt his forehead. "Are you all right?"

"I don't think I should do this."

"Of course, you should. It was your idea and I for one think it's a good one."

Mr. Simpson drew off the cigarette and spoke as smoke chugged out of his mouth. "What are you afraid of?"

Those voices of caution got the better of him. "It's a lie," he said.

"I knew it. I can see fear all over your face. Saw it a lot in the conflict. You're a fraud."

"Reggie, the boy is doing us a favor. He's our possibility. And what's wrong with that?"

Mr. Simpson wriggled his shoulders.

"Couldn't you read it?" she said, fighting tears.

"I'd better not," Henry said. "And I'm not a fraud. Wayman already came back. If I read to him, he might disappear."

Mrs. Simpson snapped open her eyes and Mr. Simpson rolled in closer to the bed. "What did you say?" she said.

Henry slipped off the bed. "Come with me." He was so secretive about it; just to be sure, Mr. Simpson pulled the pistol out of the blanket and held it breast high as he followed Mrs. Simpson to the window. He rolled his chair between the other two.

"Thank the Lord," said Mrs. Simpson.

Henry peered out. There sat Wayman, still astride the bike, still with a big finger in his nose.

"What is it?" asked Mr. Simpson.

But his wife was already flying from the room. She tore out the back door and was on the road so fast, that Henry was able to see the mother and son reunion in real time. In her rush, Mrs. Simpson hit Wayman so hard that she bowled him over and they tumbled to the road in a heap of arms and legs.

Henry thought there was music he needed to face. He walked out of the house, Mr. Simpson not far behind. He stood in the gravel while Mr. Simpson wheeled over to his family. Mother and son managed to right the bike and get to their feet.

"Oh, my boy," Mrs. Simpson cried. "You're back with us. Praise the Lord."

Wayman cast his eyes over to Henry and formed them into daggers. "Yes, praise the Lord," he said.

PART II

NEW PROSPERTY

THE NEW PROSPERITY MUSEUM

TWELVE

Despite Henry's laudable feat of bringing back his friend, Wayman Simpson stopped speaking to him. It hurt Henry more than he imagined. Phone calls were brief with many hang-ups. Attempts to corral Wayman at the Simpson farm were met with a stonewall of unprecedented proportion.

One time he did manage to keep Wayman on the phone, only to have him talk about alternate universes and a life far superior to the one he was back to on the Tulane Road. This was a story Henry was frankly getting a little tired of. Henry wanted their old life back. Wanted a confidante to help him through this famous part of his life. Wanted his friend to appreciate what Henry had done for him and for the world, for that matter. Where would he find such a person?

He had told Miss Bright that Wayman had returned but she wanted proof and Wayman was not about to provide it. Henry did talk Miss Bright into accompanying him to Mrs. Obregon's and she sat placidly with her cameraman as Henry worked his magic on an older woman whose hair was falling out because of the extreme chemotherapy she was undergoing in hopes of curing her lung cancer.

"So, the day in the vacant lot was no fluke," she said to Henry as she watched him select the right book for the woman, a Mildred Haines. "Your process is always the same?"

"That's right," he said. "But I'm going to need you to be quiet please."

He held the book in his hands. He had to admit with the presence of Miss Bright, he felt a bit shaky, but it didn't last long. Who could feel shaky with Shakespeare preparing to do his work?

"But why Shakespeare?" she asked, this time to Mrs. Haines.

"Because I've never found anything better," she replied in a hoarse voice. "I want to always be able to read so I can always have something that makes me feel healed."

"I ask that you not talk to the patient," Henry said. "It may get in the way of a cure."

Miss Bright nodded and sat back while Henry began to read:

"And this our life, exempt from public haunt,
Finds tongues in trees, books in the running brooks,
Sermons in stones, and good in everything."

Henry felt the words hook into him, was happy that he never had to explain what he was reading because Shakespeare's verse was at times confounding. But his patient seemed to enjoy it. She lay on Mrs. Obregon's bed, a smile glued to her lips, her hands crossed at her chest, as if she were ready to say goodbye to the world if that's what the gods requested. When Henry was finished, Mildred rose.

"Thank you, young man," she said. "That was hopeful."

Mrs. Obregon stood at the entrance to the bedroom, a look of concern blistering her face. She unfolded her arms, said goodbye to Mrs. Haines and slipped into the room. She glanced at Miss Bright. "I wonder if I could speak to Henry," she said.

"I don't want to be a problem," said Miss Bright, as she left, cantering toward Mrs. Haines.

Henry put the book away and waited. It didn't take long.

"I don't think having this woman here is helpful," Mrs. Obregon said.

"I was thinking the more people who know, the more people who can be helped."

"That may be how you're thinking about your gift, but it is not how Skookumchuck thinks. You are breaking the rules."

"But what are the rules? No one has told me."

"If you are in fact the chosen one, then you should already know the rules."

Henry wondered if he might challenge her. "Okay," he said. Together they stood in front of the window and watched Miss Bright interview Mrs. Haines.

"You see what happens with special gifts," Mrs. Obregon said. "The world wants to take it on and make less of it. This you don't want, and we don't want. Please, young Henry, do not make your gift less than it is."

"Can you do this, Mrs. Obregon? Can you cure people?"

"I am a *curandera*."

"But I've never seen you actually do it."

"Your friend, Ray, Jr. I am his *curandera*. You've seen that."

"Am I a *curandero*?"

"Not if you use it so you can wear it like a badge. Then you are nothing more than a charlatan. A circus sideshow."

That revelation stung. Henry knew he didn't want to be anyone's circus performer. A larger picture was coming together now. A *curandero* meant more than simply curing people. Maybe he should lend a more empathic ear to Wayman. He decided to give it a try.

Henry pedaled down the Tulane Road to Wayman's house. As he did, he recalled the time Wayman's mother had jumped him on that very road and marveled at how much the world had changed since that day. It had certainly changed for Mrs. Simpson.

The happy mother herself was out riding the tractor when Henry arrived. She spied him, waved, and pointed to the hayloft of the barn. Henry rounded the place, immediately seeing his former best friend sitting on the hay at the high loading door of the barn. He looked like he might be contemplating a jump, but Henry threw him an enthusiastic wave anyway.

It took Henry little time to navigate the ladder to the loft, and soon he was sitting next to Wayman, and both stared out the window watching Mrs. Simpson cut even rows of hay. Over the sound of her tractor, the boys could hear her singing a church tune.

"She seems happy," Henry said.

"At least somebody is," Wayman said. He picked a piece of straw out of his hair and examined it.

"You're still mad at me?"

"What do you think? I told you I was. Man, you stole me right out of the best thing that ever happened to me."

Henry prepared for the juggernaut of complaint. "I said I was sorry then and I'm still sorry now. But I had to do it. How else was I going to prove I'm not a murderer?"

"Well, that's pretty much what they call you where I was."

"Okay, now. Why do they call me that? I haven't even been there."

"They call you a murderer and The Great Imposter. And they say they haven't called anybody that since the *suyapi* stole our land."

"I don't see that as very funny," Henry said. "And that's what I am? A *suyapi*? What's that?"

Wayman rose and spit out the window. "White person. Plain and simple. If you're expecting me to sugarcoat it, I'm done with that. I've thought about it, and I'm done being nice just so you'll give in and send me back. We're all done with sugarcoating."

"I'm sorry, Way. I really am. But I think I did it for her too." He pointed to Mrs. Simpson. "Doesn't that matter to you?"

He looked at Henry then, shoved one of his hands in a pocket, slouched. "I don't think I can believe you now."

"But why?"

Wayman shrugged. "Because maybe I think the same about you that they do. I think you might be an imposter. You're not supposed to be a *curandero* and before you ask me why, I think you already know."

Henry thought about irony. After all this rigamarole about him being a killer and he still ends in the same boat of ridicule, but this time the scorners live in a different dimension. Henry tried to shrug it off. "Tell me what it was like where you were."

"Nah. You got important people to talk to. You've got to build on your fame. It's a waste of your time and mine. I'm surprised you're even here. Big shots like you never come to our house."

"Don't be that way. It was driving your mom crazy not having you around. You know that."

Wayman chewed the straw. "Maybe so. But you're not hearing me. There, in that other Rochester, there was a place for me, man. I belonged. Finally, I belonged. Believe me or don't believe me but it's the truth."

"I said I'm sorry."

"You know what I am now? I'm still the freak show I always was here. No work. No girls batting an eye at me. People think I ran away and came back. Big deal. I wouldn't be the first kid to leave home. So, I ask you again. Which place would you want to be in?"

"But there can't be two Rochesters," Henry said. "That doesn't make sense."

"Oh, and everything else does. You curing people of deadly diseases? Me flying into the universe happens every day. Yeah, right."

Henry leaned back against the wall. Soon, all he could hear was the putt-putt of Mrs. Simpson's tractor. He had not thought this all the way through. He heard Wayman, felt pain in his own gut. But what could he do about it?".

He recalled the vision he saw in Mrs. Obregon's eye. It was he who was lifted from the Andersons' hayfield, not his friend. It was like there was some mistake. But how could that be when here he had been all this time fielding calls from Mrs. Obregon? Doing interviews on TV and radio?

"You know what pisses me off the most?" Wayman said.

"What?"

"You didn't even ask me if I wanted to come back."

"How was I supposed to ask your permission? I didn't know where you were. No one did."

Wayman kept shaking his head. "It ain't right. You don't do that to your best friend."

Maybe not. Wayman had Henry in a bind, and it was nice and tight. "I didn't know," Henry said again.

This time Wayman rose, towering over Henry. "I was your best friend," he roared. "You should have known."

He had a point, and that point brought a cloud of guilt over the region's newest *curandero*. He shaded his eyes and looked at his old friend. "I need my life back, too," Henry said.

"Oh, you poor thing." Wayman folded his arms and faced in the opposite direction. "I don't want to talk to you anymore. I only pity you now."

A year later and a different kind of phone call jangled Alice out of a reverie. This call was from a friend of the museum. She had visited the place, but the building had seemed deserted. Something was out of whack. Alice assigned Henry and John to investigate.

As Henry fantasized about the coming Spring Break, the tug at the Aberdeen line was almost unnoticeable this time. Maybe Henry and Skookumchuck had come to a manageable compromise.

While Saturday should have been a busy day, only two cars were parked in the museum lot when Henry and John arrived in the Chrysler that had replaced the DeSoto as the family vehicle. The Buick was there, looking regal albeit a bit neglected; a rope chain now surrounded it.

Inside, it looked as if no one had dusted in months. The windows on the stairwell were streaked, the geraniums withered. Two couples strolled through the galleries. John and Henry rang the bell on the desk. One of the customers poked his head out and said, "Nobody's here."

John called for Mrs. Pinckney. She appeared five minutes later. She wore the same black suit as always. The heels of her shiny pumps clicked as she carefully maneuvered the stairs. The oddest thing about her was the pillbox hat with a black lace net hanging stiffly over her forehead.

"I'm so glad you've come," she said to John.

"Car's got a problem, huh?" He squinted, the way he always did when something didn't make sense to him.

"Not exactly," she said. "But that would be fine, too." She stopped not far from them and put a white hanky to her nose. "You realize I haven't been the same since the murder."

"Murder?" John said.

"I didn't do it," Henry cried.

Mrs. Pinckney crooked a finger, leading them down the hallway. They passed one of the couples. The man tried to ask her a question, but she dismissed him with her hanky.

"But we're customers," the woman protested.

At the very end of the hall, the light dimmed, and Mrs. Pinckney's pace slowed. All right," she said. "Prepare yourselves."

They walked into gloom. The room was decorated in grays and blacks. In the center hung a large poster of President Kennedy strung with black bunting. And nearby, in another picture, Jackie stood aching and proud at the curb while the cortege filed by. On her head sat the very style of hat Mrs. Pinckney now wore.

John shuffled his feet. The magnitude of her grief dawned on him. It was not crazy really; it was more crazy's uncle, *non compos mentis.* Mrs. Pinckney walked over to the giant Kennedy and arranged a piece of fallen crepe. She turned and bowed her head.

Unable to tolerate the silence, Henry said, "We're so sorry he died."

Mrs. Pinckney eased into the replica rocker and began a rhythm, tapping her toe against the floor. Henry took the opportunity to move around, checking out the displays on the walls and on the stands scattered about the room.

There were shots of the Kennedy family playing football at Hyannis Port. In another, Jackie led reporters on a White House tour.

Yet another wall showed Khrushchev and Castro and Lyndon Johnson and rockets rumbling from Cape Canaveral. Over across the room, Marilyn Monroe sang Happy Birthday and Pablo Casals played his cello for dignitaries in the East Room. There were copies of *Profiles in Courage* and pictures of Sam Rayburn.

And everyone was happy. Even Allen Dulles of the CIA when he met with the President about the Bay of Pigs. John and Jackie were smiling, the bag ladies in New York were smiling, Barry Goldwater was smiling, Rose was smiling, Bobby was smiling, the Girl Scouts were smiling, the East Germans leaping to freedom were smiling, people building fallout shelters were smiling, Grandma Moses was smiling. A preternatural shine graced all the faces in the room. Wait a minute, Henry thought. Where did all this joy come from?

Mrs. Pinckney reached into her sleeve and pulled out a new hanky. "I don't know what to do."

John jerked his head toward the door. As Henry passed, John whispered, "Go sit in the car. This is way above your pay grade."

Henry wasted no time in leaving. He was about to check out the other exhibits when he spied a couple going toe to toe in the lobby.

The woman was short and stocky and had a principal's voice. "Let's give him a ride back at least. It's not right to just abandon him."

The much taller man glanced at his watch. "You heard him as plain as I did. He said just to here. Are you wanting to miss dinner? Doreen will be furious."

"Shouldn't we call the police? Did you get a look at his face?"

"He said he was an orphan," the man said. He went right for the door and left. The woman followed.

Henry sneaked out to the lot where the pair continued the argument. He hid behind a juniper and listened. This kind of conflict seemed like a luscious discovery, more interesting even than curing people of their diseases. But the couple soon drove off, leaving only the Chrysler and the Buick. Henry walked around the lot, and as so often happened now when friction was involved, he was soon thinking of girls. Feeling an urgent need, he ducked into the thick shrubbery among the cedars.

Here he unzipped his pants and pulled out his rigid organ. Twenty, maybe thirty languorous seconds into it, he had conjured a utilitarian fantasy. He groaned. So far, this puberty thing was turning out to be a menacing delight.

He accelerated the pace and was about to climax when a voice cried out, "Hey what's going on?"

Henry clamped down hard and tried to run, stumbling and falling into a bed of scratchy salal. He scrambled to tuck himself in while behind him, he heard crashing in the brush. When he got to his feet, he glanced around desperately, but was alone.

He emerged from the undergrowth out onto the lot, brushing off dried leaves and picking fir needles as he waited. He found a twig zipped in his pants and carefully threaded it through the gap in the zipper.

His father was soon with him, his face ashen. He grabbed Henry by the sleeve and led him to the Buick.

"What's wrong?" Henry asked.

"Beats me. If I didn't know better, I'd say she had Steilacoom written all over her." He remembered himself then, and they exchanged a cautionary glance. "Or maybe not. What the hell do I know? All I know is she says she can't leave John-John."

"She's Steilacoom material."

"Anyway," John said, "she wants me to tune the old Buick." He pulled out a cigarette and lit it. He breathed out the smoke slowly, closing his eyes and shivering. "I may have to spend some time with that old tit-sagger. You keep yourself busy."

Henry went back inside. Mrs. Pinckney appeared after a while and shuffled some papers on the desk. She seemed on the verge of tears.

"Herman," she said, "what am I to do?"

"It's Henry."

"Henry," she repeated. "Do you think I should give up this museum?"

"No! You can't."

"There's nothing left. Everything new is so darn modern. Before, when they came out with a fresh idea, it seemed already like an old friend. Now, what can you do with a camera that doesn't even make you wait? That was half the fun, waiting for the drugstore to develop your pictures." She reached for her cigarettes on the desk, rattled the pack once and set it back down.

Henry didn't care about cameras or new ideas. He was thinking of what the museum meant to him and how when Mrs. Pinckney asked that question about it, he could almost see The River o' Life receding at its banks so much that big salmon flopped on the cracked bed. "You can't do it," he said.

"Oh, no?"

"It would be awful." But why? he wondered. Was he becoming attached to the museum? And if so, for what reason?

Mrs. Pinckney moved aside the net on her hat. "I suppose I could keep it open. But what kind of museum is it when the curator spends all her time in bed? People will stop coming and that will be that. A museum needs people and activity to give it life."

"Maybe you need some help," he said. "It's getting to be a big place. Too big for one person."

"Help?" She shook her head. "No, all the other ladies are younger. They have husbands and children to take care of. They don't have the time."

"Don't have time for the Bi-County Sorority of the Home and City Improvement League?" Henry knew he was being a smart aleck but couldn't help it.

"It was a beautiful name when we were younger. We had so much time. Time is it, Henry. Nothing else. Well, artifacts. That's it. Time and artifacts."

"I'd be happy to help," he said. "If you ever need me, you know where I am."

Mrs. Pinckney put her arm around his shoulder. "What a thoughtful boy you are." Then she pulled him along the hall again, and as they walked, he told her about The Cedars and his grandfather and his Robe That Would Not Close.

"That's one reason you can't shut the museum," he said.

She ruffled his hair. "Someday I must tell you about my Howard." Her hand rested on his head for a moment. "I already hear the drumbeats, Herman. I see the look on the faces of the younger ladies of the league. I can tell what they're thinking when we talk about the future. Change is on their minds. Sadly, the only thing you can ever be sure of is that things will change. You find the love of your life and the next thing you know, he's gone. You find the home of your dreams and after a while it doesn't seem like much. You find a few years of joy and faith in the world, and the next thing you know, they've killed your president."

"I could help you," he said again. And what a life changing statement that was to be.

Deciding to stay was a blur. John had the Buick all spiffy in no time. There was barely a grease mark on his coveralls. He offered to let Mrs. Pinckney come home with them, but she would hear none of it. "I belong here," she said.

After that, John took Henry aside. "What do you think about...?"

Henry barely nodded before the decision was made.

Without fanfare, Henry became an assistant museum curator. John extracted a suitcase from the back of the Chrysler. Turned out Henry's parents had already hoped for this to happen, if not planned it outright.

"Listen, son. It wasn't my idea to pull a fast one on you, but you know your mother. Mrs. P. was your grandma's friend. Mom doesn't want anything bad to happen to her."

"It's okay, Dad."

"Best of luck," John said as he shook Henry's hand. "Don't do anything I wouldn't do."

"I guess we're holding you to your offer sooner than you thought," Mrs. Pinckney said after the Chrysler roared out of the lot.

Mrs. Pinckney took Henry up the stairs, and they walked the still-linoleumed corridor now painted a bright white. They passed one door, which he learned was her bedroom and came to another at the end of the hall. Henry would sleep in this room for the remainder of his days at The New Prosperity Museum. Two twin beds with chenille spreads lined the walls. Henry lay his suitcase on one.

"This is sensational," he told Mrs. Pinckney.

No patrons came for the rest of the day, so he had plenty of opportunity to get his bearings. For the first time, he explored the back of the building where an overgrown lawn languished like a forgotten haircut. The trees were not growing as close to the building's foundation, and he soon figured out why. As he walked through the grass, he could make out the vague shape of a gigantic jewel. He stood in the middle until it came to him.

He wound up, as he'd seen Whitey Ford do so many times on TV then lobbed an imaginary pitch toward home. He pictured the old men at The Cedars with their robes whipping open, carelessly loping from base to base. Maybe his grandfather had other things to do in his last days besides hide from visitors.

Later, he and Mrs. Pinckney enjoyed dinner in the upstairs kitchen, a room awash in a blinding circus yellow. Mrs. Pinckney set a casserole of tuna surprise in front of him. "Do your best," she said. "I'm afraid I've never won any awards for my cooking."

He tasted it. "My new favorite dish."

"It was Howard's favorite." She put her chin in her hand and looked at the cupboards. "He was such a good man. His business did very well. It allowed us to explore. Do you know, Herman, I have been all around the world."

"Henry," he said.

"No, Howard," she corrected. By now she was in a nostalgic daze. "By train and by ship we went around the globe. But only once," she sniffed. "Unfortunately, dry cleaning offers a good living, but it also cuts your life short. Ironic, isn't it? All those magic chemicals they use turn out to be poison for the liver."

"I'm sorry you didn't get to go twice," Henry said. "My mom wants me to see the world. She says it opens your eyes to reality."

"Oh yes, it does. Will you go then?"

"I think it takes more money than we have."

"After he got sick, Howard came here to The Cedars. I visited him every day. He managed his disease marvelously well. Always a smile on his face." She seemed then to pop out of her reverie and notice Henry again. She snatched the bowl and scraped out seconds. "So, you see, Herman, it's your grandfather and my Howard who are the reasons we can't let go of the museum. Wherever would they go?"

Henry guessed that we meant they were a team now.

He finished his dinner and went back to his room. Supposedly, it was lights out at ten, but he had a hard time going to sleep in his new surroundings.

Once his eyes adjusted to the dark, he noticed a soft glow coming through the windows, and he rose to investigate. The dark cloth of the sky was pinpricked a million times by the stars. Their light brought the cedars to life, making them look like undersea fans. He slipped back in bed and watched them sway hypnotically.

He eventually fell asleep but awoke sometime later and lay listening to the sounds of the night. He was only half-awake when he heard the door creak, and in his stupor, figured it was Mrs. Pinckney pretending to be an actual mother. "I'm OK," he said groggily, and drifted again.

After a few seconds, he felt a hand spider across the end of his bed. He jerked away, but whatever it was quickly found his leg again. When it grabbed at his big toe, Henry kicked out and a voice squealed in shock.

Henry shouted, "What are you doing?"

He heard only a bare influx of breath, in and out.

"Mrs. Pinckney?" he said.

No answer.

The hair rose on his arms. "Wayman?"

Again, not a sound.

"Honest to God, Wayman, if it's you."

"Who?" It was a kid's voice, reedy and unfamiliar.

"All right. What's up?" Henry said.

"Buttercup."

"Who are you?"

"That depends."

"Depends on what?"

"Depends on what you do with the information."

Big words for a small voice. "I'm going to turn on the light," Henry said.

"If you have to."

"I'm not going to stand here all night talking to a ghost."

There was a short pause, quiet where words were concerned, but noisy if you considered what else had been going on in Henry's thinking. When he closed his eyes and leaned forward, he could feel there was something big in this creature's life, something supernatural, maybe. Like he was transmitting an important message to Henry a spray of light might unwittingly spoil.

"I'm no ghost," the voice said.

"Who are you, then?"

The bed creaked and Henry could now make out a form in the star glow. "I'm really starved. Is there any food?"

"Yes. But you're not getting any until you answer my questions."

"You sound like one of them. When I saw you out there, I thought you'd be different."

Henry hopped on the other bed and snapped on the overhead, ready for anything. What he saw took away his caution instantly.

A boy stood, puffing out his chest even though he had no chest to speak of. He was almost as tall as Henry, but skinnier, and his dark hair curled out wildly, like Medusa's if Medusa were younger. He wore a striped surfer shirt and a pair of Sears toughskins whose pant legs hung in strings at the hem. When Henry studied his face, the boy's hands quickly covered it.

"Don't look at me."

"What happened?"

"Never mind." His voice was muffled through his fingers. "Can't you just give me something to eat?"

Henry stepped from the bed. He pulled away the boy's hands, revealing a purple-yellow bulge around the right eye. "Did I do that?" Henry asked guiltily.

"I had a little accident before," the boy said. "It's nothing."

"Who are you?" Henry said again.

Now he seemed eager to answer. "Philip Anthony Charles. But you can call me Phid Tony Chuck if you want. Everybody else does. Or just Phid. That's what I call myself. Phid the Kid."

"Phid."

"Yes."

"Does Mrs. Pinckney know you're here?"

"Who's Mrs. Pinckney?"

"She runs the place," Henry said. "How'd you get in?"

"That's my secret."

Henry couldn't keep his eyes off the mess on Phid's face. "You're the kid those people were talking about earlier. They gave you a ride and left you here."

"I'm starved to death. Just a bowl of Shredded Wheat. That's all I want. Please."

But before Henry could go, Phid's eyes fluttered, and he caught himself on the edge of the bed.

"You're sick," Henry said. "I'll go get Mrs. Pinckney."

Phid fixed on Henry with his good eye. "Please don't."

"Why not? She could do something for your face."

"She's an adult."

"So?"

"She'll turn me in."

"Why would she? What have you done?"

He studied Henry for a moment. "I just really need something to eat."

Giving in, Henry tiptoed the hall. He was rummaging around in the cupboards when he felt a tap on the back and shouted. Behind him, Mrs. Pinckney had her hand over her heart and was backing away. When Henry explained his hunger, she made a ham sandwich for him. She wanted to sit and talk, but he told her he had to get to his room.

As he hurried back through the hall, he had a strange feeling roiling on the inside. He kept hearing the kid's name in his head: Philip Anthony Charles. Phid Tony Chuck. Outside his family, he had never run into anyone else who had three first names. This could get interesting. He slipped into his room and held the sandwich out.

But there was no one there.

As the days passed, Henry kept an eye out for Phid, but the kid was good at making himself scarce. Henry left food out at night and since it was gone by morning, he knew Phid was around somewhere. And he had the feeling the boy was watching them because the hair on Henry's neck sprang up from time to time.

Meanwhile, Mrs. Pinckney did her best to get Henry acquainted with the museum. She took him on his own personal tour, a business one this time, lingering at each exhibit and explaining its importance in the minutest detail, so that by the time she tested him on each one, he could recite its story like a pro.

"Remember it all," she said. "You'll never know when I'll hover with a pop quiz."

Henry was curiously mesmerized. He grew to love the Frontiers in Space Exhibit, studied the Eisenhower Room, adored the Appliance Wing, knew the All About the Movies Gallery with its special John Garfield and Franchot Tone walls. But one day, as he got to know the I Surrender Room where General MacArthur accepted the Japanese humiliation and the replica of the USS Missouri was proudly displayed, he heard the chug of a car out in the lot. It was a familiar sound and Henry tried to place it before giving up and walking out to one of the big windows.

It was an old Plymouth, humped at the rear. He sucked in a breath as Mrs. Obregon crawled out of it. She stood and stretched her back. Then she focused on the window and Henry knew that she had caught up with him and would not let him go until he went out to see what she was after.

"I have missed you," she said.

"I've been busy."

"Yes. I've seen what your life is now."

"It's hard to get away."

"Yet here you are. Away. I must tell you there is a long line at my door. I have tried to contact you, but you've been avoiding me."

"I guess I was thinking you were mad or something. Because of Miss Bright."

"You're learning," she said. "One does not toss aside a student who is just learning."

They had this conversation as they walked into the museum, but it was momentarily halted when Mrs. Obregon stopped and gazed around. And when Mrs. Pinckney led a group of visitors from the Eisenhower Room, her face lit up as Henry had never seen it do before. Mrs. Pinckney stopped somewhere near the staircase and said: "Do I know you?"

"Your husband perhaps?"

"Yes, of course. You made Howard so comfortable in the end." She turned to Henry. "Herman, maybe you would like to show Mrs. Obregon around?"

"But..."

"An excellent idea," said Mrs. Obregon.

"But I'm supposed to be working here," Henry said. "Mrs. Pinckney needs me."

"It is part of your job," Mrs. Pinckney said. "Maybe we can meet again when you're finished."

She left them alone then and Henry shrugged. "Where would you like to start?" he asked.

He carefully steered her to the Washington Gears for the Future display. She stood in front of the diorama showing the Grand Coulee

Dam. She played with her chin as she studied it. "It's so big," she finally said.

"Biggest in the world," Henry said proudly.

She turned to him. "But why? Why so big? It faces the river head on and defeats it. Is that how it must be? Man versus nature and nature loses?"

"We like to think of it as progress. Without the dam, some years the river floods." *In the winter, she floods. In the summer, she ebbs.* Henry shivered.

"Yes."

"Progress is a good thing, isn't it?"

"It can be. But don't ask the Chehalis. Or the Colvilles for that matter. Think about what this dam did to them and their land. They were not given the chance to forge their own kind of progress."

"But..."

"It's all I want from you, Henry. I want you to think about things differently. I just want you to know that there are other ways to look at the world. Perhaps that is what Skookumchuck has in mind for you." He looked about to speak, but she beat him to it. "I think you hide from me here because you are afraid."

"Ha," Henry said, but he knew there was truth in her words.

"It is fine to be scared, but you must not let your fear win out. There is more to life than keeping safe. Ask those of us who fight against the thieves who stole our existence."

How could he say no to this idea? "I'll come back," he said. "I do want to learn from you."

"Then a promise will do and I will let you proceed," said Mrs. Obregon. "When you are finished here, come to see me. There is work to be done."

Ah. In the midst of what she said, there rose the specter of Qone again. Henry had started to develop a low-hanging cloud feeling of doom about Qone. But he nodded his head and watched Mrs. Obregon as she left the room. Still at the window, he saw her pull out of the lot and chug away.

One of Henry's responsibilities at the museum was to make sure that the Buick had survived each night. The Buick: his father knew what made it run, Henry soon learned what made it special. Mrs.

Pinckney treated it like a member of the family. A master at vicarious learning, Henry ministered to the car with dignity and care. Whenever he opened the driver's door, the smell of deteriorating rubber hit him, and he reveled in it. On this day, he quickly slipped inside and shut the door to preserve the air intact.

The Buick had a deep green dashboard. Henry could see his face in it, and all the instruments were plated with shiny chrome. It was a spacious car and for a moment he fantasized what he and Anita Bush could do in the back seat.

On this final morning before his father came to pick him up, Henry was performing his daily check of the Buick, sitting behind the wheel, twisting it this way and that, fantasizing he was driving the road to Rochester. He was not paying attention when a voice called out from the back.

"Is it safe?"

Henry swiveled around. Phid's head rose like a gas-filled balloon.

"Don't yell," he pleaded.

"What are you doing here?"

"Hiding."

"From what?" Henry noticed the bruise was more yellow now, his face less swollen.

"You told on me, didn't you?"

"No, I didn't."

"I heard you talking with that old lady."

"I didn't tell her about you."

"Are you sure?"

"Listen," Henry said, "why do I have to explain myself? I don't know who you are. I don't know where you come from."

"I'm not used to talking to people," Phid said.

"Are you going to tell me?"

He shook his head.

"Where are your parents?"

"Why do you have to know everything?"

"Because you just materialized out of nowhere and you look hurt."

"I'm not hurt. Nothing can hurt me."

"Don't be so sure," Henry said.

"All right. I'll tell you." Phid paused, and a wicked smile slinked over his face. "I saw what you were doing in the woods."

Henry sensed denial was not going to work. Phid's was obviously the voice he'd heard in the brush. "That's none of your business," he said.

"If it's none of my business then you shouldn't be doing it out in the open like that."

"I was hidden."

"By the way," Phid said. "Your technique was very good."

"Shut up."

Henry wanted to say more but at that moment, a car slid into the lot. Phid's eyes went wide, and he ducked behind the seat. In a moment, one of the doors opened and he tumbled out, running awkwardly toward the woods. As he did, a man jumped out of the other car, blocked his way, and then dove, snatching him by one of his feet. They struggled for a moment, but the other guy was much too big. He snapped a pair of handcuffs on Phid's wrist. A hint of metal gleamed on the man's chest.

Henry scrambled out of the Buick. "Hey!" he shouted. The deputy looked at him, sort of half-saluted, then pulled Phid to his car where he stuffed him in the back seat. Puzzled, Henry watched them drive away.

THIRTEEN

Henry kept his promise to Mrs. Obregon. As soon as he and John arrived at the farm, Henry hopped on his bike and pedaled all the way back to Porter. If he thought there'd been a long line a couple of years before, the one now on the trail to the cabin was much longer.

He passed people with casts on their arms, bandages on their heads, sadness printed on their faces. Old and young, man and woman, boy and girl. It seemed that life was not kind to everyone during this time of prosperity.

Mrs. Obregon and her cat met him at the door.

"Here you are," she said as she took him by the shoulder and escorted him inside. "And to what do I owe the pleasure of this visit?"

"You asked me to come."

"Ah, yes, I did."

"Who are these people?" he asked, surveying the crowd.

"My patients," she said. The accent on my was not lost on Henry.

"But how do they know to come here?"

"Do you really need to ask that question? Are we too far advanced to have forgotten how to communicate without a telephone, a letter?"

Henry wasn't sure what she meant, but what with the line outside and his experience with the Triangle, he had no clear answer for her.

"Perhaps you would like to help me," Mrs. Obregon said.

"Help you?"

Now, Henry was sure the word my meant he was not to be running this show. He felt miffed at the change.

"Maybe you could see how it's meant to work," she said.

The day was a long one. The line began to move as Henry set each patient up by finding out what the problem was and directing them into Mrs. Obregon's bedroom. People for the most part were polite and forthcoming.

As the shadows stretched longer in the afternoon, Henry found himself growing tired, both physically and in his mind. Mrs. Obregon operated more like a naturopath as opposed to someone with supernatural skills. He noticed, however, that each patient looked forward to what she could do for them. Some quivered. Some were chatty. Some kept dead silent. All had hope.

Night came and finally it was only Mrs. Obregon and Henry left in her cabin. To his surprise, just as he had when it was him who was doing the actual work, Henry felt exhausted, but good and accomplished. He decided there was something about this type of healing that superseded the satisfaction of achieving a cure in front of television cameras. A kerosene lantern glowed in the corner. Somewhere in the house, the cat mewled softly.

"I can see it on your face," Mrs. Obregon said as she dished up soup and placed it on the table in front of him.

"What do you see?" Henry liked this. Two *curanderos* discussing their day.

"Smug I might call it.'

"Smug? I don't feel that way."

"I must warn you again. It is best not to make your gift appear to be popular. To be a gimmick. It is dishonorable to these patients to treat them that way. I've warned you before. Don't wear your accomplishments like medals on your chest. This is not special. This is simply your job."

Henry, of course, wanted more than this. He was, after all, only thirteen years old and recently pubescent boys want to own the world and feel they deserve it. "I won't," he said. "I like what I do."

"And your friend?"

"Who, Wayman? I still don't think he's very happy with me."

She took a noisy sip of the soup and laid her spoon next to the bowl. She watched as Henry bowed his head and ate. "Maybe it was dishonest to bring him back."

He stopped in mid-slurp. "Not you too. What do you mean?"

"He was happy where he was. His life was better. He was accepted by the others. Almost as if he had found his people."

Henry considered this, but at that moment was having difficulty seeing beyond his own nose. "I had to do it. His mother wanted it and I needed to prove myself."

"Prove what? That you had power over him?"

"No, not over him. Just that I had power. That it wasn't my fault what happened to him in the first place."

"I see. Was it your fault?"

"I've been thinking about that, and the answer is no." He finished his soup and pushed the bowl ahead. "How can it be my fault if his parents are happy now? Mrs. Simpson doesn't run me down on the road anymore."

"I see. So, you did it to protect yourself."

"It isn't good what I do? I shouldn't be a *curandero*?"

"I am not saying that. I'm just saying to know your reasons for the things you do in life. It is not only you who lives in the Triangle."

"Qone?"

"Yes, of course Qone is watching."

He took a chance. "Maybe it's Qone's fault what happened with Wayman. I wasn't even looking when he disappeared."

"Careful," Mrs. Obregon said.

"It's a free country," Henry said. "Wow. I have to be careful of other kids because I could be a murderer. I have to be careful of Qone because I'm not supposed to be a *curandero*. What can I do? Didn't you see me at the museum? I don't have to be careful there. I was happy. Am happy there. Mrs. Pinckney never makes me be careful of what I say or what I do."

Mrs. Obregon scratched at her head. "You have much to think about. Did you learn anything today?"

Henry thought hard, then brightened. "Don't you get in trouble with Qone because you charge people for what you do?"

"What are you saying?" she said, a bit defensive.

"What's the difference between curing in front of a camera and getting paid for a cure? Doesn't Qone have anything to say about that?"

Mrs. Obregon raised her chin. "Maybe it is time for you to leave."

He stood. His bravado stayed in the chair. "I'm sorry. I just don't know what to say."

"Thank you for today. From time to time, let me know how you are doing."

"I'm not coming back tomorrow?"

"Skookumchuck doesn't need you tomorrow."

He left, then stood outside the cabin for a few minutes. It was changing, this power of his. But it was still a power, still his salvation, still his ticket for a good life. Weren't cures everything he ever dreamed of?

Not long after Henry's day in Porter, Uncle Ray gave Mrs. Obregon the boot and brought in what he called a real doctor. It happened the day she announced that Ray, Jr. was allergic to certain substances in the house, but she couldn't pin them down. She said he had to undergo an expensive series of herbal tests, and even then, she wouldn't be able to state for certain from what malady he suffered. Uncle Ray's confidence in Mrs. Obregon had waned over the years, while his suspicions about Ray, Jr. had increased. The day Mrs. Obregon wanted thirty dollars per visit was the day Uncle Ray dragged Ray, Jr. out of bed.

"Get up!" Uncle Ray bellowed.

The commotion scared the birds out of the trees in a disorganized mob. Mrs. Obregon stood by the rear of her Plymouth, her hands extended, the fingers pointed and splayed. For a moment, she looked like a combination of spirit people. She bared her teeth, hissing through them. If it had been dark, sparks might very well have jumped from her fingernails. She said a few words under her breath but only one stood out: "Skookumchuck."

She narrowed her eyes as Uncle Ray pulled Ray, Jr. out into the yard. She waited a moment, then slid into the car and backed away from the grisly scene.

What'd I tell you?" Uncle Ray said. He stood in front of his son. "This boy's been faking it." They glared at each other for what seemed a long time. Uncle Ray's hands were curling and uncurling, and on one curl he looked about to punch Ray, Jr. in his pointed nose.

But before he could, Ray, Jr. said, "I'm going to do it."

"Do what? You're not going to do nothing." He put his face in Ray, Jr.'s. "And you guard your backside. Cause when you forget to, that's when I give you grief."

"Just watch me," Ray, Jr. said. He walked back to the house, mounting the stairs with ease. When the door closed, Aunt Peg sneered at Uncle Ray, "You did this to him. Making him see that crazy woman."

"You don't know nothing."

The next week, Aunt Peg took Ray, Jr. to Dr. Minard who pronounced him, besides being undernourished, fit to live a normal life. When Aunt Peg brought Ray, Jr. home and told her husband the news, Uncle Ray hopped in his Pontiac and left for Aberdeen. When he came back a week later, he had dark circles under his eyes and looked heavier. He didn't speak to Ray, Jr. for another month.

Henry was a sophomore when Ray, Jr. returned to school. Everyone was skeptical. It had been years since they'd seen him in class and a lot of guys tried to take advantage of it. They expected a moron and, as people go, especially teenage people, they got upset when their expectations didn't jibe with reality.

As it turned out, Ralph Underwood notwithstanding, Ray Jr. was one of the smartest kids ever to set foot at Rochester High. He had the teachers baffled, and some of them stayed up nights just to devise special lesson plans to stump him. He was way ahead in Math, so Mr. Meenach had him doing Calculus. He was way ahead in Contemporary Problems, so Mrs. Vitale had him studying the American involvement in Indochina. He was way ahead in English, so Miss Atwood had him writing blank verse and correcting sophomore papers.

He applied early to Stanford but was rejected because there were no records of his previous high school years. Mr. Meenach stepped up to the plate and arranged a special SAT testing for Ray, Jr. Perhaps it was the nearly perfect 1580 he scored that convinced Stanford to take a closer look at the young man. In any event, Ray, Jr. soon received a letter granting him an early acceptance to the most prestigious university on the West Coast.

"In spite of his uneven history, we see the formation of genius in this young man," the admissions committee said. "Even without evidence of an ongoing formal education, he has the kind of native intelligence we admire here at Stanford."

Henry was not appreciative of what Ray, Jr. had set up as far as college expectations. "And all you can do is moon over that Anita Bush girl," Alice said. "That non-speller. Look at Ray, Jr. He didn't even go to school for half his life."

The only one who had nothing to say about his acceptance was Ray, Jr. himself. He had gone about the whole thing as if it were just another problem set. Relentlessly, he sat poised over his desk, waiting for someone to pass a paper across it, so he could plunge to the task of finding a solution. His pencil was sometimes writing in the air before the paper even hit the table. When he read, he was clocked at 1250 words a minute with 90 percent comprehension, thus tying him with Ralph Underwood's school record.

As his academic success widened, Ray, Jr. grew more distant from Henry, distant from everyone. He walked around with a look that led one to believe he was carrying on a far more interesting conversation in his head than he would ever have with anyone else. Henry tried to cheer him up, but Ray, Jr didn't believe he was depressed.

"God, the whole world is yours," Henry said. "Mrs. Winkle always told us we're the blessed children of the future. That includes you."

Ray, Jr. looked at him dubiously. "And your idea of my blessed life would be what, Hankie? Ralph Underwood's life? Am I going to be so geeky no one can stand to be around me? Will I have a group of scientists over for dinner just so I can show them I speak French? Am I going to spend my nights trying to make tiny computers that everyone will want in their homes? All due respect, but do you want me to take out a book and read to someone I can't see so he'll come back from some other dimension?

"No, Hankie, I'm not going to do any of those things. And you shouldn't either. I know you're not asking for my advice, but here it is. Do a different kind of reading. Talk to real people. Listen to that voice in your head. Think about the snake on my back porch just waiting for its chance to swallow us all. You'll find out soon enough. Good things are not going to come."

Henry withstood the stinging rebuke and as it turned out, Ray, Jr. was right. But that was the last meaningful conversation anyone would have with Ray, Jr. for a couple of decades. The River o' Life, be it the Chehalis or the Hamma Hamma or the Mekong, was poised to float him away for a good long while.

FOURTEEN

At age 16, Henry motored along the highway toward Aberdeen on a day after school was dismissed for the summer. One elbow rested out the window of the DeSoto, which had been gifted him as promised on his birthday. The day was cloudless, about 70 degrees, and his spirits were high. He faced a full summer as an assistant to Mrs. Pinckney, his meager salary underwritten by the donations that still flowed in. But he knew he would have taken the job without any kind of compensation attached. Since his week as an assistant curator a couple of springs before, he was now a full-fledged fan of the museum, although he might be hard-pressed to explain his attraction to it in any logical way. Notwithstanding the truth that he still enjoyed the idea of being a *curandero,* the fact that the museum rested outside the unpredictable Triangle remained a beckoning siren.

He had visited Mrs. Obregon's cabin on two further occasions, although the lines were shorter, the problems less acute. His job remained as her assistant. Since his own period of brief notoriety had ebbed, he had no options to use his curing gifts other than as an ordinary assistant to Mrs. Obregon.

As it was, Henry was allowed to live the kind of life he desired, and what he desired more and more was to be off at the museum where he could think of other things besides cures. He was also keen to be away from home since Suzanne had withdrawn into her own select world. This pleased Alice, who ignored Suzanne's peculiarities given her daughter's new preference for home and isolation.

"I think it's a good thing she's staying around here more," Alice told Henry. "What kind of trouble can you get into at home?"

And something unusual had happened at Uncle Ray's house. After securing Honors-at-Entrance to Stanford, Ray, Jr. sent a letter refusing the gift, stating he had a change of heart and would not be entering their freshman class in the fall. He also declined an invitation to speak at the high school Commencement in June. The hard money had him as Steilacoom material, but there were bigger things in store for Ray, Jr. It took no time at all for him to figure out what they were.

The day after graduation, Ray, Jr. marched to the recruiting office and joined the Army. There was no mention of ROTC or OCS or anything else that might have been more fitting. He wanted to be a grunt and received no argument from the folks in charge. He chose the infantry and shipped out to Basic Training less than a week later.

Beside Henry now on the seat of the DeSoto, sat a box of novels his mother insisted he bring. She still seethed because Mort Gunderson of the Rochester Weekly Guardian rejected her review of *Black Like Me*. She had decided the best guard against depression would be tapping into her literary gifts. She critiqued book after book although it looked to be that Rochester was not ready for an erudite reader like Alice George. Mort Gunderson tossed them aside just as quickly as she cranked them out.

Henry was enjoying his ride, so much so that he forgot what usually happened to him at the Aberdeen border. At least in the old days it had, though not since he'd brought Wayman back. But there it was. Just before Henry left the Triangle that day, he felt his neck constrict again. The Triangle put its strong arms around him and started pulling him from the seat. And as he was lifted, he heard those strange voices again, murmurs really, just as he had during his first cure with little Simon in Mrs. Obregon's cabin.

It must have been quite a sight. Surely other motorists could see him struggle to keep his hands on the wheel. He was frightened, of course. He couldn't decide if the Triangle was friend or foe, although he now leaned toward foe. In any event, fighting the invisible beast within his car was a familiar winnable battle. Today, he managed to hold his own and as soon as he crossed out of Aberdeen, the pressure subsided. But the fact it was still there, trying to pull him back into the Triangle was a problem Henry preferred not to deny.

When he arrived at the museum, the lot was full, thanks to Mrs. Pinckney. With the extra care she once again gave the place, and a human-interest article in the Seattle Times, the swallows were returning to Cosmopolis. The donation coffers brimmed. Henry found a place to park close to the highway and hauled his bags across the lot. Inside, the lobby was buzzing. Groups hovered around the reception desk and gathered in clumps along the halls, and folks strolled in and out of the rooms. Someone exclaimed, "My mother had one of those!"

Mrs. Pinckney was nowhere in sight, so he set down his bags and walked to the Appliance Wing. She wasn't there. Nor was she in the Frontiers in Space Exhibit. He might have gone directly to the Kennedy Memorial, but something caught his eye and transfixed him in the doorway to the Eisenhower Room.

A rapt audience followed every word spoken by a young guide at the front. This guide was none other than Phid the Kid. Henry stepped inside, but Phid didn't notice.

"People everywhere love the bald-headed man called Ike," Phid said. "His wide grin and friendly disposition put everyone at ease..." He went on, as Henry watched from the doorway. Phid finished with, "Even his critics never questioned his honesty and sincerity."

Then Phid was quiet a moment. He seemed to wait for everyone to notice his silence. Then he whispered, "And everything I just said about the man is a pile of steaming doo-doo."

A gasp sprang from the front of the room, and some of the older Mamie look-alikes headed, chins raised, for the door. "Well, I never," one of them said. Their husbands filed out more slowly, a few of them snickering behind their hands. Soon the gallery had cleared, and Henry faced Phid.

"I take it by the look on your face you don't agree with the truth," Phid said.

Henry lowered his voice as fresh visitors entered. "How could you say that?"

"Easy," he replied. "Steaming doo-doo. What, do you think I should have said horseshit? That didn't go over that well before."

"They'll never come back."

Phid scrutinized Henry. "Don't you go to school? Don't you read? Ike's a Nazi. He couldn't care less about you or me. He only cares about people who have money. He also caused the deaths of thousands of young Americans."

"People think he's a national hero," Henry insisted. "And, he had a heart attack."

Phid his palm outward, said, "Before you get any more excited about this, Mrs. Pinckney and I have struck a deal. She's letting me stay in exchange for work. Now, start acting like you're pleased as hell to see me, and get upstairs, change your clothes and get to work."

Frustrated, Henry walked to the end of the hall where he found Mrs. Pinckney. She was chatting amiably with a couple, and he had to get next to her before she noticed him.

"Why, Herman," she said with delight. "How nice of you to come. Just look how busy we are. Schools must have let out early because they've been coming in droves. What a stroke of luck it was to find that Philip. Thanks for referring him. He knows so much about the museum. He even knows the speeches."

"I didn't refer him," Henry said.

"He thinks you did, and I couldn't be happier. Well, you'd best get started. I left a copy of the new speeches on your bed. Oh, Herman, now you won't be so lonely."

"New speeches?" But she had turned away and was rattling on about Jackie as she adjusted her pillbox.

In his room, Henry snatched a sheaf of paper from the top of the dresser. Under his name was the Appliance Wing, the Washington Gears for the Future Display, the At the Movies Exhibit, and the I Surrender Room. And next to his name was Phid's, with his own impressive list of galleries to monitor.

Henry was worn out by the time night fell. During that week in spring, hardly anyone had come to the museum, but now each of his galleries was full. He stood in the Appliance Wing and watched strangers browse through the exhibit. He stumbled at first, but eventually developed a rhythm. He didn't cringe when it came time to say, "And it's not even Apricreme, that exciting new go-with color of the forties."

Mrs. Pinckney lingered by the main door, bidding extended goodnights to the inevitable stragglers. She locked the doors at eight, and even then, after she'd collected the donation box and brought it upstairs, still wanted to rehash the day over ham sandwiches.

Henry tried to pay attention, but his concentration was on Phid, who sat across the kitchen table. He was more filled out now and would be formidable competition should Henry try to challenge him to a fight. His face had cleared too, and his smile glowed brighter. He obviously had charmed the pillbox off Mrs. Pinckney.

As Mrs. Pinckney counted the money, Henry excused himself and went to his bedroom. He wondered if he should be peeing in the corners. Phid's appearance in his territory made him speculate. What was the guy doing back? The police just didn't arrest people on a whim. He must have had a criminal record. What if he wanted to steal from the museum? He considered going back to the kitchen to supervise the counting of the money, but eventually slid into bed and pulled the thin covers tightly around him.

Sometime in the night, he awakened to hear what he first thought was the mewling of a small animal. He checked out the window, but the empty lot was quiet. He cracked the door and stuck his head out in the hall. The tiny nightlight near the kitchen cast a feeble glow against the wall. Henry followed the sound to Phid's room.

A muffled cry issued from inside. Henry tapped on the door. "You all right in there?"

The crying stopped, but there was no answer. After a minute, Henry returned to bed. Now he couldn't sleep. A breeze began and the sea fans moved in the current outside.

Soon there was a knock at his door. "Henry? Can I come in?"

"Is something wrong?"

"Just could I?"

"Come on in."

Phid sat on the edge of the other bed. "This is nice."

"That was you crying earlier," Henry said.

You think I'm a baby, don't you?"

"Why were you crying?"

"You're going to laugh. I'm afraid of the dark."

"I'm not laughing. Sleep with the light on."

"I was. I hate it that I'm afraid."

"You want to stay in here awhile?"

"Yes," he said and scooted back on the bed.

Fear was nothing new to Henry. There was after all the recurring vision of his dead sister on the beach. "You want me to turn the light on?"

"No. If I'm with someone else, it goes away."

"Why are you back here anyway? It was so weird when the cop came and got you."

"I ran away," he said. "My dad's a cop if you can call him a dad. Somebody reported me. Was it you?"

"I didn't turn you in," Henry said. "And why was your face all bruised then?"

"My dad likes to think I'm his little prisoner."

"Your dad hit you?"

"He disciplined me."

"That's horrible."

"That's life."

He stayed the night. When Henry woke up, Phid was curled in a ball on top of the blankets, his arms tight at his chest.

"Do you mind if I sleep in here for a while?" Phid said.

"All right by me."

It did get better. The two talked or Henry talked. Phid operated at his own pace. He offered tidbits about himself, a snack here, a nibble there. Meanwhile, Henry told him of his past where cures were concerned, and Phid simply saw it as another step in Henry's development rather than a grandiloquent twist of fate. A gift deserving of a pat on the back instead of a ticker tape parade. Henry also told of his lifelong love for Anita Bush.

Phid nodded but as far as his story was concerned, he seemed focused on merely one thing. "I don't have a girlfriend," he said.

"I do, sort of. Well, Anita will be."

"But I do have a friend." Phid winked, which was at once unsettling for reasons Henry didn't understand. Yet. "You want to be my new friend?"

Phid sparingly doled out these revealing glimpses. One or two a week.

And, even better, he was the hit of the museum, a natural orator when necessary but with a sprinkling of ham that won over the older set. They seemed to like order and rule-following in their own children but found the breaking of convention charming in the children of others. Phid thrived on their attention.

They grew close, Henry and Phid, as often happens when people are thrust together in a protected environment. As June wore on, Henry put together the information Phid doled out to him. He was from Longview. School bored him and he only went to avoid punishment and please his parents. He was enormously interested in sex and could describe people from his hometown as if they were sides of butchered beef.

He was well read, revered Jack Kerouac, found Holden Caulfield a fascinating character. Slowly, Henry began to understand the difference between being smart in school and smart as a way of life.

On Mondays, Phid and Henry took the DeSoto to the beach and Henry showed him the spot where the Georges always picnicked when he was young. He told him about Anne and the riptide. They bought ice cream in Moclips and walked to the beach where they threw driftwood into the surf and played Axis PT gunners trying to sink the 109. Boys at play. Happy and relaxed.

Phid had kept to a ritual borne out of his fear of the dark. Every night before Henry nodded off, he opened and closed the door softly. Henry was developing a good sixth sense, so he knew when Phid sneaked in. He listened to the soft padding across the floor, waited for the bed to creak, waited for the rhythmic breathing.

But one night it didn't happen in the usual way. When the door opened, Henry smelled cologne. Maybe Hai Karate?

"Phid?"

"It's me," he whispered as he snapped on the light.

"What's up?"

"It's okay," Phid said. Henry felt something odd on his bedspread. Like on the first night they met, a giant spider scuttled toward him.

Henry sat upright and there was Phid, completely naked, sitting on the edge of his bed, his hand finally reaching Henry's crotch. He kept it there and wiggled it.

Henry snatched the spread away.

"Relax," Phid whispered. "Just let it happen."

"Uh, no."

"You're such a candy ass."

"Phid, your hand's on my dick."

"You want me to take it away?"

"Yes," Henry said quickly.

"I thought you would like that," Phid said.

"Why would you think that?"

"For one, you never told me to mind my own business. You never called me a queer or a homo. You never told me you'd stop being my friend. We've been dating for weeks."

"What? We haven't been dating."

Phid stood and smiled.

Henry looked away. "Put some pants on."

Backing up to the other bed, Phid fell on it. "I don't get it."

Henry collected his thoughts. This guy was a friend. He came from violence. Henry could use some clarification. "Well, are you?"

"Am I what?"

"Are you a... homo?"

Phid pulled the bedspread over himself. "Not to piss you off or anything, but you're kind of uptight, Hank."

Henry took a deep breath that did little for his anxiety.

"You might as well go ahead and say it," Phid said. "You think I'm a freak."

"Normal guys don't spy on other guys," Henry said.

"I didn't follow you into the bushes," Phid said. "You came right over where I was hiding."

"I did not. I would never do that."

"You've got a nice cock, Hank."

"I don't want..." He wondered how many guys in the world had this kind of conversation with a friend. "I just don't want you to try anything."

"Okay," Phid said. "I won't. You know that day I first met you, I was hitchhiking out by Humptulips and I saw the stupid sign for the museum. I got a ride with that dumb family who wanted to see their future in the past. I was going to stay with them. Make them mine. I was all set to live the rest of my life in their house but then I saw you. You and your dad. He looked pretty funny in those coveralls. Do you know he talks to himself a lot?"

"We know," Henry said.

"I learned a few new words while I was waiting for it to clear out. Only not everybody left. You stayed."

"Oh boy."

"Is that too weird for you?"

"Yes."

The word vagina popped into Henry's brain, and he worked it repeatedly. Vagina. Vagina. Vagina. Ad infinitum, forever and ever. It cleansed him. He thought of Anita Bush and her vagina. He laughed.

Bush. Vagina. No connection could ever be sweeter. He felt his penis expand. Relief flooded his gut.

"I'll leave tomorrow," Phid said.

"You don't have to. Anyway, Mrs. Pinckney loves you. She'd never let you go."

"Then are we still friends?"

"Just get over your fear of the dark."

"Oh yeah," said Phid. "My fear of the dark."

Henry survived the summer. Mrs. Pinckney was pleased with the boys' work. They had taken a load off her shoulders and were good company. When Henry left on Labor Day, she held him for the longest time and insisted he come back to visit more often.

"Your father will be coming up," she reminded him. "You come with him."

"I will," he said.

Henry drove home in the rain, through squall after squall sweeping across the highways like silk curtains. He had mixed feelings. He knew where he was going. Back to the land of cures and dreams about alternate universes. But his family was there, and he had missed them. It buoyed him, made him think that somehow, he could find out why these supernatural events had fallen on him and nobody else. It was at least worth a try.

FIFTEEN

Henry walked innocently down the hallway and thought he was one lucky guy. He had friends now. He had a place at school. What could be better for a sixteen-year-old?

He turned a corner and there it was. The crucible. The arrow through the heart. The ant trail to the picnic basket. He heard sobbing, some screaming, words unfit for academic ears being thrown around the counselor's office. He paused and wrinkled his face. He knew that voice. Shock became his newest friend.

A few days before Thanksgiving, the school counselor had called Alice to his office, where Suzanne admitted, after ten minutes of continuous sobbing, that she was pregnant. Alice dropped her book to the floor, and it was one of the few times she was able to focus completely on one of her children. But while her head was swirling with why, how and who, Suzanne was shouting out how sorry she was: "I'm sorry!" she yelled. "I'm goddamn sorry! I'm sorrier than ever!"

Alice clamped a shaking hand over her daughter's mouth, but it was too late. Within minutes, nearly every kid in the school knew of Suzanne's plight before she and her mother left the office.

John and Alice flushed her out of eighth grade and confined her to her room while they consulted with the school district on the best way to handle the situation. Number one on the list was the inevitable search for the culprit, and if there had been tears during Suzanne's confession, there were now shouts of anger from parents who threatened suits against the district and the Georges for suggesting their sons could be responsible for such an outrage. For Suzanne's part, she refused to name the father, so, even though it was narrowed to a sophomore named Earl Pitts, and he so much as confessed to the whole sordid affair, he received nothing more than a punitive stare from John, who would have liked to jump across the table and strangle him. But Earl's father was a Golden Gloves champion.

After a month, the Georges decided Suzanne should stay at the Melody Bartlett Home, located in a small town north of Seattle. Alice bundled Suzanne to the Trailways station where they were met by a social worker who rode with Suzanne. Alice was allowed to phone her once a week, and the reports were encouraging. She said that Suzanne's spirits were high, and she was getting the best of health care from the kind staff. But Henry spoke with Suzanne once and learned the truth: she had been taught how to smoke, how to get the examining doctor to blush, how to sneak out for a few hours and meet some of the young n'er-do-wells who hung around the gate because they knew they didn't have to give one thought to birth control.

Henry had concerns for his sister, but he had his own life to contend with. His old paramour, Anita Bush, was back. Despite her tendency to move away and return every year or two, his feelings had burgeoned. She was on the cheerleading squad, a position she was born to inhabit. But she confused him as she was an abysmal student. She became an embarrassment at football games when she shouted out the fight songs.

Anita inevitably yelled, "F-I-H-G-T!" in her most earnestly dyslexic manner. Over time, the other girls on the squad learned to raise their voices so that it became Henry who was the only one to hear her mistakes. No one dared take her off detail. She was too friendly and cute, and everyone expected her family to move again soon, so it wasn't an issue.

The endearing part was that she was oblivious to her flaws. She performed her routines with vigor, spelling out Warriors, W-a-r-y-e-r-s, with such passion that every cell in his body cried out for relief.

And it was a blessing that she shied away from books. To be able to concentrate on a pair of eyes that didn't forever rove across the printed page, now that was something. She was his only love, and at Christmas he asked her to go steady. Her affirmative answer sent his spirits soaring.

During the Christmas vacation, they attended a basketball game and Henry watched her bounce across the floor as the Warriors proved once again there was talent in the hinterlands, just not within the boundaries of the Rochester School District.

But Anita did not relent. While the other cheerleaders sat depressed at the sidelines, hair matted with sweat, she implored the fans to dig deep for that last bit of loyalty and cheer the Warriors on.

"Let's go!" she commanded. "T-r-o-n-c-e, let's trounce 'em!"

After the game, they shared a bag of fries and a coke at the Interstate Burgermaster and Henry started in about the fans not following her lead, but she raised her hand.

She fake-slapped his face and said, "Silly, that's not their job. It's mine." Henry looked forward to the two of them being blessed adults in the future.

One night, near the end of basketball season, he drove her home through the pounding rain. They parked in front of her house and kissed passionately while the wipers flapped. He drew back once just so he could see her long eyelashes, her perfect lips now slightly puffed from their kissing. He reveled in her delicate touch as her fingers glided along his cheek. He couldn't tell himself enough about how much he loved her.

"This could be love," Anita said when they broke apart. "Who would have thought you and I could fall in love? I mean who? We're the most unlikely couple."

"Maybe not that unlikely," he said over the throb in his groin.

She snuggled closer. "I guess if Wayman can come back, we can fall in love."

He kissed her again. "God, I love you," he said.

But she bowed her head.

"What's wrong? Is it the game?"

"No. It's not the game."

"We did lose pretty big this time."

"It was close till the end."

"I wouldn't say a thirty-two-point difference is close."

"You're not very optimistic." She lay back against the seat and sighed. "Besides, it's not the perfect anyway. It's the effort."

He whispered those words to himself as he breathed in her perfume. It dazzled his senses, made him want to crawl closer. "We could seal our love," he said.

Her head rolled toward him. "What do you mean?"

"I mean we've been going out for a while. We've known each other since we were babies. You know, we could make it official." He took her hand and inched it toward the tent in his pants.

But she snatched it away and Henry felt the oddest pitch to his stomach. Outside, the rain pounded the DeSoto in torrents again. He clicked off the wipers so the rest of the world could disappear as they slipped under the deluge.

She took his face in her hands. "I love you so much, Hankie. I don't know how I can live without you."

"Maybe you don't have to."

"We're moving."

"What? Again?"

"We're moving. My father wants to be in Manson by the time the apple trees bloom."

"Manson? What do you mean?"

"I knew I should have told you sooner. But I just couldn't."

"We're only sophomores. You just said you loved me. You can't leave until you graduate."

"I'm not as lucky as you are. My dad doesn't have a steady job. He sits for days and stares out the window. Mom says it lifts him to think he can get a job over there."

Henry looked at the soft lie of her hair, and he couldn't resist touching it. He liked the silken feel. It was like touching the future. "So, you're not joking."

"No, Hankie, it's real. My family needs me. My sisters. My mom. Wherever they go, I go."

It felt so wrong. They'd come too far, and Henry feared he'd never be able to fall for anyone else. He could hear her quiet crying. He gathered her in and whispered in her ear. "I know a way."

"What way?"

"Marry me," he said. The words sounded perfect. They bumped along the ceiling and threw a party in the back seat, not to mention the little soiree in his pants.

Anita sat straighter. "Marry you?"

"Yes. We could go somewhere to do it."

"My parents would never let me. Yours neither. Besides, you've got people to cure. You have an obligation."

"Screw the obligation."

"Now, now. Look, Henry, you're famous and I'm not. People know you and I'm the disappearing girl."

"None of that matters to me. I could work at the museum. I could add more hours. We both could live there."

"Oh, man alive." She leaned in and touched his forehead with hers. Her voice was an urgent whisper. "I'm not ready to choose between you and my family. I can't do that. Maybe I'll come back after I'm old enough and if it's still good between us, yeah, it would be fun to be married to you."

She kissed him and slid out of the car. He clicked on the wipers and watched as she tented her jacket over her head and hurried across the yard to the front porch. She stopped and waved. Henry lowered the window. She stood there a moment, cocked her head. It was like the two of them were taking those mental pictures that eventually fade like the real ones.

"I love you," she called out before slipping inside the door.

"I'll miss you," he said. But there was no party left. The words had blended into the upholstery in the back. Henry pulled out and drove along the Tulane Road for a mile or so before he stopped. He got out of the car as the rain fell and fell and fell. The rain could hurt you sometimes. It melted you, stung you, left a barbed hook in your skin. But, as they say, Henry had no sense to get in out of it. Even the dyslexic girl was too smart for him. He needed it pouring over him as he leaned against the front fender and cried.

It may have been the most difficult year of Henry's life, although it had stiff competition. Having first opened himself to love, he now felt the kind of betrayal only true love can bring. Anita Bush was gone as was Henry's sense of well-being. He tried to blame it on Skookumchuck, but he watched her leave in her parents' jalopy, not kicking and screaming to the sky. His answer to his abandonment: she didn't love him enough, or worse, he didn't know how to love her well enough to make her stay. Or maybe being a *curandero* wasn't all it was cracked up to be.

Henry finally heard from Ray, Jr. It was his first letter from overseas, and it came from Vietnam, a place beginning to get more press on the Inland Washington Coast.

While most soldiers were writing home about the lousy food, the lousy weather, and homesickness, Ray, Jr. was telling Henry about the topography, the nuance of the Vietnamese people, and the spirituality and peace he found there. His stories revealed such rich detail that Henry was carried away, flipping page after page as he lay on top of the blankets.

"...and some nights it is like nowhere else I'd ever want to be. For three straight duties I'd been hearing something moving in the hedgerows. I told Sarge about it the next day and he was gung-ho on setting a mechanic trap to catch whatever it was, but I thought some of our guys might be out trying to take a piss and get caught in it and it's not a pretty sight when a claymore flays you. I don't like bloodshed. I don't like guns even. So, I asked him if I could check it out one more night before we tried the trap.

"About halfway through my duty, I heard it again, so I grabbed my scope and scanned the reeds across the track. That's when I saw it. Hankie, the most beautiful animal you ever saw spread out on its belly right at the edge of the road. The tiger was perfectly sculpted in straight black and orange lines. Every now and then one of his paws would jerk and for a second I thought maybe he'd seen me and was planning an attack. But when I focused in better, I could see he had some kind of little shrew or mouse and was playing with it like a house cat would. Gently, to keep it alive. I sat there for a half hour watching before it stood, stretched itself out, and then lumbered off down the trail. I had an impulse and almost gave in to it: I wanted to follow that beast into the jungle. Because that's what you're supposed to do when a leader beckons you to follow. There could be so much to learn from him. Oh, this place, this war, this solitude is more than I could ever wish for."

When Henry was finished, he was confused by what Ray, Jr. was writing. He found peace in a war zone? Where was the enemy in his report? What was happening to his mind?

Life dribbled on. He had one more day at Mrs. Obregon's, but he grew less fond of his role as assistant. First at The New Prosperity Museum and now with Mrs. Obregon's work. Was she trying to teach him a lesson, because if she was, he was not buying it. Her cures were still not as dramatic as his; they took longer, and he mostly wasn't around to see how they turned out. What did it mean? And what did it mean that Mrs. Obregon was no longer asking him to come to her cabin to help people?

That spring, Henry took third in the 880-yard run at a track meet that happened to coincide with his seventeenth birthday. He started out like a galloping pony – clocked his best quarter mile ever – and was way ahead of the pack. But it was hard to keep the pace and by the 660 mark, his legs were cartoon rubber bands and he hoped simply to make the finish line. He barely staggered across it and crashed onto the cinders. His knee hurt so much he stayed down. The coach pushed people aside and examined Henry's wound, embedded with pea gravel. "Fuck oh dear, you got to get this flushed out," he said.

He helped Henry to his feet and led him to the infield, where the trainer worked on his knee. Henry closed his eyes and listened to the sounds of the meet as it unfolded. This was his life now. Noises with no apparent connection to him.

Back in Rochester, he heard another kind of misery when he carefully stepped out of the DeSoto. Suzanne was screaming through her bedroom window. He quickly ran inside.

"What's she doing here?" Henry asked John who sat by the wood stove with a beer in his hand and helplessness on his face.

He ran his free hand over his thinning hair. "Came home today, big as a whale."

Upstairs, Suzanne cried out again, and Henry grimaced.

"God damn," John said. Here was a man who had reached his limit long ago. Now he could do no more than moan and worry and the masculine chore in crisis after crisis fell to Uncle Ray despite Ray's tendencies toward physical abuse of his wife.

"Ain't a goddamn doctor in miles going to help her out," Uncle Ray said as he exited the bathroom and headed for his favorite armchair.

"Is it bad?" Henry asked.

John turned. "She won't go to the doc for it."

The kitchen was alive with steam from boiling kettles. Alice descended the stairs carrying wet towels. "Ah, Hankie," she said. She wiped her forehead.

"Is she okay?" Henry said.

"I don't really know. They usually had me medicated by the time I got to this point. You want to see her?"

"Yes, I do."

"Come on then." She took him by the hand in a surprisingly delicate way, and they climbed the stairs. At the doorway to the room, Aunt Peg stood with her arms crossed. Her face was flushed and wet and she bit her lower lip.

Once inside, Alice took a stance on one side of the bed, Suzanne on the other. Suzanne waved a clown lamp she'd taken from an end table.

"Get away," she said.

"It's all right, Suzie," Alice said. "No one's going to hurt you."

"Yes, they are!" She doubled over and held her ample belly.

"Those pains are coming pretty close," Aunt Peg warned. "Something better happen. She's not a big girl."

"I want it, I want it, I want it," Suzanne moaned as she leaned against the bed.

"Honey, you're so young," Alice said. "You've got a whole big life ahead of you."

"I want it, I want it, I want it."

"Want what?" Henry asked.

"She wants to keep the baby," Aunt Peg said. "And your mom says no."

Henry took the opportunity to sneak back downstairs. John and Uncle Ray now sat closer together.

"Well?" Uncle Ray asked.

"She wants to keep the baby."

John bowed his head and wagged it back and forth. "She's Steilacoom material."

"Not Steilacoom," Uncle Ray said. "She's just slow. It's the damn horse."

"Can't she die if she doesn't see a doctor?" Henry said.

John snapped to attention. "You think so?"

"Oh, for Christ's sake," Uncle Ray said. "She's not exactly a baby anymore. She's just hurting. Somebody's got to take charge." He took one more pull off his Olympia, hiked his pants and pushed through the doorway to the kitchen. Henry followed close behind.

Upstairs, Uncle Ray's blustery attitude turned to sugar. He bumped Aunt Peg aside and filled the doorway. "What do you need, princess?"

Suzanne burst into fresh, agonized tears.

"Raymond," Alice cautioned. "I really think the women can handle this."

"Not exactly a super job so far," he said. Crooking his finger, he signaled Alice over and whispered in her ear. She immediately shook her head, but he persisted, and she eventually stopped. She looked over to Suzanne who just then threw the lamp to the floor.

Now Alice approached less assured. Wringing her hands, she said, "Suzie, honey. It's okay. It'll be okay. You need to get to the hospital or there could be trouble. I don't want trouble for you."

"I want it, I want it, I want it," Suzanne insisted. "Please, Mommy."

Alice glanced to Uncle Ray and bit at her cheek. "All right, Suzie. All right. You can. We won't stop you."

"I want it," Suzanne said again.

"I said you can have the baby, Suzie. Just let us help you. We'll take you to the hospital. Everything will be all right."

Suzanne swallowed hard and gritted her teeth until a contraction passed. She drew a deep breath. "I want it and I mean it," she said one more time. Then she sank to the floor, unconscious.

Uncle Ray and Henry carried her gingerly down the stairs, while the women cleared the way ahead of them. John popped to attention, and took her legs, while Henry ran outside and opened a back door of the Pontiac. She was all tucked in before she came to and started howling again.

"Got a book you can read her?" John asked Henry.

"Leave me be, Dad."

"I'm serious. What the hell good is that talent you've got if you can't make it work for family?"

Uncle Ray hopped behind the steering wheel and John slid in next to him. Alice grabbed Aunt Peg by the hand and pushed her in to be with Suzanne.

"You coming?" John asked Alice nervously.

She pointed to Henry, and then flicked them away with her hand. Uncle Ray sped off in a shower of muddy gravel.

Henry and his mother scooted along in the DeSoto as if Henry were taking lessons again, his hands tight at the wheel and his mother staring out the window with a curled fist at her mouth. "Twain's in the glove box," Henry said.

She gingerly opened it, fingering the paperback before she pushed the button closed. "There's something not right here, Hankie."

"She'll be okay."

"This shouldn't be happening to her." She fiddled with the upholstery. "Something is wrong. She's growing up too soon. My fault I think."

When they got to the end of the gravel road and turned onto the highway, Henry looked at himself, realizing he still wore his track uniform. Goose bumps crowded around his wounded knee. "She'll be all right after it's born."

"No, that will be the worst of all." She took a deep breath. "Things would be so much better if Raymond weren't around."

"Why?"

But she didn't answer because ahead of them, barely off the side of the road, Uncle Ray's Pontiac idled. His broad behind exploded from the backseat. When they pulled close, Henry heard the cry of a baby, mixed with the most plaintive wail he would ever hear in his life, that coming from his kid sister.

"What now?" Henry asked his father.

"God damn," he said. "She's gone and had the fool thing. Alice?"

But Alice would not leave the car. John tried to yank her door open, but she grabbed the handle and held her ground. So, it was Henry who ended up with a squalling bloody baby in his arms, wrapped in Uncle Ray's work shirt.

Uncle Ray twisted Henry's wrist. "Take it to the hospital! Pronto!"

"But what about Suze?" Henry asked, looking past him to his sister who by now flirted with hysteria. Aunt Peg petted her as she held her head.

"We'll get her there. You go!"

Henry hurried around to his door and slid in clumsily, handing the baby over to Alice, who at first refused, but then took it. John managed to hop in the back and leaned over the seat.

"What the hell," he said. "Step on it, Hankie!"

They raced away, barely stopping for lights and signs, weaving in and out of traffic. All the while, Alice held the baby in her outstretched arms, studying it carefully.

"No, you don't," John warned. "Grandkid or not, we can't keep it and you know it."

"Shut up, John. All right? Just for me." She shifted the baby to one hand and ran a pointed finger around its coarse facial features. She shook her head and plunged the tip of her finger in its mouth, trying to calm it. She turned to Henry once and he thought she might ask him to read to the little one.

Henry stopped the DeSoto in the middle of the ER driveway and they all hopped out, rushing across the asphalt, the baby held ahead of them. Miraculously, the young woman behind the desk was able to decipher most of what they were yelling.

A few minutes later, Uncle Ray burst through the doors, shouting about Suzanne who was bleeding profusely in the back seat. But they had been warned she was coming, and a gurney was at the ready. Within minutes, Suzanne was whisked away to the far reaches of the hospital, and the rest of them were left in the plastic seats of the waiting room, looking wan and shaken. When their breathing calmed, Alice reached over and smoothed the loose bandage on Henry's knee. "Happy Birthday, Hankie," she said.

When Suzanne came home, she slept on the floor for a week until John made her another crib. It was spacious and comfortable, with short wooden sides she could raise or lower at will, and it was probably this that lifted her out of her funk.

As for Henry, he could not shake the feeling of betrayal that dogged him. In the hospital, Suzanne cried and cried like a newly weaned puppy howling for its mother. She was not allowed to keep the baby, and Henry felt a conspirator in an unfair game.

It affected the rest of his life, too. His world was askew. He tried more than once writing to Anita through Manson General Delivery, but the letters always came back with no explanation. He imagined his love drifting out in the rich fruit and vegetable fields east of the Cascade Mountains, an expansive place where he could easily slip from her mind. He desperately needed someone to talk to.

But who did he have? He had no confidence in the counselors at school. His family was off limits for this kind of conversation. That left only one person in the whole Triangle who would understand.

145

SIXTEEN

It had been a rainy spring, and the woods and grasses were deep green and lush. At Porter, Henry got out of his car and stretched. He shivered in his T-shirt and glanced to the hill where a thin curl of smoke rose from Mrs. Obregon's cabin. He climbed the steep rise, batting away the salmon berry bushes and the Himalaya brambles, soaking his pants in the tall, dew-laden grass. Near the cabin, the fruit trees were in ferocious bloom; a few petals lay decomposing on the ground. Not a soul stood outside her door. He smelled burning cedar as he knocked.

"Ah yes," Mrs. Obregon said when she opened it.

Something rich was cooking on the stove, and she receded to a dark corner of the kitchen, stirring the contents before clanging a lid back on the pot. She wiped her hands on her apron, started braiding a hank of her mostly salty hair, and motioned him to a seat at her table.

"I don't exactly know why I stopped by," Henry said.

"No matter. I have no cases. But it is good to see you."

He rubbed at his arms.

"You don't believe me?" she asked.

"Well, I don't know."

"Smart boy. It pays to be skeptical." She held out a box of sesame crackers and lifted a bushy eyebrow.

He took a handful, even though he wasn't hungry.

"Explain, please," she said. "You are unhappy with your power?"

"I'm still happy with it," he said. But he had to turn from her stare. For when the words left his lips, he realized that he wasn't being honest. What power, after all?

"As long as you are good to it, Skookumchuck never leaves you. But it ebbs from time to time."

"She ebbs and she floods."

Mrs. Obregon lay her hands flat on the table and rose. She walked over to a bookcase and sifted through a pile of papers. "I have a letter from the other one."

Henry recognized Ray, Jr.'s handwriting.

"Go ahead, you read it. I'll peel onions."

So, he did. It was a different Ray, Jr. between the lines of this letter. No monologues about the flora and fauna, no topographical sketches. Toward the end was a paragraph that almost made him cry:

"Sometimes I wake up screaming and thrashing around until I realize where I am. That's my worst nightmare, that I might awaken and find myself back in Rochester under my dad's roof. But when I come to, I know I'm over here and that calms me. There are some things worse than seeing people die, killing people, watching people slowly go crazy. I hope this blasted thing goes on forever. I think about what you told me, and I know now I've found my home."

Henry laid the letter on the table, humbled.

Mrs. Obregon returned with a mirror of tears in her eyes. "A vegetable that can make me cry," she said, wiping them away, "is a vegetable I can be friends with."

"I don't get what Ray, Jr. is saying."

"What is so hard to understand?"

"Well, for beginners, he's in a war. And he sounds happy."

She leaned back and folded her hands in her lap. "I would not thrive in a war. You would not thrive in a war, but some do. Otherwise, would there be wars?"

"I don't like this," Henry said. He felt restless again, and stood, going over to a window, and looking out at the drizzle. "He wrote me about a tiger he wanted to follow into the jungle. I'm worried he's losing his mind."

"Don't worry. If you were going to follow something into a jungle, wouldn't you want it to be a tiger? Think of what you could learn from it."

He turned to face her. "I'm troubled about Qone. I spent the summer at the museum, and it was the best summer I've ever had. That can't be good, can it? Aren't I supposed to be happy here?"

She nodded. "Yes. But you are also growing older. That could be the reason. How much do you know about Qone?"

Henry shrugged. "Only what you've told me."

"He is Transformer Moon."

"That doesn't tell me anything."

"He made the world. He made life back when all animals were people."

A bolt of anger zig-zagged through Henry. "Is life always a myth?"

"You think I'm lying? Be careful." She came over to the window, grabbed his hands. "To many around here, he is the only god. He still lives but people like you don't believe it. And you, of all people, should know when you need to believe something."

"Because of my power?"

"Especially because of it. Where do you think it comes from?"

"Skookumchuck."

"An imperfect answer. You need to learn more. As I've said before, you are not native. If you were, you would not slander Qone as you just did. Perhaps it is a mistake you have the power."

"Why do I have to be native?"

"This is our land. We decide what happens here."

Henry looked at her, wondered if she was fooling him somehow. "So, it is true, I am a mistake. I'm not supposed to be able to cure people."

"Your power is good but sometimes imperfect. There must be a mistake."

"You just said Qone was a god. Gods don't make mistakes."

She picked at the corner of one eye. "It looks like you still need lessons. And lesson number one: gods are not perfect. Qone is not. Look around you. He can make a mistake. The gods of the ancients, the Greeks, for example, made mistakes. How are people supposed to trust their gods if they don't make mistakes that are relatable?"

"Isn't it natural to trust gods?"

"That's for you to answer. You are the one who was not taken away when it seems you were supposed to be."

Henry thought of leaving but guilt kept him in place. "We lied to my sister and told her she could keep her baby. But she didn't get to keep it and now she's miserable."

"And how would you help her?"

"Read to her. Cure her."

"But you can do that. Why haven't you cured her? Why aren't you reading?"

"I don't know. I wish I did. Maybe I'm just afraid."

"And what is it you are maybe afraid of?"

"That I might lose someone again." He pictured Anne on the beach and shivered.

She laughed, a deep, throaty genuine laugh. "It's not just the gods. Life itself is not perfect. Those of us who live it either. You are not perfect, yet you blame others for your own imperfections."

"I don't want to blame anyone."

"Fair enough. But you just blamed the ones who've left you. Let me tell you something that is not a game. Your power."

"And..."

"Outside of the Triangle, it has no force."

"I think I knew that. But why?"

"Outside of here. At the museum for example, that was never our land. We don't control it."

"If that's true, then I don't need to worry if I'm not here?"

"Why would you need to worry?"

"Here's what I'm thinking. If I'm not native and I'm meant to be native, but I've been given this power anyway, someone's going to be mad at me and I worry that something bad will happen as a result."

"I see."

Later, she walked back over to the stove and took the lid off the kettle, releasing a tantalizing steam of carrots and onions and celery and bits of chicken. "I've been thinking about what you said earlier. You come looking for something you think you don't know. But you already know it. You don't feel frightened outside the Triangle. Do not ignore what you already know."

She was right, of course. Henry thought about his summer at the museum, his other times away from Skookumchuck. He felt comforted.

Mrs. Obregon brought a pair of white porcelain bowls. "Perhaps in all your longing for answers, what you really want is soup."

"I do?"

She clucked her tongue. "Yes. So many want answers, so few want soup."

She ladled a spoonful and dabbed at it with the tip of her tongue. "You've got to change your relationship with the spirit. You must be with the spirit. Next time, just let it go. When it circles your neck and tugs on your body, just let it go."

His toes curled. His throat constricted remembering the times he'd felt the pull at the Aberdeen border. "I couldn't," he said. And he gave her the reasons why he couldn't let Skookumchuck spirit him away; the dream where he went instead of Wayman, the fear of the unknown, the awful crawling feeling that he might never see anyone again.

They ate the soup, and it was fresh and delicious. As he swallowed the first spoonful, it was as if the concoction awakened taste buds all over his body. He was ravenous. He asked for seconds, and as they chatted more about the Triangle, a relaxation took hold. His shoulders loosened. He breathed easier. He stopped between gulps and peered into the bottom of the bowl. Mrs. Obregon laughed.

He asked for thirds, slurping without manners, burning his tongue and not caring. When, after his fourth bowl, he was finally sated, he pushed away from the table and groaned.

"There now," she said. "You feel better?"

He admitted he did. He looked around the room. A thought came to him. "Can you tell the future, Mrs. Obregon?"

"Yes," she said.

"Would you tell me mine?"

She stroked her chin, chewed on her lip. "It is not how you imagine. No crystal ball or shaking table. But I see you. I see you with others. Helping them. You are alone. Speaking out. You use your... special voice. All around, night fills the cracks of the earth."

He tapped on the table. "That doesn't really help."

"I cannot explain it. I cannot pluck random answers from the void. I only stir it for a better look."

"Okay," he said. "But I need more answers. I want to pray, but I don't know to who."

"Pray to what you can't explain. That's what humankind always does." She stopped and smiled, throwing him off guard. "And in between prayers," she added, taking him around the shoulder, "have a little soup."

He sat back and welcomed bowl number five, and it was as delicious as the other four, but now there was something else in the taste. Not bitter exactly, but not so sweet and comforting. Like the taste had changed color and hung over him like a dark obligation.

When he was finished, Mrs. Obregon said, "Perhaps pray to Qone."

"Why?"

"Because it might keep you from swimming upstream."

"What?"

"Upstream is where you find the weirs. You don't belong there, and you may become trapped."

When he left, although he felt the tweak of a profound disillusionment, he did wonder what she meant about helping others in the darkness. And what the heck was a weir?

SEVENTEEN

On the way home, Henry stopped at Wayman's. There was no guarantee that his old friend would even talk to him, but Mrs. Simpson had grown even more fond of Henry, and she led him to Wayman's bedroom door and asked him to open it.

"He's not feeling the best," she said. "Poor boy won't even leave the house now."

Henry entered and stood over by the dresser. Wayman was spread out on top of his covers. Hands behind his head, he stared at the ceiling.

"What do you want?" Wayman asked.

"I came to see how you're doing."

"How do you think I'm doing? I feel like shit."

"Come on, Way. It's been six years since you came back. Can't you just let it go?"

Wayman swiveled his legs over the side of the bed and stood to a great height. "Can you let your goddamn curing gig go? No? I didn't think so. I had a good thing going, Henry, and you had to go and yank me out of it."

Henry felt both his friend's animosity and his pain. He struggled with which side should win. Should he try to help Wayman get back to wherever he had been? Or should he leave things the way they were? Both Wayman's parents had never been happier. Even they had been on the television all those years ago telling the world how great it was to have their son back. "I'm not God," he said.

"Who you kidding? Of course, you are. Who else would have the power to bring me back? You're God. But I'd have to say not exactly a fair and decent one."

Henry took this in, rejected it. "I'm sorry, Way. I don't know what happened. We were friends and then something got in the way. It's all so spooky and it scares me. What do you want me to do?"

"You said something to me once and I never forgot it. You said if anyone tries to get after you, Wayman, just let me know and I'll take care of it."

"I did?"

"Great. Now, you don't remember."

"But you're so much bigger than me. You don't need me to take care of your problems."

Wayman sat down again, shook his head. "You don't get it, do you? You don't know how to be a friend."

"Yes, I do."

"I think curing people has gone to your head. It's filled you with ideas like you're better than everyone else. Than me. Like you matter more than I do."

"God, Wayman."

"It's true. Even my mom was more important than me. You were always a better friend to her than to me."

Unable to tolerate this criticism, Henry carried this humbling back home and sat in his bedroom with it, thinking about his gift and its burden. Once again, there lived something dubious in his power. Maybe Mrs. Obregon was right. There was more to being a *curandero* than met the eye.

When summer arrived, seventeen-year-old Henry left his family for the museum where he found Mrs. Pinckney in bed with the flu. Her forehead was hot, and the whites of her eyes held a yellow aspect. "You'll have to take over for a while," she breathed. "Till I get my strength back."

It seemed an easy enough task, but Henry hadn't counted on such a glorious Saturday. When he awakened, the parking lot was already filling. There was a 9:00 starting time and he only had ten minutes before the day began.

At 8:59, he unlocked the door, a piece of peanut butter toast just disappearing down his throat. There entered a throng of about twenty, relatives of a retired couple from Pysht, taking a turn around the peninsula. Henry gave them the standard welcome spiel and sent them on their way.

The visitors spent most of their time in the Appliance Wing. He overheard snippets about the hits and misses folks had with the fantastic new products when they first came out.

"Herb tried to put a bone down the Waste Away once," one woman said as the others teased Herb about his lack of sophistication. "I can still hear that horrible noise."

"Like a Chihuahua birthing an elephant," Herb roared.

Although the museum's double doors opened and closed with regularity, Henry felt he could manage the flow. He saw it as a challenge as he directed them to form one line each, coming and going, so there would be no clumps in the halls. He'd had experience, of course, in managing lines, and it came back to him naturally.

After his Kennedy speech, which he delivered on the hour, he could always slip off for a breath of fresh air. When the last patron left in the evening, he locked the doors, ran upstairs, and made dinner for Mrs. Pinckney. He told her of the success. She seemed satisfied and ate most of her hamburger. After dinner, he helped her back to her room, read to her from *Profiles in Courage*, and tucked her blankets tight at her neck before she nodded off to sleep.

One night, soon after a busy Fourth of July and the recovery of Mrs. Pinckney, Henry snuck out back for some much-needed alone time and stood in the middle of the baseball diamond. The air was soft and seductive and smelled of cedar and the ocean breezes. This was a day he missed Anita Bush with an explosive passion. He missed Wayman too, and Anne, of course, and something else less substantial he couldn't name.

He put his hands on his hips, tilted back his head, and spoke to the building. "You think maybe they'll get along without me? All the needy people in the world, I mean."

"Left ankle, Hankie," came the reply in his grandfather's voice. "Just a wee trickle now. Left ankle."

"Does everybody go through this?"

"There's a wee boat," Grandpa said. "There's a wee boat that can hold one or two, and when ye are young, it's like big rapids, sure ye can hear 'em screaming with joy in there, but when ye get to be an old crotch, they start complaining, 'Where in God's name did all thee fun go?'" His voice rang with laughter.

"All I want to know is how come I'm not as happy as I used to be?"

"Don't you know that's how the world works?"

Henry whirled around. The voice was not his grandfather's. And clearly not inside his head. He peered into the darkness. Something tapped hard on the ground.

"Batter up!"

"Phid?"

Another tap. "I said, batter up. You going to toss me one?"

"I don't have a ball."

"That would be plural, young man. Balls. Just roll your sock. That way I won't hurt you when I send it to Powder River."

Henry slipped off his shoes. "Did you graduate?"

"You bet I did."

"And now what?"

"Well, after I thumbed my nose at all the bastards in my life, I realized I haven't figured out what I'm going to do. You ready yet?"

"Just about. I don't know if I can reach the plate from here."

"You always were a weenie."

Henry made a windmill out of his arm. "Can you see it?"

"Doesn't matter. I can sense it."

Henry made a great underhand toss and could almost feel the air move when Phid missed it. "I think that's a strike." The sock fell quietly in the weeds next to Henry. "You going to stay here for the summer?"

"You want me to?"

"Yeah, sure. Of course." But Henry paused.

"Don't be so enthusiastic."

Henry wound up again, exaggerating his moves. "It's not a problem. Why the question?"

"Last time you weren't so sure. I think I scared you."

Henry threw the ball into the darkness, heard Phid run toward it, then a soft thwunk! "Ha!" Phid cried. "A home run!"

Henry located him when he dashed into the wash of light near second. "Wait a minute! I can't see where it went!"

Phid danced around second, hesitated, taunting, then sped off toward third. "That's supposed to be my fault?"

Henry stabbed around in the darkness. Phid rounded third now, heading for home. Henry chased him down.

They collided a few feet in front of the plate and tumbled to the grass and hard-packed dirt. Behind Henry's lids, bright yellow lightning bolts flashed. The two became a jumble of arms and legs, stinging with pain. Unlike Henry, Phid lay still. "You okay?" Henry asked.

"When did you get to be so fucking competitive? Would you get off my goddamn leg before it breaks?"

Henry managed to unlock them and lay panting beside his friend. High above, the stars tried to overcome the light from the museum.

"We can't go on like this," Phid said. "One of us always gets hurt." He moaned, but it didn't sound very genuine to Henry.

"What did you mean you scared me last time?"

"The sex thing."

"I wasn't scared."

"Sure, you weren't," Phid said. A moment later, he added, "You okay? I mean, you were talking to no one out here."

"I'm mostly okay." He told Phid about Anita and missing her.

"Ah, you just missed me is all. You missed me and you need a new project. You'll find one. Me and you always know what we want. And when we do, we go get it."

"I'm not doing much going these days," said Henry.

"But how much coming are you doing?"

Henry glanced over at Phid's big, juicy smile. He wished he had his friend's casual manner. "I'm horny all the time."

"Join the worldwide men's club."

At that moment, Mrs. Pinckney opened the door and called to Henry. Phid answered instead, but she didn't notice.

"Come on," Henry said. "Let's get this over with."

You would think President Kennedy had been resurrected, the way Mrs. Pinckney carried on once she saw Phid. She was in the kitchen in a flash, making Phid everything he liked; ham sandwiches, canned corn, mashed potatoes, and imploring him to catch her up on his life. He responded with his trademark stories. Henry observed him and was shocked once more how much he had changed in the year they'd been apart.

He was taller, and his hair now brushed thick against his neck. His biceps stretched the sleeves of his shirt, and the way he laughed showed a young man with more confidence and control. He had turned into the kind of guy the girls at Rochester High whispered about. It wasn't until Phid said, "Can't keep your eyes off me, huh?" that Henry looked away sheepishly.

Henry snuck to bed while Mrs. Pinckney and Phid continued their reunion. He slid under the thin summer blanket and listened to the soft voices from the kitchen. An astonished gasp erupted from Mrs. Pinckney as Phid told her about his single-handedly catching a robber in his home in the middle of the night. Another lie, Henry was sure.

He thought of Anita instead, her perfect creamy skin, her tender luscious lips, her soft and seductive voice, and he felt the sharp pain of her absence. He knew he was languishing, and he also knew he could not go on forever missing her and waiting for her return. Couldn't people die from unrequited love?

Henry needed to do something. He thought he might jump into the DeSoto and take off across the mountains in search of her. He was seventeen now; the car was his. He'd find Anita and this time convince her to marry him. He just needed to combine the right set of words and she would have no choice but to give in. Why wait? Every day he hesitated was another day alone. He fell asleep to the music of his plan.

Later, Henry awakened when the door creaked open. He listened while Phid removed his clothes and dropped them to the floor. He feigned sleep during the moments of silence that followed.

The floorboards whined as Phid tiptoed over to Henry's bed. Henry struggled to think of something to send him away. A simple "stop right there" would have worked fine. But he didn't say it.

He sensed Phid dropping to his knees and felt the hand on his bed.

"I know you said no before, but I've missed you, bud."

"Just shut up," Henry murmured. "Just... please." His self-control turned off its engine.

Phid tried to move away but Henry grabbed him by the arm. The arm was warm and pulsing. Henry ripped back the blanket and guided Phid's hand over.

"What's this about?"

"I said shut up. Don't say anything."

Phid slowly moved his curled hand up and down.

"I don't know what to do," Henry said hoarsely.

"I know. I know."

"I'm stuck." Henry whimpered. The pleasure was overwhelming. He wrapped his fingers around Phid's. "There's nothing I can do."

Phid leaned in closer. Henry let go and shut his eyes tightly. Phid's intense grip enclosed his brain. He sucked in a hard breath and cried out.

"Oh God." A terrible wonderful pain flamed in his chest. The sensation was thrilling, rapturous, and uncontrollable. "No…" But there was no stopping it. With a cry of pure anguished pleasure, Henry exploded. Visions of his power pulsated in his thoughts. He rushed back and forth and spun in his own mind. He clutched for Anita as he begged and begged and begged again. "Let me go," he whispered hoarsely.

"Hang in, man," Phid said.

"I can't do this. It's so wrong." Henry gasped and winced and jumped in electric starts as his breathing slowly came back to normal. "Phid?"

"It's okay, bud."

But abruptly, Mrs. Pinckney knocked on the door. "Are you boys all right in there?"

Overwrought, Henry whispered, "Get out. Now."

Henry worried about a repeat of the Lost Night, as he now called it. But he shouldn't have. He stayed awake the next night, listening closely for the creak of the bedroom door, but it never happened again. He was flustered, unsure of his behavior and motivations. He hadn't talked to Phid and wasn't sure he could.

About the third night after, Henry woke to the sound of a car door slamming. Through groggy eyes, he observed Phid, out on the road with one hand in a pocket, the other waving off a sleek green MGA. He walked across the lot, kicking at a stone that rattled noisily against the asphalt, Henry saw a bright smile plastered across his face.

Henry left the window and waited outside his room. The front door opened and closed but Phid didn't come up the stairs, and after a while Henry crept down.

He went from room to room, peeking his head in. Just outside the Appliance Wing, he heard Phid giggle. He rested on the floor, next to the Admiral Fridge, on top of a comforter made into a mattress, reading a paperback, a wicked smile still hugging his face.

"I know you're there," Phid abruptly said, setting the book aside. "You might as well come out of stalker mode."

Henry stepped in; one of his hands drifted to cover the front of his boxers.

"Oh, for God's sake," Phid said. "Don't worry about it."

"But it wasn't right."

"Really?" He grabbed up the book again, flipped through the pages. "You want to know what Kerouac thinks?"

"Not really."

"Well, I'm going to tell you. I think it applies." He ran a finger along a line. *"Give them what they secretly want, and they of course immediately become panic-stricken."*

"Uh, no."

Phid slapped the book closed. "Think what you want, but it was your hand that dragged mine over."

"I don't secretly want that."

"Whatever you say. The proof is in the pudding, so to speak."

"God. It's not me. It's not."

"You just keep telling yourself that." Phid stared at Henry, then sighed. "Maybe it isn't you. But aren't you glad you found out?"

In all his worry and confusion, Henry had not thought of it this way.

"Come on, let's approach this intelligently, shall we? Through a sharper lens, a hand is just a hand, a tongue is just a tongue, a mouth is..."

"I get it," Henry said. "I was hoping maybe we could declare a truce."

"It isn't war, you know. It's just sex."

"Can't you help me out here?"

"Okay. Besides, I don't really want to do it with you again anyway." He sat primly. "I now believe that sex between friends is a bad idea."

"Thanks for the homily," Henry said. "But you're right. It can ruin everything."

"Yeah, exactly. So, can we still be friends?

"Never again, right?"

"Never again."

"Okay. I guess we can be then."

Phid shook his head. "As an aside, I think you should know you're a tough one, Hank."

The museum was closed on Mondays. Phid had gone to Moclips on an errand, something having to do with unguents, and wouldn't be back for most of the day. Henry was feeling lonely and puzzled again, still bewildered over the doings with Phid. But his reverie was interrupted by Mrs. Pinckney as she hurried down the stairs.

"Okay, Herman," she ordered. "You want to get that door?" She arranged the pillbox on her head. "We've got visitors."

Henry stood from the reception desk chair and fiddled with the neck of his shirt. "How many?"

"One car. It shouldn't take long. I'll go start the phonograph."

Henry walked over to the window and peeked out. Uncle Ray was removing a piece of luggage from the back seat of his Pontiac. Suzanne stood beside him with her hands clasped behind her. John had just slipped on his coveralls and slid under the belly of the Buick. "What a world," he said as he disappeared.

Uncle Ray led Suzanne to the door Henry had just opened. "Well, I'll be screwed," Uncle Ray said. "The welcome wagon we all know and love. Say hello to your sis."

Suzanne was pale, her hair appeared even darker now against her face. She brushed it away. "Hello, Hankie." She glanced, embarrassed, at her bag. "They thought..."

"Can't seem to control her." Uncle Ray reached into his pocket and removed a crumpled piece of Big Chief tablet. He snapped it open and held it out to Henry. It was a letter from Alice.

Dear Rosal,

I know this must be a terrible imposition, but please try to understand my predicament. Suzanne seems destined to be unhappy this summer. She pines and cries and genuinely misses her brother. I would have called, but my husband seemed to think this would be the best way to handle it.

You have been so kind with our Henry. I will send money along with this note with the hopes it will cover the expenses of an unhappy girl. She is a good little worker and good company when she's feeling well. Tell Henry he is to look after her.

I'll always remember the ladybug pin you gave me when I was young. I still wear it occasionally. If there is anything ever, I can do for you, please let me know. I hope this finds you well and the museum prosperous.

With Kindest Regards,
Alice George

Henry faced the two of them. "What's this?"

"She needs a rest from the house." Uncle Ray moved aside so Suzanne could sneak in.

From under the Buick, John said, "Tits on a boar. She needs to take this cocksucker out." Tink-tink.

Inside, Uncle Ray set the suitcase down near the desk and looked around. "It ain't what it used to be. Who did the decorating?"

"I'll get Mrs. Pinckney," Henry said, but she already stood at the doorway to the hall.

A half-smile dallied on her face. "Don't worry with your names and addresses," she said, "we'll get that from you later. We'll pretend it's Sunday, so it's free. Herman, you're not charging them, are you?"

"Herman?" Suzanne said.

"They're not staying," Henry said.

"Be kind," warned Mrs. Pinckney.

Uncle Ray walked over to her. "You don't remember me?" he asked, winking.

"I'm afraid I'm not the woman I once was."

"Well, you're in luck because I haven't changed a bit. I sold your old man his life insurance policy. You remember?"

She quickly glanced to Henry and then to Suzanne. Behind her, the dirge expanded along the hallway. Henry handed over Alice's note while Suzanne snaked her fingers into his.

"John's out fixing the Buick," Uncle Ray said. "You wouldn't want to trade pink slips, would you?"

Mrs. Pinckney was not listening. She finished the letter and folded it. "Am I to become a foster mother then?"

Suzanne squeezed Henry's fingers even harder.

"She's a handful," Uncle Ray said. "Won't argue with that. Used to be a fine girl. Got herself in the family way, though. Now she don't pay attention to nobody. She's still good, mind you. Won't get in the way. And she can sing, too."

Mrs. Pinckney walked past him, lifted the curtain with a finger and observed John underneath her car. "This is your sister then, Herman?"

"Yes, ma'am."

She turned. "I can't pay you a thing. I barely have enough to feed the boys." She examined Suzanne hard. "Is all this true? Do you want to come here?"

"Course she does," Uncle Ray interjected.

Mrs. Pinckney stopped him with her eyes before she slipped out the door. Suzanne and Henry crept over and watched as she kicked at John's heels. He came sliding out, a spattering of oil on his nose. They chatted for a moment.

"Do you think she'll let me stay?" Suzanne whispered.

"What happened at home?" Henry asked.

"I just can't face it anymore. What's the use of living?"

Outside, John dug into his pocket and took out a small wad of bills.

"It looks good for you," Henry said.

"Is it nice here, Hankie?"

"It has its ups and downs, mostly ups."

The transaction complete, Mrs. Pinckney returned with a smile. She wasted no time in brushing past Uncle Ray and confronting Suzanne. "There is a lot to learn here," she said.

"I know."

"Well, come along then." Mrs. Pinckney pulled her up the stairs, her suitcase banging against each of the risers.

Uncle Ray watched them go, then turned to Henry. "That woman's Steilacoom material."

"Stop it." Frustrated, Henry went outside and stood by his father's feet.

"Oh, Hankie," he said, not missing a tink. "How's it hanging?"

"Is Suzanne okay?"

"Sure thing. She's just making your mom a little nervous is all. She sits by the phone all day, waiting for a call. Poor kid. Figured the change'd do her good. Look what it did for you."

"Was there something wrong with me?"

Pound, pound. "Not exactly. It just came different for you is all. You know, all that curing nonsense." He hammered again.

After a while, Uncle Ray emerged and they left, peeling out from the lot, the clink of bottles already audible before they got past the sign.

Mrs. Pinckney stationed Suzanne in a room in the nurse's left breast, a part of the museum Mrs. Pinckney never got to anymore. Henry cleared the room of unmemorable memorabilia, artifacts that had not made the grade: a Kefauver photo, a movie poster for The Rose Tattoo, a Pogo stick, a 45 of Olympia's Fleetwoods singing "Come Softly To Me". The room was a mess of clutter, and the dust roiled around them when Suzanne helped him later. Beneath all of it, they found a curved iron bed with a white spread monogrammed with The Cedars in the corner. From the closet, they pulled a worn nightstand with faint rings discoloring the wood where glasses of water once sat waiting to wash down pills to keep old folks and their many ailments under control.

It took two hours to get it all cleared and another to store the memorabilia in such a way that some of the pieces could be easily fetched if their stock suddenly rose in Mrs. Pinckney's eyes.

When Phid came home a half hour later, they'd just sat down to dinner when Suzanne walked in. Phid had his fork halfway to his mouth and there it floated as his eyes bugged and his face flushed.

"This is Herman's sister," Mrs. Pinckney said. "She'll be spending the summer with us. She is quite the singer."

Phid put down his fork. "Suzanne?"

Suzanne blushed and tossed one lock of hair over her shoulder before she sat next to Henry. "Sorry I'm late." She looked down at her plate. "What's this?"

"Roast beef," Henry said.

She was tentative, trying to get it to crumble like a patty with the edge of her fork. She clearly captured Phid's attention as she toyed delicately with the meat.

"She's not used to exotic foods," Henry said, noticing Mrs. Pinckney's concern.

"Let me," Phid said. He walked over and sliced the roast with sure strokes.

"Thank you," Suzanne said, and they all watched as she brought the first piece to her lips.

Long after Mrs. Pinckney and Henry had washed their dishes, Phid was leaning on the table, studying each move Suzanne made. She performed quite a ceremony, relishing every mouthful, not once showing teeth as she chewed. Henry left for his room and read *Flowers for Algernon* on top of the covers.

An hour later Phid snuck in, leaning against the door. "That's your sister?"

"They say we're alike."

"Hardly," Phid said, dropping on the other bed. "She's great."

Henry tried to keep reading, but Phid wouldn't stop talking. He wanted to know everything about her and Phid was too earnest and charming to be held off for long.

Henry reminded him of that spot at the beach where Anne buried her, told him about the horse and the baby and just about everything else he could think of. Phid lay on his bed with his chin in his hands, his eyes dancing with the reflection of Henry's waving arms.

Phid soon went to the window, parted the curtain. "I'd like to take her to Moclips someday." He glanced down at his watch and rubbed at his lips.

"I don't think so," Henry said.

"What? Why? Oh God, you think I'd take her to do that? Never. You know, there are other things to do in Moclips besides having sex."

At that moment, a car pulled in and honked. Phid pushed open the window and hung out. "Not tonight!" he called into the growing darkness. There was an exchange of words, but Phid was adamant and soon the car thundered away.

He turned back inside and, for the first time since the Lost Night, started removing his clothes. Henry nervously shoved himself under the covers.

"She's pretty cool," Phid said.

He turned out the light and Henry heard him rustling the blankets. After a minute, Phid left the room.

Later, Henry went out to check on him. After searching the usual places, he found him in Suzanne's room. Phid sat on the end of her bed, his back against the iron footboard. Henry listened to their excited voices; she was telling him about the Melody Bartlett Home, and he was telling a tale about Moclips. For a moment, Henry had a fantasy of them all being patients at The Cedars, better yet, relics at the museum. For the first time, he wondered if the blessed children of the future were as blessed as Mrs. Winkle thought.

But when he crept away, he felt happy for his sister to have found a friend.

As the summer progressed, the three of them took Monday trips to Moclips and walked up and down the boardwalk, like the rich Seattle vacationers who tumbled out of their Cadillacs. They sat for hours at the end of the main pier, Suzanne in the middle, watching the eastern sun pass to the west and then put itself to sleep in the warm cozy glow of the distant oceanic horizon. Once or twice, Suzanne slipped her hand into Phid's and squeezed it tight. He turned each time and rested his forehead on hers.

"Love," Henry whispered to himself.

Suzanne was happy that summer. Henry was happy. Phid was cheerful and optimistic for a change. When September came, none of them wanted to leave and Phid spent most nights with Suzanne, cherishing every moment. But happiness encouraged everyone to grow sanguine. Suzanne, newly energized, had her heart set on going back to school, and Henry looked forward to his senior year.

The night before they left, Phid bade them goodbye and walked across the lot to the side of the road where he waited for the mysterious MGA to whisk him away to some beckoning pleasure. He was still not back when the morning dawned gray and quiet. Suzanne and Henry waited longer than they should have, but eventually left for home. Their arrival was subdued. Aunt Peg had heard from the Army.

Ray, Jr. was now a prisoner of war.

EIGHTEEN

Henry drove his mother to Aunt Peg's house. She was quiet most of the way and he could tell it was an important trip because she hadn't brought along a book. She wrung her hands together like Lady Macbeth and finally said, "If you so much as think of going in the military, Hankie, you are no longer a child of mine."

"Mom."

"No, I mean it. When I said you must see the world, I did not intend it that way. You will not do this to me."

Aunt Peg sat on the front porch rocking and when they climbed to her, she pulled up her apron to hide her face.

Alice gathered her in and the two cried. When it looked as if they'd never stop, Henry snuck inside. He arrived at the back of the house in time to see Uncle Ray pull a leghorn out of a sack.

The glass door to the cage was framed in iron rebar painted white. For years and years, Henry had helped Ray, Jr. look for the key that Uncle Ray now used to unlock it.

"No one touches this key," Uncle Ray said once, holding it in front of Henry and Aunt Peg. "You two don't know your asses from a snake hole. You get hold of this; we'll all be snake shit."

Now, while the leghorn flapped hanging from his fat hand, he unlocked the door and flung the chicken to its doom. Instantly, the big reptile dropped from the old apple branch. The chicken squawked and flopped around, but that forked tongue had him trapped.

"Go get `em!" Uncle Ray urged, finding a chair, and sitting back to watch the spectacle. "Look at 'em go!"

Henry squinted, hoping that a murder through an eyelash-covered haze would be less of a murder. The ill-fated chicken bumped against the glass with its clipped beak.

The snake was a master, relishing the hunt. It took its time, head erect and riveted toward the bird as it settled among the rocks placed around the perimeter of the cage. Soon the chicken grew tired and stood, feathers drooping, as the constrictor coiled in big meaty circles around it.

And then the constriction began, tightly from the bottom until the chicken was lost in the coils. The snake turned in on itself, stretched that gruesome face and engulfed the bird until it was nothing more than a picayune lump migrating slowly toward the tail.

Henry looked over to Uncle Ray who was wiping sweat from his face with a damp cloth. He stood, kicking the chair back. "No more cluck," he said.

"I'm sorry to hear about Ray, Jr.," Henry said.

"Why should you be sorry? He's right where he belongs."

"With the enemy?"

"That kid'll do anything to get out of duty." He walked over to the cage and tapped his blunt fingers against the glass. The snake rose and flicked out its slippery tongue. "This guy could eat three or four more."

"Do you know anything about what happened?"

"Nope, and I don't want to." Uncle Ray made clucking sounds to the snake.

"I wish it didn't."

Uncle Ray hung his head for a moment, then backed into the chair again. Dust roiled when he plopped down. "I believed in her," he said.

"In who?"

"That Injun. Obregon. I sent my boy to her."

There was a timbre to Uncle Ray's voice Henry had never heard before. "But..."

"Ah, go on," Uncle Ray said. "Go on and talk to the ladies. Calm `em." Then he struggled to get out of the chair and left, walking disconsolately toward the barn where the chickens were kept.

On the front porch, Alice and Aunt Peg had stopped crying. Alice sat on the top step, holding her knee in her hands. "It isn't fair. This shouldn't happen to your Junior. Not after everything he's been through."

"Murderous heathens," Aunt Peg breathed. "Snatching a boy like that. He's just so frail."

"He'll be all right," Alice said, and she cast Henry a threatening glance, aware that he had recently read a novel about prisoners of war.

"Why would he volunteer to be on sentry?" Aunt Peg said.

"Well, somebody's got to make sure the coast is clear."

"But the coast wasn't clear. They came out of nowhere and took him away. I bet they stabbed him with those bayonets of theirs."

"Now, Peggy, you don't know for sure what happened. Don't torture yourself about it."

"Ray, Jr. liked to be out at night seeing what he could see," Henry said. "He loved it. He saw a tiger once."

The women stopped and studied him for a moment, too long a time for Henry.

"Well, he did."

"We shouldn't let their kind over here," Aunt Peg seethed. "They should all be shot."

After a short pause, Alice said: "Do you need anything?" She jerked her head toward the back of the house. "Are you going to be okay?"

Aunt Peg considered this for a moment and shook her head. "I don't care what happens to me now."

When Suzanne returned to school, she became a teacher's assistant and her grades along with her spirits soared. It was a perfect fit. She took Home Ec where she assisted Mrs. Shipley in the preparation of all her foodstuffs and in the fine sewing for her demonstration dresses. She took Office Assistantship and spent countless hours poring over tardy slips and running errands for Mrs. Buckley, the real assistant, who was developing plantar fasciitis and was not as fleet of foot as she was in her heyday. She took Nurse's Training and was an aide to Mrs. Trueman who could never keep track of her stethoscope. She got an A in each of these classes, which helped her weather the difficult adjustment of being an unwed mother with a touch of brain damage, back at the scene of her shame.

Adolescent boys on the Inland Washington Coast were relentless in their pursuit of gracelessness and often gathered in packs to show off. Suzanne had always been a favorite target. Many of them had never forgotten her haunting beauty at a community wedding. They followed her noisily until the day she'd poured out her heart in the counselor's office.

After the baby was born, she returned home with a target on her back for the snarling band of near men that hovered in every open doorway at Rochester High. To be fair, it wasn't just Suzanne who was the object of their desire, it was girls in general. But some girls were better able to defend themselves. Suzanne was especially vulnerable to the kind of sex-charged hooting that went on in high school hallways.

During the middle of December, the boys got more physical with her. The Warriors had a home basketball game against Oakville, and everyone's blood was aching for the match. The gym was of a fine 1930's vintage, outdated and cramped. A communal cheer of R-E-B-O-N-D led by a now-absent Anita Bush might very well have brought down the crumbling roof.

It was jammed for the Oakville game. The spectators were sweating before the opening whistle. Henry was dressed in a white shirt and dark tie because he had been chosen to call out the winning raffle number at halftime and present a yard-size crèche made by Mr. Vernon's shop class to the winner.

Suzanne agreed to dress up as well and took great pains to sew a Peter Pan collar with the initials SG onto a frayed blouse. She wore a black sweater and a glistening false amethyst locket which, when opened, revealed a generic baby picture. She sat in the stands next to Henry.

The game did not go well, as was the case with so many of the Warriors' slugfests. Form was not a selling point to these fans. It was desire, and the Rochester team showed plenty, mostly in their desire to maim opposing players. The top scorers often fouled out before the end of the first half and after that, the games took on a circus quality.

Henry hadn't noticed the shop class sitting behind them, but they had noticed Suzanne. At halftime, he carried the squealing mike out to the middle of the floor, had one of the cheerleaders dig deep into the hopper of ticket stubs, and announced the winning number amid a chorus of excited shouts coming from the Oakville bleachers.

After the announcement, the crowd milled on the floor and Henry picked his way through the bodies back to his seat. Suzanne was gone. He waited for her until the team returned to the floor. He cast a nervous glance toward the doors as the nicotine crowd shuffled in. The second half was two minutes old when he stood and hurried out, asking after his sister. Finally, the girl selling hotdogs told him Suzanne left with a group of boys.

Adrenaline poked his heart as Henry sped across the parking lot. It was dark and cold; his breath exploded into white beneath the light.

On the edge of the field, he stopped and listened. Soon, he heard shouts and laughter and ran in that direction.

They all had a bottle of beer in their hands and were in a Zorba the Greek stance, arms slung over shoulders in a circle. There were ten or twelve of them, an odd fairy ring of boys under the glaring December moon. Suzanne was on her knees in the middle of the circle, her hands over her face, and they were taunting her as they pranced, taking swigs of beer.

Henry thought he had arrived in time, that he could save his sister from this torment, but soon discovered he was wrong. Earl Pitts broke from the group, and danced over to where she huddled, sobbing. He held his bottle over her head, stroking it earnestly as the others hooted to the cadence. When he was ready, he gave the bottle a shake and squirted streams of foamy beer onto her shoulders, her hands, and onto that carefully stitched Peter Pan collar.

Horrified, Henry ran shouting into the crowd and there followed a melee in which he was kicked in the gut and the face and rendered unconscious. When he came to, he and his sister were alone, except for a presence Henry never exactly saw, but felt, humiliation given shape. Suzanne still cried and he crawled over to her. Her sweater was a mess, her hair even worse. He pulled the sweater over her head and used it to clean her off.

"Christ," he said.

Suzanne pulled on her blouse. "Did you see what they did?"

He felt the first real pain of his injuries. "They're animals, Suzie."

"They never go away. You promised me they'd go away."

"What?"

"You said all my problems would go away with books. You said nothing could touch me if I read them. When you read to me, most of my problems do go away, but the boys still bother me."

"That's not exactly what I meant."

"Well, what did you mean then?" She snatched the sweater back and wiped more of the foam away.

Henry thought hard about her question as he listened to the dull roar coming from the gym. "What I meant was it takes you away from your problems when you read. I don't think it solves them."

She lay back on the ground, began to shiver in the December air. "Then all those times you read to people and cured them was a lie?

You tricked me too? Like everybody did when they said I could keep Diana?"

"Who's Diana?"

"My baby. I named her after Diana Ross of the Supremes."

"Suzie," he said with delicacy. "Your baby was a boy."

She rolled over to him. Her eyes glistened in the moonlight. "A boy?"

"I thought you knew."

"Uncle Ray told me it was a girl, a pretty little girl with lots of hair and chubby cheeks." She rose on her elbow. "Are you sure?"

"I drove him to the hospital. I know."

She crumpled again, this time rolling over and sobbing into the brown grass of the practice field. Henry watched over her, wondering if he should get her home, but he let her cry there. Maybe Suzanne needed to do her suffering closer to the earth.

Finally, she sat upright and tossed her hair. "Can you read to me?"

"Now? We don't have a book.

"Then what good are you? You're famous and everyone thinks you're some kind of magician, but what good are you if you can't make your own sister feel better?"

They were quiet for a while. Henry knew she might have a point. While he still performed some cures, it seemed that the world around him, his own world, wasn't in the best shape.

"I can read to you later," he said.

"Forget it."

And it was later, right before the game was over, Henry helped her to the DeSoto. She sat in the front; her feet barely scraped against the floor. A mile from their house, she turned to Henry and said:

"Thank God I have Phid. He'll take care of things for me when we get married. And he won't be reading any books."

"What?"

But she was already ripping the Peter Pan collar off and slowly unraveling her initials until they were just a wad of red thread caught between her fingers.

It was a busy season. A Rochester school bus skidded off the road and people blamed John. Nobody was hurt, but something was wrong with the steering mechanism. John was summoned before a district tribunal and received a warning about paying closer attention to his duties. After that, he spent most of his free time either out in the toolshed or with Uncle Ray, which was probably most of the problem to begin with. Since the news about Ray, Jr., the two of them drank together almost daily.

Alice, on the other hand, finally persuaded the editor of the Rochester Weekly Guardian to print one of her reviews. It wasn't her favorite, but it was a start, and the local bookstore had a two-book run on the works of Anne Morrow Lindbergh. It may have been a sign of the times. Rochester, at Christmas 1967, was awakening to the world around it; its longtime slumber being its implied eventual fate. Subscribing to its changes was never in the cards. But Alice was ecstatic. She spent even more hours tapping away at her Remington, convinced of her future career as a literary critic.

That spring Henry was accepted to the University of Washington, which pleased his mother. When Henry got the news, her second review had just been published in the Weekly Guardian. The review was chopped to the bone in a blur of editorial frenzy so the average Rochester reader could understand it. But Alice was in the trance of publication wonderment. One night she handed Henry her review of *Travels with Charley*. He thought it was good and told her so.

"Thank you, my Hankie," she said. "Oh, I wish I had enough to send you on a trip to Europe, to somewhere else, just so you can see what the world is like."

"I know, Mom. But it's okay. I'll have Seattle."

Before she left, she asked, "Do you think there's any chance I could go to college, too?"

He thought she was kidding.

"It's a pretty stupid idea, isn't it?"

"Yes," he agreed. "Moms don't generally go to college."

But the friends of assistant museum curators did. As soon as Suzanne told Phid about Henry's matriculation, he dashed off an application and was accepted at the UW as well.

Henry's graduation was anticlimactic. He sat with his fellow graduates and watched Ralph Underwood rake in all the scholarships and prizes. It wouldn't have been so bad, except Ralph carried them around at the Senior Party. Henry remembered the dinner at the Underwoods and the day at the assembly when he blamed Henry for

Wayman's disappearance. It still rankled. After a couple of kids corralled Henry in the bathroom and had him swallow a few shots of whiskey from the flask they'd snuck in, Henry confronted Ralph the next time he stopped by to gloat.

"Why did you tell my secret to everyone?"

"Be careful, you'll become an alcoholic," Ralph said. He dropped one of his envelopes and Henry stooped to retrieve it. "Go ahead. Take a look."

Henry opened it. It was a full tuition scholarship to the school of his choice.

"Harvard," said Ralph. "Just in case you were wondering."

Henry handed it back. "But why did you do that? The whole sociological study? Why me?"

Ralph stepped back. "You're not going to hit me, are you?"

"Cut it out."

Ralph put his cards in order again. "Seems to me you can't do much sitting in a chair with a book. Seems to me, you'd better get up on your feet. I didn't make it to the vacant lot when you performed your so-called miracle." He laughed out loud.

"Wayman came back."

"But from where? You didn't fool anyone with a brain. He was hiding out is all. Give it up. Admit that I beat you fair and square, that it's rationality that always wins the day."

The whiskey had loosened Henry's boundaries. Never had Henry felt so close to using his fists. "Someday, you're going to get yours."

But Ralph had already drifted off, leaving Henry with a sour and unsatisfied taste in his mouth.

"Listen," he called after Ralph. "You can't have it all. That bunch of cards you've got isn't everything."

"I'm telling Mrs. Winkle," Ralph said. "She said I could have it all."

Henry bit his lip until he tasted blood. "You've never believed I have power, have you?"

"I believe in science," Ralph said. "It isn't scientifically possible. It's like you and that ridiculous museum. It's just wood and nails. It'll never come to anything. The New Prosperity Museum. Come on, Henry. Everyone knows the real prosperity is yet to come."

"You're a geek," Henry said.

"I know. But someday, I'm going to be a very rich geek."

Henry returned to the museum for the summer. There the craziness started up with Phid again, the late-night forays into Moclips, the raucous behavior. They each had their assignments and Phid stuck close to his. He couldn't shut up with Mrs. Pinckney, but with Henry, not much talk.

Henry grew more pensive. He spent most of his time up in his room where he sat in front of the window and watched the sea fans.

"Left arm, Hankie," came his grandfather's weak voice. "Listen to her now." Henry put the crook of his elbow up to his ear and listened. No rush. No river. No thub-dup.

Maybe it was time to take a serious look at life. Time to put away the childish notions about magic and powers and gifts. Henry wondered again if he should have been paying more attention to the likes of Ralph Underwood. He wasn't feeling blessed at all.

In his circle of family and friends, things were not moving in a linear direction. His younger sister relived the torment of her poor adolescent choices and planned to rely on the love of a guy who would never have any sexual interest in her. His father was losing his grip at the bus garage. One of his best friends was sitting in a lonely cell somewhere in Southeast Asia.

And Henry? He was about to embark on a college career. How would it change him?

He put the crook of his elbow to his ear again. Still nothing. Maybe his grandfather meant to call it the stagnant Pond o' Life and not a rushing river at all.

All he knew was he wanted to get away. Seattle would do for now, but he had bigger plans working in his brain. Some place where they spoke a different language. Some place far away from powers and disappearances and women who couldn't be caught. Alice said she had started a travel fund for him. That was good, wasn't it? It might propel him toward his goals. But then again, maybe he could land where Wayman had gone. He shivered. Time to focus. Time to move ahead with his life.

PART III

CURES

NINETEEN

On a rainy November morning, Henry awoke to a loud rap on his door. He unhooked his arm from around Romana and drug himself out of bed.

"Don't answer it," Romana said groggily. "I need another hour or so." She pinched him on the butt.

"You always need another hour," he said. He'd met her in class when she asked for a cigarette. It was the first time he could recall wanting one. After class, he accompanied her to the store and then to his room where he watched her plug the cigarette into her mouth and smoke like a movie star.

Now, he pulled on his shorts and found his mother on the other side of the door.

"Can I come in?" she asked. "I've left your father."

"You what? It's Friday." He quickly looked behind and tried to will the covers back over Romana's breasts.

"I don't care what day of the week it is. I've left him. I want to have a word."

He ushered her into his dorm room. She cleaned off the chair in front of the desk and sat, untying her plastic rain scarf. It wasn't until mid-snap, clearing it of water, that she noticed the girl in Henry's bed.

"Oh," she said.

"Oh, yourself," said Romana. She hadn't bothered to cover her breasts, the smallish ski-jump variety Henry loved. She sat up, pulled back her long blonde hair, and lit a cigarette. She offered the pack to Alice who shook her head.

"Sorry, Mom. If you had called…"

"It's not like you interrupted anything," Romana said. "Your boy here is one and done."

"Rome," Henry warned. She spoke the truth, though maybe not mother truth.

"What? It's something we're working on. I take it all out of him, I guess." She stretched her arms high, nearly burning the curtain above her.

"Oh my." Alice turned the chair around so her back was to the bed. "I was in a hurry. I wasn't thinking."

"You left Dad?" Henry dropped to the floor.

"He and Raymond are on a binge, and I can't stand around and watch them ruin their lives. It's the last straw."

"But why now? They've always done that crap."

She toyed with the fringe of the scarf as she glanced back at Romana who seemed not to be listening. "Your father has been suspended from the school district, Hankie. For conduct unbecoming a bus mechanic."

"Not the drinking?"

"He's been taking it in his thermos."

"Why does he do that?"

"He's always done it, only not as much as now. He has demons he can't get rid of."

"From the war."

Alice considered this possibility but decided she wasn't in the mood. "Now he spends all his time out in the toolshed doing odd jobs for people who want good work done cheaply. It's all too much. I had words with your father, Raymond stepped in between us, and I left."

She stood and opened her handbag, removing a few sheets of paper. She thrust them at him. "I want you to take these. They're reviews the Weekly Guardian doesn't see fit to print. I want you to take them to your English professor and see what he thinks."

"No."

"What? Why not?"

"We met in that class," said Romana. She looked at a clock on the wall. "As a matter of fact, we'd better get going if we want to make it on time."

"It's today?" Alice said.

"Hey, that's a good idea. Why don't you come with us? You can give them to him yourself."

"Oh, I don't know about that, Hankie."

Romana laughed. "Old people," she said. She dropped the long ash of her cigarette on the bed.

As it was, it did thrill Alice to be on campus. She watched students as they milled and talked and smoked between classes. They rushed as the time for class grew near. The three of them found seats toward the back of the huge bowl-like theatre.

"I can barely see him," Alice said, shading her eyes.

But she endured the fifty minutes of talk—mostly from the professor—about Faulkner, Melville, Steinbeck. During the lecture, whenever she recognized a famous writer, Alice rapped Henry on the leg.

When class was over, Alice tried to hurry them along, but when they reached the bottom of the room, the professor was nowhere in sight. At the doorway, Henry spied him and shouted out his name.

"Dr. Blatt, wait. Dr. Blatt."

A man with a severe haircut turned and waited. He sported a Van Dyke beard with sharp points, and a look of tiredness across his features. He said: "I'm in a hurry. Walk with me."

While all three started to walk, after a few seconds, it looked to be only Alice who had his attention. She pulled out her purse and removed the sheets of paper, talking all the while. Henry finally stopped and watched as she disappeared with his English professor.

"Oh God," he said to Romana. "This could go bad for me."

"I think she's great. She knows what she wants."

Alice returned a few minutes later. "What are you going to do now, Mom?" Henry asked.

"I thought I might try to find a little place in town and do some reviews," she said with a sparkle in her eyes. "There are a couple of nice apartments above the cafe that haven't been used in years. I'm sure Mr. McDonald would give me a deal if I cleaned them up."

"You'd move out?"

"You don't believe me either, do you?"

"Can you afford it?"

"I have to be able to afford it."

"I don't know, Mom. I don't want the two of you to split up."

She left him with a reminder to always answer the door in pants.

As it turned out, she was serious. At home, she packed up her belongings and took a walk-up over the Garabedian Cafe in downtown Rochester. She was right that it needed work, but she was not lacking in enthusiasm, and by the end of the first week, had fashioned an attractive home.

By day, she cooked for Mr. McDonald—Mr. Garabedian had long since left this world. The menu was like any other café menu. The problem was that Alice, aside from hamburgers, was not a good cook, and many a customer could be seen spitting their deviled egg or ham patty sandwich into their napkins.

By night, Alice sat by her two windows that looked out over the main street, and composed reviews, which she mailed to Henry. Dr. Blatt thought they were fine, his favorite word, one that could be bandied about easily in a class of eager freshmen. But Alice, when she learned of it, thought the word gilt with gold. The word fine became for her a beacon by which she could write her reviews and live her new life above the Garabedian Cafe. During this period, she composed one a night until the streetlight winked out, calling all decent Rochester citizens to their beds.

That next spring, after a bitter break-up with Romana, Henry struggled with what he should do for the summer. The museum was an option, but for the first time, he considered other possibilities. He heard of work in Seattle being a gopher for a construction crew. He was offered a job at a mechanic shop, busting tires and repairing inner tubes. Neither seemed right, seemed special. What was he to do if Mrs. Obregon called for his help? In the end, he headed for the museum.

The place seemed eerie and lonely. But when he walked into the Appliance Wing, it was a visit to an old friend. A single light shined on the Waste Away. He didn't suppose this device was fashioned by any great artistic mind, but now it took on a certain ethereal quality he'd missed before. Here was an instrument of popular culture that gave time as a reward. No more separating the wet from the dry garbage. No more keeping smelly chickens you go sloshing through the weather to feed. This invention was at your command. You stuffed it with garbage, and with a flick of a switch, it gave you back your time, your energy, your peace of mind. And it didn't shit and mess up the back porch either. The Waste Away was a glimpse of the American genius: Avoid as much as possible contending with things that had a heart and soul; live as if sweat and toil and suffering were not normal consequences of living; and pile onto this an affordable price and ready availability. He was indeed back.

He did some general cleaning and rearranging of artifacts before having dinner with Mrs. Pinckney. He was pleased with everything until she said:

"Herman, I had a talk with the ladies of the League."

"Oh, oh."

"I'm afraid so. It looks like we're becoming the Waste Away of community action."

Henry chomped on his tuna surprise. "Meaning?" He was, of course, curious about the museum's future. Mrs. Pinckney seemed less able to manage it on her own. More than once, Henry had awakened to hear what sounded like the scratching of a kitten at the back door only to discover the arm of the phonograph ceaselessly rasping the smooth edge at the end of the Kennedy dirge.

"The nerve of those girls, and I do mean girls. The new ones hardly look twenty years old. They seem not to care what's going on around them. They see other, more pressing issues to face. Like vagrancy laws to kick out wandering tribes of hippies from settling around here; facelifts for community statues; voter registration; anti-drug lectures. They're spending all the money on garbage. Without the donation box, the museum might turn into a ghost town."

Henry swallowed noisily. "They'll come to their senses."

"Tell me when, please. What really could happen is that they may close the galleries and kick us out of this museum place."

Could that be possible? That night, hours passed without sleep for Henry until he finally sat up and looked out the window. Across the road, only one light shone against the billboard, and it illuminated the young boy to the side of the Buick. The paper was peeling from his jacket, and he looked to a mother whose face had completely torn away. Come See You In The Past, it said, the request having lost an r and its Future to the elements. Something lay lost within Henry as well. By reflex, he held his elbow to his ear.

"Right arm, Hankie," it said, loud and steady. But just then, the phone rang and soon, Mrs. Pinckney called out. He hurried to her room and raised the receiver.

"Mr. George?" a woman's voice said.

"Yes."

"This is Grays Harbor General. I'm afraid we've got a problem."

"Problem?"

"Do you know a Phillip Charles?"

"I do."

"Well, he's asking for you."

Phid had been beaten and he needed his friend.

At the ER, Henry learned the prognosis was fair: Phid was covered in lacerations, contusions, but suffered nothing major internally. He'd need only one tooth replaced. Henry dozed in a hardback chair in the lobby and was allowed to see Phid when the sun broke briefly in the morning. He sat next to his bed while a nurse tried to spoon mush through the slit of Phid's mouth. But she was not successful and eventually left the two alone.

Phid's head was shaved in spots to allow for stitches so that he resembled somebody's long forgotten rag doll, but when Henry gave him a hand mirror to survey the damage, Phid said, "Not as bad as I thought." He dropped the mirror to his bedclothes, ran his tongue through the space left by his broken tooth.

"Look, Hank," he said. "About what's happening."

"It's okay."

"There you go again."

"Okay, okay."

"Listen. I know we haven't been close lately and that's mostly my fault. It's just that school has been superior and there are so many people to meet and hang out with. And you don't want to do much of that. Anyway, I'm sorry."

"Not necessary, but done," Henry said. "More importantly, who did this?"

Phid waved a bandaged hand. "Doesn't matter."

"It does matter. You're just going to give in?"

"You don't get it. A cop was already in to talk to me. There's not a thing they're going to do. Zero. You want to know how I know? He looked at me, spit in his hands, rubbed them together and said, 'Is a little man-juice worth all this to you, Nancy boy?'"

"Asshole."

"I had to lay here and listen to all his stories about homos. They get off on shit like that." He winced and rubbed at his damaged cheek.

"Who were they?" Henry asked again. "If the cops won't do anything, maybe we can."

"They're just guys. Guys hanging around the rock at Moclips. You know the rock? That big sucker at the end of the public beach? Just high school boys there for a drink. Staking out their territory. My friend and I were in the wrong place at the wrong time."

"Again?"

"It's just sex."

"Yeah, I know you think that. But somehow it always turns out bad. Don't you think you should figure out why?"

Henry braced himself for the barrage that usually came now, but Phid was quiet. He held a mirror again and touched near his eye. "Guys get killed in San Diego. Sailors gut them and leave them to bleed out in the sand." A rare tear spilled from the hole at his eye. "Goddamn it, Hankie. I can't control myself. Like the way you feel about Anita. Only worse. I need it. I have to have it."

"But what's "it"?"

Phid poked his tongue through his teeth again. "Can anybody answer that? I always thought it was sex, but it sounds like you're thinking it's something else."

"I'm the last person you should be asking about sex. Besides Anita, I don't have enough libido for any girl. I've tried to work on it, but nothing changes. After a while, I get back nothing but indifference. I guess what I'm saying is I'm not one to criticize. I've got my own sexual problems. I even researched possible solutions."

"What kind of answers did you find for your problem?"

"Stupid stuff. Like finding a girl to work with me." Then Henry brightened. "Speaking of solutions. If you want to, there's something you can do about your deal. I saw a possibility that might work." Henry told him what he learned while researching for his psych class. He'd read about some new treatments called counterconditioning.

"A cure?" Phid said.

"That's what the guy in one article concluded. You want me to ask?"

"Jesus, you and your cures. What book you going to read to cure me of this?"

"It's not a book. It's science."

"I'm tired," Phid said. "I've got to figure out how I'm going to pay for this mess. What would I be cured of? I don't feel like there's anything wrong with me."

"Suit yourself. But it'll probably be me who has to identify your body someday."

Phid thought for a long time. He tried to rub at his mouth, but his hands were too thickly bandaged. Henry leaned in and gave his lips a little scratch.

"What the hell," said Phid. "It's what I called you here for anyway. I'm getting sick of it too. And if I was honest, I'm scared. Besides, according to you, my best friend, everybody needs to be cured of something, don't they?"

Maybe so, Henry still thought, as they returned to school and searched out a therapist together. It wasn't until well into winter quarter that they visited Dr. Sweeney. He had an office on Ravenna, within walking distance of the university.

That day they slipped into the good doctor's office and Henry made himself comfortable in a waiting room adorned with all things male; sports pictures, checked gray and brown carpet, hunting magazines. An hour later, Phid came out visibly shaken, Dr. Sweeney at his side. He was younger than Henry expected, maybe his father's age, and he seemed fit for a guy making his living out of a chair. He had a neatly trimmed beard, but there was a devilishness about his eyes that put Henry off, like maybe he enjoyed what he was doing, and nobody should really enjoy that kind of work.

He shook Henry's hand. "Your friend would like you to come in with him the next time and I wondered what you thought of that."

"Sounds fine to me."

Phid made himself scarce for a couple of days until one night, he arrived at Henry's room with the fistful of articles Dr. Sweeney had run off for him.

He spread them on the bed and began reading, punctuating his silence with cries of, "Oh, my God!" or "Jesus!" Henry's interest piqued, and he read over Phid's shoulder.

"Get this," Phid said. "Here's one from England. This doctor treated wienie-waggers with what they call aversive counterconditioning. Sounds horrible, doesn't it? Anyway, he has these poor saps go into a room, one at a time. He has them flash, I mean drop their drawers and everything, and guess who's standing at the other end of the room? A bunch of volunteer nurses."

"God," Henry said, trying to reach Phid's location in the article.

"And as soon as his dong flops out, the nurses start laughing, I mean doubling over like it's the funniest thing they ever saw."

"That doesn't sound very professional to me." Henry ran a finger along one of the last lines. "And all ten of the guys noticed a reduction in their impulses to expose."

"Well, wouldn't you? If a bunch of chicks were standing there laughing at your dick, do you really think you'd feel like getting it up anymore?" Phid chose another article.

"What are these for anyway?"

"They're supposed to make me feel comfortable with the program. It gives me an idea about the history of behavioral conditioning before they got to the point they're at now."

"Which is what?"

"That's what I'm supposed to find out next time. The equipment and stuff."

"Equipment?"

"Yeah, that's the weird part."

And it was weird. Curiosity drove their next visit to Dr. Sweeney's office. They walked in like two of the Three Stooges; their steps nearly synchronized.

Phid went in alone for a time while Dr. Sweeney gathered more information on his background and such. It wasn't long before the two of them emerged, collected Henry, and walked to a room further down the hall.

This room was small and dark and windowless. A La-Z-Boy occupied the center and behind it, on a cabinet stretching the width of the room, sat several contraptions with wires growing from all sides.

Phid hitched his brow as Dr. Sweeney explained the process.

"This is the slide projector. I insert the appropriate slides in here and then flash them on the screen over there on the wall."

To demonstrate, he clicked on the power and a small white square came into focus.

"Simple enough," Phid breathed.

"These other two you probably haven't heard of," Dr. Sweeney continued. "The first one is the apparatus by which the faradic stimulus is administered, and this second, the plethysmograph. Any questions?"

Phid looked to Henry. "Ask him what the hell that means."

Dr. Sweeney cleared his throat, straightened his bow tie. "It's as we discussed the first time. Here, I'll show you." He lugged one of the machines over to a small end table next to the La-Z-Boy and had Phid sit there. He unraveled the wires, separating three of them. Taking a tube of gel, he dabbed three spots on the inside of Phid's wrist. "Helps the conduction," he murmured.

Interested, Henry crept closer. Each of the wires had a small circle of metal soldered to the end and these Dr. Sweeney pressed over the jelly on Phid's wrist. He secured them with a piece of opaque tape.

"Now," Dr. Sweeney said, "as I told you, the purpose is not to punish you in the way the electric chair punishes a guy." He paused but neither Phid nor Henry responded. "It's just a small shock, a gentle reminder. Shall I proceed?"

Phid nodded and closed his eyes tightly.

Dr. Sweeney positioned a dial on the machine and, ever so slightly, turned it. "That should be about right." He lifted a gadget, depressed its plunger and Phid's wrist cramped.

"It's like a frog," Henry said.

"I beg your pardon?"

"It's like the frogs in Biology. You touch a piece of electrified copper to a pithed frog's leg, and it hops."

"Great," Phid said. "Now I'm an amphibian."

"That wasn't so bad, was it?" Dr. Sweeney said. "Did it hurt?"

"Not really."

"It'll never be much worse than that," Dr. Sweeney said. "Now, the plethysmograph I've already explained, and I'll be designing paradigms to match your needs."

"Tell Hank about the plethysmo-whatever," Phid said.

"Oh. Well, the plethysmograph resembles a lie detector." Back over at the cabinet, he patted the top of another machine. "This piece of latex is called the strain gauge. It fits snugly over the penis and this wire coming from it registers penile blood volume. The more aroused a fellow gets, the more the needle moves higher. If a man says, 'No, that doesn't turn me on anymore,' all I do is look at the readout to tell if he's truthful."

"Oh," Henry said.

"We're running out of time for today," Dr. Sweeney said. "There is one task for next time. I have some slides of my own I'll give you to look over, but I would like you to purchase some explicit magazines depicting both women and men, and I'd like you to go through them and pick out ones that appeal to you on a 1 to 10 scale. Let's say twenty of each for now."

"Men and women?" Phid asked. "You mean nude pictures? Sex pictures?"

"That's right. Here, let me see if I can dig out a few examples." He pulled open a drawer in the cabinet.

Phid removed the electrodes from his wrist. Henry plucked a tissue from the box and gave it to him to wipe the jelly away.

Dr. Sweeney held a slide to the projector's light reflected on the wall. "Yes, here they are." He fiddled with the projector. "Okay, this is what I mean."

Later, Phid and Henry fought to be the first out the door. The whole experience was one of those that one thought about in the privacy of one's own home. But Phid was smitten with the assignment of going to an adult arcade, and the two had a good time walking the aisles of the Lucky Lady Novelty Store. Phid studied magazine after magazine, book after book, pamphlet after pamphlet with considerable alacrity.

In Henry's room, they spent the evening leafing through the bounty. Some of the pictures had stories to go along with them, and Phid frequently paused to read them.

"You're supposed to be getting away from that," Henry said.

"Do you ever cut a guy any slack?" said Phid.

Phid had trouble with the hetero attitude he had committed to adopt. He breezed through the pictures of the men, assigning them numbers with great ease. But when it came to the women, he stumbled, dawdling with each picture until he finally threw the magazine aside.

"I just don't know," he said. "There's only one number to describe the feeling. Zero."

Henry pointed to the picture. "Look here, she was Playmate of the Year. Look at that body, here, this pic is a side view."

But Phid glanced away. "You number them."

"Come on. Give her a score." Henry held it out, so Phid had to face it.

"All right," he said. "I guess a three."

"A three?" Henry pulled the magazine back. "With those legs?"

"Hank."

"You're right, we'll give her a three." As they continued through them, Henry began to see the problem. They did look an awful lot alike, statuesque women with endless legs and ample breasts and straight white teeth. The hair color was different, the scenery was different, but that was it. They were not inherently interesting. But the two finally managed to get the assignment done and Henry was hopeful the next time he accompanied Phid to Dr. Sweeney's office.

This time, Phid looked stricken when he emerged. "Let's get out of here," he said, grabbing his jacket. He was quiet as they walked up the street. It was foggy and a light mist soaked the air. He thrust his hands in his pockets and cursed at the drivers who tried to spray them.

"Well?" Henry said. "So, how was it?"

Phid pulled open the cuff of his shirt. Three dark red welts decorated his wrist, as if he'd been tortured with hot nickels.

"Jesus," Henry said.

"It felt none too pretty." Phid walked on. They passed gardens of tulips arranged in fiery patterns of color. Henry peered in their black throats and saw they had collected the mist. Unlucky bugs swam there.

They got back to Henry's room and Phid headed for the shower. Ten minutes later, Henry found him there, still standing beneath the cooling stream, scrubbing and scrubbing his wrist with a bar of scratchy soap. When Phid noticed him, he quickly put his face under the stream. But he could not hide. Henry could tell he'd been crying.

It was then Henry realized that without the use of his power, he was pretty much helpless, unable to do anything to really assist another person. And wasn't that what being human was all about? Helping. Shouldn't he be able to do something to lighten his friend's load?

He snuck back to his room and returned with a Kerouac book. Was he turning into his mother whose fingers still spidered across a desk to snatch a novel when she was confronted with any difficulty? No matter, Henry thought. We do what we can.

He slipped into the bathroom and sat on the floor with his back to the bank of showers. He started to read, felt a comfort enter his body.

In a moment, though, Phid was leaning around the tile wall. "What the hell?" he said. "Cut it out."

Henry slammed the book shut. "Okay, okay," he said. Maybe he had made things worse. "I have a proposal. Just this time. Couldn't we go to the Triangle and let me read to you? To cure you. Just this once and then I'm done. I promise." Henry smiled weakly.

Phid thought for a moment and Henry believed that maybe he had struck a chord with his friend. But in the end, Phid simply shook his head. "I've got to do this on my own," he said.

Phid adjusted but the procedure made him pensive, and he and Henry went for days exchanging only perfunctory snatches of conversation. Phid rarely attended classes; he didn't open a book during the month of May. Henry missed Phid's sense of humor, his positive take on the world. He now feared the cure would turn his friend into a completely different guy.

Toward the end of May, Phid asked Henry to come in with him again.

"Not usually the way we do these things," Dr. Sweeney said under his breath. "More of a private occasion."

"I need support," said Phid.

Back in the gadget room, Phid tapped out his nerves with the heel of his shoe. He hooked himself to the machine, and Henry helped him tape down the electrodes while Dr. Sweeney dropped slides into the carousel.

"We've come quite a long way since last you were here," he said. "We've moved from a strict punishment paradigm to a combination of punishment and reward."

Henry nodded as did his equally confused shadow on the wall.

"I think we're about set," Dr. Sweeney said. "Are you ready, Phillip?"

Dr. Sweeney clicked the carousel and they set off on a lurid junket into human sexuality. Some of the photos Henry and Phid had chosen jumped onto the wall like a slap in the face.

A man posed with one foot on a chair. He smoked a cigarette and wore a jockstrap. Then another. Seated, legs spread, his testicles spilled over the front of the stool. Phid fidgeted. Three men, standing in a circle, heads raised, masturbating.

"I want to be there," Phid squeaked.

Dr. Sweeney depressed the plunger and Phid's wrist flopped like a dying chicken.

The slide changed. A woman this time, standing in spiked heels in the sand. Behind her, the ocean curled toward the shore. A bright golden amulet rested between her dark, be-sanded breasts.

"I like her," Phid said.

The slide quickly disappeared. Men again, a tongue touching the tip of a penis.

"Yes," Phid said. Again, Phid's wrist kicked. Plunger: kick.

And on it went for forty-five minutes. Piles of men like newly harvested crustaceans, their limbs sprouting from the mass, twitched and grasped. When they flashed on the wall, Henry grew impatient for them to be whisked away. He silently called for Dr. Sweeney to be done with the men and move on to the women. Come on, come on, he urged, and soon he was rewarded with one, all sweetness and longing, bright, colored female delight.

When the men came on, they leered at Henry, they challenged him; we know about the Lost Night, they said. In black and white, they appeared gritty, brazen. They cupped their genitals, laid them over another man's shoulder, let them hang from leather underwear, used them to probe pleasure spots. Henry was soon ready to sprint for the outdoors.

Henry understood Phid better after that. Maybe he understood himself better as well. The subject of Phid's transformation was now a painful one and they kept quiet about it from then on. Henry realized the hope surrounding Phid's change could be his own selfish hope. Their future together as friends, his future. But what kind of friend dictated that to another? He was ashamed of himself. Ashamed of Dr. Sweeney. Someday, he would make it right for Phid. He would.

TWENTY

The school year ended. Henry did well, Phid less so. The university suffered occasional bomb scares and demonstrations. Angry students, including Phid, flocked to the streets and freeways, lying across them like martyrs as they chipped away at the injustice they perceived to be the fault of the government.

Maybe it was a way for Phid to relieve the electrical tension that flowed through his body due to his still visiting Dr. Sweeney. The doctor was shocking Phid less, showing him more pictures of voluptuous women. Phid now made himself scarcer. Henry did not accompany him to another session. Maybe treatment was one suggestion Henry made that was going to turn out well.

Henry assumed he wouldn't see Phid for the summer, but when he mentioned the museum one day, Phid said he was anxious to go. And so, even though Dr. Sweeney would have preferred Phid stay in Seattle, they left together the middle of June and gave the DeSoto a chance to burn the carbon off its valves.

Mrs. Pinckney met them at the door. "Come in, come in," she chattered. The place smelled of disinfectant. "They'll be here before you know it."

"Who?" Henry asked as Phid headed for the staircase with his luggage.

"The Bi-County Sorority of the Home and City Improvement League."

"But why?"

"Well, Herman, they do own this establishment." She looked at him as if this year of college had been a waste of money.

She grabbed a broom and started sweeping the already pristine floor. "You better follow Phillip's example and take your things to your room. Make sure it's straightened before you come back."

When he returned, Mrs. Pinckney was in the At The Movies Exhibit, leading Phid on an inspection. "Some little brat almost tore off Patrice Munsel's signed photo. Came in here without parental supervision. As if everything's a toy."

Down the hall, the dirge started to play, and Henry smiled. There was something comforting about the familiar beat, and even though the room was still strung with black crepe, Henry felt delighted when he walked through the door.

"They're going to be paying close attention to some displays," Mrs. Pinckney said, dusting off John-John. "There have been complaints."

"I thought they were all about dead," Henry said.

"There has been some recruitment."

"Oh-oh,"

"Yes, new sixties mothers."

"Hellish thought," Phid said.

"There have been infiltrators. A lady or two has visited in disguise and spied on us."

"Aren't you still a member?" Henry asked. "Don't you have a say?"

"I live so far away I don't get the announcement until the day after the meeting. I've called and tried to get them to let me know sooner, but something always comes up."

The ladies of the League were to inspect for a few hours. Henry straightened and re-straightened the photos of General MacArthur on his wall in the I Surrender Room. He could never remember a review, let alone an inspection being held, in fact, it was only one time a few years before when he ever saw any of the ladies of the Bi-County Sorority of the Home and City Improvement League.

In mid-afternoon a fleet of cars pulled in; sleek new Eldorados and Thunderbirds, a Delta 88, a Bonneville. They parked in spaces next to the Buick and the ladies tumbled out, clicking open umbrellas even though the rain had not progressed beyond a mist.

They crowded in, one after the other, and Phid and Henry took on rain gear until it piled up to their throats. The two dashed awkwardly to the storeroom, returned for another load, and caught up with the group in the At The Movies Room.

They were typical, these ladies, bunchable into subgroups of three: Those Who Do All The Talking, Those Who Summarize, and Those Who Nod. They numbered maybe a dozen, ages scattered across a wide range.

"Why Cary Grant?" an obvious talker said. "Is he from this state?"

"Now, don't mind us," a Mrs. Wright said, ignoring her. She was thirty, wearing pounds of beads and gold earrings that flashed under the overhead light. "We just want to wander and take notes. As you know, most of us haven't ever been here." She tossed her head as she spoke.

"I've made coffee," Mrs. Pinckney said, trying to rein in her hands that fluttered like butterflies. "Help yourselves in the Kennedy Room. I'll be glad to guide you, or maybe one of our employees, Herman George or Phillip Charles, could lead you through."

The group studied the boys critically. Mrs. Wright, however, declined their guidance, and the ladies were off.

They eavesdropped, Phid and Henry. Mrs. Wright expressed herself with volume at every opportunity. Henry heard the words pathetic and undesirable and excessive and pointless more times than he could count. Mrs. Pinckney heard them, too. She sat at the reception desk, a pack of perhaps the same ancient Parliaments waited on the table next to her. She lit one and leaned back, one arm lofted in the air.

"I hope they like it," Henry said.

She shook her head and blew out an explosion of smoke. "They won't, Herman. They won't like it because they don't understand it like you and I do."

It was true, of course. This bevy of ladies tramping through the hallowed halls saw only a pathetic, undesirable, excessive, and pointless grouping of artifacts. Mrs. Pinckney, Henry and Phid saw a genealogical line.

"They will try to tell us what we have here is not important. Our vision is our vision, not the vision of the West Coast." She took another long drag. "Now, if Jackie Kennedy said that a nice museum like this was her vision, well, I don't need to tell you these ladies would fight to be the first to second it."

"Is it a matter of visitors?" Henry asked.

"Heavens no. Thanks to the mention in that retirement magazine and the Seattle papers, we have considerably more than the Dinosaur Haunt and they're still going strong."

The ladies returned to the lobby, quarrelling like starlings, scribbling notes. Each of them wore the same type of jacket, same hat, same shoes. Only their colors were different, like a litter of kittens.

Mrs. Wright pointed toward the other wing and off they trotted to the Our Friend the Atom display.

"I heard them," Mrs. Pinckney said. "The Kennedy Room is too somber, too funereal. Using such language." She stubbed the cigarette out and clucked her tongue. "And who cares where Cary Grant is from?"

"It'll work out," Henry said.

Phid whirled from the window. "Do you always have to be so goddamn positive? Can't you just face facts? Sometimes it's best to know the truth and accept it. Sometimes, it's all just shit."

"I know that."

Phid strode past them. At the stairs, he leapt them, three at a time.

"He's upset," Mrs. Pinckney said. "Poor thing. It's like inviting people into your home when it's for sale. Strangers soiling your carpets. When they leave, he'll be better."

"I think it's something more than that."

She took out another cigarette and set fire to it.

"I don't care what Phid says, it'll all work out."

Mrs. Pinckney took a deep puff and held it a moment before releasing it into the room. "I can see where you might be right. But this is 1969. Next month we try to put a man on the moon. And Mrs. Wright will wonder why we don't have a moon exhibit. There are all sorts of complications."

And she was right.

The ladies stayed two hours and left without a word. They would discuss the museum and most likely forget to include Mrs. Pinckney in the back and forth.

Later, after dinner, Henry roamed the halls looking for Phid. He had been quiet all afternoon, keeping to his bed, reading magazines. Now, he was nowhere to be found. Henry even checked Suzanne's old bedroom, but it was cold, and dust flew up when he opened the door.

He stepped out to the parking lot and leaned against the Buick. The rain had stopped hours before and now the moon and stars winked through a layer of cirrus clouds. He felt the anxiety leak out of him, loosening its grip. He could not imagine a life without the museum to come home to.

When he turned to go back in, he nearly ran into Phid. "We've got to talk," Phid said.

Together, they navigated around the building. In the back, as if this would always be their personal boardroom for working things out, Henry walked to the pitcher's mound. Phid made his way to home, picked up a stick and tapped the plate.

"Batter up!"

Henry had already kicked off his shoe and was rolling his sock into a ball.

"This won't take long," Phid said.

"You always say that, and we go on for hours."

"So sometimes I stretch the truth. It's not like you've never done that."

"I challenge you to come up with one thing I've ever lied to you about." Henry windmilled his arm, preparing to throw.

"Okay, why do you really come back here year after year?"

"That's easy. It's fun here. It's..."

"That's a lie. And on my first question no less."

"Okay, bud. Why do you think I come back?"

"Because you're afraid. You think the boogeyman is going to snatch you up and fly you to Never-never Land or wherever it was your friend Wayman went."

"I'm not so sure about that," Henry said as he lobbed the sock. He missed the imaginary plate by a wide margin. "You forget I'm a famous man."

"I haven't forgotten," Phid said as he retrieved the sock and pitched it back. "Your aim gets worse the older you get."

"I can't see you," Henry complained. "If I could see you, I'd pitch better."

"Well, isn't that the problem now? That you can't see me?"

"I'm not afraid, by the way. I'm cautious."

"Yeah, well, caution is just fear wrapped up in language."

Henry threw the sock again and this time heard it softly hit the stick.

"Foul!" Phid called, but he didn't run after it. Instead, he plodded over, picked it up, and stared at it. "How come we've never gotten a real baseball?" he said.

"This always seemed to work okay."

"Like your DeSoto. Why get a new car when an old smoky one will do?"

"Well, there's the issue of money."

"I know, I know. It's a bad example, but you know what I mean."

"Explain it to me."

Phid took a deep breath and tossed the sock back. "I'm not sure you can hear it."

Henry wound up and pitched once more. Phid connected and it sailed over Henry's head. He ran back to it, preparing to send it home, but saw that Phid was sitting, tapping the stick against the inside of his foot. In a moment, Henry was at his side.

"I can't do it, Hank. I just can't do it."

Henry squatted on his haunches. "With Dr. Sweeney you mean?"

"I just don't think I can be normal."

"What does the doctor say?"

"All Dr. Sweeney wants is to rid the world of another little fag. I think he loves to zap me." He stretched out on the ground. "It's killing me."

"Then stop."

Phid rolled over and faced his friend. "At first, I was gung-ho. Who wouldn't want to be normal? But, let's face it, I'm just not fucking normal. I sit up nights thinking about guys. I try to think of girls, but there's no feeling that goes with it. It's one-dimensional. With guys, it's 3-D. I don't want a one. What I want is a three."

Henry stooped to the grass next to him and stared him in the face. "I don't want you to get hurt."

"Why don't you let me worry about that part?"

"Okay," Henry said. They both rolled onto their backs and studied the sky. "You should go on out and have some fun. You've earned it."

"I have been."

"I knew it," Henry said. He chewed at his lip. "God, Phid, what if I tried harder than you to get you to change? Sounds kind of selfish now that I say it out loud."

"There may not be cures for everything," Phid said.

"No cures?" Not an idea Henry was prepared to entertain.

Back inside the museum. Henry thought Phid might pack up and leave but he surprised him by crawling into the other bed. They stayed up late, talking about sex, about girls, about boys, about Suzanne, who Henry realized was like a sister to Phid too, and how much better she was doing, about the great mysteries, until they dropped off to sleep.

Henry woke up sometime after midnight and heard Phid's gentle snoring. He thought again about the past year, playing its parts over and over in his head. It was all going faster now, as if his memories were moving through swift rapids. He turned on the lamp and waited for Phid to rouse, but he didn't. What had he done to this poor guy? He knew Phid wanted to keep their friendship, and this touched Henry. Phid did something against his will because he was a good friend and didn't want to lose their bond.

Henry pulled a book out from under his pillow: *Gargantua and Pantagruel.* The beast on the cover reminded him of Uncle Ray. He opened the book and sniffed it, but he pulled back in horror. Again, with the reading?

He looked over at Phid. The guy was probably right. To push someone to be normal might be the worst thing you could do for him.

He put the book away, his heart no longer in it. The best thing he could do for Phid was to be his unconditional friend. To watch him live his life the way he wanted and needed to live it. It wasn't a bad circumstance to be left with after all.

TWENTY-ONE

Later in the summer, Mrs. Obregon called Henry for the first time in months. She told him he was needed back in the Triangle.

"What's the problem?" he asked as he usually did.

But her answer was different, more circumspect. "It is a very difficult case. A kind you have never been willing to proceed on. But I think you should come and see for yourself."

He took an afternoon off and drove the DeSoto to Porter, fully expecting to see a line outside Mrs. Obregon's door. Instead, the front yard of her place was empty. He walked up to the door, knocked, and was surprised when Wayman Simpson opened it. Wayman stood for a moment, staring.

"Hello," said Henry. He peeked around him, looking for others, but saw only Mrs. Obregon seated on the sofa.

"Come in," she said.

When Henry had stepped inside and Wayman closed the door behind him, Henry noticed a fresh red band of skin around Wayman's neck.

"What's that?" he said, concerned about what it could mean.

Wayman touched his neck. "You've got to help me get back," he said. "I can't take it anymore."

"You tried to kill yourself?" Henry glanced over to Mrs. Obregon who was nodding vigorously.

"I think your friend may have been right all along," she said.

"But why is that so?"

"Because in the balance of life, you may have been wrong."

"Riddles," Henry said.

"All right then," Mrs. Obregon said, standing. She walked over to Henry. "I can see I have to be direct with you. As you know, Wayman here is native."

"He's adopted. We know that much."

"Indeed, he was. And he is native."

Henry looked closely at Wayman and saw signs that what Mrs. Obregon said might be true.

"Therefore, I think it's important to give this young man what he wants." When Henry hesitated, she added, "Maybe this means you were meant to be the chosen one after all. So you can send Wayman back where he can be happy."

Wayman walked over to the kitchen counter. He pulled off a book and held it up. *The Velveteen Rabbit.*

"You're serious," said Henry.

"You've sentenced me to a horrible life," Wayman said. "Without even asking me if I wanted it. Please. For the last time. I'm begging you." Afraid of the prospect of his own tears, Wayman grabbed the book and ran out the door.

"Wow," said Henry.

"As time passes, I am less and less sure why you won't do this one favor for him," Mrs. Obregon said. "Is it because he's native?"

"No. Not that at all."

"Then why?"

Henry thought for a moment. His sentiments those years ago now seemed to carry less weight. No one followed him around these days and called him a murderer or a bad friend. But what might happen if the opposite occurred? If Wayman disappeared again? There was no guarantee that it would happen, and if it didn't, there would be nothing lost as Wayman was already home.

He opened the door and stepped out as well. Wayman stood beneath one of the apple trees. "So, you're not even the slightest bit happy to be home?"

"I'm not. I never have been. I'm sleeping in my parents' house. I'm eating my mom's cooking. I'm watching their damn TV. I have no life, Hankie. Please help me. I need a life."

Henry heard a noise behind him and turned to see Mrs. Obregon in the doorway. "You two should come in now. I have prepared for you."

A smile grew on Wayman's face as he hurried past Henry. When Henry reached the door, he saw that Wayman already lay on the sofa, his hands at his sides. His ankles twisted back and forth. He had placed the book on his chest, and it sat there, waiting.

"It's up to you," Mrs. Obregon said. "But what you should consider is this: what your friend has in the other world is more than just work and girls. It is spiritual. It is healing."

So, Henry changed his thinking that day in the Triangle. He got on his knees next to his old friend and pulled the book off his chest. When he held the pages, it all came back to him. The way his own life changed. He recalled the people who wanted to hear his words after the miracle happened. The power that wasn't only magical but seemed to apply to others as well as the needy. They wanted to watch. To see something unprecedented happen. Well, this now was unprecedented.

He glanced up at Mrs. Obregon and opened to the first page.

There once was a velveteen rabbit, and in the beginning he was really splendid.

As he read, Henry noticed a leaden feeling in the pit of his stomach that grew with each page. At first, it did not seem to affect his reading voice, but after a while, he had to stop and clear his throat. He began to feel nauseated, and a pain developed along one of his legs. Then his head throbbed in rhythm with the erratic beating of his heart. He stopped and looked at Mrs. Obregon and witnessed his own concern mirrored on her face. He took a deep breath, turned another page, and everything went black.

He awoke at St. Joseph's in Olympia. Instead of Mrs. Obregon, his mother sat beside his bed.

"Oh, thank God," she said, putting her book aside.

"Mom? What happened?" Henry tried to shift to a sitting position but didn't have the energy. He lay back and sighed.

"An ambulance brought you here from Porter. They called Garabedian's and said it was an emergency. When I got here, you were undergoing all kinds of tests."

"How long have I been out?"

"This is the third day," Alice said. "Nip and tuck, they said to me. Like you weren't going to make it." A tear formed on an eyelash and fell when she blinked.

"Third day? I don't remember anything."

Alice nodded. "And they don't know anything either. Your tests all came back normal. Hankie, what were you doing there at Mrs. Obregon's?"

"I was..." He stopped, wondering how much he should disclose. Maybe Skookumchuck was searching for him in Olympia. "I was doing the usual thing."

"I don't understand. Why did this happen? The doctors thought you might die. It was horrible." She grabbed hold of his arm. "How do you feel now?"

"I feel okay," he said. He tested out his arms and legs. "Just a little tired." Again, he tried to move up on the pillow. This time he was successful. "Can I ask you something, Mom? Have you heard anything about Wayman?"

"Now, that's interesting. I wonder why you ask, since it looks like Wayman ran away. His mother was at the café looking for him."

"Oh no."

"His parents are fit to be tied."

After Henry was released, John drove him back to Mrs. Obregon's. Henry quickly got to the point. "What happened? Where's Wayman?"

"Gone," said Mrs. Obregon.

"Is he...?"

"Gone. Yes. He will not be back."

Henry shook his head. "Something's sideways. Did I do something wrong?"

"I don't know if it's wrong. All I know is this has not happened here before."

"I could hardly breathe. It felt like I was dying. I had no..." Here he stopped and felt his torso, thumped on his chest, kneaded his abdomen. "It was like I had no substance."

"Yet you are here now," she said.

Henry stayed the night at her cabin. In the early hours of the morning, Mrs. Obregon heated up a kettle of her soup and fed it to him. As he left, he thought this had been an experience he would never forget, much like the time he brought Wayman home from that other Rochester. He wondered if Skookumchuck was not happy with him and speculated that it might be a good idea to stay away from the Triangle for a while.

In May, after he turned 22, Henry sat in the sunshine in the middle of five thousand other graduating students on the turf at Husky Stadium. He'd finally earned his degree in education, but not one member of his family was there to witness it. All around he saw mothers and fathers and grandparents praise and applaud their children for this milestone in their lives. More than once, he was the one to take the group picture so that Grandpa or Aunt Tess could pose with the rest of the relatives. He had sent out invitations and received cash hidden behind congratulations, but beyond that, his graduation dance card was without one entry.

When the long ceremony was over, Henry drove south so he would be on time for Suzanne's ceremony. She had attended a six-week nurse's aide course at St. Joseph's and graduated at the top of her seven-member class.

A celebratory picnic was planned, and the weather cooperated, sending sunshine to the Inland Coast. The DeSoto had been unreliable lately, coughing in the mornings, running a temperature on trips over twenty miles. Henry wanted his father to diagnose and fix the problem.

He went the roundabout way to his parents' farm. It was clear that the more he kept away from the Simpsons, the better off he would be. It had been nearly a year now since he had last talked to Mrs. Simpson, but he didn't want to chance her fury.

When he arrived at the farm, the driveway was filled with a procession of mechanical paraphernalia hemmed in by high ridges of dried mud. John now repaired these machines for a reasonable price. He worked out of his toolshed and even had a sign attached to the barn wood:

J. George
The Fix-It Man

An ancient picnic table dominated the backyard. There, Aunt Peg snapped a sheet in the air, trying to lay it perfectly over the top. But a breeze kept lifting and carrying it to the side. Henry ran over to help, and they positioned plates along the edges to keep it secure.

"Where's Suze?" Henry asked her.

"She had a meeting at the hospital."

"How are you?"

"You know. Day to day. Just life, I guess." She cleared her throat.

He was on the verge of saying, "It's okay," but he remembered how Ray, Jr. was always upset by those words. Instead, he reached out and touched her arm, startling her. He wondered if Aunt Peg had ever been touched affectionately.

Alice came later, driving the Garabedian Cafe Volkswagen with its hand-painted advertisement on the side. The lunch rush must have been a busy one. She removed her spotted apron and folded it neatly before laying it in the back seat. She smoothed the front of her pantsuit, picked up a book, and walked toward the table.

"I thought maybe you at least would show up for my graduation," Henry said when he spied her.

"Oh, I'm so sorry, Hankie. But you know how life can get sometimes. I just couldn't find a way to get up there." She gathered the book at her chest. "Come on, though, I've got a surprise for you."

They sneaked into the house and up to his parents' old bedroom. Here, Alice opened the book and removed a fat envelope. "This is for you," she said.

Henry dove into it, discovered a stack of bills. "Mom?"

"You know how long it took me to collect that?"

"But you didn't have to."

"I know, I know. But I'm proud of you. You don't have to count it. There's enough for you to take a trip like college graduates do. Plus, there's some spending money as well."

"Europe maybe?" Henry put his arms around her.

"Haven't I always told you it's important to travel?"

"Yes, but you haven't actually travelled yourself." He tried handing the envelope back. "Maybe this should be for you."

"No. I want you to go and then come back and tell me about it."

"Thanks, Mom."

"I know it hasn't been easy for you. You deserve it." She closed the book and went back outside.

Uncle Ray's Pontiac announced itself long before it hove into sight. He laid on the horn and did not let up until he was parked behind the Volkswagen. He struggled out, wearing a white short-sleeve shirt and Panama hat. He pranced around to the other side and helped

Suzanne, holding her hand as she stepped across the deep ruts in the driveway. Twin circles of fire blazed at her cheeks.

"Guess what you're looking at here?" Uncle Ray asked. "Anyone want to guess? Hankie?"

"I give up."

"The newest employee at St. Joe's Hospital, that's all."

Embarrassed, Suzanne dropped her head and started arranging the food. She had prepared most of the meal the night before; fried chicken and potato salad, deviled eggs with a rust of paprika, celery stalks with processed cheese spread inside their ribbed channels, apple pie and Kool-Aid. Everyone managed to squeeze in around the table, except John.

Alice sat next to Henry, taking a bite or two of potato salad and reading with her book hidden below the table. Uncle Ray and Suzanne sat across from them.

From the end of the table, Aunt Peg's eyes moved between Suzanne and Uncle Ray. For his part, Uncle Ray grabbed another bottle of Olympia beer and filled his glass until the foam erupted over the sides, soaking Aunt Peg's carefully laid tablecloth.

"Should've seen how they made over our little princess," he gushed. "You knew they'd hire her without an interview. What was that they said about you, darlin'?"

From the toolshed came a gentle tink-tink.

"Oh, Uncle Ray."

"Come on, what was it?"

"That I was made to tend babies," she said. "I aspirate better than any of the others."

"Oh, now, goodness," Aunt Peg said. Her fingers dallied at her mouth.

"Congratulations, Suze," Henry said.

"Well, I'm sure it's meant to be an honor to be complimented that way," Aunt Peg said. She pushed her plate away. "A real honor."

Now a different sound drifted from the toolshed; a murmur-tink, murmur-tink; John's complaint topped with a hammer. They all stopped for a moment and recognized it as his music.

"What about you, Hankie?" Aunt Peg asked. "How was your graduation?"

"Ah, it was only college. No big thing."

"Where will you be teaching?"

"Wishkah."

"No fooling," said Aunt Peg. "That's not all that far away."

"Come on now, I think your jealousy is showing. Don't ruin Suzanne's celebration," Uncle Ray said. He patted her on the shoulder. "Pay them no mind."

"What grade?" Suzanne said as she leaned away from Uncle Ray's arm.

"Combined fifth and sixth."

Aunt Peg found an empty plate and loaded it with food. "Teaching is honorable," she said. "We need good teachers."

Uncle Ray shook his head. "What we need are good students. Decent kids who don't run around like wild apes."

Suzanne turned to Henry. "Did Phid graduate?"

"Yes."

"Where's he going to teach?"

"I don't think he is. He interviewed a couple of places, but then gave it up. He'll probably do something else."

"Well, I hope he doesn't go far away. I hardly ever get to see him."

"Who's Phid?" Uncle Ray asked.

"Only the nicest, sweetest, kindest guy you'll ever meet." Suzanne took a big bite of potato salad and let it rest in her cheek like a chipmunk would.

Aunt Peg shoved a plate over closer to Henry. "Your father will be hungry."

Henry hurried away, losing a couple of chips in one of the tire ditches. At the toolshed, he kicked on the door. John opened it quickly and hustled him in. He was skinnier, and it made his eyes look buggy. His hair had thinned dramatically in the last year.

Henry handed the plate over and John took a bite of chicken leg "What are you doing out here?" Henry asked with more venom than he meant to.

"Lot of work staring me in the face. Can't stop for little parties now, can I?" He pulled up a nail keg and sat down hard, washing his face with his hands. "What's the big deal? Something eating you?"

"I thought maybe somebody might come to my graduation, that's all."

"You know how I don't like the city. All the cars and people. Seattle used to be a nice little town." He coughed and avoided his son's stare. "Suzie said she sent a card from us. Did you get it?"

"Thanks for the money."

"Well, you're welcome. I thought maybe you could get yourself a nice shirt and pair of slacks for when you start teaching those hellcats."

Henry looked around at the tools on the walls and the gadgets lying in pieces on the bench. As greasy and as disorganized as it all was, it also fit John well. The nail keg was his throne, the wrench his scepter. "Mom's out there," Henry said.

"I know. I heard her come up. That Garabedian character needs a good mechanic for that bug."

"His name's McDonald."

"Big fucking deal. I don't care."

"Are you still going to AA, Dad?"

"Why? Isn't three years of meetings enough? Do you smell something on my breath?"

"No, just wondering."

"You know, if a guy wanted to get hooked on cigarettes or coffee, all he'd have to do is go to a meeting a couple times a week. You can't see for the smoke. And that damned Raymond's uncorking beers like they're bound to be rationed."

"What's he doing here all the time anyway?"

"Peg won't have him. He's there two minutes and they're fighting. She says he's got to get rid of the snake and he says over his dead body."

"I hate that thing."

"You seen it lately? Big as a telephone pole around. I don't blame old Peg. I think I'd kick him out too."

"So, he's living here?"

"Part of the time. We feed him, and he sleeps on the couch and runs to the store now and then."

"I don't think Suzanne likes him very much."

"A lot you know. The two of them are giggling like kids half the time. I can hear them all the way out here. You ask me, Raymond's good for her. She mopes around a lot, Hankie, like your mom used to."

"Mom looks pretty good."

John bit his lip and then washed his face again with his dirty hands. "If you say so. To me, she looks like she's getting older, just like the rest of us."

"Maybe I better get back. Uncle Ray was about to go off the deep end."

"Just a sec," John said, jumping up from the keg. He rolled it out to the center of the room and pried at the top. He dove in with both hands and pulled out a book.

"What is that?"

"A goddamn torture chamber in words," he replied. "*A Tale of Two Cities.*"

"Dad?"

He held up his hand. "I know, I know, just don't ask any smart-ass questions." He flipped the pages and a marker fell out. "Do you think your mother's read this one?"

"You remember that trouble at the beach? She had me read it that day."

"Damn, I was hoping to find one she hasn't got to yet."

"Dickens is a pretty important writer."

"You know what I have to say to that? Could he grind a valve in a John Deere? Pretty sure the answer is no."

"Where are you?" Henry asked, trying to look sideways at the page.

"Oh, I don't know. Some people are doing something to some other people. It's not going anywhere."

"So, why are you reading it?"

He rubbed behind one ear. "I'm trying to educate myself."

"Why?"

He tossed the book back in the keg. "How the hell should I know? Ask me later when I'm finished reading that shit."

Henry went for the door, but John rushed there with him. They peeked through the cracks together, a pair of cops on a stakeout.

"Just look at her," John said. "How can a gal sit there with all those people and still get what she's reading?"

"She's had a lot of practice."

They watched as she turned page after page with a stiff, wetted finger. John's eyes softened; his whole face became more relaxed. "Damn I wish she wasn't so stubborn."

"What, are you thinking of getting back together?"

"Not a chance," he said. "I don't want a woman who smells like she lives above a cafe."

"Ah, I see."

"Well, I don't."

"The DeSoto's acting up," Henry said.

John wagged his head. "I don't guess they taught you basic mechanics up at the big school."

"No."

"Goddamn worthless education." John flung open the door and marched out to the car. He had the hood up and was struggling with the engine before Henry could close the door and walk back to the table.

That night, Henry stayed with his mother at the Garabedian Cafe. She was unaccustomed to guests and had to dig far back in her closet to find an extra blanket and pillow. She was living a Spartan life. She didn't scrimp on paper or typewriter ribbon, though. Piles of them surrounded her chair.

It was a comfortable place. The springs of the sofa sank nearly to the hardwood floor and Henry lounged there while she read aloud her latest critiques. She was getting better, having found the proper rhythm for her arguments, and she seemed to understand more about language and life. Henry told her so.

"Really? Well, that makes me feel tingly all over."

"How are you learning this?"

"How do you think? I read."

"Who?"

"You ready? Trilling, Sontag, Baldwin, Vidal, Mailer, Broyard, Mann, Ransom, Ponsot."

"Ponsot? Who's that?"

"Oh, Hankie. You need to get out more. Marie Ponsot. A living doll."

"With a list like that, shouldn't you be expanding your horizons. I mean, Mort Gunderson is no Marie Ponsot."

She knew he was right, but she still struggled with the marketing of her product. It did seem that her life's goal would be the gradual wearing down of the Weekly Guardian's publisher by the sheer weight of her submissions. Every new book that hit the public library she tore from the shelf and read with vigor, and within hours she was standing at the newspaper's reception desk with a copy of her analysis hovering over the blotter. Mort Sanderson rarely saw her since he no longer cared to engage in loud literary struggles with a woman he considered a danger to his heart attack prevention regimen. As soon as the door closed behind Alice, her latest submission floated to the wastebasket.

Only once had she appeared in print again and this was when Mr. Sanderson did suffer an infarct on the Thursday of publication and there was left a rather wide gap on the back page, which the frantic secretary filled with: Valley of the Dolls, What Have We Come To?

After his recovery, Mr. Sanderson printed an apology to Jacqueline Susanne, along with a recommendation for the purchase of her breakthrough work.

Alice eventually grew tired of reading and set her papers aside. "Do you think you'll be happy in Wishkah? I thought you told me you liked the city."

"I do. Only when it came to it, I wasn't sure. When I went to Wishkah to interview, it felt right."

"It's also outside of the Triangle."

"Could be why it felt so right."

"But then so is Seattle."

"What are you getting at?"

"A friend of mine once told me you'd be living a pitiful life if you let your fears control it."

"What if I said I chose Wishkah for you?" Henry said.

"If it was for me, and I notice you didn't consult me, I would have chosen Seattle or some other place further north. But I suppose your fears have a basis in fact. How are things with Mrs. Obregon?"

"I don't really know. She and I haven't had a lot of contact."

"What happened with Wayman Simpson. That changed things?"

"I guess. Mrs. Obregon gives me the shivers with what she says. Did you know Wayman is native?"

"I knew he was adopted." She looked out the window. "And so, you'll become an elementary school teacher. After your life as a healer, why do that? Don't take this wrong but it seems like a step back for some reason."

"I think because of Mrs. Winkle. Remember her? She was so dedicated. I want to be dedicated to something."

"That's admirable, I guess. I don't suppose you can figure out a way to use your gift as well?"

"Haven't yet. But being a teacher beats being the local murderer."

"Hankie, you're not still on that, are you? He came back."

"Please, Mom. All I want is a new start."

"Then you should have stayed in Seattle."

"Maybe, but thanks to you, I'll at least be seeing some of the world. I thought about it at lunch. I think I'm going to tour as many countries as I can."

"I hope you do." But she seemed preoccupied. She reached to the floor and snatched a bit of typewriter ribbon. "Can I ask a question?"

"Of course."

"Can you explain Suzanne to me? Listening to her today, it was almost as if she's in love with your friend, Phid."

"I don't know about that, but that time she was at the museum, we all did a lot of things together."

"Did you know that the two of them call and write each other regularly? I thought the young man was..."

"He is," Henry said.

"I hope he doesn't hurt her."

She soon turned out the lights and they crawled in their beds. Henry lay listening to her steady breathing from the alcove. She talked to him as if they were siblings, possibly roommates. He wondered where she was headed.

In the morning, Alice fixed him a grilled burger without the bun, and he left in his newly repaired DeSoto. But besides the beautiful day, despite the fact the DeSoto purred along at a solid fifty, despite the fact his whole life now spread out to the horizon, something his mother said bothered him. Something about, *if he wanted a new life, why didn't he stay in Seattle*? Why indeed.

When he got to the museum, he pulled over across the road from the sign and got out. It was the boy he was most interested in. His face was peeling. A narrow strip had fallen off his nose and he now stood like some victim of leprosy, a toothy smile, one rosy cheek, his fingers floating by themselves, grasping his sister's hand. The sign itself was sturdy enough; John came out once and reinforced it with metal struts, but no one seemed to pay much attention to the characters on the board. It now said.

CO S YO   IN THE PAS

"How can we just sit around and watch this happen?" Henry said out loud. He thought of his father's shocking features, the loss of weight, the buggy eyes and wondered if all things, even inanimate objects, aged together. This sign, the artifacts inside the museum, even brilliant ideas grew rusty and old with the passage of time.

But he did not want to accept it and instead felt a burst of energy, a new-college-graduate kind of energy, and he stood on his tiptoes, flexing his brain. "We'll see about this."

Mrs. Pinckney sat at the reception desk, smoking a cigarette. Her hair was now a silvery gray, which contrasted nicely with her pillbox, like onyx and sterling. She seemed surprised to see him.

"I meant to go to your graduation," she said. "But the ladies were here again, and I couldn't leave."

"I think we should do something about the sign," he said, pointing over his back.

"We?"

"Yes, I think we should have it fixed. It's falling apart."

She stood and walked around the desk. "Oh, isn't that sweet. But please don't feel obligated."

"What do you mean?"

"Herman. I understand. You're a graduate now. You have places to go." She took a puff and slanted her head toward the ceiling.

"I don't feel like that."

"Phillip was here yesterday, and he broke the news to me. I can't say I didn't spend a restless night, but I always expected it. People do come and go in your life."

"What did he say?"

"That he wouldn't be able to stay. He has an opportunity in California. And I just shooed him out, told him that was what a college education was all about, getting ahead in life. I wished him luck and Godspeed. He left a note in your room."

"This is all news to me. Who's going to take care of the visitors?"

"What visitors? We seem to get fewer and fewer."

"That's why we have to make repairs. People see the condition the sign is in, and they think the whole place is like that."

"I understand. But what are we to do about it? There is no money for maintenance. The ladies are hinting even more that they want to do something else with the building."

"But what about your husband? What about Howard?"

She stubbed out the cigarette and looked around. "I think he may have forsaken me."

"This can't happen," Henry said.

"Maybe not, but it's been happening for a while."

Well, we've got to do something about it," he said as he left to get his bags. Upstairs on his bed, he found the note from Phid.

> *Buddy,*
> *I think it's time, don't you? Time for us to go off and find our fortunes in this world. I've got an itch and I think only California can scratch it. Thank you for caring for me when no one else would. It really, really meant a lot. Sorry about you-know-what. I'll catch up to you later on.*
>
> *P the K*

TWENTY-TWO

Henry sat alone in a bar off the main drag of Torremolinos, Spain. Deep into the last week of his three-week European sojourn, he felt anxious and a little drunk on *vino terreno*, the local raisin wine Bernardo kept bringing him in a clay carafe.

"*Sigue*," Bernardo said. "*Tarde o temprano todas las mujeres se verán hermosas.*"

"*Si*," Henry said, and he nodded, smiling broadly, the international language of the overwhelmed. "Where to pee?"

Bernardo spread his arms out toward the street. "*Te espera la calle*," he said.

Henry stumbled to the door. It was midnight and only a few people walked this dimly lit back street. He leaned on the wall as he unzipped and thought about his trip: Denmark, Holland, France, Andorra. Did they even compare to this place? Finished and back in the doorway, he stopped.

Bernardo said, "*Hay un bar americano en la calle para allá.*"

"English," Henry sputtered.

Bernardo shook his head and pointed out the door. "American bar. Go through. You want?"

Henry saluted Bernardo. He left, a little drunk, and feeling he had truly communicated.

He liked it here, liked paying mere *pesetas* for beer and *tapas*. He liked the friendly drone of another language romancing him. It seemed, well, free. He marked that as something he would tell someone as soon as he found someone with whom to converse.

Henry lurched down the alley Bernardo had pointed out. It was maybe five feet wide. He tripped over a concrete stoop. As he passed, he heard scratchy *Sevillana* music, chattering Spanish, smelled potato omelets laden with garlic frying on braziers. Soon, the alley opened on a much wider street. He heard more than Spanish here. Northern Europeans maybe. Was that Swedish?

Ahead of him he saw it, aptly named: Bar Americano. He walked in. The place was lighter and brighter than Bernardo's. He blinked and stumbled to the first empty table where he could put his back to the wall. He settled in and took stock.

A tall swarthy young man in black pants and white shirt came over to him. He wiped the table and then waited; arms crossed.

"*Cerveza*," said Henry.

"Beer?" the young man said. "*Una caña?*"

"What?"

"Draught?"

"*Si.*"

Not bad, thought Henry. Maybe he could live somewhere else. Get by day to day. A loud group of English speakers was gabbing in a far corner. His age. Mixed men and women. Their accents American. He tried to listen, but quickly grew bored. Students most likely. Talking about student things. He suddenly missed Bernardo.

The waiter returned and set a wet glass of beer in front of Henry. He leaned in. "The woman at the end of the bar, this *cerveza* is from her."

Henry peeked around him and mouthed, "*Gracias*" to her. She sat with her legs crossed, her skirt hiked to mid-thigh. She wore a beret. She was dark with bright red lipstick that accented her smile. A smile Henry thought he might know.

He took a second look as the waiter walked away. It was possible he was too drunk, but she did look familiar. He lifted his glass and took a long pull. She turned in her stool and walked over to him.

"You've got to be fucking kidding," she said as she bumped into the table.

She came into focus and his heart raced. He had hoped it was Anita Bush, but Natalie Underwood pulled out the chair opposite him and sat down.

"What are you doing here?" he said.

"Are you scared?" she said. She drank something stronger and tipped it back to drain it. Her tongue snaked out and corralled a bit of ice. When she set the glass down, she said, "You don't want to know what I had to do to get all that ice."

"You're right, I don't. What are you doing here?"

"On break," she said. "Took the train down from Salamanca. Those are my cohorts." She pointed over to the group of students Henry noticed earlier.

"Why aren't you sitting with them?"

"'Cause I'm sitting with you." She snapped her fingers and brought the waiter over quickly. "*Otro,*" she said. "*Y una mas para el subnormal.*"

The waiter smiled as he left the table.

"One more for..." Henry said, trying to translate.

"For the retarded guy, that's right."

"I've got to learn this language. So, what's Ralph up to now?"

"Do you really want to know that? Don't you want to know about me?"

"Okay. What are you up to?"

When the drinks came, she quickly chugged half of hers. "You actually do what you're told, don't you?"

Henry was struck by how well she fit here with her dark hair and confidence. He could do without the beret, but no matter.

"I'm doing some post-graduate stuff," she said, "through the University of Chicago. International Relations."

"Ah, it's your year as a broad. I mean abroad."

"No, I'm only there a few months." Her lips set in a straight line. "Listen, Henry, I don't think you're as stupid as you're coming across. Maybe you should cool it with the bum-fuck routine."

He sat back, stung. "I'm drunk, I think. But aren't you supposed to be the French girl? *Chapeau* and all. You should be in Paris."

"Studied there already. Not just on the Continent, I've been to West Africa. Senegal. I'm Frenched out. This is a nice change."

Henry lifted his glass. "Here's to change."

"What are you doing?" she asked. "Are you traveling with somebody?"

"No, I'm seeing the world before I settle into teaching." He told her about Wishkah. And in the telling, it did not seem as magical as he believed when he first learned he was hired. Here in an obscure bar in Spain, it seemed inconsequential.

"Well, at least you're here."

He stood and she grabbed his wrist. "Where do you think you're going?"

"I'm about to piss my pants."

"There are worse things. Can't you just stay put a while? I'm warming to you."

He stayed and used his best hold-back muscles.

"My dad has cancer," she said. "Do you think it's wrong of me not to want to go home?"

"Is it bad?"

"He'll probably die soon. It's in his pancreas. An automatic death sentence."

"You might regret not seeing him before he goes."

"Ralph says I'm selfish. We have rules in my family. You don't wander outside the lines. Not going means I'm wandering." She finished her drink and looked to be at her limit. Her face grew serious as she stared at the empty glass.

"You're old enough to make your own decisions." he said. Laughter rose from the table of students. Natalie sneered at them.

"They say the stupidest things. Money and houses. Guys with money and houses. Like that's all there is to the world. There's a war on for fuck's sake. That friend of yours is still over there, isn't he?"

"Ray?" He nodded.

"Well, these asses couldn't care less about him or any other prisoners. The war's a bother to them. It gets in the way."

The waiter came back to the table. "*Algo mas?*"

"It's up to you, Henry," she said. "I'm about done."

"If I could just pee, I might have more room."

"*Este mamón no quiere nada más,*" she said. "*Quiere jugar con su pene.*"

"*Muy bien,*" said the waiter.

Natalie pulled *peseta* notes out of her bag and laid them on the table. The waiter picked the tab out if it and then disappeared. "Come on, short stuff," she said. "Come with me to the beach."

He followed her out the door. Standing made him have to pee again and at the first opportunity he relieved himself against a wall. They crossed a narrow highway with asphalt badly cracked and heaving. A pair of mules stood yoked to a wagon, swishing their tails. They passed a makeshift cabana with a cold hotplate inside balanced on a rickety table.

"I'm amazed more things don't get stolen here," he said.

"Not me. It's a dictatorship. You steal, you might die."

"But it feels so free."

She stopped on the sand. The weak lights illuminated only a few feet of water. The darkness beyond was all frothy sound and mystery. "You can do anything you want here but speak against the government. How free is that?"

He started to walk away but she leapt out and pulled him back. "Just listen to the waves a second."

Control. That's what Natalie Underwood was about.

"I don't want you to leave my side. I'm very fragile right now." He got the sense that for Natalie, it was always right now.

Soon, they walked again; the sand was deep and dry. "It gets lonely sometimes, doesn't it?" he said.

"It's lonely everywhere. Not just here." She stopped yet again and this time took his shoulders and straightened him to face her. "Shouldn't you have a TV show or something? You know, where you heal people on crutches. You could be a rich man."

"Maybe I don't want to be rich," he said.

"So, you'll just sacrifice who you are to be a teacher. There's ambition for you."

"You want me to cure your loneliness?"

"Could you?"

"It doesn't work outside Skookumchuck."

"Figures."

They took off once more, walking parallel to the town and the lights. Beached dories loomed to the sides. When they got close to one, Natalie leaned against it. "I can be alone, you know. I like peace and quiet. It's just the loneliness that gets me."

"What can you do about that?"

"Well, there's you right now. Come to my room why don't you?"

Her hotel was a few blocks from the Bar Americano. They hiked to the second floor where she struggled with the key before kicking the door open. She turned on the light to reveal a bed, a dresser, a small table.

"Looks like mine," he said. "I'll just be a sec." He headed for the bathroom door.

"Again?"

He might have been more nervous than he would like her to know.

"Wait."

"I really can't." He was already unzipping his pants.

He did stop when she pulled her blouse over her head revealing a lacy black bra. Her breasts spilled over the top of it.

"Uh." He turned and escaped into the bathroom. In a moment, he heard the door open and close behind him. His mind worked hard. What just happened? In the corner of the bathroom, a small, curtained shower stood. Natalie was turning the water on. She came to him and pulled his shirt off his shoulders, waited as he slid off his pants.

He stepped in and stood under the water, his chin against his chest. He found a tiny remnant of soap and lathered, then rinsed under the spray. Behind him, he heard the curtain part and Natalie joined him.

She moved in close, and he leaned against the wall to give her room. She purposefully avoided his eyes.

"It's the loneliness, Henry."

"Don't worry about it."

"No, I owe you an explanation. When I saw you walk into that bar, I was flooded with this feeling, this warm kind of homey feeling, and I haven't felt that in a long time."

"It's okay, really."

"You don't get it. That feeling? I can't deal with it."

Henry shivered as she drew him by the penis under the water. Ignoring the spray, she tilted her chin and kissed him on the lips. The silky slippery feel of her made him instantly hard and she smiled around the kiss.

As if they had played it out for years, she turned, and he bent her over and entered her smoothly. He wanted it now, now, now, but Henry purposely slowed, found comfort and pleasure in that warm place. Later, he shouted to the gods, the ripples of pleasure making his legs shaky. The water cascaded over his nose and mouth, but he could have drowned then and been happy with it. After a moment, he circled her waist and lifted her under the water. He found her ear and nibbled it. Ah, this was the best it could be.

"I come halfway around the world to fuck the girl next door."

"Don't make too much of it," she said.

Eventually they shut off the shower and stepped out. She turned away and he dried off her back. He felt each bone in her spine. "I could get used to this," he said.

She turned back around and kissed him full on the mouth. "Better not. My husband won't like it."

"You're married?"

"Yes." She opened the door and walked out. "To one of those guys who can only talk about money and houses."

Henry followed her and pulled on his trousers. "Is he here now?"

"No, don't worry. He's back in Chicago. He's kind of a homebody." She rummaged in her purse and took out her wallet. From it, she removed a picture. "That's him."

Henry glanced at it, felt guilty.

"Handsome, no?"

"I guess so. Listen, I didn't know about him. I'm sorry."

"Cool it, Henry. You didn't do anything wrong. But I don't want you to tell anyone about this."

"You don't have to worry."

"Because I will hunt you down and flay you alive."

"I believe you," he said. He tarried a moment. "Well then...thank you, I guess."

"Just go."

"*Adios.*"

Henry didn't see Natalie again, and on TWA out of Madrid, he tried to make sense of their time together. What did it mean that the most significant part of his three weeks in Europe was the couple of hours he spent with his neighbor from Rochester? He felt a curious attachment to her, as if, for the first time ever, they were able to connect on a level not filled with rancor. He was convinced he saw the real Natalie Underwood and he both liked her and felt for her. But, about the middle of the Atlantic, he fell asleep and when he landed, he was almost sure he and Natalie Underwood never happened.

TWENTY-THREE

Henry was in the middle of his first year of teaching, but this was beside the point. Bigger events were afloat in the world. The war was stuttering, a peace accord had been signed, and the news trickled forth of all those POWs who were being sent back to the homeland. Beginning sometime in February, Travis Air Force Base in California would welcome the men to free ground.

One day, the intercom in Henry's classroom broadcast word that a phone call awaited him in the principal's office. He instructed all the Back Row kids to behave and left them, finding his mother on the other end of the line.

"Isn't it wonderful?" she said.

She was hardly an exclamatory person and had never called him at work, so he figured either Mort Sanderson had another heart attack or Suzanne had received an additional promotion and was now teetering at about as lofty a position a nurse's aide could achieve in the local hospital system.

Neither was correct. Aunt Peg received a letter from the president, advising that her son had been included in the North Vietnamese list of POWs and she could expect another letter apprising her of the date and location he would be delivered to American soil.

Henry banged the receiver into its spot. At last, his old friend was coming back. Mrs. Hoskins, the secretary, stared at him suspiciously, as she had from the day he met her, and he smiled and said, "God Bless America!"

Henry dawdled back to class, examining snippets of artwork hanging from lockers, feeling the pulse of the future in them. It was a great country that could track long lost soldiers and return them home. This must have been how his parents felt at the end of the war. Hope, and, yes, a sense of impending prosperity.

Back in class, he walked toward the front, ignoring the Back Row students, and tapped on his desk. When he had their attention, he pulled the map open and tied the string to the nail he'd pounded into the wooden trough of the chalkboard. He took his pointer and positioned it on the lubricated vagina of Puget Sound. He looked at them all solemnly. "You are the blessed children of the future."

"Vancouver Island looks like a dick," one of the Back Rowers said.

On February 10th, they all saw Aunt Peg off at the station in East Olympia. She was to board the train and travel down the coast to California. It would take over 24 hours to get there but everyone agreed it was worth it.

She tried to carry herself with authority and a modicum of grace, but her skin was tightly bound to her bones, and she floated adrift in a yellow flowery dress. Alice guided her hand all along the platform to keep her company.

In her purse, Aunt Peg kept the second letter she received from the president, directing her to Travis Air Force Base as a guest of the U.S. government where, on February 12, 1973, she would reunite with her only child.

John carried her valise and helped her onto the train. They eventually found a comfortable seat in a row with no other passengers. Before John was off the train, she snapped open her purse and read the letter once more, as if making sure there was no error about the date or the time or the place. Satisfied, she folded the letter and stared out the window.

Minus Uncle Ray, they all gathered at the Georges' house to watch the live broadcast of the great homecoming of the prisoners. John sipped a club soda contentedly at the back of the room. He was clean-shaven and natty. His old blue suit still fit him even though he was gray at the temples and had put on a few pounds. Beside him on the table, lay the same well-worn copy of *A Tale of Two Cities*, with the bookmark only slightly farther along than the last time they'd all gotten together.

There in support of Peg, Alice sat in the middle of the couch. She wore glasses now for reading and writing and was deeply engrossed in Erica Jong. Her cheeks flushed brightly as she looked to be preparing for one hell of a critique.

They ate hamburgers from the Garabedian Café, which Alice hauled in from the Volkswagen and dumped in a pile in the middle of the table.

John bought a new TV to watch Ray, Jr.'s arrival broadcast, and it threw out a sharp, bright color. The camera panned on the flat surface of the tarmac lined with big, lumbering battleship-gray planes that had last seen action in World War II and now were pastured like domesticated elephants. The skies were clear and celestial blue. A band waited to the side, bright golden horns reflecting the sun.

Soon, the conversation in the room died down. The band began to play, and out of the corner of the picture, a transport plane flew out of the distant mountains. The crowd gathered at the base cheered, and everyone in the George living room clapped, as the big plane circled the base once and dipped its wings precipitously.

They gasped in their anxiety, but the plane managed to circle magnificently, and all was clear for a landing. The wheels popped out as the plane coasted in, its tires barely making a smoky fuss on the runway. The patriots were home.

The camera focused on the crowd as the plane taxied; a throng of excited nervous faces were painted with both joy and caution. They caught sight of Aunt Peg at the very back. She still wore her yellow dress—they found out later her bag was put off the train accidentally in Medford and she hadn't enough money to purchase anything new. The back of her hair was matted, as if she had been awakened at the last minute and rushed from the train to the air base. Alice put Erica Jong aside.

The important people got off first, those who facilitated the surrender of the prisoners. Their medals glinted as they stood at the top of the stairs and waved to the applause.

"Here, here!" John said. He began to relate the story of a man he'd known who'd been taken prisoner by the Japanese, but they all shushed him, for the announcer was coming on and reading the name of each man who walked out the door of the plane.

Henry was surprised these men didn't resemble the prisoner photos from World War II. Instead, though thinner than normal, they seemed to be in decent health. Of course, they had been housed for a time at Clark Air Base in Manila for decompression, fed good

American food, and allowed to watch re-runs of the television shows they'd known since childhood. These were men far into transition.

The crowd milled behind the rope. Their individual jobs were to wait until their loved one marched to the microphone, saluted, and stated his name, rank and hometown. Then, when this soldier approached the crowd, the loved one was allowed to walk/run to him and throw their arms around his weary neck.

Henry felt jealous of these men, the same kind of envy he had for his father and Uncle Ray when they talked of the war in their drunken stupors. Soon the stories of these men would be pouring forth and they would call fellow prisoners at Christmastime in years to come and recount, over shots of bourbon, the grisly days of war and how hardship created and solidified friendships that never ended.

On the screen, they proudly stated their names, some shouting, some more mechanical, some timid and unsure. The breeze was amplified as it passed through the mesh at the end of the mike, so each soldier had a natural white noise to contend with, but nobody complained.

A prisoner wheeled an injured soldier across the runway and the injured one spent what seemed like long minutes extricating himself from the chair before he stood at wobbly attention as the crowd noise surged in appreciation. After loved ones met, they clutched and cried and held on tightly as they walked to a spot beyond the rope, under a red, white and blue canopy.

The crowd of family gradually grew smaller, and the Georges saw more and more of Aunt Peg. The breeze was throwing her hair into disarray, and she finally gave up trying to keep it in place. She stood on tiptoes, looking over those in front of her, but even the group in the living room could tell the muscles in her bony legs were failing. Finally, she stood flat-heeled, her bag hanging loose at her fingers.

And then she was alone as the band played a John Phillips Sousa march.

"Oh, God," Alice breathed.

"Is there another plane?" Suzanne asked.

The camera was under the canopy now, capturing the full, relaxed smiles of a few of the reunited. There was strawberry shortcake, which only the children were eating, and it slid from paper plates onto the ground. Some soldiers appeared rigid, stoic in their crisp uniforms, and their wives merely squeezed their hands and spoke softly to them.

"I don't see Ray, Jr. anywhere," John said. "Did he miss the flight?"

"I wish they would show us Peg again," Alice said.

And they did. Bewildered, she grabbed at her hair and turned a full circle. She opened her purse and balanced it as she dug in and pulled out the letter. You could see her lips move as she read it.

"This is horrible," Alice said. "Someone needs to help her."

As usual, everyone then looked at Henry. There was always an air of expectation about them when a problem appeared that seemed unsolvable.

"No, it would never work," said Henry, and they turned back to the screen.

The band switched to America the Beautiful, and the commentator came on, rehashing the event. They only saw the spectacle in the background now. But Aunt Peg stood out in her dress. Two dignitaries finally approached her and talked animatedly for a moment before someone else in a lesser uniform rushed in, and Aunt Peg was whisked off on the arms of the U.S. military.

The house was stunned.

Alice sat back and stared at the screen. "Someone's got to be there with her. I am so angry with Raymond."

"Raymond?" John said. "He's not even there."

"That is my point, John."

She stood and gathered her book in her arms. She spoke to everyone. "There has got to be an explanation for this."

There was. When she came back on the night train, still wearing the dress—they never found her bag—Peg collapsed in Alice's arms and spent three days at the hospital in Olympia. On the second day, she said Ray, Jr. had been prepared along with all the others, but the night before he'd asked permission to take a walk in the darkness. He never returned. They combed the island but found nothing. It was far too unusual for the military to understand, so they assumed he'd been kidnapped. They wanted to tell Peg beforehand, to save her the trip to California, but Peg was already on the train and couldn't be contacted. The man who'd answered her home phone had hung up on them.

"We're the U.S. military," they told Peg. "We'll find him by God."

"What possible reason could anyone have for kidnapping Ray, Jr.?" Alice asked.

What possible reason, indeed. Soon, they suspected the military of some hanky-panky. Newly released prisoners-of-war simply didn't disappear on the eve of their departure for home. It was this suspicion that brought Aunt Peg out of her stupor and back to life on the Inland Coast. Even Uncle Ray got into the act. He came crawling out of his hole a few days after Aunt Peg was discharged from St. Joseph's and said he saw the whole thing on the television and, as a veteran, he deserved to be told the truth.

Well, sometimes truth had no bottom to get to. The military chased a multitude of erroneous leads and got nowhere on a consistent basis. The Ray, Jr. affair flared up and flagged with regularity over the ensuing months, but it always returned to the same conclusion. The problem was Ray, Jr. There was no way the military could misplace a soldier unless the soldier was complicit in his disappearance.

Finally, they placed his name among the others who were presumed still to be prisoners and time fashioned a different story on Ray, Jr. Most came to believe he was too important to the Vietnamese and was back in their custody.

PART IV

CHANGE

TWENTY-FOUR

Years passed and life moved on around Henry. Some weekends he worked close to a phone in case Mrs. Obregon might need him, but ultimately heard nothing. No word was forthcoming from Phid either. Instead of a flowing river, Henry's life was fast becoming a stagnant pond.

He grew accustomed to teaching fifth and sixth graders, sometimes wondered if he hadn't developed a fifth/sixth attitude about life. He missed Phid who could generally set him back on course if he strayed into more juvenile territory.

Once a year on his birthday, Henry received a postcard from Phid. He was in the Bay Area and apparently having a delightful time. He taught school for a year and then resigned. He was selling real estate now and bought and refurbished one after another of the old Victorians in Pacific Heights. "The money," he wrote, "is growing out my ass", was all that appeared on one card. Henry was certain the Wishkah postman got a kick out of that one.

From time to time he thought of Natalie Underwood, especially when he heard of her brother's growing notoriety. Suzanne told him a friend had told her that she had overheard that Natalie was unhappy in her marriage, was contemplating divorce, was getting to be aimless, visiting her mother only occasionally. At one moment, Henry thought of calling her, but stopped the thought before it could bear fruit. He entertained an occasional vague feeling that he might miss her. But did he really?

He was missed at The New Prosperity Museum, though. He visited as often as he could. Mrs. Pinckney outsmarted the budget and hired an old hippie living in a step van who spent an entire day on a ladder, restoring the sign to its previous glory. The Bi-County Sorority of the Home and City Improvement League was committed to their mission again too. While other projects like war memorials distracted them for a time, now they were back with a whole new agenda. Visits and donations were climbing, and this excited them. But along with that came more pressure on Mrs. Pinckney to add new exhibits.

For example, there were advances in camera equipment, electronic marvels in kitchen appliances, look at Nixon and Ford and maybe Carter if only he would have acted more like a real man. And there were all those new gadgets being invented by that whiz with local ties, Ralph Underwood. Henry felt a creep in his bones, though. He felt he knew this group and was sure it wouldn't be long before they changed their minds and decided to close the doors forever.

Thirty-one-year-old Henry lived in a one-bedroom former house for forestry workers on the edge of Hoquiam. It was manageable enough, a place he didn't have to worry about. He paid cheap rent and had few bills to pay. He stashed money away each month. He believed a low profile might be helping him. When he swept the street in front of his place, he also swept his neighbor's section. Whenever there fell a surprising snow, he shoveled his neighbor's driveway as well as his own. No one in the neighborhood thought of him as a *curandero*. He was simply the guy who rose every morning and came home every night, the bachelor who taught over in Wishkah. Nice guy, they said. Wasn't there something about him back in the sixties? But nearly fifteen years later, that kind of memory had leaked out of people's brains. It was a good life, Henry thought. It was no Europe, no Seattle, but it was a life, and it was his.

Once Henry had been teaching a few years, he came to recognize that students fell into definite categories. Every year, without fail, he got the same brand of kids. And no matter how hard he tried to fight it, and how liberal his attitudes were regarding the education of children, he eventually gave in and accepted the natural order. There were some kids born to please. There were some kids born to cause trouble. And there were some kids in between who were born to become the champions of the middle class.

It wasn't a colleague who taught Henry this, nor did he read it in any educator's primer. It was Carla Reinbold's mother.

All summer, Henry had been pondering the deep well of loneliness before Carla appeared in his classroom. She seemed older than the other students. Her dark hair was lustrous, her teeth pearly and well cared for. She had a full-lipped mouth and took out a compact and practiced kissing it if she grew bored with, say, the American Revolution. As if this wasn't enough, what infuriated most of the faculty was that although she barely paid attention in class, she could ace a quiz along with the best Front Rowers in the room. But she did have an Achilles heel.

Henry was getting better at conferences. Anything would be an improvement on his first, which he swam into like a shooting gallery duck, thinking, in his blessed naiveté, all parents were respectful and admiring of elementary school teachers. This was not so. He thrusted and parried with most of them as he heard accusations about other students, other parents, about his teaching style, and some unfounded suspicions about the criminal records of his colleagues. In 1981 he was more prepared. That is, until a woman walked through his classroom door who would change his life forever.

Carla Reinbold had a problem with spelling, and she came by it naturally. Her mother, Anita Bush Reinbold, looked stunning as she stood, eyes fluttering, in his doorway. She had changed, but barely. Her face was more mature which, to Henry's way of thinking, made her even more lovely. Her eyes remained intense, and Henry could still read the kindness in her glance.

"Hankie!" she cried.

He stood awkwardly and braved her fond embrace; his mind went to the stern warning on page eight of the Wishkah Valley School District Teachers' Handbook. There was to be no extra-curricular activity between teaching staff and parents. He abided by that rule at this moment. Even so, Henry blushed crimson, for despite having accepted the notion that he might never see her again, as soon as he sensed her surrounding arms, he felt himself come alive.

"I guess I didn't make the connection," he stammered as she took the seat across from him. He dropped into his chair, grateful to the clunky wooden desk for hiding him.

"Well, how could you?" she chirped. "I mean, her last name's not the same and us being new and all. But isn't it the best, Hankie?"

She sat forward slightly. He couldn't take his eyes off her. She caught him looking and smiled.

"I was just thinking about your parents the other day. How funny they were. How are they?"

He explained their current situation. About Alice who, in 1979, read *The World According to Garp* and how it threw her into a literary daze that kept her awake nights pondering how does one critique the work of an artist, or better yet, why does one critique such work? Alice finally reached her *Kairos*, her point of change, and it entered her body over the Garabedian Cafe in the middle of an essay on Mr. Irving's book. She left for Seattle a week later. Now, she took a creative writing class at the University of Washington and worked at an off-campus burger joint to make ends meet.

"But they're still married?" she asked.

"They're still married."

In Wishkah, teachers got fifteen minutes in the fall and fifteen minutes in the spring to apprise parents of their children's progress, but Anita chatted on as if they had hours. When an impatient mother tapped imperiously on the door, though, Henry knew they couldn't keep her waiting. Anita, realizing this, promptly invited him to dinner.

They lived one street off downtown in a white two-story house with black trimmed windows that stared like sunken, exhausted eyes. The fence sagged and the gate didn't latch. But Henry saw signs of Anita everywhere. A message in the window identified her as a block mother, even though theirs was the only house on the block, and the fall crocus beside her porch grew in a perfect line, like a regiment of song girls cheering for a touchdown.

Her husband was an itinerant worker named Rich who currently candled eggs in Humptulips. He was a beefy man let go at the middle but was congenial enough and, according to his wife, understood the problem of blood in yolks better than anyone. Carla was their only child and obviously spoiled, although she had good table manners and a sense of knowing when she should excuse herself from adult conversation. They ate pork chops and rice and talked about the local economy, which was not prosperous but promising anyway.

Henry didn't hear much from Rich because Anita needed to get out all the words left unsaid in the years they were apart. No sooner were the dishes cleared away than she drug out their junior yearbook and enough photo albums to keep them occupied for hours. Rich excused himself and left through the back door.

"Gone to Billy's," Anita said. Billy's was the town tavern where egg candlers and loggers sometimes mixed.

She pored over the annual. "Oh, look," she squealed and pointed to a photo of the two of them lighting a bonfire. "I think we were happy then, Hankie," she said, before moving on to another picture.

Her yearbook was well-used, even though it was only sixteen years old. She read aloud the dedications written before she left Rochester for good; all of them assured her of a life filled with children and success. Some of them discussed Henry:

Ask the idiot to undo the spell he has on you so we can go out sometime.

She saved Henry's for last:

Dearest Anita,
Maybe someday fate will tell us why it turned out the way
it did. I know we could have made it as an old married couple.

Roses are red,
Violets are blue.
Till the end of time,
It will always be you.
Love, Henry J. George

"Oh, God," he moaned.

She giggled. "I think it's the cutest thing. See that lipstick stain there? That's when I kissed it."

"So, what's it like?" he asked when she reluctantly closed the book. "Being married and all?"

She tilted her head. "Oh, it's a lot like you think it's going to be, and then a lot not like you think it's going to be."

"Mr. Quigley wouldn't have let you get away with an answer like that."

"Oh yes, he would have. Mr. Quigley let me get away with everything." Her eyes sparkled and Henry could feel the years peel back. "Is he still there?"

He shook his head. "That's right. You didn't go to the reunion."

"Couldn't make it."

"I kind of hoped you would."

"Rich wasn't interested, so we didn't. We were in Manson and it's so far away."

"Manson again? What were you doing, picking fruit?" Henry laughed, but she didn't.

"We move around a lot," she said, looking at her hands. "We haven't found the spot for us. Wishkah's nice, but it's so isolated." She looked at him. "You know what I mean? I'm going to be straight with you, Hankie. Rich has a hard time holding onto a job."

"That's too bad."

"It keeps us on the move."

Carla came in, dressed for bed. Her hair hung straight to the sides and reached far beyond her shoulders. "Have you got those spelling words done?" Henry asked her.

"Sure. But it's no use. I'm brain disabled. Like my mom."

"Now, is that any way to talk about your mother?"

"She says so herself. Just ask her." She kissed Anita on the forehead. "Mr. George, some kids were saying you're famous. Is that true?"

"Famous. I don't know about that."

"You've cured people."

"Yes, I used to. Not so much anymore."

"No kidding," said Anita. "You kept doing your old trick?"

When Carla left for her room, Henry caught Anita up on his extra-curricular activities. He finished with: "And don't call it a trick. It was for real."

But Anita may not have been the best audience to convince. "Whatever you did. I'm happy to know you."

After a moment, Henry stood. "Maybe I should be going. God knows what the town would say if they knew I was here talking to you while your husband was at Billy's."

She walked with him to the door. "Let them think what they think. They're all a bunch of cretins anyway. C-r-e-t-a-n-s. How's that, huh? A girl can learn a few new things." She stood with her hand on the knob. "I see you still have that DeSoto."

He parted the curtain. "The one and only." As she turned to peek out, her hand settled on his chest for a moment before she pushed against the door.

"Oh, yes. That was sure a machine."

"Still is," Henry choked. He was surprised by her move, but also flattered, and stammered like an unprepared student as he stumbled his way outside.

"I hope Carla's spelling gets better!" she called as he got in the car.

Henry wondered if Anita Bush had spent too many nights alone while Rich was at Billy's. She called him the following week and begged him to come to dinner again, but he declined, saying he had lesson plans to contend with. That was a lie. He hadn't made a formal lesson plan in years, and by now was flying by the seat of his pants, relying on his experience and his power over children to stay current. Anita Bush bothered the hell out of him. He felt schizophrenic around her. His dream of having her walk back in his life had come true, but the rules against going further were there and flashing like a neon sign.

She started coming to school to collect Carla, even though Carla was clearly capable of walking the few blocks home. Anita stood outside the classroom while Henry finished giving instructions for assignments. He admitted to only weak attempts to keep from thinking of her and he couldn't help but glance out the door. She waved whenever their eyes met.

Who knows about this sort of thing? Henry was a lonely man, Anita, a lonely woman. Or did it even need an explanation? He was a teacher and she a poor speller. Teachers in small towns were not allowed to be real people. They, more than any other, had to set an example for their charges. Which is why so many small-town teachers could be found in the nearby cities on the weekends where, perhaps, there were no examples to be set.

They could have gone over to Olympia or south to Kelso, but after so many years, they had no defenses. Anita was tired of moving around, and Henry was tired of this lonely stretch of river. Somehow, he managed to get it in his head that they were once practically engaged. Now they both were ripe again. So, what could they do but start the harvest?

When Henry decided to pursue an affair, a part of his brain shut off, the judgment part, the intelligent part, and he coaxed from the shadows the side of himself he didn't know very well. He dusted it off, shaped it, argued about the propriety of it, and it became recognizable as the friend who slept under the sheets with him in his adolescence.

He re-learned to rationalize, justify, deny. Alibis quickly became important.

With any other woman Henry was close to, it never felt like an affair. With Anita, it was nothing but. All these cerebral events happened in the weeks before he gave in to an impulse and clicked the lock on the door to the supply room. He trapped Anita next to the mimeograph machine after school. It was a simple maneuver, a flick of the wrist. A flick of the wrist and he had the door locked, a flick of the wrist and he had her blouse unbuttoned. A flick of the wrist and she was pressing her breasts tight against his bare chest. And it felt like home.

The passage of time left him. With Anita, it had not been a decade and a half since they grappled in the DeSoto, they were there. And they still had teenage energy and they still giggled and shushed themselves and didn't feel the press of the table against their skin or hear the soft purr of the furnace as the heat hissed into the supply room from the vent over their heads.

She lifted her long, flared skirt and knotted the hem around his waist; her ankles locked at his lower back. "Hankie," she whispered, "make me happy."

Henry pushed the mimeograph further across the table and they leaned back. It was more uncomfortable than the DeSoto, but it might as well have been the DeSoto, and he hadn't felt such ardor since those cherished moments. They bounced and bucked, flinging judgment out the window. He believed Mrs. Hoskins couldn't help but hear, or any other after-school stragglers for that matter.

When they finished, he stood, his pants at his ankles, shaking with relief. Sweat clung to his eyebrows. Anita's head lay next to the mimeograph's handle. She grinned and took hold of him; he was still hard. "This is so evil," she said. "Here at school, I mean."

"Where else would you suggest?" he said.

"My bed's more comfortable."

He backed away while she rearranged her clothes. He pulled up his pants and snapped them. "Oh, Mama," he said.

"Don't ask me to spell what just happened. But I want to do it again."

"I guess I don't need to tell you I'll get canned if they find out."

"I know. But times like this, I've learned to keep my mouth shut."

"Aha, so you're not a virgin with this stuff."

"You would be the one to know the answer to that," she said. She walked over to the door and pressed her ear against it. "I love what you were saying."

"What was I saying?"

"You didn't hear yourself?" She steepled her hands at her mouth. "Right at the end, with your teeth on my ear?"

He shook his head.

She slinked back over and leaned to his ear. "Marry me, marry me, marry me." She pulled back. "Just like old times, Hankie."

"I said that?"

"Did you mean it?"

"I did."

"Be careful. I might take you up on that offer." She pinched him in the front of his pants before she danced out of the room.

Even with extra attention, Carla Reinbold was slow to become a good speller. But Henry's dreams about her mother may have been making him a better teacher. He became more creative; his optimism blossomed. Even though they were underwater for a good part of the winter, he didn't notice.

He couldn't name the point he jumped from loving Anita to being crazy in love with her. Maybe he always was. But it knocked him over one day and was as if he had sunk his teeth into life again. The taste was sweet. It gave reason to his existence, re-imagined his youth. It brought back his old buddy hope. And hope was generous this time.

His Back Row students were the first to benefit. Every afternoon they gathered in a circle, and he read to them. They complained at first, but soon settled into a rhythm. The rest of the class was jealous, and it wasn't long before they drifted over to listen. And that was not all. One afternoon, Mrs. Julius, the mixed third/fourth grade teacher, stopped by, ostensibly to deliver some workbooks, but she lingered in the doorway, rested her head against the jamb, and nearly fell asleep listening to that day's chapter.

Did it work? It seemed to. His Back Row students became better spellers, better readers, better listeners. And so did Mrs. Julius's students. By now, Henry allowed her class in at the end of the afternoon to lie on the floor as well. As a precaution, Henry paid close attention to make sure that nothing out of the ordinary happened. But there was no loss of energy, no stripping of his soul like with Wayman the second time. He was, after all, beyond the boundaries of the Triangle. So, he just felt a pleasant sense of accomplishment. Henry hit the local discount stores, found rugs to cover the floors, bed pillows with arms, low tables. Watching this whole pleasant result unfold filled Henry with satisfaction. Imagine. Reading for hours and nothing bad happened. He would have to check into it further. He started believing, for the first time in a long time, that anything was possible. That he might be able to make a career out of this.

He appointed Anita as a volunteer teacher's aide. She was a natural at it. He only had to shoo her away from tutoring spelling and she did fine. She was especially effective on the playground where she carried a bright silver whistle on a string around her neck and trilled it enthusiastically whenever she saw an infraction of what she considered the rules of life.

Since the afternoon Mrs. Hoskins urgently rattled the doorknob, the supply room had been off limits. When the affair became serious, Henry started taking its possible demise more seriously. He made it more like a marriage. He managed it. They became inventive. They ended up in her bed a time or two, but only when it was assuredly safe—Rich out of town. Once, during a particularly violent rainstorm, they drove out to the gravel pit and left the car running as they engaged themselves to the rhythm of the DeSoto's wipers. Anita was an isometric lover, and this was useful in the tight confines of the DeSoto. When he sat propped against the window, gasping for breath, he heard Anita whisper something that gave him a sure footing with her for the first time in his life.

"I love you, Hankie. I always have."

"Then marry me, Anita," he blurted out.

"I'll tell you what. I'm going to think about it real hard and see what I decide."

But none of it was right, of course. There was abandon, to be sure, and hope, but what was that voice of reason that popped up soon after Henry drooped down? Perhaps it was Rich Reinbold's. The voice of every cuckold.

It was spring and Henry needed a field trip. In the fall, they'd gone to the offices of The Daily World in Aberdeen and learned how a newspaper runs. Trying to accommodate Carla's wishes, this time he chose the McVicker Egg Plant near Humptulips, the only egg producer in the state that still hired candlers.

Anita accompanied them as the official room mother. They sat at the front of the bus and chatted with Lou, the veteran driver, who wore a porkpie hat and kept a greeting card with a picture of Our Lady of Hope tucked in the visor above him. The children were rambunctious this day; a field trip did that. A child could live on a dairy farm where he had to arise at ungodly hours and plod through cow manure, hating every minute of it. But give this same kid a field trip to a dairy and he's the most inquisitive, happy child you've ever taught.

It was March and raining; the giant wipers were splashing the drops from one side to the other. Henry, as usual of late, was experiencing mildly prurient thoughts. Anita must have shared them as she squirmed with desire at his side.

"Did you hear about it?" Lou asked, scratching his head under his hat.

"Hear about what?"

"Those gooks?"

Henry quickly checked, but the children weren't listening.

"Heard it on the radio this morning. Feature that," Lou added.

"Feature what?"

"You didn't hear?"

"No!" This time the kids did quiet down and Henry turned around and gave them his Middle Row look, stern but forgiving. They relaxed and went on tormenting each other.

"Yep," Lou continued. "Told my old lady, them gooks been hiding 'em all along."

"Who are they hiding?

"American soldiers."

Now Henry was on full alert. "What did you hear?"

"They gave one of our guys back. About ten years too late if you ask me."

"Who was he?"

"Beats me. Beats them, too. Bunked down and all bandaged up. Bet they tortured the poor sap."

Lou turned the blinker on and jounced onto the road to the egg farm. Henry sat back and clung to the underside of his seat. He had a sense running through his body. This part of his power never left him. He knew things. He knew Lou was talking about Ray, Jr. even before his release was announced to the public. Maybe it was the talk of bandages and a cot, sure signs of Ray, Jr. Poor guy. He went through all that just to wind up in bed again.

But Henry had children to lead and after Lou guided them through the potholes, they wound up at the McVicker Egg Farm.

"Oh no," said one girl when she looked out the window.

"Do we have to? Can't we go back to the newspaper?" said another.

They might have been expecting low, sleek shiny metal buildings with the constant whir of an exhaust fan to keep the inside at a reasonable temperature and humidity. But as they descended from the bus, it was clear McVicker's was less than that.

What greeted them were the moldy white sides of a series of low wooden sheds whose old windows were flecked with fading green paint. The smell of many chickens in close quarters bowled them over. They were welcomed by Mr. McVicker the Third who was completely covered in camouflage rain gear. His teeth were as white as a leghorn's eggs, and he clucked in the manner of his constituency. Tall and skinny with big feet, he rubbed his hands together as he gathered his thoughts.

"They've just come out of their winter slump," he said happily. "And they'll be so proud to have you."

He was a natural with fifth and sixth graders raised on television. He gathered in a couple of the best Front Rowers who peeped in appreciation and let him lead them toward the first shed.

As soon as the group stepped inside, they all threw their hands up to pinch their noses. The school's best and most tender reader leaned over and vomited onto the wood chip floor. McVicker the Third pulled out a hanky and wiped her mouth.

"Sorry about that. The aroma takes a little getting used to."

The low sheds had deceived them, for arranged in rows of modern cages, thousands of white hens clucked a greeting. McVicker the Third searched for Henry over his flock. "I don't know what you had in mind!" he shouted. "But I can start them out with a little history!"

As Henry listened, he wondered if McVicker the Third didn't belong in one of the agricultural colleges. His knowledge of the chicken was extensive. He led the children through the bird's early history in Asiatic jungles, as observers of the Roman's gladiatorial times, right up to the good old American breeding know-how. "These are white leghorns," he said at the end. "They're Mediterranean. They lay a lot of eggs but have no meat on their bones." Through the laughter, Anita bit her lower lip and looked toward the exits.

"I don't like this," she said.

"It'll be fine," said Henry.

"You don't know Rich like I do."

McVicker the Third led the kids down the middle row of cages, tapping one here and there and calling out names to humor the kids. "Come now, Matilda, no egg? Bad girl. Good job, Ruby. No pecking, Lottie." The kids followed behind, two or three of them poking their fingers in to taunt the birds out of McVicker the Third's sight.

Anita and Henry stayed back. "I'm worried. I think Rich knows," she whispered.

"Has he said anything?"

"He was too nice this morning. Too... something."

"You're imagining things."

"He doesn't go to Billy's anymore. He stays home now. He even offers to take me to Aberdeen to go bowling."

"It's the chicken poop. It's gone to your head."

"Funny. Just be careful." She walked ahead and disappeared through another door.

Henry caught up with the group in a warehouse, just like the other, only this one with fewer cages of brown hens.

"Rhode Island Reds," McVicker the Third said. "An American invention. Decent layers, and more meat." As they walked through, Henry picked up and examined a large brown egg. At the far side of the room, McVicker the Third had the children standing in a circle. One of the Middle Rowers chewed on her nails. "Some producers nip the tips of their beaks right off the chicks when they're barely a day old."

"Oooh!" the girl screamed.

"Yes, that's right, so they can't peck each other. That'd be like the doctor snipping off the end of your tongue when you were a newborn."

"Gross!" came in unison from a few of the boys.

"But not here at McVicker's. We keep our chickens as natural as possible. No debeaking, no forced retirement. Look out here." He motioned through a series of dusty windows to a huge pen occupied by hundreds of hens in a state of molt. "If they do a good job for us, they get turned out to pasture, to live out their final days as real chickens. We appreciate the job these girls have done."

A hand flew up. "How long do they live," a girl asked.

"They normally live somewhere between eight to ten years. Especially if they get to have some time to play in the sun."

Twenty-seven little heads nodded at once and from then on, the children saw McVicker the Third as another St. Francis of Assisi. Anita strayed back to Henry, and they lingered once more while the class moved on.

"Are you really that worried about Rich?"

"He's a Back Rower, Hankie. Just watch out."

Henry thought on this while McVicker the Third walked the class to the very back barn. There he bid them goodbye and left them in the charge of Carla Reinbold's father. His room was darker than the others and some of the kids were reluctant to enter. Not so Carla. She was a proud egg candler's daughter. "Come on," she said, stepping right in. "There's nothing in here but a bunch of dumb eggs."

Inside, Rich was seated at a low table with several trays of eggs positioned around him. "Spooky, isn't it?" Light bulbs reflected in his eyes. "Scary territory, Mr. George?"

"These are tough kids," Henry said.

"All kids are tough." Rich grabbed one of the boys by his shirt and pulled him forward. "You got a light, kid?"

The boy shook his head and broke free while Rich searched in his own shirt for a book of matches. He used one to ignite a tall white candle.

"In olden days, they used this to check the eggs."

"Don't scare them, Rich," Anita said.

"Scare them? Who's scared?"

A chorus of denial followed, and Rich crossed his arms.

"There, you see. No one's scared here, except maybe Mr. George." Rich smiled and scooted in his chair. The kids gathered in closer.

"The reason we like to peek inside these things is because we don't want to let any little spots sneak by. Sometimes it goes wrong inside the hen, and she lays an egg that isn't perfect. Well, McVicker's likes to sell perfect eggs. Can't have Mama breaking one of these beauties in the pan and have a bumblebee come flying out now, can we?"

The kids cheered.

"Most egg farms don't do this by hand anymore," he said. "They have big lights and the eggs come bouncing by on a belt that goes round and round. Some guy stands and picks out the ones that don't have the right kind of silhouette. You know what that is? Well, it's like if you have the shades pulled and there's a light on in your room and you decide to walk in front of the shade. The whole world can see you standing there."

"Yuck," said Carla.

"You bet it's yuck, kid. And it's a damn shame when you find out, too." His hand trembled on the table. "It's the same with an egg. When you put a light behind an egg, you can see inside and tell what's there without breaking it." He blew out the candle and switched on the overheads.

He took a couple of eggs and rose slowly. "Once in a while, Mr. McVicker wants us to check and see how the yolk stands up. It's the rule around here." He walked over to Henry, so close Henry could smell his sour breath. An angry curl bloomed on Rich's lips. "So, what we do is crack one open and judge it by how it holds up." Quickly he broke one on Henry's head.

Henry stumbled back, reaching for something to hang onto. Part of the shell tumbled to his shoulder and then to the floor. He felt egg ooze over his hair and drip off the end of his nose.

"I'd give that one a Triple A," Rich said, laughing. "See how the yolk is nice and yellow?"

As Henry wiped the egg from his face, he forgot where he was. Instead of the McVicker Chicken Ranch, he was battling some unknown spirit in the middle of the Skookumchuck Triangle. He lunged for Rich, caught him around the waist, and brought them both to the floor. They rolled over and over, Rich connecting with a punch to Henry' cheek, and Henry laying a solid hit over Rich's left eye.

Carla screamed. "You're hurting him!" But neither of the men knew which one she was talking about.

When the rolling stopped, Anita was at Henry's side in a flash; the kids were squealing with glee. Rich stood up and squeezed hard and cracked the miraculous egg that survived in his left hand. The yolk dripped from his tight fingers like yellow blood as he rolled his eyes in exaggerated circles.

"He's her teacher, for Christ's sake," he said to Anita as he wiped blood from over his eye.

 Henry jumped up, feeling invigorated, yet doomed. He clapped his hands at his students. "Time to go back."

By now, the kids were hysterical with laughter. McVicker the Third appeared, searching for Rich who had disappeared out the side door. Henry dried off with a towel and after receiving an assurance that the culprit would be duly punished, he gathered the children and took them to the bus where Lou, roused from a mid-morning sleep, cranked up the engine and powered them away. Anita did not accompany them on the trip back.

The ironic part of the whole affair was that Carla Reinbold's spelling improved. Henry found this out on a note she passed him a few days after the chicken farm incident. It said:

Dear Mr. George,
>*I know about you and my mother.*
>*So does my father.*
>*Everybody is about to.*

>*Yours very truly,*
>*Carla Reinbold*

What could Henry do? He gave her an A and handed it back.

It got ugly. Within the week, Henry was called into the superintendent's office and the man danced around the point like Baryshnikov, finally suggesting Henry read the Code of Conduct of the Wishkah Valley District and that the phrase proper decorum might jump out at him. He also suggested Henry consider legal counsel.

Henry fought back with a plea concerning a certain lack of evidence and his rights under the law, but this idea met a solid wall. He was invited not to renew his contract and, even though it was close to the end of the year, was let go with a severance compromise and the promise of a non-judgmental recommendation.

Henry stayed mostly at his house until the foggy rain drove him to the phone. He called Anita and she agreed to see him in Hoquiam. They met at a burger joint but neither of them ordered. Instead, they sat at a picnic table overlooking a park.

"I'm so sorry," she said. "I should have known."

"No, it was my fault. You suspected, but I didn't pay attention to the signs."

"What are you going to do?"

"I don't know. Probably look for another job." He grabbed her hands and brought them up to his lips. He felt the same deadly urgency to connect. "Marry me, Anita. Let's make it right. Let's go on with life together."

Her hands went limp. "I can't."

"Why not?"

"Because it would never work. I think I'm becoming a Back Rower and that's no good for you. I had my chance in high school. But not now."

"Can't we meet in the Middle Row and be together?"

"I can't leave Rich. Carla would die if I did."

"For Christ's sake, Rich doesn't love you. I love you."

"Oh, Hankie."

"Listen, we'll take Carla with us. Even if I don't get a teaching job, and I might not be able to after this, I can still help her with spelling."

She smiled. "You're such a sweet guy. Do you think it could work?"

"I know it could work. You're the love of my life. Isn't it true for you too?"

"I think so. Yes."

"Then let's m-a-r-r-y."

"All right. Let's do. Damn Rich and his stubborn ways. I want a real life."

Henry told her he would pick her up in three days and walked on a cloud as he packed. He figured the three of them could go to Rochester and find some way to support themselves. When it was time, he loaded up the DeSoto and motored into town to pick up his intended.

All the way in, he thought about the kind of place they would live in, the kind of jobs they would get. He even had the new puppy named as he pulled up in front of her house. But something was wrong, and he felt it when he parked at the curb.

He vibrated as he walked up the steps. He knocked and heard an echo inside. He cupped his hands at the front window. The furniture was gone. At the bottom of the stairs, he turned around. His own vacant eyes stared back at him in the reflection of the front door panels. What did you think? they seemed to say. That she would come to the door wearing a new Sunday dress, wrap her arms around your neck, and kiss you like she intended to kiss you for the rest of your life? No. This is your lot. Empty windows and empty rooms.

TWENTY-FIVE

It was nine years after Aunt Peg waited at the air base in California, hoping there had been some mistake. Apparently, there was. When Henry got to town, his tail between his legs, he snuck into the Rochester Tavern and ordered a beer. Now several days after his fight with Rich Reinbold, his cheek still throbbed, and he had already developed a habit of rubbing it which only agitated the nerves.

Toying with the beer on the polished counter, he looked up to the television perched in its aerie overhead. The sound was off, but he didn't need it. Ray, Jr. filled the screen, shoulders hunched, his fingers dabbling in front of him.

It was a poor quality black and white film, produced by the Vietnamese prior to his release, showing Ray, Jr. enjoying the sights of Vietnam. Henry asked the bartender to turn up the sound and they listened together while the tale unfolded.

"What do you bet he's a red?" the bartender said. The man hid a scar with his goatee.

"They're saying that?"

"Why else would a guy stay after the war was over? He's a red for sure. Look how he's dressed."

Ray, Jr. wore a suit a size too small and more fashionable in the 50's. Henry's first thought was that it could be an artifact in the museum.

"That's what they're saying."

"Who's saying?"

"Guys who knew him during the war. Said he was a pet of the VC. Shit, even his old man says so."

"Ray says that?"

"Was in here last night, drunker'n snot. Had his dukes up the whole time. Hell, I thought he was gonna lay out the first guy who said his son was a red. But it was the other way around. He was daring anybody to call his kid a patriot."

"Did anybody take him up on it?"

The bartender shook his head. "Nah. Seemed unanimous to me. Course, what do you expect? You remember what that guy was like."

Henry knew of other POWs coming back and the charges filed against them. From what he could recall, they had all been dismissed or reduced to a slap on the hand. On the screen, Ray, Jr. stood in front of a fountain, his arms around a couple of Asians. It seemed unlike him to be that congenial. Henry could not recall a single time when Ray, Jr. ever touched him.

"Says they were trying to take his kid away and they roughed him up pretty bad. Kind of proves it all right there, don't it?" the bartender said, as he handed Henry his second beer.

"Ray, Jr. has a child?"

A group came in then and the bartender got busy. Henry soon said his goodbyes.

Now he felt at loose ends. The DeSoto was missing and banging and even knocking again. But he didn't want to have to explain anything to his father, so he passed the turnoff and drove to Porter.

The afternoon smelled of last year's silage, fir sap, and a precocious lilac or two. He walked up the path and stood beneath the apple tree already sprouting its new nubs. Mrs. Obregon sat in the sun near her porch, plucking a chicken. She stopped, wet feathers coating her palm.

"Hello," he said. "I'm here."

"I have been waiting for you."

Henry squatted and toyed with the grass. "I guess you heard about Ray, Jr."

She ripped the smaller feathers from the carcass in a methodical motion.

"He's back with us."

"Yes, he is," she said.

Henry peered into her face. "You don't seem so happy about that."

"The government is interested in him. It is suspicious when one doesn't adhere to the rules." She laid the chicken down and it sighed through the gash at its jugular. "Before I was not worried. Now I worry."

The sun loosened Henry's muscles and he leaned back against her house. The flies approached brazenly, daubing at the chicken blood with their unfurling tongues. "I'm worried, too," he said, flicking one away.

"They do not let you go." She was looking out to the yard where several other chickens cocked their heads and eyed her warily. "They take you and make promises, but what they don't tell you is you can never be free."

"Who?"

She picked up the chicken again and examined it, turning it over and over, its wings and head flopping from side to side. "You need to ask me that question? The ones who don't live by the rules."

"I do want to ask you something."

"All right."

"Skookumchuck. Is it going to end up killing me?"

Lines creased her face. "Perhaps."

"But why?"

"You know why."

"There you go again. It wasn't my fault. I didn't do it on purpose."

"You brought your friend back for selfish reasons. As if you are in charge."

"But I sent him away again. Doesn't intent count for anything?"

"It is never what you intend. It is what you do that counts. And you are not who you should be. Therefore, we must defend ourselves against the likes of you, even from the grave. Qone lives even if you don't believe in him."

"Sounds Christian to me."

"It is far from Christian. Qone is native. This was our land. You came. You stole. You reaped the benefit."

"I didn't do any of those things. My ancestors did, but not me."

"You are your ancestors. They are the only religion." She wrapped the entrails in the newspaper and handed it to him. "Please go under the trees and give this to the cat."

The cat jumped as he walked, finally snagged the paper, and brought it to the ground. Henry looked back to Mrs. Obregon's cabin. She stood in the doorway, brushed her hands together. When he returned, she held up one of them. "There might be another way for you," she said. "I have seen you, remember when I told you this? You were in the darkness with people all around."

"Yes, I remember."

"Don't forget that. But I want you to listen now." She pointed to the doorstep. "Sit. There is information you need to know."

He obeyed and waited.

"Close your eyes. Look into them from the inside."

He saw specks of yellow circulating behind his eyelids.

"Now listen carefully for the wind. It blows backward. Close your ears. Close your thoughts."

He did. A strange rush of wind came. He reached out.

"Good," she said. "Now listen. Not with your ears. Do you hear it?"

Amid the sounds whispering in his head, he did make out a voice, as if someone were talking while sucking in air. It startled him, and he snapped open his eyes.

"You are not blessed," Mrs. Obregon said. "You are not the future. None of you is."

"The voice said someone is dying. Who is it?" he asked.

"You already know."

Frustrated, he wiped his hands on his pants before he bid her goodbye and walked the path to the DeSoto. He sat in the front seat for a while, soaking up the warmth. But he was not sure there was enough heat to ever warm him again. The backward wind, the backward voice. When he thought of it, he was chilled more deeply. That strange voice could have belonged to Wayman, speaking from his parallel happiness.

But he couldn't explain it. It was not English he was hearing, so why could he understand it? He glanced up the path. Mrs. Obregon slowly raised her arm and held it aloft. Henry started the car and drove away fast, in the direction of his safe place: The New Prosperity Museum.

PART V

THE SAME BUT DIFFERENT

TWENTY-SIX

Ralph Underwood was on every network talking about the revolution in computers. But it wasn't just the machines he talked about; it was everything that went along with them. Not that Henry understood this, being a typewriter man himself, but the interviewers were impressed by the news. Apparently, Ralph Underwood's invention was on the verge of making him a wealthy man. And here Henry was, back at the museum in the same old room with only Mrs. Pinckney and a secondhand TV to keep him company.

He was about to turn off the set when a picture flashed on. It could have been the billboard at the museum. On the screen were Ralph and his lovely wife, Linda. And three little Underwood kids, a girl and two boys. His nemesis was a total success.

Mrs. Pinckney had a lump on her left breast. She felt exhausted most of the time and was not approaching her duties with her usual vim. This hadn't gone unnoticed by the ladies of the Bi-County Sorority of the Home and City Improvement League. Before Henry could come up with a viable plan, Mrs. Wright announced that Mrs. Pinckney had been relieved of her responsibilities. An ambulance transported her to the hospital where her condition was formally diagnosed as breast cancer. The Buick was gone. One of the ladies drove it away. Henry was left alone at the museum.

When Henry lost his job at the age of 31, he didn't immediately need another; he needed peace. And the museum offered him that. It was like snuggling beside his grandfather again, the way its roof was thinning, and its foundation exposed a crumble or two. Even its own river, its plumbing, was no longer reliable, and the electrical system rarely could last an entire day without some short in the circuits.

On the third day, a Pacific storm blew in and the lights blinked out. Using a candle, Henry stepped carefully into the musty basement, looking for the fuses. He located the box but couldn't seem to get the lights back up.

Around back, spring had been kind to the baseball diamond, but summer had been ruthless. At this point it resembled a real field, with paths and bases covered in heaps of green grass. The cage behind home was rusty, the wire mesh torn. Henry tasted the worn metal on his tongue. The rear of the building was cracked and peeling. A window above was left open and a white curtain hung out of it partway, a handkerchief of surrender.

That night, Henry read aloud from John Kennedy's *Why England Slept*, sitting on Mrs. Pinckney's empty bed in meager candlelight, hoping the words might find her. He fell asleep and sometime during the night, the book fell from his lap and landed pages-first, steepled at his feet.

The next morning, after finally getting the electricity back on, he started the process all over again; walking among the exhibits, dusting them, typing up new cards to replace the old ones that had faded. A few customers visited from time to time but didn't stay long. All the while Henry sensed an approaching denouement.

On the morning of the fourth day, a Suburban drove up and parked behind the rope chain. Through the window, Henry watched Mrs. Wright climb out and stretch. She looked up at the facade and tilted her head before dragging out a pad and making a note. From the passenger side, a man emerged carrying a portfolio. Short and trim in olive gabardine, wearing small round wire glasses, he seemed intent on every word Mrs. Wright uttered.

"This is Mr. Lewis," she said, pointing to him. "He's my assistant."

"Well, not assistant exactly, I'm the architect."

"Mr. Lewis, Mr. George," said Mrs. Wright.

Mr. Lewis did not bother with a handshake even though Henry offered one. "What is it you do?" Mr. Lewis asked.

Glancing at Mrs. Wright, Henry said, "I look after the place."

"How nice for you," Mr. Lewis said. He scratched at a sandpaper beard and rolled his eyes.

While Mr. Lewis scribbled notes, Mrs. Wright glided from room to room and dictated recommendations. "Look, up there in the corner. Is that water damage? No need to dwell. This has to go. Absolutely has to go. There is no rational excuse for it."

"But with a little TLC..."

Mr. Lewis grabbed Henry's arm before he could finish. "Please don't interrupt us. We're trying to do a job here."

Henry snapped his arm away and looked at Mrs. Wright.

"They tell us Mrs. Pinckney is doing well," she said.

"Yes, I know. I check on her progress every day." They had removed one breast and a few lymph nodes, and she was taking liquid nourishment now. The prognosis was encouraging, though the final test results had not yet been released.

Henry begged off and the others spent two hours going upstairs and down, and even outside where Mr. Lewis made sketches of the grounds. When they finished, Mrs. Wright wore a flush of satisfaction. "I'm always impressed with this place," she said.

"Some might think so," said Mr. Lewis.

"What's going on?" Henry asked, sidling up to them.

"We're figuring out our options. Taking an inventory. Mr. Lewis here is a commercial architect and he's consulting with us."

"Oh, so you're going to have it renovated?"

"Hardly," Mr. Lewis said, snorting.

Mrs. Wright snuck a glance at her consultant. "That's always been an option."

Henry asked to speak to her a moment and, hesitantly, she walked a few feet away. "Are you telling me the truth?" he said.

"Yes, of course."

"Mrs. Wright. Please. This is Mrs. Pinckney's home. It's practically mine. I need to know if you think you will hold on to the museum."

She opened her mouth but caught herself. "Mr. George, don't take this wrong, but I'm not responsible for your lives. We at the Bi-County Sorority of the Home and City Improvement League have never been able to promise either of you a home nor a livelihood. In truth, I'm here to see what repairs need to be done before we put this sagging lemon on the market."

"Ah."

She turned back and Henry followed her dusty footprints in the carpet.

After they left, Henry ambled into the Appliance Wing and stood in front of the Waste Away. He noticed what looked to be Mr. Lewis's chubby fingerprint smudges on it. Henry rubbed them away with his sleeve. "All the appliances must go. Preposterous!" had been the man's words.

He was not sure if rubbing a retired Waste Away had the same effect as burnishing the brassy sides of an old Middle Eastern lamp, but Henry heard the heartbeat there in the Appliance Wing, heard the rhythm of the old building as the river passed slowly from room to room. He gave the Waste Away an extra rub for good measure.

"Left arm, Hankie! Wheee!"

"I hear it, Gramps!" he whispered.

Thub-dup, thub-dup. It echoed around the building, drawing closer and then farther away, closer and farther. But each time it came, it was a little duller, a little less resonant, as if that heart was slowing, the river diminishing to a trickle, until finally it faded altogether, leaving only a languid kind of tinnitus, like what is left after the church bell chimes the passing hour.

TWENTY-SEVEN

Henry received a post card from his mother. "Please come and dress up," it said. They all got one. All in the same beautiful calligraphy. When Henry arrived at the house, Suzanne was holding hers in her trembling fingers.

"Sounds like a funeral," she said. Suzanne had developed a nervous palsy, not to any noticeable degree, but the family could tell life was not going well for her. It affected her leg as well and there were times she walked with the old limp and by nightfall had her brace strapped on for support as she stood at the stove and cooked for John.

"It's a mystery," Henry said.

"I think it's unfair that Phid didn't get one."

"Phid? How do you know that?"

"He told me when I asked him. I think I'm going to invite him anyway. He needs a visit."

"So, you've stayed in touch with Phid?"

"He calls. We write. I love him, Hankie. He loves me. Why wouldn't we keep in touch? Hey, I got the strangest call the other day. They were looking for you."

"Who was?"

"You know. That Underwood girl."

"Natalie?"

"Yeah, that's her. She sounded drunk. She wanted to talk to you but wouldn't leave her number. She was kind of crazy sounding."

"How so?"

"Oh, she said why does your brother hate me so much?"

"That's normal for her. What else?"

"One more thing she said before she hung up. She said, if he thinks he hates me now, wait till later."

"Nothing more?"

"No, she just said goodbye. Why would she call you, Hankie?"

To the side of her, Henry noticed a framed certificate. The hospital had honored her with a citation for cleanliness, patient respect, her specialty with children. In addition, her bi-yearly evaluations set records for perfection, and she was well-respected by her supervisors.

"It's a mystery," Henry said again.

"I guess. Are you staying or going?"

"What?"

"Do you want dinner?"

"I think I'm going back to the museum," he said.

They took two cars to Seattle. Suzanne and Henry piled in the DeSoto, and John and Uncle Ray sat in the front seat of the Pontiac. Aunt Peg rode alone in the back. Suzanne had not heard from Phid.

The address turned out to be a burger bar in the University District. They located Alice in the house next door, standing in the living room wearing a black robe and balancing a graduation cap on her head. When they walked in, the tassel hung directly in front of her nose.

"All of you?" she said, as an incredulous smile formed slowly on her face.

"Mom," Henry said, walking slowly toward her. "What's going on?"

"I'm joining the ranks of the educated."

He gave her a kiss. "This is a treat."

"For me, too." She gathered in Suzanne and kissed her lovingly on the cheek.

"Are you serious?" Suzanne said.

"I'm completely serious. I'll be graduating this afternoon from the University of Washington with a degree in English."

John's chin dropped, and Aunt Peg smiled weakly. Uncle Ray had remained in the Pontiac.

Alice glanced at her watch. "You're late. I thought we might have lunch, but there's no time."

She took Henry's arm and led him out the door. In the front seat of the DeSoto, they chatted amiably about school while the others followed along behind to the parking lot.

As Alice and Henry walked across the lot, they heard loud voices behind them and turned to see Uncle Ray stomping off in the opposite direction.

When Alice said goodbye and the rest had found seats, Henry noticed the front page of a recently discarded Seattle Times. He picked it up and what was he faced with? A head shot of Ralph Underwood. Henry chewed at his lips as he read a few paragraphs. Ralph was going to center his business in Seattle, which would be a great boon to the economy, and "so much more spacious than my dad's garage." Henry flung the paper to the floor. He'd had enough of Ralph Underwood.

The ceremony was the same long test of endurance Henry remembered. There were simply too many graduates and each of them took too much time getting up to the podium to receive that diploma.

They eventually spotted Alice in her own line and tracked her progress. When her turn finally came, they all stood up. It grew a little quieter before her name was called; the regent was going to announce her *summa cum laude* honor. Henry took a deep breath, prepared to hoot and holler, but someone beat him to it. A few sections to the right of them, a man rose and whistled. Henry stepped to another riser and picked the man out. A newspaper jutted from beneath his arm and reading glasses were perched at the end of his nose. Henry knew this man from one of his first college classes.

"Who was that?" John hissed, as he extended his neck, trying to locate the guy.

"He's just a professor."

Later, they waded through the robes to find Alice on the field. They almost lost Aunt Peg who was swept up by a riptide of happy families and friends of others and left to fight against the current. If not for John, bulldozing his way through, no more Aunt Peg. They found Alice, flushed and triumphant, holding a bouquet of long-stemmed roses in her arms.

"Where did those come from?" John asked.

She ignored him and faced Henry. "Well, what did you think?"

"Beautiful, Mom."

"Do they give those to all the graduates?" John asked, brushing the dark red petals.

Aunt Peg kissed Alice and the two of them clutched each other for a moment. When they broke, Aunt Peg was in tears.

"Must cost them a mint," John continued. "There must be thousands of people to buy for."

"Oh, would you please stop? They are a gift from a friend." Then Alice broke into an effusive smile. "And I'd like you all to meet him."

They turned as one and there was Dr. Blatt, Henry's freshman English professor. Twin dots of red blushed his cheeks and he still wore a Van Dyke beard with razor-sharp points. "How do you do, Henry?" he said. "I trust the world is treating you fairly."

Dr. Blatt shook hands as Alice introduced him to the others.

"You should be very proud of her accomplishment," he told them. "She is a remarkable woman."

"I guess you've read a lot yourself," John said, hiking up his dress pants.

"Yes, a fair amount."

"You ever read *A Tale of Two Cities*?" John said, jeering.

"Please, John," Alice cautioned.

"Why, Dickens was the subject of my doctoral dissertation."

John screwed up the corners of his mouth and grinned. "Say, do you guys remember the time Suzie here flushed the book down the john? She was just about fed up with her mom reading all the time. Called it pure crap, she did. So where does crap go? Why down the old john, sure as hell."

"I don't remember that," Suzanne said.

"Sure, you do. You're the one who came running in when the toilet was flooding the hall."

"That's very funny," Dr. Blatt said, feigning a smile. He turned to Alice, who looked at him as though she were looking at Mr. Dickens himself. "We do have reservations."

Alice nodded, a smile soft on her face. "Indeed, we do. Let's all go."

They found Uncle Ray in the Pontiac, finishing a bottle of blended scotch. The car smelled like he hadn't bathed. Splotches of alcohol stained his shirt. He offered the bottle to John, who knocked it aside and climbed in. Alice and Dr. Blatt left in Dr. Blatt's car and the rest followed in the DeSoto.

They wound up back at the burger bar, where a table of honor had indeed been reserved for them near the jukebox. It was festooned with purple and gold crepe and a sign hung from the ceiling overhead,

Congratulations Alice! The family members were all too stunned to understand the proceedings, so they sat quietly.

The burgers were excellent, which meant a lot for a crowd whose burgers were their signature dish, and it was clear Alice was a big favorite with the locals, and even the patrons who were not there for the party called out her name.

John spilled ketchup on his blue suit and smeared it into a stain vaguely shaped like Texas. "Where's Raymond?" he asked.

"Probably off looking for something to drink," Henry said.

John's nostrils flared and he bit at his lip. "He's a goddamn drunk."

"How's that going for you, Dad?"

"It's either die or stop drinking. Some days I want to choose death."

"Dad."

"Don't start in. Most days, especially a day like today, I could use some alcoholic refreshment. But I made a commitment not to and it's made my whole life better. Ray chooses death."

They both heard Uncle Ray's voice above the din. "Fucking Anzio," he shouted.

"How did he manage in the war if he was such a drunk?" Henry asked. "Isn't that kind of dangerous?"

John wiped a spill up with the napkin and then played with his glass of cola, coasting it along on its condensation. "Alcoholics get through all kinds of things when they're drinking. They hold jobs, marriages, companies, kids. I did it, until I couldn't."

"He's a vet, though."

"You know something, Hank? You're always asking about that. Of course, he's a vet. But being a vet can be different than being in the war."

"So, he wasn't in the war?"

"Let's just look at it this way. Raymond and I were in the service during wartime. And that's that." John left the conversation as his eyes roved to the end of the table. Dr. Blatt was making yet another toast to Alice who had come back from the kitchen. "He's not such hot stuff," John said. "So what if he knows so many books?"

Henry was still mulling over the revelation about the war but decided to save it for later. "All I know is he was a good teacher."

"He doesn't seem like much. Skinny as a bone. No muscle. Bet he can't fix a carburetor for shit."

"You're not going to try to take him, are you?"

"But we agree I could."

Later, Henry took some air outside the restaurant. The whole affair was a surprise, and he wondered where he had been that he'd missed his mother's accomplishments. He stayed on the sidewalk for a while until the sound of voices rose and shouts emanated from the restaurant, shouts that didn't sound like anyone was having fun.

He raced back in time to burst through the door where he found Dr. Blatt flat on his back near the jukebox. Uncle Ray was standing over him with his fists clenched, and John was trying to yank him away.

"You leave this girl alone!" Uncle Ray shouted. "She's got an old man already." He broke from John and bent to grab Dr. Blatt's lapels.

But John took him by the arm and spun him around. Henry saw delirium in his father's eyes as he reared back and socked Uncle Ray right in his meaty cheeks. Uncle Ray's lids fluttered as he staggered away from thejukebox before he dropped to the floor like a stone icon.

TWENTY-EIGHT

The case of Ray, Jr. vs. the United States of America occupied the headlines. It was big news, mostly because the ultimate penalty for treason was death. Ray, Jr. would need the very best counsel to keep him from the firing squad. Much of the pre-trial fanfare was not reliable: the caricatures of him drawn by the court artist always added a bit of an almond shape to his eyes that seemed to put a guilty stamp on Ray, Jr before he even got his day. No one saw much hope for his survival.

What the Army was trying to find out was this: had Ray, Jr. willingly stepped over to the other side and forsaken his country in a time of war to give aid and comfort to the enemy? It was a simple question but blessed children of the future could not leave a simple question to its own trappings. Anxious to make a name for himself, a young federal attorney from Chicago jumped into the middle and muddied the waters with anti-American hyperbole to solidify the government's case against a man who they believed worked for the enemy during a time of war. And because of this seductive jingoism, the whole trial went on much longer than it should have.

Uncle Ray came over to watch it on TV even though Aunt Peg was the one invited. Everyone thought Aunt Peg was seriously ill. Cancer ill. As Uncle Ray increased his bulk, she withered. Her legs were such popsicle sticks she had difficulty keeping her stockings above her calves. She was nearly all bone now. The doctors found nothing. They recommended more nourishment. She spent most of her time collecting magazine stories on her son, which she pasted into a scrapbook she hoped to leave to him someday.

It was easy to side with the government and its witnesses. The POWs were convincing. While they had lain wasting in bamboo cages and steaming heat, they said Ray, Jr. chatted and smoked with the Vietnamese guards. They'd seen him going out on patrols carrying a machine gun, or weeding and monitoring the camp garden, making sure his captors and he ate well while his compatriots were reduced to begging scraps and foraging for bugs.

Ray, Jr.'s attorney did not fare well with them. It was extremely hard to refute a statement like, "But I was there. I saw it."

"Could your eyes have been deceiving you? Could your state of mind have been affected by the conditions?"

"No, sir. I saw what I saw. I was a U.S. soldier first, a POW second."

For even questioning them, Ray, Jr.'s attorney was branded anti-American by some pundits.

Most everyone in Rochester believed Ray Jr. had been held prisoner after the war, but new witnesses came forward claiming to have seen him free on the streets, wearing the common attire of a Vietnamese citizen during the time he was supposed to be held captive. When Uncle Ray heard this, he threw popcorn at the screen. "Fuck this shit." He stomped out without saying goodbye.

The trial was postponed for a few days so that a witness who had been in an accident could recover to testify, and Henry took the time to go to the museum. He had avoided it in the weeks since his run-in with Mrs. Wright, but Ray, Jr.'s trouble made him wistful.

He shouldn't have gone. The guy in the step van had not done a job that would last. The sign was practically unreadable; the once proud family crowded around the Buick now resembled the starving Joads in *The Grapes of Wrath*. But he paid too close attention to the museum billboard. He missed the worst part. Only when he got close to his car did he notice it, and a hollow spot opened in his stomach. He walked over and touched a For Sale sign hanging at the entrance to the lot.

He stood in front of the head nurse. She was peeling even more now; a grayish-white primer was exposed like leprosy. Dust streaked the tall windows, and garrulous swallows nested in the crevices. He peeked in the front. The lobby was bare, except for Mrs. Pinckney's desk, now tilted at an odd angle to the wall. He looked through the windows of the Appliance Wing and the Kennedy Memorial Room. The whole place sat empty, the walls bare, dust bunnies on the floor. Nowhere was there evidence of Franchot Tone. What happened to the museum the whole West would be, should be, talking about?

He tripped and nearly fell as he hurried back to the front and noticed, for the first time, an official sign taped to the door:

THESE PREMISES ARE THE PROPERTY OF THE BI-COUNTY SORORITY OF THE HOME AND CITY IMPROVEMENT LEAGUE. TRESPASSERS WILL BE PROSECUTED TO THE FULL EXTENT OF THE LAW. IF YOU OBSERVE LAWBREAKERS, PLEASE CALL:

After jotting down the number, Henry stood for a long time just looking at the crumbling edifice. To him it was a living thing gone to waste. The signs were obviously a mistake. He leaned against the building and put his ear up to it. He heard nothing. Its breathing had stopped. The heart was stilled. Grandpa's River o' Life had gone dry.

He drove to Moclips and called the number. It belonged to Mrs. Wright. She told him there was no money left to do anything to the museum and when he argued that nothing ever needed to be done, there was a strong silence in which he heard his own voice coming back to him.

She cleared her throat. "In these times," she said, "a place like the museum simply makes no fiscal sense."

"Then what you told me was the truth all along," he said, a little too loudly. "You never were going to fix it up, were you?"

"Mrs. Pinckney was asking after you, Henry," she said. "I visited her a few weeks ago."

"Did you tell her what you've done to the museum?"

"No, I didn't. I didn't think it would set well."

"That was kind of you," he said. "But the reason I called was I want to know if you've had trouble with people breaking in? I mean, why the sign on the door?"

"Yes, we've had some trouble."

"Has anything been stolen?"

"We can't exactly tell."

He waited a moment and then asked the inevitable question. "Is anyone interested in the place?"

"Yes," she said quickly. "A resort chain showed some interest. You know how popular the Lake Quinault Lodge is."

"But there's no lake."

"They can build one."

Before he hung up, he asked where Mrs. Pinckney was. Mrs. Wright wished him luck, but he thought luck played a very small part in his life.

Mrs. Pinckney resided in Aberdeen, in a nursing home on a hill overlooking Grays Harbor. She was cared for well enough, but the place dropped a blanket of gloom over Henry. He found her in the solarium in a wheelchair tucked in among the leaves of a grove of tropical plants. She was looking out the wide-paned window, watching Japanese ships load cedar logs for a trip across the Pacific.

"Herman!" she exclaimed when she saw him. "I was just thinking of you."

He pulled up a plastic chair. "How are you feeling?"

"As well as can be expected. Those wonderful ladies were so gracious. They found me this nice spot, and someone is paying the bill, because they haven't kicked me out yet."

"Well, it was the least they could have done, after all those years you put in for the League."

She waved him away. "This is fine for me. I get to see the rain fall in the harbor."

The subject of the museum came up although he tried to avoid it. It was their only common ground. At first, she didn't want to know, but like witnesses to a horrible accident, her hands slowly dropped from her eyes. She picked at pieces of lint that dotted her blanket as he described the place.

"That's enough," she finally said. She sat and pondered the water for a while longer, her finger tapping at her teeth.

"Well, what are you thinking?"

"I'm wondering what Howard would think about this," she replied. "He wouldn't want to stay around a place that lonely."

"Or my grandpa."

"Do you suppose they're still there?"

"Somewhere."

"What about Phillip? What will he think?"

Henry hadn't thought about Phid in a while, and he felt sheepish when she brought up his name. He'd received the last postcard four years before, sent to the museum and forwarded by Mrs. Pinckney.

"Now, now," she warned. "You were always jealous of him. I could hear it in your voice. He loves the museum as much as you and I do. He simply has his priorities. Remember how he made them laugh with Eisenhower? That was an accomplishment. Imagine, Republicans laughing at themselves."

"I miss that place."

"As do I. What do you do with your summers now?"

"I help around my parents' place. Nothing formal."

She frowned and wheeled her chair further toward the window. "I guess I'll die here," she said.

"Sorry, I don't think there's anything I can do."

"It's not what I had in mind. I thought I'd go at the museum. At home, you know."

"Mrs. Pinckney..."

"You young ones had me fooled. When Howard rose at the foot of my bed, I told him, look at them. Look at how angry they all are. Even now, look at the outrageous things that Phid told the customers, and they didn't even flinch, they took it, some of them even giggled! That's intelligence and skill, mind you. He had it in spades. I remember telling Howard, aren't they fresh and exciting? They don't care what they say or do. To hell with convention. Oh, to have all that emotion. They're destined for good things, I said. Just you wait. They're going to channel that energy and save this country and the world."

"Are you saying we let you down?" he said. "If we did, it's because of money."

"Tell me something I don't already know. You young ones also led the charge in making money. You make more than we ever thought we could. And you spend more, you buy, you die, in credit debt. Look at that boy from Rochester, what's his name, Underwood.

"Ralph."

"Yes. How is he different? He's making all those electronic gadgets, those computers. People say he'll be the richest man in the world soon. As if that means anything. Guess what? That part's not the least bit unique. People have done that since time began. And here I thought you would be so inventive. You had so much more to work with than me and Howard did. All the opportunity, all the knowledge, all the resources. And what have you done with it? Corporate takeovers. Stealing the workingman's pensions. Unions operating as businesses. Ruining the beauty around you."

He was speechless. What she was saying was hard to deny. He wished he could hide behind the potted plants on behalf of his generation. He wanted her to be grateful for his visit, to thank him for thinking of her. This was more a call to arms.

She stopped picking at the blanket and looked at her lined hands. "Please, do something, Herman. I don't want to die here."

"It's Henry," he said.

She jerked up her head. "I know that. I've always known that."

"But why all these years..."

"I'll tell you why. Because it always got to you. You leave yourself open. I love that about you and I don't think it'll change. And, because I tease the people I love."

He kissed her goodbye and sat outside the nursing home on a concrete bench. He watched the port where the last of the cedar was being loaded on the ships. Brisk and busy American workers sending our resources to a distant land. The natural was all going away, replaced by the synthetic. Logs for cars and cameras.

When he left, even though he had planned to take a leisurely drive back to Rochester, he couldn't get the DeSoto to obey. Damn that Mrs. Pinckney. Bringing up the talking points his own inner voice had been blabbing about. She had tattooed another layer of guilt all over his thoughts. At Cosmopolis, he turned right and arrived at the museum again. He took a walk around it one time and felt the kind of need Mrs. Pinckney was talking about. He must do something. He couldn't let the museum slip away. He patted the side of the building and jumped back in his car.

In Moclips, he was on the phone again. "Mrs. Wright," he said. "I have a proposition." And by the time he signed off, he was the building's new night watchman. No pay, but all the glory an old museum could give a young man was his for free.

On his way home he stopped and picked up the keys from Mrs. Wright. Later, in Rochester, he packed a suitcase and brought it downstairs.

John looked at him from the stove where he picked bits of chicken from a steaming pot. "Where you going?" he asked.

"I'm leaving for a while."

"School starting back up, is it?"

Although Henry had been out of teaching for some time now, John was slow to come to conclusions. "Something different," Henry said.

"Good for you. Listen, did you hear the news about Peg?"

"What news?"

"Ray can't find hide nor hair of her. Even your mother came and looked, but she's disappeared. Ray thinks she ran off or, you know, they got her."

"They?"

"Indians maybe."

Finally, Henry thought as he raced along the road to Cosmopolis. Aunt Peg had clearly had enough, although he did feel the creepy-crawly of Skookumchuck as he thought about it. Why would she take off just when her son was put on trial? Maybe she was there with him, even though Uncle Ray forbade it.

Once at the museum, he set about investigating the place. True to what he observed through the windows, there was not an artifact to be seen. He climbed the stairs and walked along the hall, checking each door. Most of them were locked; the ones that weren't were as bare as the rooms below.

At the end of the hall, he tried his old bedroom door and it, too, was locked. He searched above the frame and found the skeleton key still hidden there. He slipped inside, eyes closed. Expecting the worst, he opened them slowly. It was untouched.

He plopped on his bed, raising a cloud of dust. He jumped up again and wiped off the dresser and the chairs and the frame of Phid's bed. Somewhere in the back of his mind, he expected to find him lying there when he opened his eyes. What was he doing now? What would he think of all the changes?

Henry was tired, so he stole the small black and white television from Mrs. Pinckney's old room. He set it up on a chair at the foot of the bed. He settled his hands behind his head and watched the news about the trial.

It was an unusual feeling to watch a childhood friend fight for his life framed between splayed feet on a twin bed. Henry saw glimpses of Ray, Jr. as he was led from the courtroom and he could tell the year back in the country had returned his looks to him, had taken some of the foreign quality out of his demeanor, the quality the court artists had snuck in to make him look more guilty. He still walked with a bit of a hunch as if he now carried the weight of the world, of the different, the unusual, the outcast on his shoulders. He certainly appeared that tired. The anchor said he had been through a grueling examination, and this by his own attorney. The cross-examination was yet to come.

What did they know by now? They knew Ray, Jr. had been out on an outcrop some distance from camp. He said he had been sketching the countryside and was captured, almost soundlessly, by a group of four individuals from the North Vietnamese Army. Witnesses testified they never found a sign of a struggle.

They knew that Ray, Jr. quickly learned conversational Vietnamese, and yes, this came about by speaking daily with his captors. They knew he had served as an interpreter for his fellow prisoners and sometimes had to deliver harsh statements to men in advanced states of decline. They knew he was moved from camp to camp in the South, but unlike many foreign prisoners, was never transferred to the North.

Then it got hazy. Ray, Jr. admitted he was released along with the other Americans in 1973. He was in the process of debriefing in the Philippines when he decided he could not go back. From one enemy and into the hands of another were his words. So, right before he was to be shipped to the United States, he escaped from the hospital and became a Vietnamese *cause celebre* when he appeared at the NVA encampment once again.

"Why would you do that?" his attorney asked him at the end of hours of questioning.

"You see where I am now," Ray, Jr. replied. "I was confused as to who was the actual enemy."

"You were confused?" said the federal attorney, when he took over the questioning? "Where were you born, son? What country reared you? Whose soil are you on now?"

"It's more complicated than that," Ray, Jr. said.

"Are you a U.S. citizen?"

Ray, Jr.'s eyes darted around the courtroom. He licked at his lips. "I consider myself a citizen of the world."

"The world? Vietnam is part of the world. Does that make you a citizen of Vietnam?"

"I'm talking about in the abstract," Ray, Jr. said.

Henry lay anchored to the bed, thinking about Ray, Jr.'s testimony. There was something anachronistic about the whole affair. His friend was captured in 1968, barely out of high school, unable to vote his own destiny, and here he was fifteen years later, on trial before a scapegoat-hungry military. Henry thought they should leave him alone.

He switched off the set and did his rounds. He made a quick run of the lower two floors and then found the door to the third.

It was dark and when he tried the light switch on the stairs, nothing happened. He rummaged around in the kitchen and found a flashlight, which magically worked, albeit with a waning light. It barely illuminated the pockmarked plaster walls. It smelled old and damp and the stairs creaked beneath his feet. He could feel his heart beating hard in his chest and at first, he thought it might be the sound of the museum itself. When he arrived at the top, his own sounds drifted away.

He stood at the head of a long hallway. Toward the end, only the reflection of the night sky through the window shined off the old wood floor. Henry walked along it, hearing his footsteps play music with each loose nail. All the doors were open and empty along the way. He stopped at the end. Confronted by a paneled door, he tried the knob. It was icy in his palm and would not budge. He put his shoulder against it, thinking it was jammed, but it was obvious that someone had taken the pains to put a real lock on this one. He shined the light and examined the new deadbolt. He tried the keys, but none of them fit. On his hands and knees, he jammed the light as close to the floor as he could. It picked up only balls of dust and the tips of chair legs. He was too close to fail now, he thought, as he got back up and dusted his knees.

He had managed to get inside the museum, and that counted for something. So there, Mrs. Pinckney, he said to himself. Try to tell me I've done nothing.

He found *Profiles in Courage* in the tilted desk in the lobby. Back in his room, he lay down and started to read. Although he didn't expect them to because the power never did work outside the Triangle, the words took shape. He felt a thrill as he imagined them going up and out the windows on Mercury wings. And each one of them had

Mrs. Pinckney's name on it. His couriers would make it to Aberdeen, envelop her, and bring her back home. He was almost sort of pretty damn sure of it.

The most miraculous thing about justice is the legal truth often wins out. Ray, Jr. told the truth and that is probably what got him through the next day of testimony, when the government of the United States pitted itself against a frail young man from the Inland Coast who spent most of his childhood in bed. The government had righteousness dripping from its briefs as it sized up its opponent. The smug attorneys took turns picking Ray, Jr. apart.

First, they wanted to know what was his affliction that he should have been crippled in bed all his young life, and why no real doctor was ever able to pinpoint a malady. And they wanted the court to know his treatment was administered by a witch doctor that wheedled his unsuspecting family into believing her powers and then continued to haunt them long after they saw their error. Wasn't Ray, Jr. in cahoots with her? Hadn't he always been in conflict with authority? Hadn't he always sided with the more, shall we say, socialist side of life?

Ray, Jr. said yes and yes and yes. In fact, he answered yes to most of their questions. He sat there placidly with his hands folded and answered yes to the question of whether he willingly tried to get back into Vietnam after he was released to the U.S. He answered yes to the question of whether he took up the life of a Vietnamese. He answered yes to the question of whether he married a Vietnamese woman and had a son by her.

It's probably easier to tell the truth in a court of law. It makes one sweat less, and Ray, Jr. was not sweating even though the government attorneys were having a field day. They were drawing new questions out of a hat just to hear him answer yes to them. But eventually he did reach his limit. When asked if he was a Vietnamese communist, Ray Jr. said no.

"I am not a communist," he said. "I belong to no party. I subscribe to no theory of government."

"Ah," the attorney said. "In that case, that would mean you are not a believer in the democracy you sprang from, wouldn't it? And if that's the case, then you must not uphold the values of the flag, the values you promised to protect as a soldier. That would make you not a patriot, and in time of war an enemy of your own state."

The courtroom grew quiet, as if all present were practicing what they might answer when given such a question to consider. "I am no one's enemy," he said.

"Were you an agent of the enemy during time of conflict?"

"No."

"Did you defect?"

"No."

"Are you guilty of treason as defined by statute?"

"No."

"How do you explain your behavior in the prison camps?"

"I was a prisoner myself. Have you ever been a prisoner?"

"The Code of Conduct states you cannot give the enemy any information beyond the minimum. Did you not break the Code of Conduct in your dealings with the enemy?"

"The Code was not written while under the influence of those who want to kill you. The Code is theoretical. It is designed for people who are inflexible of thought."

"Do you even know the Code?"

"I have a code, yes."

The attorney wrinkled his forehead, making sure the judges saw this. "Are we talking about the same thing, young man? What I want to know is did you learn the military Code of Conduct?"

"Yes," said Ray, Jr. And before the attorney could speak again, he added, "It was taught to me by a snake."

When an attorney is rolling down a slippery, seamless slope, he does not expect that kind of response from an individual who is fighting for his life. He stopped and cocked his head. "Did I just hear you right?"

"I said a snake taught me. He lived, lives, I assume, on the other side of the wall from my bedroom growing up."

The federal government wanted no part of an insanity defense and the attorney struggled to set the cross-examination back on track. He stuttered out his question. "So, well, let's see, you are trying to obfuscate these proceedings, aren't you, young man? Much like you did with the enemy during a time of war."

"My father would bring in fully grown live chickens and offer them to the snake to play with, much like my captors figuratively did. What I'm saying is, I was quite clearly the chicken. I was just confused about who the snake was."

Henry tried to imagine himself in Ray, Jr.'s place and knew he would never measure up to such courage. The testimony ended ambiguously.

Ray, Jr. was found guilty. But not of any high treason. It became like the difference between a felony and a misdemeanor. It amounted to a kind of AWOL. He was AWOL when he was captured, and he was AWOL when he voluntarily left the safety of the hospital and re-entered Vietnam.

He was sentenced a month later, and by that time, the furor had died down and no one in grocery store lines was interested in what was to become of him. Neither was the Army, who ended up denying him his pay for all those years and giving him a dishonorable discharge. The year in prison handed down meant nothing since he had already been in lockup even longer.

In a whisper, Ray, Jr. was free. But his troubles were far from over. He still had to face the consequences of his actions on the Inland Coast.

TWENTY-NINE

Whenever Henry passed by Mrs. Obregon's cabin, he yearned to stop, not to talk to her, but to Ray, Jr. who now lived there. Before a decision was handed down by the court, Mrs. Obregon had gone out of her way to contact Ray, Jr. and let him know that there was a place for him at her cabin and, since nowhere else seemed appropriate or safe, he landed there once he was released from jail. The first thing he did when he arrived was to petition both the U.S. and the government of Vietnam to allow passage for his wife and child to the Inland Coast.

One day, Henry could not put off a visit any longer. The glaze over the sun made it hotter in the DeSoto and he opened the window. He fought with himself, wondering why he hadn't visited Ray, Jr. but knew it was probably because of Mrs. Obregon, the person he believed he had let down in his life.

He pulled over at Porter and tapped his fingers on the car door frame. Porter was just a store and a tavern now; there was talk of widening the two-lane road. Logging trucks were tearing apart the crumbling asphalt at the edges. Henry stepped out of the car and walked the path through the drying weeds.

He stood beneath the apple tree; its fruit was hanging heavy. Ray, Jr., shirtless, split perfect wedges of cedar at the woodshed next to the house. He was slender and sinewy; his bare torso glistened with his effort. He stopped for a moment and pulled a shock of dark hair away from his eyes. He cocked his head and spied Henry.

He dropped the axe and walked over, a shuffling kind of gait, all wrong for his proportion. "How are you?" he asked.

Henry surprised himself when his eyes filled with tears. Ray, Jr. was intrigued.

"What is it?"

Henry grabbed Ray, Jr.'s hand. "Sorry. I missed you, I guess."

Ray, Jr. squeezed hard. "Never apologize for the way you feel."

Henry realized that they had quite possibly never touched before. They stood, awkward, until Mrs. Obregon stepped out of the house. She shaded her eyes.

"She worries about me," Ray, Jr. said. "She thinks someone will take me away."

"Sometimes she's right."

Ray, Jr. twisted two apples off the tree and rubbed them against his pants. He abruptly squatted and peered at Henry. "Shall we share?"

Henry was less limber and sat directly on the ground. "Are you all right?" he asked.

"Now, I'm all right," said Ray, Jr. "Tran and Ky Duc are coming."

"Your family?"

"Yes. I've just received notice that since the government would not allow their passage, they escaped from Vietnam. Our representative was kind enough to speak for them. They can have asylum with me."

"That's great," Henry said. He took a bite of the apple, and it flooded his mouth with both tart and sweet. "What will you do now?"

"I will try to make a living. Take care of my family. Raise my son." He reflected a moment. "Try to understand what's happened to me."

"What has happened to you? We were all wondering. I saw the trial on TV, but it didn't seem like you."

"That's because I've changed."

"But you just took off in the middle of the night. Why? Weren't you afraid?"

"The tiger," said Ray, Jr. "You remember I wrote you."

"Yes."

"It was all the tigers. They came back. I couldn't tolerate being with the other POWs, so I snuck outside, just to be with myself for a while. Everyone was happy to be free of captivity. They were celebrating. It was too much. I crept out and imagined the world was mine alone. I saw it. It crossed the compound light and stood a ways down the lane, staring into me. And I thought, here is this grand animal willing to risk its life to come so close, to bring me a message. I had to."

"Had to what?"

"It turned and started walking the other direction, just as it had the first time I saw it. I remembered the pain I felt to see it go, and I didn't want any more pain. So, this time I followed."

"Wait. You followed a man-eating tiger into the night?"

"I know what you're thinking. There are no tigers in the Philippines. But it was there. I saw it."

Henry was not thinking that and was about to say so, but Ray, Jr. kept going.

"It led me away from all the drinking and shouting and celebrating, all the mindless noise. I left and went to Vietnam, went into the jungle and found something new, a stillness, a peace. I didn't want to go back to noise."

Henry thought maybe the pressure had been too much for his friend as he took another bite of the apple.

"Your letters were nice," Ray, Jr. said. "The ones you wrote before I was captured. It was good to know what was happening at home." His eyes lit up briefly. "Whatever happened to Suzanne's baby?"

"She gave it up for adoption."

"Ah, too bad. Poor girl."

Henry decided Ray, Jr. had a lot of catching up to do and filled him in on the goings-on in his family since the late sixties. He eased into the telling naturally and was aware the whole time he had missed this, missed having a friend he could share life with. Why hadn't Phid answered back? He clasped his legs in the net of his fingers and talked with his old friend about the town, the people, about himself until the sun shined fiercely at an angle beneath the branches of the apple tree.

When he stopped, a smile graced Ray, Jr.'s face. "You never change, Hankie. You're like the storyteller in the old villages, the one everybody relied on to keep their history straight. You'd be a valuable commodity almost anywhere else in the world."

"People here just think I'm weird."

"That's because they don't understand. But they will. The time will come when this country catches up with the rest of the world."

Henry found that an odd thing to say especially after he'd just informed Ray, Jr. about how the future of the world was likely to fall into the hands of the Ralph Underwoods, the brave new entitleds the planet spreading misinformed condescension, class wars in what was supposed to be a Shangri-La for freedom. It seemed to Henry that the world would be catching up to people like them.

Ray, Jr. must have read Henry's mind. "People like you, Henry. You're the hope for change in the world. People will come to you. And your time will arrive with them. I've heard about you, about how you've changed people's lives, changed things with just your voice. It's a power I wish I had."

"Nah. I think that may be all behind me now," Henry said.

But Ray, Jr. reached over and put a finger to Henry's lips. "Maybe not. They were not ready for you."

Henry flushed with gratification. He was so impressed by Ray, Jr., what he'd been through and where he was resolving to go with his life, that he was overwhelmed by a feeling of tender protectiveness. Henry wanted to defend him against all the people who had turned their backs on him, especially the ones whom he knew Ray, Jr. loved most in the world. He wanted to run over to Uncle Ray's and shake him into understanding, saying, get off it, you jerk, your son's back and he's a real live person with actual memories and a love for humanity, in all its frailty, for all its faults, yes, that includes you.

"Let me talk to your dad," Henry said, standing up and brushing the grass from his pants.

"No. Don't do that. It's too dangerous."

"Have you heard anything from your mom?"

"I have," he said. He swept his arm toward the door and there she was, Aunt Peg, squinting against the sun, wearing an old caftan that she swam in. She still was hollow and gaunt, but now there was color in her cheeks.

"Wow. Everybody's looking for her," Henry said.

"It would be best if you told no one you've seen her."

From the edge of his vision, Henry saw Mrs. Obregon walk over to them. Her lips were tight. "Skookumchuck has you," she said flatly.

"Me?"

"Yes, you. Did you see your friend?"

"Yes," Henry replied, remembering the strange backward voice the last time he'd come. "But she's fine now. She's in a nursing home."

Mrs. Obregon made a sign, a circle, which she crossed with the long finger of the other hand. "Remember what we talked about. I saw you speaking in the darkness. I saw you helping."

Henry looked to Ray, Jr. for relief, but these two, the warrior and the witch, prisoner and Cassandra, both tormented, both courageous in the face of Knowledge, as the federal attorney suspected, appeared to be in cahoots.

"She's told me your friend is very ill," Ray, Jr. said. "I'm sorry."

"How does she know these things?"

"This is what I've learned," he said. "We all know."

Henry shook the confusion from his head. "It's good to have you back. I hope you can be happy."

"I have never been this happy," he said. "But there is one thing I think you should know. Now I have perspective. It's a demon that plays in my intelligence." Then he turned back into the house, taking his mother along with him, and as he did, Henry smelled the aroma of Mrs. Obregon's soup as it swirled around him, daring Skookumchuck to do its dirty work.

And do it, it did.

On the way back, an emergency message came over the DeSoto's staticky radio. A woman was perched on the I-5 Bridge over the Skookumchuck River. Drivers were warned to steer clear. Henry sensed Skookumchuck at work. He immediately made a U-turn and headed in that direction.

It was not exactly chaos, rather chaos's favorite niece, tumult. He saw the flashing lights before he got there. The flow of traffic slowed; ahead, a state patrol directed cars away from the right-hand lane. Once past the bridge, Henry pulled over and parked among the cluster of vehicles. The first one, a black Jaguar, had been ditched right up next to the span.

He had a feeling. Later he would tell Mrs. Obregon and she would nod knowingly. But right now, Henry had another feeling and when the police tried to stop him, he said, "I know this woman."

He should have said, "I feel I know this woman", but an equivocal statement might have directed the police to force him back. As it turned out so often in the Triangle, he did know her after all.

Natalie Underwood, with her cloth purse hanging around her neck, had a firm grip on the green rails of the I-5 Bridge as she overlooked the running river below. It was not a long drop, nor was the water particularly deep, so Henry wondered what the commotion was about.

After he explained his connection to her, they allowed him through, and he boosted himself over the rail and maneuvered the narrow concrete channel to get closer. A news camera at the other end pointed at him. "Natalie," he said.

She turned and studied him. Her long dark hair floated in the breeze. He saw a delicate sadness on her face, the intricate design of her life since they'd seen each other last. "Fucking get away," she said.

"*Chapeau*," Henry said.

A glimmer of smile touched her lips. "You asshole."

"What are you doing? I mean, come on. This is a little dramatic, isn't it?"

"I'm making a scene," she said. "And if you fucking try to stop me, I'll take you too."

"I'm not here to stop you."

She looked to the water again. "Of all the places to end up, huh? Who would've thought?"

"But why here? There's a river in Chicago."

"Fuck Chicago," she said fiercely. "Don't say anything about Chicago again."

"Okay, okay. I hear you."

After a moment, she said, "I'm unhappy, Henry. I'm unhappy and I can't get out of it. Every day. Unhappy."

"Maybe you should talk to someone."

"That's so lame. Just go. Leave me in peace."

"Looks to me like you aren't really interested in peace," Henry said. "You wouldn't be doing this in public."

"You have no idea. Don't try to pretend you do."

"It can't be this bad."

"Haven't you been listening? I'm unhappy. How much worse can it be?"

"We had that time together, Natalie. We had fun for a while."

She closed her eyes and bit at her lip. "You thought I was a slut."

"No. Never. And I understand what you're doing here."

"I've got to hand it to you," she said. "You always had compassion. Too bad compassion isn't enough." She adjusted her purse strap as around them, emergency personnel moved closer. Below, a crew drug a bright yellow rubber boat toward the water. Natalie watched them for a moment. "Henry, you're going to be so mad at me when I'm gone. I want to tell you right now how sorry I am. It was never malicious. It just couldn't be helped."

He remembered a conversation with Suzanne. "You called me once. What did you want?"

"I wanted to tell you something, but you weren't there."

"What did you want to say?"

"You didn't kill him," she said. "I know that. It's just that you're so damn easy to get to."

Who did she sound like? Henry recalled what Mrs. Pinckney had said to him in Aberdeen: *Because it always gets to you. You leave yourself open. I love that about you, and I don't think it'll change.* Maybe it was this naivete, this gaping wound, this tender vulnerability, and not his curative power, that was his real weakness— but if Mrs. Pinckney loved him for it, if the Underwoods were willing to lie about what they reasonably doubted in order to accept it, maybe there was something to this openness after all.

"Thanks, I guess." Once again Henry flushed with a bit of gratification that Natalie had given that much thought to the ancient, wrongful accusation, especially that she was giving it this much thought at this moment. He knew that she was Natalie Underwood, moneyed elite, wearer of *chapeaux* and pouter of lips. A woman in whom fragility and self-hatred could appear instantly. He could go on but remembered who was on the ledge and who was not. He'd been on his own precipices a few times in his life, and suddenly he knew what to say. He pointed toward the water. "It's not that far down."

"Don't you think I know that?"

"What I mean is, you probably won't die. So, why don't we just settle whatever it is in some other way?"

"What, are you going to read to me? Poor, sweet, naïve Henry. The world needs more of you. When this is over, please think of me kindly."

"As a matter of fact," Henry said. And from his back pocket, not unlike his father, he pulled out a paperback."

"Jesus. If that's *The Future Is In Eggs,* I swear I will kill you instead of me."

"It's not. I don't carry around your favorite author just on the off chance I might run into you."

"You remember Ionescu?"

"I remember almost everything," Henry said.

"Who is it then?"

"Who else? Faulkner."

The boat was afloat now, and the two men dropped an anchor in the shallow stream.

"Oh God," she breathed.

Henry took a step forward. He judged he could probably grab onto her and even if she jumped, they'd hit the water at the same time, and she'd be saved. "Now, wouldn't you rather go somewhere together and listen to me read instead of in that stupid raft? Don't laugh. Maybe I can cure you after all."

She didn't laugh. "I want a do-over."

"When? When do you want to start from?"

She looked up to the sky. But in so doing, it was as if she finally realized the ruckus going on behind her. A news helicopter buzzed over Centralia. More cars slowed down, and a real jam was forming on the freeway.

He stepped closer; he was only a few feet away now. But his movement startled her, and she fumbled with her bag.

"Natalie?"

She looked up. "Call my mother," she said.

"What?"

"Call my fucking mother. She'll tell you."

"Tell me what?"

But Natalie drew a pistol out of her purse and jammed it right into her temple.

"It's still the loneliness," she said.

"Jesus," Henry murmured. "Wait."

Just then, she clamped shut her eyes and pulled the trigger, and a lot of Natalie Underwood's head found its way onto the rumpled dungarees of Henry James George, who was standing so very close to her, there on the I-5 Bridge.

THIRTY

It was Henry who jumped into the river, the blessed Skookumchuck. The panic from the gunshot loosened his grip on the rails and he wailed and leapt into the water, Faulkner spinning in the air before it fell. He had been right; the drop was not far, and the water was not deep. His feet hit the rocky bottom and sprang him back up. When he surfaced, the guys in the boat grabbed hold of his arms and pulled him in. Meanwhile, Natalie's body caught an eddy and circled close by.

Henry wanted nothing to do with law enforcement or any of the onlookers anxious to get a peek at him and what was left of Natalie on his soaked clothing. Somebody wrapped him in a blanket and escorted him to the back of an ambulance and he was transported to the hospital in Centralia, where he was pronounced slightly in shock but fit to live.

The state patrol questioned him afterward, but he had nothing to add to what they already witnessed, and he was let go with a promise to return if needed.

The drive toward the museum was a jumble. He couldn't seem to divorce what he saw from what he had just suffered. Familiar sights and sounds and colors took on a disenchanted tone. He noticed everything in its minutest detail, or he noticed nothing.

What Henry noticed: the old trees were gone alongside the repaired, widened blacktop. The trees were replaced by a less hardy variety, stunted by vehicle exhaust and a lack of protection from the winds. Newer houses dotted the valleys, houses made of T-111 siding, which weathered into a muddy mixed and muted color within a year. The bridges were wider and a darker green and didn't creak and groan when he crossed them. The rivers flowed at a permanent low water mark. More direct roads now skirted the smaller towns, and they lay breathing their last as the shake mill teepees sputtered smoke in a dying cough.

What Henry didn't notice: how much Natalie's suicide had affected him. And how vulnerable he was to the whims of Skookumchuck.

Outside Aberdeen, he did not prepare for it. Just as Mrs. Obregon once suggested, he decided to let go. When the strangled feeling came, instead of responding with his usual anxiety, he relaxed his body.

Again, there was the clutching at his neck, but since he wasn't resisting, he also lifted from the seat. He choked down a rising panic and held onto the steering wheel long enough to pull over to the side of the road. The car lurched to a stop. All the anxiety of the day coalesced into this frightful moment and Henry, aligning himself with Natalie's decision, released the wheel.

And he floated – it was no rough and tumble ride to the ceiling of the car – he floated in an easy, drifting manner, like Natalie's body in the eddy. He heard voices, saw oily pastel colors. The ceiling stopped him; he did not float through it as he imagined he might. His body flattened against the fabric. He heard music as well. Colors and sounds galore, an unorthodox sojourn at the Aberdeen line. He closed his eyes and passed into unconsciousness.

Henry awakened to a tap on the DeSoto's glass. He now lay in the back seat. He wiped his eyes and peeked out to see a sheriff wearing a tall brushed brown hat. The man rapped on the glass again.

"Open the door," he said.

Henry struggled to right himself. When he opened the door, the sheriff backed up.

"Step out, please."

But Henry was wobbly; his legs could not sustain his weight and he plummeted to his knees. The pea gravel bit into his flesh. "Ah," he cried.

"What's going on here?" the deputy asked as he squatted, got close to Henry's face and sniffed.

"Had to pull over. It's Aberdeen, you know."

"You're all wet. Smells like fish in here. He picked something off Henry's shoulder and brought it to his nose. "Fish guts?"

"Skookumchuck," Henry said.

"Really. Didn't think there was much to catch in that stream."

"I got lucky I guess."

The deputy took another whiff. "You been drinking?"

"Me? No."

The deputy stood up and offered his hand.

"Because if you have been, it was smart of you to pull over. Don't get in trouble that way." He brushed off his hand and squinted. "Do I know you?"

Henry tried his legs again and stood with dubious potential. "I don't think so."

The deputy pushed his hat back, revealing an expansive forehead. "Sure, I do. You're the reader kid. That day in Rochester. I volunteered in the Coke concession for the Lions Club."

Henry regained his strength. "I guess you do know me then."

"Pretty good stunt," the deputy said. "Hot day. Middle of summer. Do you know how much Coke we sold? Gallons."

"Thank you."

"Don't hear anything about you these days," the man said.

"Yeah, I kind of gave it up." Where did this guy come from, Henry wondered. Everyone was a philosopher.

"I hear her son took off again. Some folks just can't be trusted. Old lady Simpson's one of them. You ask me, she was the one we all should be taking a closer look at. Just give me five minutes in a bare room with a five-hundred-watt bulb blistering her face, I'll find out what happened to her boy."

"Can I go now?" Henry asked.

"You fit to drive?"

"Yeah."

"You can go then. Take my advice though, no drinking and driving. You pay a hell of a price if something goes wrong." He patted the DeSoto as he left. "Nice rig."

Henry watched the deputy get in his car and held up his hand as the man passed. Then he looked back toward Aberdeen. No roiling thunderclouds spitting fire. No gods in their chariots. But he knew something was changing. He failed to save Natalie Underwood. He failed to bring Ray, Jr. back on the tarmac where he would be greeted as a hero by God, Aunt Peg, and the United States of America. But humans fail, Henry thought. It was normal. Maybe, therefore, he was normal too.

"I think I want to live," Henry said to no one.

THIRTY-ONE

When Henry arrived at the museum, he was wrung out. Many questions ran through his mind. Where was he headed? Would he be a night watchman for the rest of his life? He was so preoccupied with these thoughts that he didn't notice the SOLD announcement draped across the FOR-SALE sign. He went upstairs where he showered and changed into his robe. He took his wet and tainted clothes and stuffed them in the garbage can like a murderer ditching evidence.

He attempted a cursory inspection of the place, but he kept pacing back and forth. Why would she do that with so much life ahead of her? How could anyone be so unhappy? Could he, in fact, have saved her if he'd read Faulkner there on the I-5 Bridge? With every step, his nerves combusted.

Back in his room, he lay on his bed. He was sure he would not sleep tonight and might never be able to sleep again. Shock wore you down, he remembered hearing once. One shock after another and you were ready for the grave before your time.

He pulled back the covers, just as he heard the squeal of brakes out front. He hurried to the window in time to see the old MGA, its side door open, parked on the road. A small shadowy figure ran from the driver's side, opened the passenger door, and pulled someone out. That person fell to the ground and was still there when the MGA took off for Aberdeen.

Henry jammed on his slippers and ran out to the lot. The figure slowly stood, wavering, unbalanced in form and function. Henry stopped, opened his eyes wider so that all the light from the heavens could filter into his line of vision. This figure, this man suddenly glowed softly, took a step. He wore loose jeans, a sweatshirt that engulfed him. "Batter..." Then he crumpled.

"Jesus. Phid?"

"Damn," came a familiar voice. "I was trying to make it out back."

Henry dropped to his knees. "Are you drunk?" He touched Phid, but it was not the body of the Phid he used to know.

"Hi." The voice was tense, distant.

"Where in hell have you been?"

"You don't want to hear."

As his night eyes came, Henry saw his friend for what he had become. "Let's go inside."

"I can't."

"What's wrong?"

"Lots. Can you help me?"

Henry put Phid's arm around his shoulder and lifted him, but Phid's legs buckled, and he couldn't stand. "Good God," Henry said. "What the hell?"

Henry had to sweep him up in his arms. He was a feather, a wisp of nothing. They passed the sign and Henry finally noticed.

"Oh, fuck. Now they've gone and sold it."

He carried him across to the front door. In the light, Phid looked like his own molted shell. Emaciation had made his skin cracked and craggy. Great bags under his eyes held the last fluids in his desert of a body. His thin hair aged him. A scruffy beard, both dark and gray covered sores.

But when he grinned, all of it disappeared and Henry saw the old Phid, his friend and compassionate colleague, metamorphose in front of him: sunlight through clouds.

"Give me a break," he said. "And quit gawking."

Inside, Henry hauled him up the stairs and into their old room where he laid him gently on his bed. Phid stretched out painfully. "You going to tell me what gives?" Henry said.

Phid's voice came from deep within a well, in fact, the whole of him had sunk to some low point. "I've got a disease," he said. "Gay pneumonia they're calling it. It's some cancer."

"Cancer?"

"They think."

"You look horrible."

"It hits me like a ton of bricks. Fine one minute, can't move the next. Must be the excitement of seeing you, Hank. Threw me right out of joint."

"I don't believe it."

"Believe what you see. We're the only ones getting it."

"I'm sorry."

He waved Henry away. "It's not that bad now. But it'll get worse."

"Isn't there something you can do?"

"I don't think so. A year ago, I was at dinner with seven friends of mine. Last week there were only three of us left. Everybody else wasted away." His eyes grew dark and glossy, and Henry saw fear in them. Phid coughed into a thin tight fist. "I don't see how I can do this with much grace."

And it was indeed a graceless disease. This became clear when Phid undressed for bed. His legs were sticks, his knees misshapen knobs, and on the inside of his thighs purple blotches rose like coral atolls. He had a running rash on his abdomen, a perfect outline of his ribs sprang from his chest.

Henry peered at his friend. "You should have stayed home. I knew you shouldn't have gone down there."

"Ah, that's it, wash it over me. I expected I would get the old mother lecture." He pulled the quilt higher. "And what do you mean I shouldn't have gone down there? Your boy did good. You should be congratulating me."

"For what?"

"For getting rich."

Henry glanced down at the pucker Phid barely made under the quilt. What constituted wealth if your body was in such a condition? "You don't look very rich to me."

"Ah well, I spend it quick as I make it. You've never heard of San Francisco real estate? Or do you still avoid the rest of the world?"

"Most of it," Henry said. "So real estate?"

"Pacific Heights. Victorians selling at a million a pop. Do you hear me, a million dollars?"

"You sound all grown up. Whatever happened to the guy who loved to trick the guests here when he talked about Eisenhower? The guy who loved this place? Who didn't go out looking to make a quick buck? Huh? Where is he?"

"You done? You ready to slide down off the lectern?"

Henry calmed for a moment. "Yes. Sorry. It's just the shock."

Phid looked hard at Henry. "I've missed you," he said. Then his face flared with anger. "What's that For Sale sign doing out front?

Who runs this joint now? Can't you do a good job for once in your life? Huh? And where the hell is Mrs. Pinckney?"

"In Aberdeen," Henry said sadly. "She's been sick." Immediately, he remembered the backward voice at Mrs. Obregon's, and looked down at the actual friend who was dying. "Fuck," Henry said softly. So, this was his sick friend whom Skookumchuck had throttled. The hairs on his neck stood at attention. Henry told Phid about Natalie.

"That's some bad luck."

Henry felt the chill of the illness when he touched Phid, and it was as deep and dark as death. He drew back and rubbed his finger. Phid was shivering so Henry searched out an extra blanket, which he draped over his friend. "They probably won't like it if you're here," Henry said. "I'm not even supposed to be here during the day."

"What a horrible predicament. I hope they don't hurt us."

Henry glanced at Phid who smirked for just a second before his mouth settled back into dying. "I don't know what I can do with you tomorrow," Henry said.

"Don't worry about it. I made it this far. We'll figure something out."

Henry watched him a moment, but Phid closed his eyes and didn't open them for the longest time. Henry went over to his suitcase. Inside, beneath his shaving equipment, he found his copy of *Sophie's Choice*. He tiptoed back to the chair and sat. It looked like a tough disease; he needed solid, resilient language.

He began to read and quickly caught the rhythm of the words. Was there ever anything better than to capture an author's cadence and be swept away? He was halfway through the first chapter before Phid stirred.

"Haven't I warned you about this?"

"You be quiet. I'll do what I want. I'm not trying to change you." He wondered if having the disease had become as much a part of Phid's identity as his gayness itself—if there were wounds he couldn't heal, needs he couldn't fulfill. Especially with the wrong book.

"You got any Kerouac? I hate Styron."

"I happen to like him," Henry fired back.

"Who's sick here, you or me?"

"I guess you but it's the only book around." Faulkner may have been still floating in the Skookumchuck.

After another paragraph, Phid coughed and wiped his mouth with the back of his hand. "Thank your sister for letting me know this place was for sale."

"Suzie?"

"I bought it," he said weakly.

Henry stopped. "You what?"

Phid lay so still that Henry thought he shouldn't ask him to repeat his news. But he knew that sometime during the night, he heard the faintest sound of a spring trickling forth from the driest parts of The New Prosperity Museum.

THIRTY-TWO

Phid rallied. Maybe Suzanne's help had something to do with it. When she showed at the door the next morning, Henry wondered if the boundaries of the Triangle had expanded somehow and the message of Phid's illness had reached her via an unknown force from this far away. But the answer was simpler than that. Phid had called her.

"We never stopped talking to each other, Hankie," she said. "That's what people in love do."

Henry thought about the conversation with his mother when he accused her of dropping her family and setting out into her own life. Maybe he was more like her than he realized. After all, a postcard to Phid every few years was nothing compared to regular conversation.

"But did you know he was sick?"

"Not until just a few days ago. You know Phid. He's pretty good at hiding."

Phid was thrilled. They put Suzanne in her old bedroom. He could often be found there, chatting away as if no time or disaster had interceded in their lives. Suzanne had to drive to work some days and stayed with John until she could return.

When the thrush growing on Phid's tongue disappeared with repeated saltwater rinses, he became good friends with peanut butter again. His lesions lightened from a deep purple to lavender. By the time the museum deal closed, he was well enough to put on his business clothes and ink his name.

Henry never asked how much he paid for it, but it had to be a tidy sum. Mrs. Wright was excessively gracious, and the ladies of the League huddled around the desk at the attorney's office, squirming with excitement as the deal was forged. They already had plans for the money; a new meeting house and investments would make their organization forever strong.

Henry drove Phid back to the museum and they stood together in the lobby. "Well, it's yours," Henry said. "I don't know why you did it, but you did it."

"It's a miracle," Phid said.

"What do we do now?"

"We find the stash." Phid dug into his pocket and pulled out a knot of keys. "One of these is to a room on the third floor. Let's go find it."

Henry supported Phid as they mounted the stairs. Together, they hobbled to the door at the end of the hall. Henry jammed the first key into the lock, but it didn't budge. Neither did the second or third.

Henry sorted through ten keys before he hit the jackpot. The door rattled open and revealed all his old friends: the Shampoo Master, the Admiral fridge, the images of Franchot Tone.

"Paydirt!" Phid exclaimed.

The exhibits were thrown together with no thought given to their relationship to each other. Much like life, Henry thought. He hurried over to the windows and threw up the shades. He scanned the room until he spotted, perched on a heap of vacuum cleaners and refrigerator parts, the Waste Away. It resembled a miniature flying saucer, gleaming in the sun. "Who in his right mind would do this?" he asked, picking it up.

"They're not in their right minds," Phid said from the doorway. "Nobody is anymore."

Henry rubbed absently at the contraption in his hand. "Do you think we're weird to like these things?"

"Of course, we are. That's the whole point, isn't it? It'll be fun putting them all back."

"Then let's get to it."

Henry started sifting through the artifacts. Phid reached for the Kennedy rocker, sat with obvious relief, and watched. The sun stole behind the cedar forest and the room grew chilly, but neither cared. Henry worked on. He was back being an assistant curator and he liked it. He may even have liked it more than teaching children.

It took weeks to organize the museum, sometimes with Suzanne's help, other times Henry tackled it himself. One by one Henry restored the exhibits. He saved the Kennedy Memorial Room for last and when it was nearly complete, he carried in a large portrait, which he placed at a politically strategic point in the room.

"That seems a little campy if you ask me," Phid said.

Henry regarded the photo of Marilyn Monroe and said, "What do you know from camp?"

Phid helped him unveil John-John and Caroline and Jackie. They polished their lacquered black frames, carefully placed them on one wall. Henry located the President's portrait. He held it out and studied it. He liked his clean-cut handsomeness, the playful wisdom in his eyes and, for a moment, saw him as Mrs. Pinckney saw him, as maybe the last truly wise leader.

Deep in December, the museum was back to its original state. To celebrate, Henry drove to Aberdeen and picked up Mrs. Pinckney. He was excited to surprise her but found her in a melancholy mood. She turned and acknowledged him. "It gets old after a while. Too much rain."

Even though she seemed depressed, Henry still played the game he had planned. "You need to go now. You can't stay here anymore."

"I knew it was coming. Nobody pays for an old woman forever." He helped her pack her bag.

Henry signed her out and they splashed away in the DeSoto. She sat with her gnarled hands folded, continuing to look out at the rain. "Where are we going?"

"I've found another place for you."

"You don't need to go to the trouble."

They drove on as the sky grew darker with a storm that had swept in from the ocean. Henry watched her from the corner of his eye as she noticed they did not take the turn further south toward the Triangle. Instead, they motored along the highway north. She glanced at him.

"I didn't mean to scare you off when you visited," she said. "I would have liked it if you came back once in a while."

"It's okay. And you're right. I should have come back sooner."

The wind buffeted even the sturdy DeSoto, and she grasped the door handle. "What did they do with my car?"

"I don't know."

"They sold it. I know they did. They sell old things. Do you suppose that's how they paid my bill?"

"They didn't exactly consult me," Henry said.

When he turned on the road toward the museum, she sat straighter. Her mouth worked in a chewing motion, but she said nothing. Hope labored hard in her hands. When they pulled into the lot, she cried out, "You've done a good thing." They parked where the Buick once parked. The upstairs lights were shining. She turned to him. "Oh Henry, I knew you would do what's best."

THIRTY-THREE

Before the last cleansing rains of winter were over, Ky Duc and Tran came to the Inland Washington Coast. There were delays in Hawaii and some final question as to the appropriateness of their papers. But there they were, standing at the end of a concourse, as retired men and women in wilted leis and failed orange tans jostled past them.

Ky Duc met Ray, Jr.'s eyes for the briefest moment and then, only slightly, as though it were giving a bit of respect to the gesture rather than making the whole gesture itself, she lowered hers. Tran bowed to his father as Ray, Jr. touched them both gently on their heads and led them through the maze of the airport into the freedom of the South Seattle mist.

Their appearance caused an immediate stir in the town of Porter, and the locals could be seen slowing near the only store and peering into ditches and bushes for a glimpse of the odd Asians. Ky Duc was a skilled forager, and soon earned a daily wage by searching for stray aluminum not noticeable to the untrained eye. Her back bent low, she was completely focused as she pulled aside the dying, wet and crushed weeds and carefully maneuvered her tiny hands into the rotting recesses to claim her prizes.

With her first month's proceeds, she walked the eleven miles to the Elma Rodeo Thrift Store and bought a Western Auto bicycle that looked to have been discarded in the fifties. She molded it back into shape and used it to ride on longer and longer excursions in search of aluminum.

Ray, Jr. could not find work. He had learned engine repair in Vietnam, so he applied at the Union School District Bus Garage. But the position was awarded to another veteran with less experience, but a more widely held view of patriotism. He found the same resistance at a mechanic shop in Montesano. So, Ray, Jr., too, began roaming farther and wider to look for work, hoping to find an employer who hadn't heard of him, or who understood the frailties of human nature and wasn't as likely to banish him with a shout of, "Go see if Jane Fonda has any work for you!"

Tran was a perfectly obedient child of nine who loved his father and took every opportunity to show it. When Ray, Jr. and Ky Duc were out ranging the countryside, Tran stayed home with his grandmother and Mrs. Obregon and learned about Skookumchuck. He was a devoted student in all respects and English came to him after only two months. He could proudly state the names of the new vegetables he was planting without error and would caution his father about roving too far into the Triangle, lest he suffer its merciless consequences.

He cooked with the artistic hand of a prodigy. Henry came for dinner once at the first of summer, and Tran followed him around, demanding his opinion, and watched as he ate, even offering to wipe Henry's chin of the inevitable dribbles of soup. Henry pronounced it excellent, and Tran replied, "Yes, Uncle, I know."

It crushed him to be parted from his father, as if he needed to make up for the time they had spent apart, as if they were inseparable now that neither ocean nor politician had managed to rend them asunder. When they were together, he shadowed his father everywhere and asked innumerable questions about American life and expectations.

"Why," he once asked, "must children go to school if there is something more interesting to do that day?"

"They don't, Tran. We can teach you here at home and everything we do will be interesting, or at least most of it—you'll see."

His clothing was simple; he loved the rain. Henry once caught him naked, making circles in the middle of it, buzzing his lips as he imitated the plane that brought them to this new land.

Ray, Jr, finally found a job at a gyppo mill near Yelm where he had to pull rough, uncut lumber off the green chain for hours at a time. On the first day, his cheap gloves were too thin and slivers from the boards pierced his palms. By the end of the shift, his hands were so swollen that Ky Duc had to cut the gloves off him. She hugged him, held him close as if they had been stitched together finely during their time in Vietnam.

Tran also attended to him, creating a concoction of Epsom salts and horsetail. He gently lowered his father's hands into the warm bath and patted his back as he winced and groaned from the discomfort. The swelling was down overnight, and, despite how expensive they were, with a new, tougher pair of leather gloves, Ray, Jr. survived the initial week of labor.

About the time the museum was ready to serve its customers, Henry heard the screeching of tires in the lot. He looked out the window; a car fishtailed and nearly crashed into the DeSoto. He peeked through the beveled glass of the front door to see Suzanne running toward the building, a bundle in her arms. When she got close, Henry flung open the doors and she sped up the stairs. He nearly caught her, but she slipped into her old room and locked the door.

Henry pounded on it. "Suzanne!" he shouted, eventually rousing Phid from his bed.

Soon, Phid was supporting his body against the jamb. "What's going on?"

Mrs. Pinckney called to Henry from her room, but he ignored her. Phid shuffled over, gently moved Henry aside, and then flattened his ear against the door as he spoke to Suzanne.

"It's nobody's fault," he said.

Henry scooted back in close. "Suzanne, open the door. Come on now. We need to talk." A baby cried.

"Let me be."

"I can't let you be, Suzie, you're the one who came here. You obviously want my help."

"Maybe she wants mine," Phid said.

Henry stepped back from the door, arms raised, palms facing out. "It's all yours, Dr. Freud."

"Not Freud. He hated people like me."

"Right now, I can understand why."

Phid took his position, spoke soothingly and before a minute passed, the latch clicked, and Suzanne appeared. In her arms a chubby new baby was wrapped in a white hospital receiving blanket. Its face was mottled red. Henry looked from the baby to Suzanne and back again.

"I might be in trouble," she said.

"How?" Henry bulled past Phid into the room. Suzanne sat on the bed, patting the baby's back. "Who exactly is this?" Henry asked, as calmly as he could.

"Diana," she said, pulling her in close. "She's my baby."

"Yours?"

"Yes. Well, I'm not exactly sure. But she's mine tonight and I want to keep her. I told you I need one, didn't I?"

Henry threw up his hands. "Oh Jesus."

"Maybe she isn't sure," Phid said, sitting next to her. He pulled the blanket back. "She's cute."

"Do you think she looks like me?"

"Where's she from?" Henry said.

"I think I'm in trouble. She's from the hospital."

"You kidnapped her?"

"I love her," she said.

Henry reached for the baby. "You've got to give her back. Tell them there was a mistake. God, you can go to prison for this."

"You're not taking her," Suzanne said. "Over my dead body they'll take her this time."

Henry stepped back, shaking his head. "Suzanne," he said.

She set her jaw. "I'm warning you," she replied.

"Don't be so mean to her," Phid said. "She's not herself."

"I don't know what comes over me. One minute I'm dreaming of Diana, and the next I have a baby in my arms. Sometimes it's real and sometimes it's not."

"But how were you planning to feed her?" Henry said. "How were you going to take care of her? Don't you think she's going to be missed?"

She stared at the baby, tapping a finger against her cheek. "I don't know. Okay? I just don't know."

"Listen," Henry said, moving in closer. "Suzie." He brushed the hair back from her forehead. "You don't need to do this. You can have a baby of your own."

"No, you don't understand. I can't have another one."

"I don't think that's true. The doctor said everything was fine. Remember?"

"No," she said. "The doctor didn't know. He was wrong."

"How do you know that?"

"He told me."

"The doctor?"

"No, no. Not the doctor, stupid."

"Who then?"

She started to cry and with that went her ability to speak clearly. She leaned her head against Phid's chest, and he petted her hair.

"I've got to lie down," he said.

"No, please stay." She grabbed for him. She cried for a minute and then straightened, wiping the tears away. "Uncle Ray told me."

"What's Uncle Ray got to do with it?"

"Diana was his baby," she said, sniffling.

It all flashed through Henry's mind, how only Uncle Ray was available for Suzanne, the trip to the hospital during her frightful labor, the way Alice ran her finger over the baby's features, trying to discern its parentage. He felt a bitter poison enter his mouth.

His?" he roared, jumping up, scaring the baby into wails again.

Suzanne kept patting its back. "It wasn't really his fault. He didn't mean for it to happen."

"But I thought it was the Pitts kid," Henry said. "I thought he admitted it."

"Him? He was just a boy. Nothing ever happened with him. It was Uncle Ray. And he told me I could never have my own babies now. It was a sacrifice what I did with him, like the way a soldier sacrifices. I was only his. I could only have his babies." She covered her eyes with one hand.

"And you believed him?"

"Why would he lie to me?"

"Suzanne," he said, sitting back and taking her hand. "It's not still happening, is it? It's not still happening with Uncle Ray?"

She grimaced through the mirror of tears. "When Dad's sleeping, sometimes Uncle Ray sneaks in. But I don't let him really. Honest. And Uncle Ray says I'm a good girl for not letting him. I do other things and that makes him happy, and he goes away."

"Oh, Suzie," Henry said. His gut thrashed with this news.

"It's okay. I'm a good girl. And he's a veteran."

"What is it with these veterans?" he said, thinking guiltily of Ray, Jr., and how the war and the world had failed him.

"They saved us, Hankie."

Henry winced. "Look, we've got the problem of the baby here. Are they after you or not? I mean, you were in a hurry when you got here."

"They're probably after me. They're going to miss the baby."

"When?"

"In a couple of hours."

"In a couple of hours from when?"

She looked at her watch. "In a couple of hours from a couple of hours ago."

Henry studied the plea on her face. "You realize we have to take the baby back."

But Suzanne clutched it more tightly. "No, I can't."

"Suzanne, you have to."

"No. I don't. The parents aren't good for her."

"But it's their baby."

"They'll scare Diana. They won't know how to take care of her." She looked at Phid. "I was hoping you could help me raise her."

"Me?" said Phid.

"You're not making any sense," Henry said. "You're sounding crazy."

"Well, maybe I am."

"Crazy or not, we've got to take the baby back."

Once again, she glanced at Phid who by now looked ready to collapse. "I was counting on you. Don't you love me?"

"Of course, I love you, but geez, Suzie, a baby?"

"Listen to him," Henry said.

"I'll lose my job. Then what'll I do? I can't go back home."

"You can stay here like you have been," Henry said, "until we figure something out." Henry gently put both hands around the baby. Suzanne let her go, finger by finger, fresh tears brimming.

"She's so beautiful. She's too beautiful to give back." Suzanne leaned her head on Henry's shoulder as he held the baby. He looked down on it and was reminded of her labor and how Uncle Ray came up the stairs and ended the conflict with a promise that she could keep the child. Henry tried to remember the look on Uncle Ray's face, tried to recall any glimmer of remorse or understanding.

"What's going to happen to me?" Suzanne asked.

"I don't know. We can only hope for the best."

Phid stayed and Henry and Suzanne drove back to Olympia under the stars. Suzanne held the baby in the backseat and cooed to her, singing her songs from her own childhood, tunes John had made up many years before along the way to the hospital to see what could be done for her damaged leg.

Hush, little baby, sleepy time's a comin'
Hush, little one, sleepy time is here.

It was not quite commotion, but commotion's uncles, hue and cry. When they arrived at St. Joseph's, a trio of police officers and a reporter and photographer were hanging around the small crowd at the front door. But they let Henry and Suzanne pass through to the elevator and up to maternity. When they stepped out, however, the head nurse lunged for Suzanne and pulled the baby from her arms. A pair of security guards bound Suzanne's hands behind her.

Henry tried to intervene, but as soon as they'd subdued her, they went for him. By that time, the photographer's flash lit up the halls.

"She didn't mean it," Henry said. "It's all a big mistake."

Which, of course, didn't impress anyone in the maternity ward. Henry learned right there that what people with minimal authority hate most of all is a disruption in routine.

They were sequestered in a nurse's lounge at the end of a hallway. A student nurse sat at a tiny table, a half-eaten cup of yogurt in front of her as she browsed through a newspaper. Suzanne and Henry sat looking blankly at each other while the security guards stood just a few feet from their straight-backed chairs.

"I think my milk's coming in," Suzanne said absently.

"Please don't say things like that," Henry said. But he automatically looked at her breasts. "I wish you hadn't done this. You had such a good job here."

"A good job doesn't matter if you're lonely."

At that, Natalie's last words resonated again in Henry's brain. He wondered if the whole world was afflicted with loneliness. "Uncle Ray needs to pay for this."

"But Uncle Ray had nothing to do with it."

"He's not even our uncle. Why do we carry him along in the family when he's not even related to us?"

"I miss Diana," Suzanne said. "I miss my baby."

"You need help, Suzie."

The police came and sorted it out, finally letting Henry go. But the hospital administration was adamant, and of course the parents had to be told. When they found out, they threatened a lawsuit and as much as begged to be allowed to burn Suzanne at the stake. They figured their baby was now scarred for life. Suzanne was beloved by some on the ward, and had won awards for her work, but those accomplishments didn't curry favor with the army of lawyers who materialized on the hospital's side. All eyes damned her now. But the fiasco eventually dissipated and by August, Suzanne was serving the first of thirty days behind bars.

Henry had been reading a lot about what was now called gay pneumonia, and each story came to the same unfortunate conclusion. There was little hope for Phid. But one of the greatest leaps a person must take is to jump the chasm between what he knows and what he feels, and what Henry knew was not what he felt when Phid started failing again.

Phid was delivering his Eisenhower pitch and he nailed it every time; somehow the illness had made him look more sardonic. He exaggerated this in the delivery of his speech, pinching his lips together and drawing his shoulders in toward his chest. But one day he stopped in mid-sentence—a brilliant turn on Mamie—and froze up. His limbs, his tongue, the saliva in his mouth stopped operating. He tried to suck air deeply into his lungs, but it was as if his throat were closing for good. His face turned dark and, before the balding men in their no-roll trousers could rescue him, he crumpled to the floor.

If Henry had said, "Please help the guy, he has gay cancer!" they all might have jumped back and stayed clear, but there is humanity in ignorance. Two of them took him in hand, while the rest of the crowd gathered round, wishing him well. The men carried him upstairs to his bed where he soon recovered his breathing and lay quiet. Henry found a book and read to him for the rest of the afternoon.

Occasionally, Phid would wince and grab at his stomach and when Henry noticed this, he said, "Let me take you to the hospital."

"I have no insurance. They'll leave me on the steps."

"No insurance? How did that happen?"

"Oh, you know. Denial is our best buddy."

"But you're rich," Henry said.

"Was rich," Phid corrected.

Henry read on, skipping across the words as he sometimes did when he wanted to solve a problem. It was as if he worked some muscle that pumped solutions from deep within.

"You okay now?" he asked, touching Phid's shoulder.

"I will be."

"What's that supposed to mean?"

Phid licked at his lips and tried to turn but failed. When he spoke, he was looking at the ceiling. "I'm going to haunt you. Be good to me now and I'll be good to you later."

"Sounds like a threat."

"Tell me about this friend of yours," he said. "The one you brought back."

"Wayman? There's not much to tell."

"What was he like?"

"He was an only child. No, that's wrong. He is an only child. His mother drove tractor and his dad was disabled. He recently died."

"But what about the kid? What really happened that day?"

"First or second day?"

"There's more than one?"

Henry explained how he sent Wayman back. "I passed out and woke up in the hospital and Wayman was nowhere to be found."

"You mean gone gone, or just gone?"

"What's the difference?"

"Gone for good."

"The first time just gone. The second, I guess gone gone," Henry said.

Phid listened closely, then said: "You haven't had the best luck in your life, have you?"

"No, I haven't. But I won't complain. I've had good luck too."

Henry thought about Wayman, about the life he claimed to love so much in the other Rochester, and how sometimes in Henry's own life it would have been nice to take off for somewhere else, where life was the same but happier somehow.

"Hank?"

Henry put the book down. "Sorry, what did you say?"

"I said, I'm going to be gone gone soon."

"Not if I can help it, you won't."

Phid pointed to the book. "I thought that didn't work outside of the famous Skookumchuck."

Henry recalled his first time, sitting upstairs at this very museum, reading Faulkner to his depressed mother. And how she came back home after that, never to be depressed again. Maybe a different kind of Skookumchuck had a farther reach than he believed. Or maybe the answer did not reside in Skookumchuck after all. "People don't die on my watch," he ended up saying.

"I wonder what it's like being dead," Phid said. "I've watched shows. They make it seem okay. As long as it's okay, I think I can do it. But no fanfare, no pain, I don't even want to like it. I want plain and simple. I fade, I stop breathing, my heart doesn't work anymore. Any questions?"

"And then the haunting begins?"

"Oh yeah. I get to see you naked whenever I want."

"Could we maybe forego the tired old jokes about that?"

This touched Phid. He grew quiet for a moment as if embarrassed. "You remember that one night?" he said.

"I thought we weren't going to talk about it again."

"We weren't. But I've been thinking, and I believe you might be right."

"About what?"

"Oh, I always said to you, come on, Hankie, it's only sex. Freaked you out and I got a kick out of it. But I think you should know I could have been lying."

"No, not you," Henry said. "You would never lie."

"Listen to me, this is important. When I said it was only sex, I was lying. I think it was love I was talking about. Have always been talking about."

"But..."

"Hold on, let me get this out. It was love I was talking about, and I want you to know that you, Hank, have been the love of my life."

Henry's throat turned to desert. "How can that be?"

"I don't know. It just is."

"But you took off, left me here."

"I think I was scared. You know? To be in love made me too vulnerable. Plus, what were we going to do given our separate inclinations?"

Henry took hold of Phid's hand, petted it for a moment. "God, we've never talked much since you left. How can that be love?" He looked about to add to it.

"Henry."

"No, you hold on just a sec or I'll never get it out. That night you're talking about." Henry bowed his head and took a deep breath. "I kept your hand there. I didn't exactly scream and try to get away."

"So?"

"So, love must be part of the equation for me as well. Christ, it's not Anita Bush after all. You, my friend, are the love of my life too." He squeezed Phid's hand, felt a rush of emotion; tears welled and spilled down his cheeks.

Seeing this, Phid withdrew his hand and hid it under the blanket. "Could you tell me just one more thing."

"What?"

"You've heard things that aren't there. You've seen things too. Now don't start denying it because it's a waste of time and that's something I don't have much of. Am I right?"

"Yes, but don't tell Ralph Underwood. It'll be all over the news."

"What does it sound like? The voice from over there."

Henry hesitated. He wasn't sure he could put it into words. "Well, it sounds like something that's on a different frequency. It crackles and there's a wind. The words move fast and sometimes it's hard to keep up with them. They move backwards."

"And what do they say?"

"Are you sure you want to know?"

"Time, Henry. Time."

"*dying friend's Your*. That's what it said the last time. I thought they meant Mrs. Pinckney, then there was Natalie, but it turned out to be you."

Phid strained to raise his head higher. "So, someone from the other side was communicating to you about me?"

"Yes. I guess so. Although I think it was just a voice. Not someone. Not flesh and blood. More like nature."

"Maybe it was that Simpson kid."

"I don't think so."

"But you don't know for sure."

Henry didn't. He was getting spooked talking to Phid this way. And he didn't want to tell him why. The truth was that Phid's voice was starting to sound like the one in Henry's head at Mrs. Obregon's. It was as if he was already joining up with the other force and he wasn't even dead yet. Why is everyone in cahoots without me, he wondered. "Let me read more," he said.

"It's no use. I can't listen."

"What do you want me to do then?"

"Where's Suzanne?"

"She's downstairs. I think she's setting up a cot in the Appliance Wing. She loves it there. Why do we all love it there?"

"We all like playing house. Naïve optimism in the form of plastics and steel. We can have better lives, and we will because it's our destiny."

"Do you want me to get her?"

"No," he said. "But I want you two to do me a favor." He whispered into Henry's ear.

"A cat?"

"Yes, I never had one. My dad killed the only one I brought home, and somehow my roommates were always allergic."

He seemed to drift off and Henry tried to rouse him, but he wouldn't come around. Henry let him sleep. He checked on Mrs. Pinckney. The blanket covering her barely moved and he wondered for a moment if she was still alive. It occurred to him the museum might be turning back into The Cedars.

Down in the Appliance Wing, he found Suzanne lying on a pallet near the Admiral fridge. He toed her hip. "Come on, Suze, we have an assignment."

Henry told his sister about the cat request, and they piled in the DeSoto and headed toward Moclips. Suzanne sat beside Henry, her leg slightly bowed, a new brace a hindrance to her movements. They exchanged important news as if it were small talk. "Where did you and Phid go the other day?" she asked.

"To the lawyer's," Henry said. "You know, to transfer the title of the museum."

"Must have been hard."

Henry couldn't really tell her just how hard it had been. He begged Phid to put it off, but Phid only looked at him with eyes that asked, did Henry know anything about the real world?

They came into Moclips and slowed. Beach towns seemed so homeless when the weather was stark. They drove the streets one by one, in first gear, headlights on bright. They saw no sign of a cat.

Suzanne rolled down the window and made a kind of mewling sound. "It's too cold," she said, rolling it back up.

"Phid wants a cat," Henry said. "And a cat he'll get."

She nodded and tried again, calling for all cats out her window, but her voice cracked, and Henry knew she was sad. They came to a cul-de-sac and made a gentle turn. They couldn't see it but could sense the presence of the ocean. They drove on to the boardwalk where they parked. When Henry turned off the lights, the night enveloped them.

He felt Suzanne's hand touch him on the leg and he shivered. "What is it?"

"I've been thinking. I think all of us have weird lives. Phid too. Something bad happened along the way."

"Well, we know what happened to us," Henry said.

Suzanne stepped out of the car.

"Sorry to bring it up," he said.

They strolled along the boardwalk. Henry could hear the surf, and the tightness he had felt in the car loosened.

They came to the far edge, but Henry had the sensation of continuing on, just stepping right off the end of the boardwalk into the sea. Instead, they sat and let their legs dangle. The dark water below strained to reach the shore.

"Do you ever think of her? Anne, I mean," Suzanne said.

"Yes. But it's been a long time. Why?"

"Because not a day goes by that I don't think about her."

"But you didn't even know her."

"Doesn't matter. It was still my fault she died."

Henry turned his head. "Oh, come on. You're just trying to feel sorry for yourself."

"You can think what you want, but if I hadn't been crying, she'd probably still be alive today."

"Do you really think that?"

"Yes."

"Well, stop. It's not your fault. It will never be your fault. Things happen, even when you have control over them, and you had absolutely no control over Anne walking into the ocean."

Suzanne was quiet for a minute. Her silence brought up the sound of the surf as it chewed at the shore.

"What am I saying anyway?" he said. "I think about her too. And I think it was my fault she died. I was reading in the car the whole time she was trying to make it to shore."

"Oh, Hankie."

"No, it's true. God, I should never have picked up a book."

"You're wrong," she said. "It's your destiny."

"Maybe," Henry said. But she had something there, this supposedly slow girl.

"He's going to die, isn't he?"

"Yes."

She whimpered, then brought herself together again. "Do you think he would have married me if he wasn't sick?"

He turned to her, took her hand. "Suzie, Phid is a gay man."

"I know that. He told me."

"A marriage between you and him could never work."

"But he says he loves me. And I love him."

"I love him too," Henry said. Then he stopped and thought. He thought about fear of contact and wasted years with his best friend. "I love him in a different way."

"I don't want him to ever leave. What am I going to do?"

Henry thought about the power and its former hold over him, and how his real life had been subsumed in a quotidian life of his own making, but not one he wanted. *I see you talking to people in the dark.* Damn that Mrs. Obregon. "Maybe something will happen."

Suzanne looked back down at Henry. "People like Phid, because life is hard for them, they're the ones who really try. And what does it get them? They put up with bad jokes and people being prejudiced and being beat up when they're practically babies. It's all uphill for them. And then when they get to the top, they get to die young."

Again, Henry had to check to be sure it was Suzanne speaking. "You're probably right," he said. He helped her up and they clomped down the planks, one-half of the crippled George family regiment.

"Well, looky there," Suzanne said as they neared the car. "Stop searching and it comes to you."

A cat was just then backing up to a tire and spraying it, twitching its tail as it shivered. It spoke to them gently and Suzanne dropped to one knee. It approached her cautiously. "It's a male for sure," she said, stroking its fur.

"It's just an alley cat," Henry said, pointing out its stripes. "I think Phid had something more exotic in mind."

Suzanne picked it up and cradled it in her arms. "I think it's perfect." She checked its neck for a collar, but it had none. "Open the door, Hankie," she said. And when he did, she put the cat down on the pavement. It looked up at her, meowed, and then hopped in the front seat.

"It better not piss in my car," Henry said. But it seemed content and curled between them as they drove away from the boardwalk.

The cat was a menace. It took to Phid, but it bit Henry squarely on the Achilles whenever he was within biting distance. No barbaric lunge, a simple set of fangs to that tender area and Henry was kicking and cursing and screaming, waking Phid and giving Mrs. Pinckney all sorts of grief.

Despite hope, the fact remained that Phid was failing. He ate very little, peanut butter and jelly sandwiches on occasion, and he drank only a few drops of water when it was forced on him. He had a wretched cough that after every spell left him a weaker person. His steep decline frightened Henry: it made him think of testing the limits of Skookumchuck once more. And Henry was still shaken with his own declaration of Phid being the love of his life. How does one cope with the death of such an important person?

As Henry observed his friend, his body stiffened; Phid's lips were chapped, grated like strips of hard cheese. His eyes followed Henry around the room and shone with tears. His once-brave take on the illness had been consumed by fear. He crooked a finger at Henry and said, "You have my permission to cure me now." A hand came out and rested on Henry's forearm, but Henry shied from the touch.

"I'm afraid now," Phid said.

"Phid. My power. You know it doesn't work here."

But the savage sadness moved forward and finally, about a week later, Henry could take it no longer. In the afternoon, he bundled Phid up and carried him out to the DeSoto.

"Be careful," Suzanne said.

But Henry was intent on his task. "Don't say anything. I don't want to think about it." Suzanne and Mrs. Pickney sent them off with apprehensive waves.

Phid was quiet. Henry had no real plan other than to seek out Mrs. Obregon. The rain fell hard and ran sideways on the windshield as they pulled off at Elma and took the back road through Malone to Porter. Henry got out and shouted toward the cabin. After a minute, Ray, Jr.'s head appeared over the weeds.

"Come help me!" Henry called, and Ray, Jr. picked his way down and they gingerly carried Phid to the cabin.

Mrs. Obregon met them at the doorway. Ky Duc and Tran were standing close by. Aunt Peg hovered near the bedroom.

"Mrs. Obregon," Henry said, panting from the strain. "He's bad."

The rain thundered against the roof. "Come inside," she said.

She cleared away a space on the sofa near the stove and here they laid Phid out. He stared right through Henry, who could still see life play in his eyes, but they were so receded he thought now it might be impossible to reach him.

"This one has been sick a long time," Mrs. Obregon said. She unraveled a scarf from around her neck and wound it around his.

"Who's this?" Phid squeaked.

"Mrs. Obregon," Henry said. "She's going to help you."

"Did you tell her I have no insurance?"

Henry stood while Mrs. Obregon ministered to Phid. Ray, Jr. handed Henry a cup of tea, which he drank greedily. When he stood straight, his head grew light, and he had to lean against the wall.

Tran came to him. "This is good," he said. "It is good when your health drains into a friend. He gets better, you get weak." If he only knew, thought Henry.

They watched as Mrs. Obregon sat with Phid and touched him lightly on his neck and chest and spoke to him in Salish. The fragrance of soup, the onion, the garlic, chicken fat, clove hung heavy in the room. Henry walked over to the stove and lifted the lid on the kettle, letting the steam rush out and shock his face. He could feel droplets laden with herbs clinging to his skin.

"Is it ready?" Mrs. Obregon asked.

Ray, Jr. stole up behind. "Ladle some out," he said.

At first Phid refused the soup. He retched when it came close to him, but Mrs. Obregon was patient and held the ceramic spoon over him until he lifted his chin and sipped slowly. He finished only a small portion.

They waited, one hour, two, and still Phid lay there, breathing quickly, unevenly, his life sinking further and further into the holes in his eyes.

When the sun was gone, Mrs. Obregon came to Henry. "He will die," she said.

"Oh no. Please."

She took him by the hand. "This is your next lesson. It is harder for your people to hear this. But sometimes, there is nothing to be done."

"More soup," Henry said hopefully, and he went for the kettle.

But Mrs. Obregon tugged on his sleeve, holding him back. She shook her head. "He will die."

"No. You're supposed to be able to cure people. Why won't you? He needs you."

But Mrs. Obregon was insistent. "My boy, he will die."

"I can't let that happen. Give me something, please." He jumped up and flew into her bedroom, searching her shelves. He wanted something, anything to read. He did not care about the consequences; he wanted just one more time to do the impossible. He grabbed a book and turned sharply, only to run into Mrs. Obregon. Behind her, he could see the others, filtered by the gauze curtain she used for a door.

"It is not wise," she said.

"But I have to. He'll die."

"You are not one of us. Remember what happened with your friend."

"I know. But I don't care, I'm not going to let him just die."

"Is this so bad?" she said. He felt a warmth coming from her fingers. "Doesn't he look comfortable to you?"

"But I can save his life."

"Can you?"

"Of course..." He wasn't sure. "I can't not try."

She stepped aside and ushered him through the gauze, onto this stage that he built as a child. He hurried and knelt by Phid.

But before he started, he looked over to Ky Duc who said solemnly, "When die want come, you open door."

He felt a singular loneliness enter his soul. He was never more aligned with Natalie than at that moment. Only Phid's graveled voice brought him back.

"We're in the Triangle," he warned.

And Henry started to cry. Soon, torrents of tears rolled down his cheeks. He spoke at the same time. "But I don't want to lose you."

Phid nodded. "I might already be gone. I always was one foot out the door to something. Funny thing is, I've never felt more present, more in the room with you all, than I do now. There is nowhere else I would rather be."

Glancing about the room, Henry saw them all watching, each of their looks told him a different story, but all had the same bad ending.

"I'm going to do this," he said, and opened the book. *20,000 Leagues Under the Sea.* He was fortified by an urgency, as if each word signified one breath made of gold:

"The year 1866 was signalized by a remarkable incident..."

It was swift and frightening. One moment he was kneeling by the tattered couch in Mrs. Obregon's cabin, the next, he felt a total dismemberment, no, more than that, a total dissolution; he became particles of himself. But within each particle was a whole self, a luminous fractal, so that he witnessed millions of Henrys scattered about randomly like stars. A rush, like a great vacuum had opened in his world and was preparing to suck him from this familiar place to somewhere foreign. The millions of Henrys harmoniously observed, "So this is what death is."

He could have been right. Along with his own disassembled selves glimpsed tiny likenesses of Natalie, his grandmother and grandfather. All the Sylvia Trestons pedaled past him, like the lady in The Wizard of Oz, a million fresh and gleaming smiles projected out as she did. Henry tried to touch Natalie, but it was a million Henrys reaching out, a million of him failing to touch a million Natalies. Much like their life together.

This place, this disjointed dimension was not at all as Wayman described. Not simply a reflection of Rochester lived on the unsilvered side of a decorative mirror, rather a million mirrors not reflecting a physical image of each Henry but reflecting instead a million feelings, a million emotions experienced by these Henrys. Geometric emotion. Now Henry could look large fear square in the eye. Rage and unlimited pain lived in other mirrors. Envy and lust crowded into yet others. The disappeared still felt, he thought. I still feel. I am one of the disappeared.

Now came an emotion that weighted him down like the strong force of a giant. But wait, was that an actual giant now pressing on him? "Wayman?"

"Hank?"

Henry looked up, and up, and up. There was no end to this unraveling Wayman; he was in the clouds, an exaggeration of himself. When he spoke, his voice boomed down hollowly like Henry imagined God's voice must boom.

"You've got to get out," Wayman said.

"Why are you speaking forward?"

"I've been practicing and now you're ruining everything. How am I supposed to be a *curandero* with you here?"

"*Curandero*? You?"

"I begged you not to come. I begged you to leave me alone. I told them you would never do this again. Now, look what's happened. Please," said Wayman. "It's my turn. Just go."

"I don't know how."

"Just do it."

Henry stood, while behind him, a million Henrys stood as well. He took a step, then another, but plummeted through what, a cloud? He pinballed off himself a million times. "Sorry, Henry. Sorry. Sorry."

Now he was spinning, somersaulting through a thick soup that made it hard to breathe.

"I am dead," he cried. "Phid!"

"Look at me," a million Phids said, all hands-out, bodies pointed at a slant toward the moon. Like Superman. "We can fly!"

"Are you ready?" said the cloud.

"Mrs. Obregon?"

"I'll send Qone to you. You'll see. You'll understand then. There is a reason for this."

And there it stood, a bright light not truly human, not pure light either. A hybrid. It spoke, and Henry instinctively knew this was not a language that still lived. This was a native language. Of God perhaps. Special. Unique.

"I am *Tsihalis*," the voice said. "This is mine, ours. You took it from us. You stole it."

Henry struggled to understand. "Who are you?"

"You should know me. You all should know. I am the one you deceived."

"Skookumchuck?" said Henry.

The light wavered, moved from side to side. "That is pidgin. Impure. I am pure. And you are not. Go. You don't belong here. You never belonged here. You cannot take this from us too. League by league, you moved on us, muddied our waters. Now, this is as far as you travel up the river."

"But what are you talking about? The River o' Life?"

And then Henry saw a vision of he and his grandfather in the bed at The Cedars.

"In the summer, she ebb," a million Henrys said. "In the winter, she flow."

"Watch out for the Injuns," said a million Grandpas.

"You are not perfect. We are not perfect, but you must give us back what is rightfully ours."

"I already know that," Henry said. "Why was I chosen?"

"You weren't chosen. The arrogance. Why would I choose the ones who killed us?"

"I don't want to be here."

"Get out then. You trespass, just like the others before you. Get out of our world. Never return."

"But where will I go?"

"Ah, there is room for that question. You will go where I send you."

Then came an enormous backward wind that blew Henry across a vast universe, filling his lungs to bursting so that he could not inhale on his own. But it was not air after all. It was water, fresh, pure water he splashed into. How easily he swam, how perfectly he darted back and forth among the rocks and under the rapids.

"What am I?" he said, but his words were underwater as well. He tried to take a breath, but he had no lungs, only gills that filtered his life.

Around him swam a million, what, salmon pushing their way against the current. He felt a part of their charge, their desperation to reach some destiny. Henry sensed this destiny as he got closer, felt it in his fins.

"I'm almost there," he cried out right before he entered the wooden weir that let him go upstream no more.

"No," he said. "No." Why was no one else trapped in this cage? Why were the others allowed to swim past to shallower water? "Mrs. Obregon! Help!"

"And now you are the one who is captured. This is where I've sent you. To the half-land. I give you, Trespasser, the quandary you must always live with. Forever, you will wonder if it is this world you are living in, or the other one. You will never know. This is your punishment for taking our life away. For being the wrong one to work the miracles that are rightfully ours."

This pronouncement was followed by tumbling, fading, thrashing, a great and timeless mournful lament that he would never ever see his home again. Despair engulfed him and then, nothing more but inky bottomless blackness.

The same, but different.

Henry waxed solid again and settled into place. And he could feel. He could physically feel his hands gripping the cracked Bakelite steering wheel of the DeSoto as it roared up the Interstate at Olympia. Just past another border of the Triangle. Compared to the warm cabin, and the spinning universe, the car was cold and one-dimensional. He pulled at the fabric of his shirt, pinched himself.

"I'm back," he said. A silent Phid lay in the seat behind him.

Henry's thoughts sped like the car, like the jumbled replication he had just experienced. Who am I now? What is this? Where is this? He wondered if he took his hands off the wheel, the car would steer itself toward a destination already mapped out.

The traffic picked up when they passed Fort Lewis; the road ahead was a constantly changing pattern of blinking reds, a million reds? In a car next to them, a pair of soldiers shared a match in the front seat.

But was it a real pair of soldiers? Was this real life he was watching? Maybe he'd been dumped into Wayman's world.

But if it was Wayman's world, he was right when he said it was the same but different. Wasn't it still Tacoma that they left so abruptly? Didn't the traffic still thin between the big cities? As they winged through the night, there came more lights, sometimes a crash of lights so that Henry wondered if he was back spinning again. But he clung to the wheel and that grounded him.

Phid stirred in the back. Henry was afraid to turn and look at him for fear it might not be Phid. It might be that Phid behind the mirror. It might be a million Phids. Or it might be a cured Phid.

They passed the turn-off to North Bend and the road to the mountain passes, cresting the hill and seeing the beginning of the long corridor that was Seattle. The lights glowed in the distance and Henry wondered what they would do when they arrived. Or whether the familiar city would in fact be familiar at all. It started to rain again. The same rain, but different. He turned on the wipers, and they clacked out of time, throwing the water while streaking the windows.

"Are you okay back there?" he asked to no reply. "Phid?"

"I'm here." The voice was a squeak. No cure then.

"I don't know. We better stop."

"We could go on forever," Phid whispered. "That would be nice."

"We should stop." And after another mile passed, Phid tried to roll on his side. But the effort was obviously painful and taxing, and he groaned.

"Phid?"

"We better stop," he agreed. And he lay quietly as Henry raced into Seattle and up to the hospital on Pill Hill.

THIRTY-FOUR

Henry stayed all night at the hospital. They wouldn't let him in to see Phid, so he slept in a narrow vinyl chair that left him creaking by morning. It may have been the chair or maybe the recent journey outside of himself that made his dreams so wild. In them, a much younger Henry and Phid were fighting over Mrs. Pinckney's pillbox hat. Phid kept shouting, "It's mine, it's mine!" but Henry would not relinquish his side of it. Fearing it would rip, Henry finally let it go and watched Phid tumble backward. He got up, smiled big, and then handed Henry the hat. "It's yours," he said.

Henry had been up and down throughout the night. Sleep deprivation was the worst enemy; it could create all kinds of tragedies, especially in a mind ripe for disorder. And so, when he awakened for the last time, Henry was sure that Phid was dead.

To calm his fears, he pleaded with staff to let him in. They finally relented, but he had to gown up. It was a quarantined ICU, for a special kind of illness, and Henry had never seen so many screens between the patient and those charged with helping Phid get better. All this forest of technology blocked his path and he had to push aside metal trees hung with plastic tube roots and fruited with bottles of clear solution, drip-dripping, like the giant cedars of the Olympic rain forest.

When Henry reached Phid, he was an anti-climax. His body was shrunken, tiny, dark and mysterious against the snowy backdrop of his bedding. He resembled a prisoner of war more than Ray, Jr. ever did. A clear plastic oxygen mask was fitted over his mouth and nose. Henry could not see his eyes, but Phid's hand raised up like a frightened insect. I-C-U: I see you. Henry took it and held it for a moment, kissed it and let it linger. But it was nobody's hand, no hand that he knew, so he let it drop.

Henry felt an eerie quaking inside, the kind that begged you to keep moving, to stay one step ahead of the inevitable. He walked to the window and looked out. The city was in glorious scope. The rain had gone, and only a few clouds hovered in waiting near Mt. Olympus where the gods of moisture serviced their fleets.

Still fidgety, he came back to Phid and noted his lips moving beneath the mask. He lifted the fragile edges. "Hi, Bud," Phid whispered. He tried to smile, but pulled the mask down tightly again, sucking for air.

"He shouldn't talk," a nurse said loudly. She'd said this before. And before.

Henry's stomach bucked. He squeezed Phid's hand. "I'm going to get something to eat, then I'll come back." He hurried from the room.

A dire restlessness captured him. But driving around would not cure it. He made a beeline for the hamburger restaurant, found it closed, then crossed to the house beside it and pounded on the door. Alice answered in her robe.

He powered past her. "A son shouldn't have to knock on his own mother's door."

"Agreed, Hankie. But what are you doing here?"

"And I think you're being a dick to Dad by flaunting Dr. Blatt."

"Hankie?"

He threw up his hands. "Fuck, I don't know what I'm doing. I can't think straight. I may be in a different dimension anyway."

She eyed him queerly. "What do you want me to do?"

"Come out with me. Drive with me somewhere. It's lonely in this town."

"Okay, just give me a minute." She returned dressed and carrying a heavy leather bag. At her bookcases, she pulled down two or three selections and stuffed them in. "I know what we can do," she said.

They drove past the university and Husky Stadium to the Lake Washington Boat Harbor and walked along the docks where sailboats the size of yachts were tied up. "I have Douglas to thank for this."

"I don't want to hear it."

"Don't worry. We're no longer together. I only inherited the mooring from him."

"Why would you take anything from that guy?"

"Because I like it down here and these are hard to come by."

They stopped in front of a slip with a miserable looking rowboat tied to it.

"This is it?" Henry said. "This is your yacht?"

"Well, yes. It's a little brisk, but I think the rowing will warm us up."

They got away from the harbor, passed through the Montlake Cut and out onto the broad surface of Lake Washington. A few others had the same idea, and they motored in their much larger and more stable craft past the modern surrealistic sculptures thrusting out of the shallow water. When they were a safe distance out, Henry put up the oars and lay back against the bow.

"Okay then," she said. "Now can you tell me. What is it?"

"Phid's dying. He's in the hospital."

"Oh, that's awful."

He stared at her. "But that's not really it."

"Well then?"

"Why didn't you tell me about all of this? Why didn't you tell us?"

"I'm not following you," she said.

"I tried to cure Phid." He coughed. "In the Triangle."

"Please, tell me you didn't."

"And something strange happened. I broke into a million pieces and scattered away."

"Oh son."

"Someone spoke to me. Told me I didn't belong."

"Well, of course you don't. None of us white folk belongs."

"So, you know who spoke to me."

She nodded. "The one and all. The creator of the world. Listen, I can't give you the best answer because I don't exactly know, but it sounds like your experience was a warning. You absolutely can't try to do that again. I'm surprised they let you come back as it is."

"They?"

"The Chehalis. The land, the air, the water was theirs, and we came and took it over. There are consequences for that. Always have been."

Henry couldn't decide if it was the motion of the waves or the revelation that was making him bilious. He grabbed the side of the boat while he listened to the slap of the water against the bow. Even though he'd heard as much from Mrs. Obregon, what his mother had said made sense to him, arranged his life in a clearer pattern.

"Are you okay?" she said.

"Yes. Well, no. Whoever it was, Qone, I guess told me I was being sent back but only to the half world. I'm not sure what that means, but now I don't know if I'm in my real life, or some alternate place like Wayman is."

"You don't want to be where Wayman is."

"Why not? He likes it better. He's going to be a *curandero*."

"How do you know that?"

He told her about his words with Wayman when Henry was disarticulated. "And you must remember when I sent him back."

"I was there when you woke up," she said.

"Believe me, his parents are still none too happy about it."

She stared off over the water. He could tell her mind was turning over this material. "He's adopted, you know."

"I know. Everyone tells me that."

"Adopted from a young Chehalis mother. That's probably why."

"Why what?"

"That it's good for him to be there. It's like his real native safe home." She seemed more troubled than normal, more so than Henry had seen since the state hospital. She looked down on her bag and abruptly pushed it off her lap, spilling the books.

"Mom?"

"None of us is perfect," she said. "I'm sorry and you're right. There's so much I should have told you."

"I'm not here to guilt trip you. But you seem to know about Skookumchuck. One thing I don't understand is why doesn't Skookumchuck mess with someone like Uncle Ray? Someone who's bad."

"I don't have the answer." She grabbed at herself and shivered. "This is a lot to take in. Please, son, can we go back? Would you row us again?"

He took up the oars and said: "Remind me to tell you about your daughter."

At the moorage, they tied the boat up and walked together back to the car. Now she seemed so on edge to him, the same mom, but different. Her hands were deep in her pockets as she walked, thoughtful. Henry carried her bag, letting it bump against his leg.

"Will you stay for lunch?" she finally asked, still sniffling. "We probably both need company right now."

"I don't think so. I better get back to the hospital."

"You're very close to that boy, aren't you?"

"Yes, I think so." He took a deep breath. "Do I seem different to you?"

"In what way?"

"I don't know. Different."

"You seem the same." They stood on opposite sides of the DeSoto. "A little bit different maybe. Most of us change over time."

"This is going to be hard," he said. "I'm not sure what to do."

"Help him be comfortable. Tell him you're listening. Tell him his life has had meaning. Tell him in heaven there are libraries full of books that haven't been written yet and what a head start he'll have on the rest of us." She stopped and looked down at the ground. "I don't know, Hankie. Who am I to say? I'm obviously not the best at helping others. I guess just tell him you're sorry his life turned out this way, that you're a better person for having known him, and that you'll never forget about him until you meet again, likely sooner than we think." She smiled weakly.

"I'll tell him, Mom," he said. And they drove off.

About halfway back to the hospital, he knew what he would do. Outside of the Triangle or not. It didn't matter where he was. It had to be done. Maybe this was the different part of his same new life. In the glovebox, he found *The Adventures of Sherlock Holmes*, all dog-eared and torn, and he carried it inside. The shift had changed in intensive care and a nurse with a shiny red face greeted him. There was no real change, she said, but Henry could see that without her help. After he gowned up, she let him pull up a chair and fight with all the tubes and wires until he'd hollowed out a space to do his work.

It was hope at work here. Maybe not hope, but hope's hapless nephew...No, it was hope.

Maybe this was a new beginning, he thought. A different way. Maybe in this world he could read outside the Triangle and the cure would work. He opened the book to the third story where all those words sat crowded on the page, just waiting to be set loose. And so, he obliged them:

"'My dear fellow,' said Sherlock Holmes as we sat on either side of the fire in his lodgings at Baker Street, 'life is infinitely stranger than

anything which the mind of man could invent. We would not dare to conceive the things which are really mere commonplaces of existence. If we could fly out of that window hand in hand, hover over this great city, gently remove the roofs, and peep in at the queer things which are going on, the strange coincidences, the plannings, the cross-purposes, the wonderful chains of events, working through generation, and leading to the most outré results, it would make all fiction with its conventionalities and foreseen conclusions most stale and unprofitable."'

They spilled from his mouth in a chain, and they wound in and through the IV drips and the looping oxygen tube and rose to the ceiling where they spun round and round the room in a slow patrol, searching out illness and sadness and hobbled dreams and driving them from the very crannies before coming round again and meeting the new words just emerging from Henry's lips. And they spiraled in on themselves and proceeded around the room again, and again, so that by the time it grew dark in Seattle, the air above was crowded with a teeming mass of animated language.

Henry stopped for a moment and snapped on a lamp the nurse brought in.

"You have a beautiful reading voice," she said.

Rustling his paper gown, he scooted in closer and watched Phid. His breathing was slower now; the blips on the screen blinked tiredly. Phid's hand found Henry's again. It was warm and dry, like Henry's gown. Phid pulled it away after a moment and pointed at the mask and Henry lifted the edge once more.

"Gone gone?" Phid whispered.

Henry repositioned the mask and bit at the inside of his cheek. "Maybe just gone." He struggled with what to say. "Are you comfortable?"

Phid looked at him quizzically.

"Hey, guess what. My mom says it's true after all. There's this spirit who's in charge of Skookumchuck. He's the reason I can't go any farther upstream. It's the salmon and what we did."

Phid shook his head. He grunted. He tore the mask off and said slowly: "What are you talking about?"

Henry quieted down. He felt a stab of shame. "Phid, I'm very sorry that your life turned out this way. I'm a better person for having known you."

Phid squeezed Henry's hand once more while Henry arranged the mask yet again. He settled back and began to read anew. His voice held up even and strong while, outside, the early evening turned to night and the sounds became night sounds, sirens and trucks on the freeways, and an occasional airplane lowering its wheels. Henry read on and drifted into the kind of mesmerizing dream state reading at night can bring. His troops were at work, his patient was captive. Henry didn't recall when he fell asleep.

He awoke to the gentle piling of snowflakes around him. They were soft and calming, and it was so real, he shivered with the cold. He opened his eyes and felt a peaceful quiet. But when he looked up to the ceiling, he saw them dropping, one by one, dropping from their circles, dropping their armor; the words he had so patiently called and placed to protect his friend were gently drifting to a mound building slowly over him. And that's how he knew that Phid had died. He did not have to check the gauge on the oxygen tank, nor the blips on the screen. He just witnessed the words, their work complete, fall back to earth in casual disarray, and die along with his friend on the pure white bed.

It was as if Henry's own heart had stopped beating. He roamed the hospital. He longed to see doctors curing their patients, nurses keeping people alive. As his anxiety grew, he moved faster and faster.

Near the elevator on the pediatric floor, he bumped into Ralph Underwood. Ralph was about to chastise him for his clumsiness, but when he realized it was Henry, his jaw moved, but no words came out at first.

"Ralph?"

"Hello, Henry."

Henry had recently seen him on every newsstand, every television talk show and now here he was in the children's wing of the hospital. "I'm glad you're here," Henry said. "My power, you know. I can't get it to work. I need help. Something's not right. I may not even be me."

Ralph's face fell. He said, "I'm here for...", then caught himself and added, "What are you talking about?"

Henry gripped Ralph's suit jacket. "Can you help me? It's not working." He felt woozy, unsteady. "Phid just died. It didn't work. I don't know what to do now."

"Phid?"

"Phid the Kid, you know."

Then Ralph did an awful thing. He glanced at his watch. It occurred to Henry that it would have been far better to ask Ralph for a million dollars than a few minutes of his time. "I just can't, Henry. I wish I could. I have too much to do right now."

He started off down the hall but turned halfway and yelled back. "Call me later. Call my office." Then he was gone.

Henry stood crying in the middle of the corridor while people rushed around him. He felt as if he'd just said goodbye to the last friend he'd ever have. At that moment, Natalie's words resonated more completely than they ever had; *it's the loneliness*. And, while he wasn't sure what his next move would be, he knew he would not be calling Ralph Underwood's office.

Henry asked his mother to handle part of the arrangements. Two days later, they met, and she presented him with a list of the people she had contacted about the death. In turn, he showed her a small brass urn that contained the love of his life's ashes.

"Apparently his folks are still living in Longview," Alice said. "But when I got hold of them, the most wicked-sounding man came on. He wanted nothing to do with anything surrounding your friend's death. He hung up on me."

"Ah, the asshole father. I hope he blazes in hell."

They walked to the DeSoto, and Henry wedged Phid on the back floor before he started it up.

"I think you should investigate it more," Alice said, leaning in the window.

"Oh, I don't know about that."

"No, I don't mean try any more cures. But maybe now is the time to find out about the rest of your life. It's such a joy, Henry, to finally figure out what you've been put on this earth for."

"I'll bet it is," he said. He put the DeSoto in gear and drove away.

He had said it sarcastically, but purpose was not a word he took lightly anymore. He thought about his own all the way back to the museum.

THIRTY-FIVE

Purpose, purpose, purpose. What a hackneyed phrase, Henry thought. Did one get up in the morning just aching to find his purpose in life? Some people might not have a purpose, he decided. Like me. Which made waking up in the morning all that much easier. But, throughout the rainy spring, he kept on hoping anyway, hoping to find it amidst the flotsam and yes, jetsam of his life.

Deep in the summer, Mrs. Obregon abruptly stood in her cabin and jerked wildly as if a penetrating force had hit her from behind. Her fingers hovered just above the table, tapping rhythmically while her eyes darted back and forth like an animal sensing danger.

Tran followed her out of the house where she lifted her face to the sky. She sniffed the air for a moment, listened to the ground. Lines of worry formed a design on her face. She looked at Tran. "Skookumchuck," she said.

He understood and stiffened, although it was his first experience with the word come alive. He walked over to the top of the path and scanned down across the valley of the Chehalis River, a green checkerboard of farms dotted with black and white cows. In the distance, red lights blinked at the tops of the abandoned nuclear power plants. He thrust out his tongue and tasted the breeze. He turned back to Mrs. Obregon.

"Where's Mama?"

"Skookumchuck," Mrs. Obregon repeated. "It is bitter."

He hurried past her to the shed where his father stored the wood, and pulled out his bicycle, one just like his mother's that represented many hours of searching for bottles and aluminum cans. He guided it down the path, avoiding the stiff prickly vines of the Himalayas whose berries were turning from hard green nubs to pale pinks and reds. At the bottom, he straddled the bike and took off.

The fender rattled as he crossed the asphalt and pedaled toward Rochester. The sun floated high and white in the sky and drew sweat on Tran's face as he climbed the rises and dipped into the depressions. At the Tulane Road, he stopped and looked both ways, finally choosing the dirt of the Tulane over the boiling tar of the highway. He rode more slowly since the Tulane had not been oiled yet and the dried puddles and stray rocks were a challenge to his skill. He got about a half-mile when the roar of a dragon sounded behind him. Frightened, he pulled off under the protection of a dusty copse of alder and soon an old Pontiac surged by, throwing up clouds and pebbles as it fishtailed along.

When it passed, Tran ran out to the road and saw the car slow, the dust settling for the barest instant. A big hand thrust out of the window, and it was then Tran noticed his mother, alone in the ditch, hands on her hips, mind in another place.

"Skookumchuck," he whispered. "Oh no."

Then a shot pierced his thoughts and he ducked. But the car engine roared again, and he saw nothing but the roiling smoke of the dust shifting in the distance, like the watery tricks of a mirage.

Ky Duc had been shot in the back at close range. John found her while on his way to visit Alice in Seattle. She was lying face-down in the ditch, clutching an empty Coke can. Tran sat close to her, his bicycle on its side, his chin resting on his knees. No matter how hard John tried to entice him into the Chrysler, he preferred to sit out in the sun.

"Cannot leave her," Tran said.

So, John hurried back home to call the sheriff. When Mr. Godfrey arrived with help, he placed a shroud over Ky Duc's little body. Soon an ambulance came, and after Mr. Godfrey did his preliminary investigation of the scene, they hauled her away. John thought for sure Tran would leave then, but even when the remains of his mother were lifted into the back of the ambulance, he did not budge.

The hot sun lazed across the sky while the sheriff's department stretched a tape measure over the boy's head and worked around him, making their calculations. Sometime before dusk, Ray, Jr., still wearing his work clothes and gloves, stepped out of the back of a green and white car.

He spoke to his son quietly in Vietnamese and finally Tran looked up, his round dark eyes blinking against the light. He shook his head. Ray, Jr. spoke more urgently, but Tran would not give in. Ray, Jr. walked over to John. "His mother's spirit has not left this spot. He's right. We can't go."

"You're going to stay here?"

"She was my wife." He walked back. Sitting down beside Tran, he folded his arms and sat vigil on the gravel.

At dusk, the authorities put away their tools and John started fidgeting. When the last vehicle left, he tumbled into his Chrysler and hurried back to the farm where he called Henry. "You've got to come. It's a hell of a deal out on the Tulane."

When Henry arrived an hour later, John waved him down. "Am I glad you're here, Hankie. Take over." Then he ran back to his car.

"Where you going?"

"Your mom's," he replied, right before speeding away.

Henry parked to the side and got out. "Ray?"

It was quiet out there and although the sky was filled with moon and stars, it took a while for Henry's night eyes to come. He finally made out the two hunched figures. Squatting down, he rubbed his sweaty palms on his pant legs. "Aren't you guys getting cold?"

"No," Ray, Jr. said.

Henry sat down next to them. "Do we know who did this?"

"My father."

"Has he been arrested?"

"No, he won't be arrested. How do you prove the measure of such rage?"

"But how do you know it's him?"

"I just know. Tran told me."

Tran looked at Henry. "Big car. Big hand. Big shot."

"Won't you tell someone?" asked Henry.

"Who else needs to know?" said Ray, Jr.

"The police. Mr. Godfrey."

"He's friends with the law, Hankie."

Henry bit at his lip. "So now Uncle Ray gets away with murder."

Ray, Jr. turned to Henry. "I didn't say that."

Those words hung heavy over them for a full hour as the night closed the windows of conversation. Henry picked at the gravel. Everything was blending together. Like the Triangle itself, it was a muddle.

Finally, Ray, Jr. talked again. "My wife can't decide if she must return her spirit to Vietnam or stay here in America. In Vietnam, she would not be walking the same streets she did as a child. In America, also true. She is a spirit without a home."

Regarding spirits, Henry thought of Phid then who now occupied a place on the mantel in the museum lobby. Henry wanted so badly to see him again, but his memories had been foggy lately. More than one night he awoke with the feeling he was once again being broken into molecules. Here on the Tulane Road in the deepest of nights, he longed for Ray, Jr.'s clarity of vision.

Henry stood. "What if Uncle Ray comes by and sees us all here?"

"He won't come by. He's a coward."

Tran stirred and jumped to his feet. "*Không!*" he shouted, and he lunged for the spot where his mother fell and rolled in the weeds and gravel.

Ray, Jr. slowly unwound himself. "She has chosen." He walked over to his son and spoke to him.

"*Không,*" Tran said. "No!"

"Look up," Ray, Jr. said. "What do you see?"

"I see my mother."

"She is always there," Ray, Jr. said. He turned to Henry. "Please take us away from here."

And so, after stuffing Tran's bike in the trunk, they all piled into the DeSoto and left the spot on the Tulane Road where Ky Duc's spirit had to choose. Ray, Jr. sat in the front seat, his hands politely folded, and Tran was in the back. Henry caught glimpses of him in the rearview. He appeared surprisingly calm given what had taken place.

Henry rolled down the window and stuck his elbow out and as he did, noticed an acrid odor in the air. They all smelled it. Ray, Jr. sat forward and tried to catch the horizon. Henry saw it too, a faint yellow glimmer. He pressed the accelerator.

"Hurry," Ray, Jr. urged.

At Porter, Mrs. Obregon's cabin was on fire. Flames leapt high on the roof and spread quickly in undulating waves.

"Oh, my God!" Henry whispered. He slammed on the brakes and the car skidded sideways. He pushed open the door before it came to a complete stop, tumbled out to the ground. Scrambling to his feet, he ran along the roadway where other cars had pulled over and people were watching the play of the fire.

He located Ray, Jr. and Tran and he scurried up the hill after them. At the top, Ray, Jr. was bent over in anguish, silhouetted against the flames. A siren sounded above the roar of the fire, but it was too late. Henry watched Ray, Jr., this outwardly calm and highly intelligent citizen of two worlds, and he knew that years and years of his father's awful poison were fermenting on the inside of him.

Ray, Jr. raised up, his hands and pointed them to the sky until the fire trucks arrived. But the hoses were released only to wet down the surrounding brush and trees. The roof of Mrs. Obregon's cabin came crashing down, sending a swarm of angry jittery sparks high in the air. Behind Henry, Ray, Jr. quietly sobbed, choosing to let loose the poison, drip by drop, as was his fashion.

When Henry finally went up to comfort him, Ray, Jr. said, "Mrs. Obregon was not in there."

"Where is she then?"

"I don't know."

"Your mother?"

"I believe she was."

Henry stared at the fire. He felt battered by the events of the day. Voices chattered and shouted all around him, but he only heard a loathsome funereal drone. He wondered yet again if this was going to be the way life proceeded in this other dimension he seemed to inhabit.

Later, when the fire burned down to coals, they got back in the car. It was a quiet DeSoto that rambled along the back roads, carrying an aimless party of mourners. Henry knew where he was headed. He glanced over to Ray, Jr. who simply nodded his agreement.

The lights were on in the house when they arrived, and the dusty Pontiac was parked in the driveway.

"I'd better make sure," Henry said to Ray, Jr.

They got out together, leaving Tran in the car with his nose pressed against the window. Henry was nervous as they approached the house. Ray, Jr.'s fists swung in rhythm at his sides. They were careful not to squeak the steps as they climbed to the porch. At the window, Henry sucked in a ragged breath.

Some scenes are remembered for life, and the moment he saw it, Henry knew this one would haunt him forever. He would never forget the image of that snake wrapped around Uncle Ray. Its jaws were fully unhinged, but they still couldn't fit completely around the big man's head. Uncle Ray hung over the arm of his chair; a bottle of Olympia clutched in one hand.

"Skookum-fucking-chuck," Henry said slowly, enunciating each syllable. Ray, Jr. stood silent as if they were dedicated voyeurs who had finally found something worth looking at.

The car door slammed, and Tran ambled toward them.

"Uh, maybe he shouldn't," Henry said, but Ray, Jr. held out his hand.

"This man killed his mother." He gathered Tran in and held him close to his side. Tran immediately focused on the grisly scene in the chair.

"Maybe we should call the police," Henry said.

"Wait," said Ray, Jr.

"For what?"

"For a little while."

Once caught, a boa constrictor doesn't like to give up its prey, so it didn't really matter when they called the police. It kept curling and shifting around, trying to get a better grip. Uncle Ray's hand flopped and flopped until the bottle of Olympia jarred loose and clattered to the floor.

Henry decided the next move was rightfully Ray, Jr.'s so he stepped down from the porch and walked around back. There, he quickly saw that the cage door was open. Uncle Ray's keys hung from the lock. As he examined it, he could see a few of the snake's thick scales that for some reason looked exactly like the molecular crystals he witnessed the night of the try for Phid's cure. As he peered closer, he thought he could see a million Aunt Pegs staring up at him.

At the same time, he was struck with a strong and curious smell of ozone. He brought his sleeve up to his nose and gazed toward the living room. The snake had just now managed to take in all of Uncle Ray's head. Beyond it, Henry saw, framed in the window, Ray, Jr. and his son mesmerized by the deadly progress.

Henry retreated to the back steps. Gradually, his shock dissipated, and he noticed the sound of the chickens clucking happily in their coop.

Later, Sheriff Godfrey had him move from the back steps in case a stray bullet from the snake shooters hit him.

"I know you," the sheriff said, taking a second look.

"I didn't do it," said Henry.

Ray Jr. had it backwards; his mother survived the fire—even though she was missing—but Mrs. Obregon did not. It was a few days later when Henry realized that Skookumchuck no longer had its *curandera*. It hit him hard. Who would replace her? Surely not Henry James George.

Ray, Jr. and Tran did not want to live in the house where the snake ate Uncle Ray, and Mrs. Obregon's cabin was a total loss, so Henry called upon Mrs. Pinckney to allow the two to stay at the museum.

"Of course, they can," Mrs. Pinckney said. "Everyone is welcome here." She still wore the pillbox and on a good day, gave tours as she always had.

Ray, Jr. immediately set to work on the building's electricity and plumbing while Tran wandered and learned and played doorman for whomever ventured in.

In September, Henry and Mrs. Pinckney arranged for a visit from a class of Rochester elementary students and was pleasantly surprised when their chaperon turned out to be none other than the famous Mrs. Winkle. The years had sketched deeper lines on her face, but her smile was just as bright and her attitude as intense as it was when Henry sat in her classroom.

She came right up to introduce herself. She shook his hand vigorously but closed one eye as she studied his face. "Hold on. You're..."

"Henry James George."

"You'll have to forgive these aging eyes of mine."

"You look just fine to me."

She laughed. "Maybe yours are going too." She turned to quiet one of her students, but Mrs. Pinckney was already doing it. In fact, she followed the students around fiercely, making sure they didn't do anything untoward to the artifacts.

Mrs. Winkle faced Henry again. "What brings you to a place like this?"

He told her the short version and she listened intently. When he was finished, she said, "We had big hopes for your class."

"Of course," Henry said. "We were the blessed children of the future." He waited expectantly for her reply. But it didn't faze her. Henry cleared his throat and said, "We all were destined for great things."

"Yes, yes, I heard you the first time."

"What you said, the way you taught it, I've thought about it a lot through the years."

"As have I," she said. She looked nervously toward her students who had disbanded and were now largely converging on the Kennedy Memorial Room.

"They'll be all right," Henry assured her.

She relaxed and leaned against the desk. "I remember you were a good little student."

"Not the best, though."

"No, not the best. Now that Ralph Underwood. There was a one in a million student. You know, it's odd. As I'm about to retire, I imagined I would think about every class I ever taught, every student, kind of like my whole teaching life flashing before me. But I'm not doing that. Instead, I'm thinking about all the cruises I'll be going on." She peered at him curiously for a moment. "And I don't expect my former students to be spending their middle age thinking about me, either; at least I hope not! I want them to be thinking about their kids, or their gardens in the backyard, whether their snow tires will last one more season, their parents who are doing poorly—my generation is a big group of long-lasting insurance liabilities, or it looks to be that way. The way I see it, my students and I collided in the sky as improbably as stars do sometimes, and I've always felt lucky to get to try to make an impression. I hope I gave you some hope, even a portion of what you all have given me, have sustained me with, for so long."

Henry told her he taught for a while and she seemed interested, but she didn't ask why he was an assistant museum curator now and for that he was grateful.

"Guess what I said on the very first day I stood in front of a classroom? You are the blessed children of the future."

"Goodness, I hope they didn't take you seriously," she said.

"I don't think so. They had other things to occupy them. I took you seriously, though."

"So often I've wished for a magic wand to wave over the students I had in the fifties and sixties. Start them over somehow."

"Why?"

She paused and clicked her fingers on the desk. "I think we heaped it on a little thick. I know I did. All this special generation business."

"So, you don't think we were the blessed children of the future?"

She shrugged. "Take a look around you. What do you see? I know I see the same kind of students I've always seen. No better. No worse."

"But look. Your generation put this museum together to memorialize post World War II America."

"But who does it memorialize? I don't see you in these appliances, in these photos of Hollywood's Golden Years. In nothing, frankly."

"But..."

"Here's how I've got it figured out now. I look around me and all my students are indistinguishable from one another. I've thought about it, and I think it was just me, just my own group breathing a sigh of relief that the wars were over, and we had won." She pointed to herself. "I wouldn't be surprised if we're the special generation. We won the war; we built the country into a model for the world. We made other countries think twice about crossing us. Yes, I think we're the blessed ones. Not you boomers. You guys are the spoils."

Mrs. Winkle's words affected Henry more than he thought they would. For two nights straight, he couldn't sleep. In the middle of the second night, he swung his legs over to the side of the bed and planted his feeton the floor.

"Let's start from the beginning," he said to himself, and then went into a long monologue about his life and the twists and turns he'd encountered. When he got to Natalie's suicide, he stopped and felt a wash of guilt spread over him. He'd forgotten to follow through with Natalie's wish.

In the morning, as soon as was sensible, Henry called Mrs. Underwood. He got no answer, not even a machine. On a Saturday filled with raging storms, Henry drove an entire hour down to Rochester to keep his promise. It seemed like too many years since his childhood visit to the Underwoods. But there it was, the rambling ranch house that still managed to impress, not in spite of but by the very virtue of its dishevelment, like a co-ed in a boyfriend's ratty sweater. The house no longer showcased a perfect privet hedge, a shiny paint job.

He knocked once and then knocked again before a child opened the door. On impulse, Henry reached out to tousle his hair, but the boy ducked and frowned. "Grams!" he called.

"Is she here?" Henry asked.

"Yep."

In a moment, Mrs. Underwood was at the door. "I wondered. Her note said she would tell you. Won't you come in?"

Henry followed them. The inside was nearly the same, but now had an edge to it, some feeling not easily defined. Gone was the well-trained family nuance, the aroma of rump roast cooking in the oven. Now, a fragrance of tragedy hovered over the house.

They passed the dining room, and Henry could almost hear the hearty conversation on the night he stayed for dinner. The rampant one-upmanship, the coy, casually disinterested Natalie. *Chapeau, chapeau, chapeau.*

In the family room, Mrs. Underwood pointed to the sofa whose covers were a bit shabby now. "What can we offer you, Henry?"

"No, I really didn't want to bother you, I just wanted to follow through with, you know, what Natalie asked me to do." He glanced at the boy and raised a brow.

"I don't suppose it matters. This little love knows about everything. He's his mother's child. I doubt you could tell us anything we don't already know."

"My mom's dead," the boy said.

"I know. I'm sorry."

"Did you make her die?"

"Now, now," Mrs. Underwood warned.

"No," Henry said. "But I was there. I tried to stop her."

"But you failed."

"Maybe you should go find something to do, Henry," Mrs. Underwood said with both brightness and steel. "Perhaps there's something interesting in your Uncle Ralph's old room." It took Henry a moment to realize she was speaking to the boy and not him.

Little Henry recognized her tone and took off. He'd inherited some of his mother's resentment of authority, but only the bravado, with the muscle yet to come. Hopefully not, Henry thought—Natalie's rebelliousness never did her much good in the end. Mrs. Underwood watched her grandson leave. When she refocused on Henry, her eyes were heavy in the lids.

"You can ask me anything you want," she said.

"His name's Henry?"

She nodded. "Is that your big question?" She bowed her head. "Forgive me."

"No, no, it's okay. It's funny. I was going to tell you the same thing. You can ask me anything you want."

This surprised her, and she perked up a bit. "What could I possibly want to know about my only daughter's last moments? She was obviously not in her right mind. That alone gives me some solace."

"She was lonely. It got the best of her."

Mrs. Underwood lowered her chin and again nodded briefly. "A loneliness she brought on herself." When she raised her head again, a fire burned in her eyes. "She couldn't have found a better man to marry. She had every opportunity a young woman could have. She traveled, she studied in interesting places, she had all the money she could ever want, parents who loved her, a famous brother. Who wouldn't give the world for that?"

Henry wondered if Natalie didn't give up her world because of all that. "I'm sorry," is what he said. He reflected on whether Mrs. Underwood was trying to be kind to him by explaining that Natalie's problems were the unsolvable kind. That she didn't do it because Henry couldn't find the right thing to say to her on the ledge. That she was already dying inside. That the two collided in the moment attempting to share hope. But sometimes such a collision could be fatal.

Mrs. Underwood finally focused again. "I don't mean to be impertinent, but could we get on with why you're really here?"

"Well, I'm here because Natalie told me I should talk to you. That you had something to tell me."

Mrs. Underwood drew her head back. "You mean you don't know?"

"Know what?"

She seemed to consider something for a few seconds and then surprised Henry by whistling. "Henry, come back here, will you?"

Soon, the boy appeared and stood between them. "Yes, Grams."

But Mrs. Underwood stared at Henry. "So, there you have it. You and my daughter met up in Spain twelve years ago for whatever reason."

"Oh."

"Yes," said Mrs. Underwood. "Meet eleven-year-old Henry. Henry, this is Henry."

"Pleased to meet you," Little Henry said.

"Okay," said Mrs. Underwood. "What more then? You've paid your condolences. Henry, you have no debt to this family, I want you to understand that." Her eyes went hard again.

But Henry was still processing what she'd told him. Could it be that this small Henry was his child? He looked at the boy again, raised both eyebrows.

"Very well," Mrs. Underwood said. "Henry, you can go back to what you were doing now." And once again, Little Henry disappeared from the room.

"Just to be clear," Henry said. "He's my child?"

"Yes, he is."

"I'm sorry, but I had to be sure."

She waved him off. "Forget it. You both were adults. You made your own decisions. I just don't like to hear the words out loud."

"I can see myself in him," Henry stammered.

"You've grown more straightforward over the years," Mrs. Underwood said. Her shoulders drooped like the girders in the roof. "She told me. A few days before she did the deed." She looked at him, then looked away. "For goodness's sake, she named him after you. What did you expect? When you do that sort of artless conjoining, you must always be ready for the possibility."

"Does he know?"

"Well, I haven't told him directly." Here her grief bubbled up and she hid it in her palms. In a muffled voice, she added, "His father knows, and he wants nothing to do with him."

To his own surprise, Henry wiped away tears. Mrs. Underwood studied him.

"What are you asking? Surely, you're not thinking of taking him."

Such a notion was blooming larger in his mind as they spoke. "Well, actually I was."

"Oh, Henry. Are you sure about that? This boy has been through so much trauma already. Are you stable? Are you in a relationship? Can you provide for all his needs? College fund?"

"I'm at the museum."

"I see. So the answer is no."

"Where in anything I've said so far did you pick out the word no?"

The sun came out again and lit up the room. It reminded Henry of different days. The sun came, the sun went. Always looking for the equilibrium. He smiled at his grandfather's memory.

"What?" said Mrs. Underwood.

"Does a kid need all those things? I mean right away."

She looked at him even harder. No more nice Mrs. Underwood. "It's not my fault my daughter took her own life. It isn't."

"Mrs. Underwood, I didn't say it was."

She stood, wobblier he supposed than she wanted to give away. "I will tell him," she said abruptly. "I'll let him decide whether he wants to see you or not. But still, you do have a reputation."

Henry stood too, and the pair looked at each other for a moment. "You know I didn't kill Wayman Simpson," he said brusquely. "And if you think for a moment that I would ever be a danger to my own son..."

"I didn't mean that. I meant whether you could provide for him."

"It was you who provided for Natalie," he said.

Her face turned to stone. "Goodbye, Henry. Maybe someday I can be a better hostess. Maybe someday you can be more polite. But I will tell him. I keep my promises."

Behind them, Little Henry sidled up to the family room door.

"Are you going?" he asked.

"Yes," Henry said. Little Henry disappeared down the hall and when Henry got to the front door, it was held open by the boy. Henry was reminded of Tran.

"Thank you, sir," Henry said. "Say, listen..."

But Little Henry had already closed the door.

It was late at night and Henry was restless, happy to have the museum, but wondering what the value of his life was. He felt powerless and alone. It occurred to him that he had no one to read to; no one could use his help, no one would again, and that notion was more than a little dispiriting.

He wondered if maybe he had never actually cured anyone, that it had been raw luck all along. A happenstance singular to the Triangle. Maybe Skookumchuck had been punishing him for being the wrong boy all those years ago.

True, he enjoyed being an assistant museum curator—Mrs. Pinckney was still officially the curator—but he now had that deep longing inside we all know. Maybe it was the disarticulation at Mrs. Obregon's and the need to keep those million Henrys corralled and happy. Or the subsequent loss of Phid. Maybe it was his doubt about the actual life he was living. Or something had lingered after the image of the snake doing its primal deed. Perhaps, and this may have been the most important, Natalie's suicide leaving Little Henry orphaned within the Triangle.

He lay watching the play of shadows on the wall, until, quite suddenly, he heard a car drive up and idle in the lot. Often cars showed up at the museum, lost or late, or even carrying young occupants wanting to explore each other's bodies in the vehicular tradition of young Americans. But usually, these cars would either turn around and pull back out or park for a while with their engines off. This one kept running. Henry got up and peeked out the window. It was a large Mercedes, its headlights still bright. He watched it for a moment before going back to bed.

As he lay there, he heard the car door open and then determined footsteps cross the asphalt. At once there rose a fierce pounding on the door. Henry wrapped himself in his bathrobe and crept down the stairs. There he found Tran holding open the door.

"This man wants to talk to you."

This man was Ralph Underwood. He was thinner than he was at the hospital and dressed in a dark blue Armani suit. He wore a long wool coat, unbuttoned. A gray hat hung from his fingers. "Hello, Henry," he said.

Henry walked over to the desk and snapped on the small lamp.

"Do you want to talk to him?" Tran asked, protective and assured.

"It's okay, Tran. You can go back to bed."

Ralph stepped inside and both he and Henry watched the young boy disappear into the shadows. Ralph took a straight back chair by the desk.

"Your car's still running," Henry said. "Do you want to go turn it off?"

"I'd like to leave it that way if it's okay."

"Okay by me," Henry said. Then he waited.

"I read about this place in the Sunday supplement." Ralph paused and licked his lips. "The photos didn't do it justice."

Henry perched on the edge of the desk. "There's a lot of work left to do."

"I wanted to talk to you."

"Sorry, I never did call your office."

Ralph blanched and his mouth curved down. "I'm the one who should be sorry. There's always so much going on. I barely have time to take a breath."

"Phid died, Ralph."

"Yes. I remember you said that." He tried to smile but couldn't. He played with his hat. Henry had never seen an Underwood take this stance before.

"I'm sorry about your sis," Henry said.

Ralph suddenly glanced up. "I'd like to buy this place."

"You want to buy the museum?"

"I'm prepared to pay a lot of money for it."

"But why would you do that? You hardly seem like a guy who would appreciate it."

Ralph hesitated. Henry could see what he was about to say was the hard part. He cleared his throat. "I figure you'll never leave this place, so if I buy it, I can have you along with it."

"You want to buy me?"

"That didn't come out right. I figure by buying the museum, I could continue to see you."

"We haven't exactly enjoyed a lifelong friendly relationship."

It was then Henry witnessed one of the great phenomena of modern life on the Inland Coast. Ralph Underwood lowered his head. His shoulders began to shake. In the fuzzy glow of the desk lamp, his tears fell onto the plank floor. Since the night of the sociological study Henry had longed to see a chink in this man's armor, but now he was not prepared to watch absolute power melting. Ralph finally looked up. "There's nothing they can do."

"What is it? Nothing who can do?"

He clenched his jaw and the hinge pulsed. "Listen, Henry. I want this place. I'm prepared to knock you over with an offer."

"Nothing who can do, Ralph?"

He reached into his pocket and pulled out a handkerchief, soaking up his tears with a pointed corner. "I'll give you five million dollars."

The words screamed in Henry's ear. "Are you crazy? Take it."

"Don't worry about me. My stock made that much and more today."

"I still don't understand."

He dabbed at his upper lip. "Ten million, Henry. We both know ten million is much more than it's worth."

Henry took a deep breath. Because he was a new prosperity kid, he briefly entertained what ten million dollars could get him. It made him laugh. "I'm not interested in money, Ralph. Just tell me what's going on?"

Ralph tried to sit up straighter, but immediately resumed his slumped position. "Does it not mean anything to you, Henry? Maybe you're the one who's out of your mind. Okay, here goes." He looked Henry straight in the eye and Henry felt what it must have been like to sit across an executive table from this guy. "I'll give you one hundred million dollars for this property. Did you hear that? One hundred million dollars. You would never have to worry about anything again. Your kids would never have to worry. Your grandchildren. You could invest it and be the richest man in all your dreams."

"Is this another one of your sociological, wait no, anthropological studies? Let's tempt Henry James George and watch what happens?"

"I deserve that," Ralph said. He hung his head again and Henry saw all things undaunted in Ralph Underwood turn to vapor and drift away. Ralph put the handkerchief over his mouth and a look of fear settled over his features. When he removed it, he said, "I don't know what else to do."

"About what? Are you ever going to tell me?"

Ralph stood. "Please. Can you come outside with me?"

Henry cinched his robe tighter and followed him through the door to his car. A bundle wrapped in a blanket lay in the back seat. Ralph opened the door. "I kept the car running so he wouldn't get cold."

Henry peeked in. "Oh, God."

Ralph gently put his arms under the child and lifted him up, the blanket trailing its corners. "It's my boy," he said, crying again.

The kid was probably ten years old but looked maybe five. His appendages were sticks, his skin pasty. The Underwood lips were dark against the backdrop of his pale face.

"That day at the hospital. I was there for him. Imagine the hometown hospital having the best experts. He's got acute myeloblastic leukemia. It's very rare in children. I've taken him to doctors all over the world for the past two years. There isn't anything I haven't done for him." He hugged the boy close to his chest, breathing in the smell of the blanket. "I don't know what else to do."

"Ah, Ralph," Henry said. "Are you sure you've come to the right place?"

"I'm sorry. I'm sorry for all the hurtful things I said to you. I was just a gawky dumb kid then."

"You don't need to..."

"I was so busy trying to get ahead of everyone else, I got ahead of real life."

Henry looked at the boy. "I'm not a doctor. What do you think I can do?"

"You could be my hope."

For a moment, Henry reasoned that one hundred million was a lot to pay for hope, but it wasn't in him to resist the simpler request. They went back inside and found the boy a place on the second floor. He was awake now and Henry patted his hairless head after tucking the blankets in around him.

"Where's your wife?"

"It's been hard for her," Ralph said.

"What do you want me to do?"

"Do what you normally do." Ralph dragged a chair over to the corner and sat down. His Italian leather shoe tapped lightly on the floor.

Henry walked over to him. "You need to remember that Phid didn't make it. The cure doesn't work from here. And I can't go back in the Triangle to try." He hated saying those words. "But I'll do what I do."

Ralph touched Henry's arm. "He's my son. I can't tell you any more than that."

Henry searched the museum for something to read. He would much rather pass this job on to someone else. His failure with Phid had been his life's failure, a career misfortune that should have forever stilled his voice.

He found a copy of *Alice in Wonderland* in Phid's old dresser. The nights reading to Phid came rushing back to him, his eyes streaming over each page, desperately searching for the one word that would set everything straight. And every morning realizing he'd failed when he saw Phid wake up again still riddled with disease. But Phid kept asking him to read, and so he had.

Back in the room, Henry sat down and began to read from Lewis Carroll's tale. He felt drawn in on himself, stiff and scared. Not unlike his patient whose little eyes questioned his every move. Ralph was leaning back against the wall, his arms folded across his chest, his eyes fixed on his boy.

The same but different.

Henry coaxed and coaxed, but the words remained two-dimensional that night. They did not take flight; they did not animate in any way. Still, though, they were true and strong and left his lips in an easy manner. By the end of two hours, Henry wasn't sure who had received the most benefit. Ralph's son was dead asleep, but his father's eyes remained wide and bright and expectant.

Henry closed the book. "I think you should take him home now."

Ralph put on his coat. He gathered his son in his arms and Henry led them to the door. They stopped before Ralph went out. "You know, I never thought about that story in that way before."

"How did you think of it?"

"Unreal," he said. "I'd like to come back."

Henry felt a strange, nearly comforting familiarity. "You can come back whenever you like."

"Thanks. And listen. Forgive me for the money thing. You are doing something good here. You never deserved how I treated you."

"I wish you the best with your boy." Henry closed the door and watched them pull away from the lot.

After that night, Henry's thoughts fell into place. His question was a common one. What is it, after all, that we are placed on this earth for? He could see the answer in everyone else. It looked to him that Ray, Jr. seemed to have magical hands when it came to fixing any manner of things. Watching Suzanne with Ray, Jr. made it clear that she was finally opening herself up. Ralph Underwood was made to lead the entire world into the age of technology. But what about Henry? Once he had a future in curing people of their ailments and this set him apart and made him special. Now, the words stayed stuck on the page, remaining just words, never changing. What could you do with that? It was perhaps an unsolvable dilemma.

The answer for Henry came late one night. Restless again, he went downstairs and picked up the urn that held Phid's ashes. With nobody looking, he gave it a little rub. Hmm, he thought. No different than the Waste Away. He placed the urn on the mantel and as he did, he sensed the presence of Natalie, of Simon, the boy he had cured of leukemia, of Ray, Jr, of Suzanne and others of his generation, alive or dead, roaming the halls of the old building as if they were also relics to be saved and admired and hoped for. Yes, there might be a museum even for relics called people.

Sometimes, when the atmosphere is right, and the stars twinkle with a certain charm and one's ears are sharply tuned, you can hear what you need to hear, and the world will right itself and set one on a clear path. It was such a night. For after he rubbed the side of Phid's urn, Henry heard it loud and clear. He heard it so well that he feared it might wake the others. It was a steady beat, pure and strong, as if it had been beating for an eternity. It beat for Henry, it beat

Henry shoved his hands in his pockets as he strolled through the exhibits. It followed him, unseen but persistent, thub-dup, thub-dup, thub-dup, and right at the doorway to the Appliance Wing, when he looked in on Suzanne sleeping in her cot, he heard a definite backward voice.

"Hankie, arm left," it said. "It hear?"

He turned around and saw Mrs. Obregon. He would swear to it no matter what anyone told him. He saw her as clearly as he did that time in the meadow after Wayman disappeared. She was standing at the bottom of the stairs with her arms out.

"I know you," Henry said.

And then he heard the other sound, the one he first cherished as a child in the nook of his grandfather's arm. A swish-swish, a gentle flow, and he looked up to see them sliding down, one by one, a man he did not recognize but knew must be Mrs. Pinckney's Howard led the way. And he saw Phid and Ky Duc and a hundred others, their arms held high, their mouths agape, laughing, playing, reaping the glee. They sailed down the curved banister, swish-swish, and into Mrs. Obregon's outstretched arms, all of them, including Henry's grandfather, who waved at him from the rear. She gathered them all in and turned to face him.

"The Cedars," she said. "It is yours now."

Yes, he finally heard it. Even when she disappeared, and all the laughter and joy had died down, he heard it. A voice backward to the wind, a kind of calling, an invitation. And he knew without a doubt that this was his job. This is where he belonged. Out from under the Skookumchuck Triangle. Doing the work he was born to do. He knew there would be many more finding their way to The New Prosperity Museum seeking their own brand of equilibrium. Because of this, he had to be here to welcome them. He had to be at the ready. He had a lot of hope to deliver to the world.

SEQUEL

During the week, John slept out in his shop. On weekends, he packed up the Chrysler and drove to Seattle to see his wife. Alice seemed more and more receptive to his visits, although determined never to return to the farm again. John was especially happy he no longer had Dr. Blatt to deal with. On one trip to Seattle, John ceremoniously tossed *A Tale of Two Cities* out the window somewhere around Steilacoom.

Ray, Jr. had Uncle Ray cremated, but didn't tell anyone what he did with the ashes. All Henry knew was that the chickens had new holes to bathe in, filled with a new gritty kind of dust that they flapped and rustled through their feathers, while Aunt Peg watched with a real sense of satisfaction. The snake was stuffed and brought to the museum, cage and all, where it lay, suspended off the dried branch of a maple. Weekly, Tran rubbed the glass to a shine. Occasionally he stopped and smiled at the taxidermist's job, and perhaps for the good work wrought by the snake.

Henry read to Ralph Underwood's boy every week for months until he finally died of acute myeloblastic leukemia. It was the kind of disease that should never be visited upon a child. He was a good patient, a trooper until the end. Ralph still came to visit Henry. In spite of the fame and fortune he had accumulated in his life; he was a lonely man in need of real company. Whenever he left, Henry found an obscenely large check in the donation box. Some might be embarrassed and want to return it, but Henry was not stupid. It cost a lot to run the place. And Henry sensed it did something for Ralph's soul to contribute.

It was the right decision to stay at the museum. It felt safe. From it, Henry had learned to be more confident, to have perspective on the world. He had learned that not just reading between the lines but listening between the lines was important. Maybe there were different ways to cure than simply saving someone's life. In short, he now knew how the world worked.

It is not the one with the most money, it is the one with the most soup. It is not the one who is most special, it is the one who makes it with the most grace. It's not the perfect, it's the effort. If it doesn't belong to you, don't steal it because sometimes you may break up into a million little facsimiles of yourself and you may struggle to remain afloat. It is this struggle that revives you and brings you back. There is no generation more blessed than the other, no one person more deserving. It is all an ancient endless process occasionally punctuated by an invention such as fire or the Waste Away. It is an inevitable changing of the guard of ideas that somehow, inexorably ends up at the same place. And that place is the fact that the truth is often what you don't see before your very eyes.

And most importantly for Henry, it was the act of reading, not its consequence. There was great power and grace in the attempt. There was more connection, soul to soul. Even though he could no longer cure anyone, he could make them feel alive and better and who could measure the real value in that? It was the same. But different.

Henry thought of Phid every day and thanked him for his legacy. He still had trouble sleeping at night, but somehow that fit into his schedule quite nicely.

Usually, the others had gone to bed when Henry slipped out of his room and paced down the stairs. The museum was at its best at night and so was he. It gave him time to think and admire the artifacts and realize once again that most museums serve a purpose to inform and educate and bring us closer to our heritage. The New Prosperity Museum did that. When Henry went into the Appliance Wing, he still picked up the Waste Away and marveled at what it brought us. He looked around the room and saw all those trinkets, but now he saw other artifacts indelibly imprinted on his soul as well.

He saw Suzanne sleeping on her cot, still dreaming of the day when she'd mount a horse and not fall off. She had started sneaking back to the museum after grieving Phid. She now spent time with Ray, Jr. as they both learned about how to deal with loneliness. Henry saw Ray, Jr. contemplating his future. He was now the supervisor of the physical plant at the museum, such as it was. He taught conversational Vietnamese to gifted children on the side. But his soul still ached more than it should have, and he spent a lot of time with Tran who followed him around asking questions like, "Why would America want to remember that its favorite president was shot?" or "Wasn't Franchot Tone's job just another job like anybody else's?" Tran had the benefit of perspective.

And Henry saw Wayman Simpson perched on an exhibit stand, as one of the few that made it out, who confounded the odds and found a better place within the same, albeit so different environment. Henry wished that one day their paths might cross again instead of that endless parallel living that Wayman thought was their future. Who knew? Because Henry was still not exactly sure which realm he lived in.

He even saw Phid's urn up there competing with the Waste Away. And there were a thousand others he could probably see if he let himself linger, other new prosperity babies growing old, standing against the Admiral fridge, sharpening knives on the Oster, rubbing pine tar on a Little League Louisville Slugger, checking for the possibility of cancer, or searching for a new love. Searching earnestly for that all important equilibrium, all relics in their own way.

And that's what he was there for, to preserve those artifacts, those images, those people even, and to make sure they had their places in the proper wing. Because, after all, somebody had to do it.

Phid not only left Henry the museum, he left him a mandate to boot. Every night in the Kennedy Memorial Room, Henry plopped down in the old rocker and scooted up to the mike. He put on his headphones and cranked up the power to begin his broadcast on KNPM radio. Occasionally, a night owl would come down the stairs and sit at his feet; sometimes folks would travel from far away, ask to stay a while, and serve as his live audience.

Normally, he simply opened a book and read. It was picked up on radio waves far and wide and was listened to by a great many people, some of whom made literary suggestions. He knew he was getting through to even the most remote parts of this world, spots hidden within charmed triangles with their own particular set of problems. On some nights, his voice crackled in a backwards way. It was like the universe speaking. It was like a secret chorus that most of us only heard in a vague whisper. We call it our inner voice, our intuition, but Henry knew it was more than that. It was real and honest and held the answers to the difficult questions. Henry was not saying he had all the answers, but he was the steward of questions and there was value in that.

Nearly every night he read, and it generally went without a hitch. When he saw folks seated before him, he always did a cursory search in the semi-darkness. He usually acknowledged whoever stopped in the room and then went on with his work.

But one night he peered into the dark room and made out a pair of young boys sitting close to each other, the strings on their tennis shoes trailing on the floor. One was, of course, Tran, and the other, on closer inspection, looked an awful lot like Henry James George. Behind these boys stood Mrs. Underwood, arms crossed, eyes closed, perhaps dabbling with a potential victory over depression.

And Henry smiled as his heart finally released its mournful ache. At that moment he believed. It is love, no matter what kind, that leads us through.

So each night Henry opened his book and cleared his throat with more purpose, and he read and read and read and he knew that those words would go out from The New Prosperity Museum and hover above the world and when they were needed, would drop, one by one, sentence by sentence, page by page into the hearts of all those new prosperity relics whose rafts were sprouting a few holes and who needed the kind of patch Henry could provide to help them float down the unpredictable River o' Life. And when he was through, when his voice rasped like sandpaper, he leaned into the microphone to sign off to the world.

"Until tomorrow, this is KNPM. Good night, Wayman Simpson. Wherever you are, you're where you belong."

THE END

ACKNOWLEDGMENTS

Over the course of the thirty-five years it took to complete this novel, many people participated in its development. There is Maria Morton, who has been there from the beginning and supervised the final draft as well. She was a winner from the word go and has been my biggest supporter since.

I thank my first agent, Liz Trupin-Pulli, who believed in this novel and took it to the ends of the publishing earth in its first iteration.

Terry Peterson, Dr. Paul Wert, Jon Quinn-Hurst, Teri Bicknell, Mari Clack, Amber Quereshi, and Jan Johnson Hopwood are among the many who gave the manuscript a read. Not to mention the scores of editors in the 1990's who, although they could not find room for the novel on their lists, were kind enough to take time to explain themselves. Thanks so much for your feedback and helping me keep this book in the forefront of my mind.

Then there is Duncan Murrell, a more recent editor, who set this novel on its head and urged me to take it in a direction that would end up being the correct one. Thank you, Duncan; your comments were both frustrating and appropriate, as any good editor's suggestions should be. Also, thanks to Carol Ann Davis, Elizabeth Smythe Brinton and Kate Duignan. And also to Kate's sister, Rose, whose connection to film and whose opinion held me captive while she read the manuscript. I am most grateful to all of you. Hopefully you will find bits and pieces of yourselves within these pages.

SELECTED TITLES BY EDWARD AVERETT

Homing

The Rhyming Season

Three Star Private Nuisance

Cameron and the Girls

Scablands

The Yellow

Level IV

ABOUT EDWARD AVERETT

A clinical psychologist writing in his free time and on sabbaticals, award winning author Edward Averett now writes fulltime in his rural home in Ecuador. His published works include several adult and young adult novels, numerous short stories, and a series of suspense novels. Critics have deemed his fiction, "thoughtful, nuanced and empathic writing that jumps off the page" (Kirkus Reviews, School Library Journal, Voya). He is the proud grandfather of three rowdy girls.